Love Me Tender

Anne Bennett was born in a back-to-back house in the Horsefair district of Birmingham. The daughter of Roman Catholic, Irish immigrants, she grew up in a tight-knit community where she was taught to be proud of her heritage. She considers herself to be an Irish Brummie and feels therefore that she has a foot in both cultures. She has four children and five grandchildren. For many years she taught in schools to the north of Birmingham. An accident put paid to her teaching career and, after moving to North Wales, Anne turned to the other great love of her life and began to write seriously. In 2006, after sixteen years in a wheelchair, she miraculously regained her ability to walk.

Visit www.annebennett.co.uk to find out more about Anne and her books.

By the same author

A Little Learning
Pack Up Your Troubles
Walking Back to Happiness
Till the Sun Shines Through
Danny Boy
Daughter of Mine
Mother's Only Child
To Have and to Hold
A Sister's Promise
A Daughter's Secret
A Mother's Spirit
The Child Left Behind
Keep the Home Fires Burning
Far From Home
If You Were the Only Girl
A Girl Can Dream
A Strong Hand to Hold

ANNE BENNETT

Love Me Tender

HARPER

Harper
An imprint of HarperCollins*Publishers*
1 London Bridge Street,
London SE1 9GF

www.harpercollins.co.uk

This edition published by HarperCollins*Publishers* 2015
2

A catalogue record for this book
is available from the British Library

ISBN: 978-0-00-754778-4
Set in Sabon LT Std by Born Group using Atomik ePublisher from Easypress

Printed and bound in Great Britain by
Clays Ltd, St Ives plc

MIX
Paper from
responsible sources
FSC C007454

Acknowledgements

This book was first published by Headline Publishing in 1999, so special thanks must go to HarperFiction and my editor, Kate Bradley, who decided to re-release these books again. I am very pleased about it. I was just starting out and the print run was quite small so I'm thrilled that a whole new audience will be able to discover this book for the first time.

The story centres on the O'Malley family who live in a back-to-back house in inner Birmingham, very similar to the one where I was born and lived in until I was almost seven. It opens just before Christmas 1937 and covers the turbulent and often terrifying years of the Second World War. The conflict rips the family apart at a time when women had to draw on resources they often didn't know they possessed in order to care for their families alone. All of this while taking up war work to ensure they had food to put on the table and to keep Britain going as whole areas of the country were emptied of able bodied men. It also deals with the aftermath of men returning to children they barely knew, who had grown up while they were away and wives so independent by necessity that the men felt they had no place in the home anymore.

It was pre-internet for most of us in 1999, so research was through literature and I thank Keith Wilson, the Birmingham historian for his series of books on various features of Birmingham's past. And then, of course, there was Carl Chinn, who used to lecture on local history at Birmingham University. As a consequence, he wrote a great many books emanating from the research he had done, which over the years helped me a great deal. When I wrote this novel he also hosted a radio show on Radio WM and he would invite me on every time a new book was released. I ended up on his show five times, though alas, the format was changed and books are no longer featured.

Left behind then are Carl's publications like the *Brummagen* magazine series where, as well as informative articles, he collates people's memories and I have always found them a great source to dip into. These writings highlight so many areas and activities in Birmingham's past, such as *Homes For People: Council Housing and Urban Renewal in Birmingham 1840–1999*, detailing the housing programmes and the problems families encountered and, of course, *Birmingham Undaunted: Birmingham During the Blitz*. The last book was so well used by me that by about books six and seven, it literally fell to pieces and then, despite the internet creeping into our lives, I had to buy myself another copy. So a huge thank you from me to Carl.

The internet does make things so much easier, and not least for checking what people tell me is correct. If it is something remembered by a person or a relative that will add flavour to the story, that's all right. But though I write fiction, I always strive for accuracy so if someone tells me something as given fact I verify it before inclusion. The web is invaluable for my own research, and I often download photographs so that I can visualise more effectively what I am writing about as well as using the internet to promote my books. It seems odd to thank the internet for being there but I have to admit I'm very grateful it is.

But without you my gallant and loyal band of readers, none of this would have any purpose – another plus point for the internet is how much easier it is to connect with so many of you and I am so grateful for that too.

I would also like to thank the great team I have at HarperCollins who work so hard for me, in particular my editor Kate Bradley and publicist Amy Winchester. Then there is my lovely agent, Judith Murdoch. Immense gratitude to you all.

My family also deserve a mention and enormous thanks for they keep my feet firmly nailed to the floor and cope brilliantly with the fall out when I'm stressed.

I feel I would be a lesser person without each one of you so a heartfelt *Thank You* again to everyone.

To my lovely husband, Denis, with all my love.

ONE

Mary Sullivan heard the dragging feet in the entry and swung the door wide to see her eldest daughter Kathy just about to push it open. The dejected sag of Kathy's shoulders told its own tale as Mary drew her inside. 'Wait, pet,' she said. 'I'll brew us both a drop of tea.'

'No, Mammy, I can't stay,' Kathy said. 'I've left Barry minding the weans.' She shook her head angrily. 'Oh God, it's no job for a man.' She looked at her mother, her deep brown eyes sombre, and said, 'D'you know, he was over at Northfield today, after a job on the building he'd heard about. Course, it was gone by the time he got there and then he walked back to save the tram fare. But the thing is, his boots are falling off his feet and I don't know whether it wouldn't have been better to pay the fare and save his boot leather.'

'Ah, girl, I'm heart-sore for you,' Mary said.

'I couldn't stand the look on his face, Mammy,' Kathy cried. 'I took the few coppers he'd saved and went down the Bull Ring. I got some bones and vegetables cheap, you know how they sell them off at this time of night. At least I'll make a nourishing meal with it tomorrow.'

1

Mary looked at her daughter sadly. 'Wait,' she said, and went out of the room, coming back a minute later with a loaf wrapped in a cloth.

'Ah no, Mammy, you do enough,' Kathy protested.

'We have plenty,' Mary said. 'Sure everyone in the house is working now but Carmel, and she's turned twelve, she'll be left school in a couple of years. Take it.'

'I will,' Kathy said. 'For the weans, at least. Barry said they must have the best food first. He's terrified something will happen to them that they won't be well nourished enough to fight. I can understand it; after all, his two young brothers were taken with TB and his da was out of work at the time. Barry said there was little money for food and none at all for doctors, or medicines, and the youngsters were too weak to fight it on their own.'

'He's a good man you have, Kathy, and a good father,' Mary said. 'Things could be worse. Maybe in the new year Barry's luck will change. God's good.'

Kathy sighed. She had no hopes for the new year, for Barry had been out of work for four long years and she dreaded Christmas, with nothing for the weans at all. She was beset by worries. Her daughter Lizzie needed new boots – the ones she had pinched her feet and Kathy'd had to line them with cardboard to keep her feet dry – and Danny only had one jumper that fitted him now, and that was ragged and all over holes. She couldn't lay all this at her mother's door and so she kissed her goodbye.

There was another worry pressing on Kathy's head, but it was nothing she could share with her mother either, or anyone else for that matter. Barry never made love to her any more. They slept side by side in the same bed and could well have been strangers. Often Kathy would long for Barry's arms around her, or his lips on hers – not of course that she could say that to him, but still she missed the closeness they used to share. She knew he wanted no more children till he got a job, but still . . .

She was not to know that Barry realised how quickly kisses and cuddles could lead to other things, and he couldn't risk it. If it wasn't for his in-laws helping, the two children he had would go to bed, time and enough, with empty bellies. It tore his heart out that he was not able to provide for his own weans. God forbid he would bring another into the world to the same fate.

Lizzie and Danny were the only ones Barry could be natural with. He'd never been an inactive man before unem ployment, and had never given much of a thought to the children either. Their rearing would be down to Kathy, like his had been down to his mother. But he'd been laid off before Danny's birth, and now the boy was three going on four, and Lizzie six and a half.

At first, like many others, Barry had gone to meetings, listened to rallying calls and taken part in marches and demonstrations, but all to no avail. He knew he had to get out from under Kathy's feet during the day, but hanging around street corners was not for him and there was no money for the pub, so he began to go for long walks.

He tended to veer away from the town, a thankless place to visit when he had money for nothing in the city centre shops. At first, his feet took him towards Calthorpe Park, or often as far as Cannon Hill, where he'd walk hour upon hour and return home tired and more dispirited than ever. However, one day, tired of the same route and with his stomach yawning in emptiness, he turned down Bristol Passage into Bristol Street and from there on into Suffolk Street, coming out at the top end of town by the Town Hall, and there he saw the lending library.

Barry had never been inside the library; there had been no occasion to. Although he could read, since he'd left school there had been little leisure to do so. Except for now, he thought, and he went in, glad of the blast of warm air, for the day outside was raw and his clothes were pitifully threadbare and thin.

It was very quiet also, quiet like Barry had never met before. He'd grown up in a small back-to-back house, first among a clutch of brothers and then with a family of his own, where noise was part of life and everyone knew everyone else's business. The silence of the library was like a balm to Barry's bruised soul, and the only sound was that of his boots on the wooden floor.

And then he saw the papers, such an array of them laid out, presumably for anyone to read. He sat down, and as he read first one and then another, his hunger was forgotten and the time sped by, although the papers made frightening reading. After a few days of intense study of the political situation in Germany, he was more aware than most of the mad little Austrian ruling the country. He knew that if only half the tales coming out of that beleaguered place were true, the man was a dangerous and vicious maniac, and he wondered how long the rest of Europe was going to stand by and watch. He said none of this at home for, God alone knew, Kathy had enough on her plate and it would serve no purpose frightening any of the family, possibly needlessly.

He progressed from the papers to books to fill the long winter evenings, and was choosing some one day when his eyes alighted on the children's section of the library. He could buy little for his children, on twenty-six shillings a week for himself and Kathy, and two shillings extra each for Lizzie and Danny, but the lending library was free, and so he began to bring books home for them and read to them regularly.

Lizzie loved her daddy. He had more patience than her mother and was gentler somehow. He'd taught her to love books and write her name before she went to school. She

4

liked nothing better than to snuggle down in the chair with him, her on one side and Danny on the other, and listen while her daddy read to them.

And that was how Kathy found them when she went in that day, and for some reason it irritated her seeing them all cuddled up cosily together. 'Get up out of that,' she said angrily. 'Sitting there and the pair of you like a couple of tinkers! Get down to the cellar this minute, you need a wash before bed.'

'Oh, Mammy!'

'Do as your mother bids you,' Barry said, scattering the two from his knee.

Lizzie glared at her mother. Mammy always spoils things, she thought, she's always shouting. But wanting to live to see her seventh birthday, the little girl said not a word, but walked across the room and took her brother's hand at the top of the cellar steps.

Barry stopped Kathy as she was about to follow the children. 'Solly came by,' he said. 'One of the men has been taken ill at the market, he says he'll put a word in for me.'

'Regular?'

'Well, till the man's better. Even a couple of days is better than nothing.'

'Is it?' Kathy snapped. 'And what if the means test people get to hear of it? What then?'

Barry was silent. He knew Kathy had a point, but he'd been pleased, almost excited, and had expected her to feel the same. After all, any job was better than no bloody thing at all. 'I thought,' he said at last, 'I thought I could buy the weans things for Christmas, a wee orange each or maybe even a skipping rope for Lizzie, I know she'd like one.'

'You know she'd like one!' Kathy repeated, and her eyes flashed with temper. 'What's this "like", all of a sudden? The things I'd like, I have to go without. The child needs new boots on her feet and you talk about a skipping rope.'

'They're only weans, Kathy.'

'I know that,' Kathy snapped. Suddenly it was too much for her and tears of frustration ran down her cheeks. She needed her husband's arms around her to comfort and reassure. He was quick enough to put them round the children, but now he held them by his side, terrified that the dam keeping his own feelings in check would burst if he attempted to hold his wife close, as he longed to.

'I do my bloody best,' he said grimly.

'Well, it's not good enough,' Kathy burst out in hurt anger. 'You make me sick. Get out of my way, I must see to the weans.'

Barry stared at his wife in silence for a minute, and then snapped, 'Oh, I'll get out of your way all right. I'm away to me ma's, where the welcome is always warm and the company's better.'

'Go to hell for all I care,' Kathy snapped back, though her heart sank.

Below, in the damp, chilly cellar, Lizzie and Danny waited and listened. Lizzie knew it was all her mammy's fault. Her daddy couldn't help being out of work, lots of daddies were, and she shouldn't have shouted at him like she did. When she heard the slam of the door and watched her father's feet walk over the cellar grating, she began to shiver, and it wasn't just from the cold of the place.

Kathy, descending the steps, was ashamed of herself. She shouldn't have gone for him like that. God forgive her for what she'd yelled at him that evening. What had he been doing that was so wrong when she'd come in? Just amusing the weans with a story while he minded them. Was she jealous of her own children? No, she told herself, that was silly, but she knew that if she wasn't careful, by the time Barry

6

did get a job, they'd only have the shreds of marriage to hold on to, and when she went into the cellar, the children's accusing faces filled her with guilt.

From then on, Barry and Kathy's relationship deteriorated steadily, though they never spoke of the argument again. Barry had been bitterly hurt by Kathy's accusation that he hadn't tried hard enough to find work, and he couldn't forgive her for it.

He did get a fortnight's work in the market, and in a gesture of defiance bought a skipping rope for Lizzie and a toy car and marbles for Danny. He put them in the stockings they hung up on Christmas Eve, together with a shiny penny, a small orange and a bar of candy each. It was a grand Christmas morning for them, though Barry hardly spoke to Kathy and his only smiles were for his children.

Kathy longed to say she was sorry, but the words choked in her throat. Later, when they went to her mother's and Mary produced the children's presents – a pair of new shoes for Lizzie and a jumper she'd knitted for Danny – Kathy was consumed with shame that she and Barry weren't able to buy those things for the children themselves, even though she was very grateful. Mary waved away her protests. 'Let us do it while we can, child. God alone knows how long young Michael will be in work, with him turning sixteen in the new year.'

Kathy knew fine what her mother meant. Her youngest brother Michael had been an errand boy at Wrenson's, the grocer's shop, since he'd left school two years earlier. Once the lads reached sixteen, they were normally replaced by a school leaver, who at fourteen would work for less money. It was no good moaning about it; that was the system. Everyone was keeping an eye out for Michael, but the family knew that he would probably be drawing the dole with Barry before long.

So Kathy said nothing more and put Lizzie's old boots away for Danny – maybe she could afford to have them soled sometime. Anyway, for a wee while longer the children were all right, and she blessed the fact that she had her close family all around her to help out all they could.

Mary knew things weren't right between Kathy and Barry, but she said nothing, not even to her husband Eamonn. Though both seemed fine with the children, there was a definite frostiness between them. Few would have seen it – there was much jollification when the family all got together, and bad feelings could often be successfully covered up – and she hoped it was just a temporary thing.

New Year's Eve was celebrated as always at the Sullivans', where all the clan and many neighbours crammed into the little house and the children took refuge under the table with eatables they'd pilfered. Pat, the eldest of the Sullivans' sons, was the 'First Foot' after midnight and arrived at the door to a chorus of 'Happy New Year!' carrying some silver coins, a lump of coal and a bottle of whisky that Eamonn had hidden away. They all drank a toast and hoped that 1938 would be a better year. Mary was glad to see Barry with a wide smile on his face for once. Of course that could be put down to the amount he'd drunk, not that it had been excessive but Mary had the idea that he and Kathy lived on bread and scrape and not much of that. On that sort of diet it didn't take more than a drop or two to knock a man off his feet. She worried they'd both become ill if they didn't eat more, and Barry needed to keep his strength up so that if he got a job, he'd be able for it.

She did what she could by feeding the children as often as Kathy let them come, and often sent round a pie or bit of stew and the odd loaf, but she had the feeling that it fed the children only. They were certainly sturdy enough and had the well-nourished look missing from many of the

8

ragged, bare-footed children one saw around. God, it was desperate, so it was, how some of them lived.

Lizzie was a carbon copy of her mother, with jet-black hair and dark-brown eyes with long black lashes, but she still had the bloom Kathy had lost. Her face was the open one of a child, not the old face of many of the urchins, and her cheeks had the pink tinge Kathy's had once boasted. She also had her mother's wide mouth, but no worry lines were there to pull it down.

Danny had his father's sandy hair, and a bit of the chubbiness of babyhood still clung to him. He was very like his father, with his round face, and he had the same-shaped nose and mouth as Barry, but his deep-brown eyes were like those of his mother and sister, for his father's eyes were grey. Indeed, Mary thought they were fine children, and enough to look after when a man had no job. Thank God Kathy had had no more after Danny.

Kathy pleaded tiredness just after twelve, and Eamonn helped her carry the sleepy children home and put them to bed, but Barry stayed on longer, pouring out his troubles to his good friend, Pat. He and Pat had been through school together since the age of five, and it was through him that Barry had begun courting Kathy. Pat's own wife Bridie was known as a nag, but he was so easy-going, it seldom bothered him. 'Water off a duck's back,' he was fond of saying, but he sensed that whatever was wrong between Barry and Kathy went deeper and couldn't be laughed off.

'I don't know what she wants me to do,' Barry complained. 'God knows I've looked for work hard enough. If I stay in she nags, if I go out she complains. If I play with the weans I'm spoiling them and I could be doing something useful.' Barry shook his head from side to side in puzzlement at it all.

'God, Barry, don't be trying to understand women,' Pat said. 'What goes on in their minds is beyond me altogether, we just have to put up with it.'

Barry wondered if he could. There had been times before Christmas when he'd wanted to walk out and leave them all to it.

'Come on,' Pat said. 'It's a new year, a new start, nineteen thirty-eight will be your year, you'll see.'

Barry chinked his glass against his brother-in-law's. 'New year, new job,' Pat said, and Barry was infected by his optimism.

'Aye,' he agreed.

It was much later when he made his unsteady way home. Once inside his own house he began to see the stupidity of thinking that way. New Year's Eve was just a day like any other, and he was just as unlikely to get a job in 1938 as he had been in '37, '36, '35 or '34. God, the dole was a living death that ate away at you inside, and now he'd got Kathy pouring scorn on him for not trying hard enough.

Upstairs, Kathy was either asleep or pretending to be. Either way, it suited Barry, and he slid in quietly beside her. God, what a life, he thought. I have a wife who lies beside me like a stranger and who hardly talks to me, and he remembered with a twinge of nostalgia the heady days early in their marriage when they couldn't get enough of each other. Now, Barry thought, Kathy had settled without complaint into a sexless relationship. Maybe sex hadn't been important to her. Maybe she'd just pretended that it had. He'd known from his limited sexual experience that most women didn't enjoy it, and he thought that in Kathy he'd found a gem. Just went to show it was all put on, a pretence, or surely she would have said something by now. Ah, but what the odds, what could he have done even if she'd said anything? Once he'd loved her so much, but it seemed a lifetime ago now. With a grunt that was almost a groan, he turned on his side away from Kathy and settled to sleep.

*

10

One raw February day, the O'Malley household was roused by a furious knocking on the door. The clock showed barely six o'clock, and Barry struggled into his trousers and ran down the stairs to find young Michael on the doorstep. Michael had been on the dole for just over a month, as everyone had expected. Now he was breathless, both because he'd run from his house and also because of excitement.

Barry pulled him inside, for the wind was fierce. He knew something must have happened for Michael to be there so early in the morning, and in such a state of agitation. 'What is it?'

'They're . . . they're setting on at BSA,' Michael panted, hardly able to get the words out.

Barry hadn't been aware he was holding his breath till he suddenly let it out in a loud sigh. He'd been expecting bad news of some sort, but this . . . He remembered how once he'd been like Michael, shooting off in all directions, chasing one job offer and the hundreds after it. He couldn't feel excitement like that again, but he couldn't dim the light in Michael's eyes. 'Where did you hear it?' he asked.

'Paddy Molloy came in this morning and was after telling Da. He was set on yesterday. His cousin told him about it.'

'BSA the cycle place?'

'Aye.'

'And this was yesterday?'

'Aye, last night.'

'Any vacancies will be long gone by now, Michael.'

'No, it's new lines, I'm telling you,' Michael burst out. 'Molloy said there'll be jobs for us all, and the new lines aren't making bicycles.'

'Well what, then?'

'Guns.'

'Guns?' Kathy exclaimed. Neither Barry nor Michael had seen her come into the room. Now she stood before her

11

brother, Danny in her arms, and repeated, 'Guns! Did you say they're making guns?'

'Aye, Molloy told us. A lot of the old workers have been made up to inspectors, he said.'

'But what do they want so many guns for?' Kathy asked. 'How should I know?'

Barry thought he knew only too well, but he didn't share his thoughts. Instead he said, 'Well, I'm away to get dressed. It's worth going for if all Molloy says is true.'

Kathy looked after him. She couldn't even feel pleased, and certainly not optimistic. God alone knew she'd been pleased enough in the beginning, when she'd thought Barry would be set on any day and he'd been flying all around the place on one unlikely jaunt after another, until hope had dimmed and dejection set in. 'Have you time for a drop of tea?' she asked her brother.

'No, we'll have to go as soon as Barry's ready. We'll need to be early to have a chance.' He'd just finished speaking when Barry entered the room, pulling a jumper over his head and grabbing his coat off the hook on the door. Lizzie was trailing behind him.

'Have you any money?' Barry asked Kathy. 'We'll have to take the tram there at least.'

Kathy tipped out her purse. 'Two and threepence,' she said. 'All the money I have in the world,' and she extracted a shilling and gave it to him. 'Good luck,' she said.

'Thanks.' Barry made no move towards her, but she hadn't expected a kiss; that had stopped some time before. Instead he lifted Danny from her arms and kissed him soundly before setting him on his feet, and then bent down to Lizzie and, kissing her cheek, said, 'Pray for me, pet, this could be it.'

Kathy felt tears prick behind her eyes as she watched Barry and Michael stride down the road. She might have been a dummy for all the notice her husband took of her.

She gave the children their breakfast, supervised their wash and helped Danny get dressed, but her mind was far away. She had no hope left that there'd be a job for Barry, and she feared he'd come back more morose and depressed than ever.

'It's all right, Mammy,' Lizzie assured her, catching sight of Kathy's worried face as they walked to school. 'I've prayed to the Virgin Mary.'

Oh, to have a child's faith, Kathy thought, but she smiled at her daughter and gave her hand a squeeze. She couldn't help wondering, though, what BSA wanted with so many guns, and why they should take on Michael and Barry when neither of them knew a damn thing about making them.

But when Barry came back, one look at his face told Kathy he'd been successful, and when he caught her around the waist and hugged her, she suppressed the thought that if Lizzie hadn't been at school and Danny at her mother's she wouldn't have got a look-in. 'I start tomorrow at six,' Barry said. 'Michael's working along with me and we have as much overtime as we can take.'

'That's great, so it is! Great!' Kathy said, and she felt the worry of the last years slip from her.

'Is that trying hard enough for you?' Barry asked, his face stern.

'Oh, can't we forget that stupid quarrel?' Kathy said. 'I was sorry as soon as I said it. God, how many times I wished it unsaid.'

'You never told me.'

'I'm telling you now, and I am sorry, Barry, truly I am,' Kathy said, facing her husband.

Suddenly Barry was seized by desire for his young wife. 'You could show me how sorry you really are,' he said, and his face was very close to Kathy's, his voice slightly husky. She could read the expression in his eyes and knew what he wanted. 'We have the place to ourselves and it's been a bloody long time.'

Too right, Kathy thought, and though she had plenty to do, she turned the key in the lock of the door to the street and the one into the entry, and followed her husband up the stairs.

Lizzie really missed her father when he went to work, though she sensed everyone else was pleased. Her mother didn't snap so much at her and Danny now, and she was friends with her daddy again. Lizzie often saw them laughing together, and Daddy sometimes kissed Mammy when he thought no one could see.

So they were all happier, and Grandma said that, 'Things are back to normal again, thank God,' and only Lizzie was the slightest bit miserable. Her father worked long hours and any overtime going, and he got home too late and too tired to play with Lizzie and Danny as he used to. Often he was so late they were in bed when he got in and he had only time to give them a kiss. Danny had often fallen asleep, but Lizzie would wait, however tired she was, for her father's tread on the stairs.

It was June now and almost Lizzie's seventh birthday. Just after it, she would make her first holy communion. She knew most of her catechism and things were going along nicely at school, but no one at home seemed bothered. Who would make her dress, Lizzie wondered, or could she choose one, in the market? She imagined a veil with flowers on the band at the front like she'd seen others wearing. She longed for white sandals, which would be the prettiest shoes she'd ever had in her life, and white socks, so different from the grey woollen ones of winter and the bare legs of summer.

Eventually she broached the subject with her mother. 'You're neither having a dress made nor am I buying one; you're having Sheelagh's.'

'Sheelagh's?' She was having to wear a cast-off from her hated cousin Sheelagh! Why hadn't she thought that could happen? Her cousin was a year older than her and so had had her first communion the previous year. 'And are the veil and the sandals and socks from Sheelagh too?'

'Yes, and you can take that look off your face, miss, before I take it off for you,' her mother said angrily. 'I know your father's working now, but there's a lot of things we need and it's silly to spend money on things Sheelagh already has.'

Lizzie knew she was right, but it made it no easier to bear. Nor did the party that her mammy arranged for Lizzie's seventh birthday make it much easier either. She'd never had a party before, and the jelly and blancmange and tinned fruit had been delicious and she should have been thrilled. But across the table sat her hated cousin with a silly smile on her face that made Lizzie want to smack her. Sheelagh was a spiteful cat, and Lizzie knew what she was thinking, and she knew that she'd tell them all at school that Lizzie O'Malley was wearing her old communion dress.

But before long, Lizzie had more to worry about, and that was confession! Miss Conroy had let all the new communicants look in the confessional box, and of course they'd rehearsed and rehearsed all they would say, but that was nothing like the real thing.

The night before, she lay in bed thinking about it, and the more she thought, the more despairing she became. It was her first confession, and for that reason she'd had to examine her conscience not just for the last week or fortnight, but for the whole of her seven years. Lizzie decided there were a devil of a lot of sins you could build up in seven years, and she thought of all the bad things she'd done.

Disobedience – she wasn't very good at doing as she was told. Not that she openly disobeyed her mother, or even her grandma – she might be bold, but she wasn't stupid, and she had no wish to shorten her life. Forgetting prayers – oh, how easy it was to slip between the sheets at night if

15

her mother and father didn't come up straight away and make her kneel beside the bed. Then, when they did come up, Lizzie, not wishing to leave her warm bed, would often say she'd already said her prayers, so that was adding lies to it. And in the morning she was up and away and had started the day before she gave a mind to them, and then something more interesting would claim her attention if and when she did ever remember. Then there was fighting – she wondered if that was a sin; if it was, her soul must be as black as pitch, she decided, for she'd fought with Sheelagh for as long as she could remember.

And who would be hearing confession? It mattered because Father Flaherty was likely to give you a whole decade of the rosary for forgetting your prayers once, while Father Cunningham was much kinder and more understanding. But did you know who it was when they had the screen between them and you, and then voices were probably muffled in the box?

Lizzie decided she'd better not say she'd been too bad, for if it was Father Flaherty on the other side, she might spend the rest of her life on her knees. She'd say she'd been disobedient and cheeky and sometimes forgot her prayers; it would be better not to say she couldn't be bothered sometimes. Anyway, three sins would do for now, Lizzie thought, as she curled sleepily in the bed. She had a mind it would take quite a few confessions to account for seven years of sins.

In the event it wasn't so bad at all. They sat in the pews in the dimly lit church that was almost as familiar to them as their classroom, and shuffled down the rows, one by one, towards the confessional box in their turn. Strain as the children might, they could hear not a word spoken, just a tantalising mumble, and Lizzie was glad no one could hear the bold things she would tell to the priest.

Lizzie's friend Maura Mahon told her that priests went blind into the confessional – it was well known, she said – and when you'd confessed, as soon as you left the box, anything you told them was wiped from their memory. Lizzie thought that very comforting, even if it was only Father Cunningham hearing the first confessions of the children.

Lizzie was given three Hail Marys and a Glory Be as a penance for the list of sins she told to the priest and Maura had the same, but Mairead Cleary had to say a whole decade of the rosary! Ask as they might, none of the children could get her to tell them what she'd said to be given such a heavy penance. Maura whispered to Lizzie she thought you'd get little more if you murdered someone and Lizzie was inclined to agree.

Certainly Mairead looked sorry enough as she knelt at the rails of the side altar with the statue of the Virgin Mary before her. She had her head bowed for a long time, but then one Our Father, ten Hail Marys and a Glory Be can't be said in a couple of minutes. When Lizzie saw Mairead make the sign of the cross and then drop a coin in the box and light a candle, her eyes nearly popped out of her head; she'd never had money for candles.

'She's just making sure,' Maura whispered. 'She's lit a candle so that Our Lady will put in a good word for her with God.'

'She must have done something desperate, all right,' Lizzie said with awe.

Her mammy had always said the Clearys were a funny bunch. She said it was strange these days to have the money they seemed to have to splash about when never a one of them appeared to be in work to earn it.

But all the same – a whole decade of the rosary . . .

The Saturday night before Lizzie's first communion was the same as every other Saturday night as far back as she

17

could remember. Her mammy would fill the boiler in the cellar early in the evening, and later her daddy would lift the large tin bath from the hook on the back of the cellar door and fill it with buckets of water from the boiler and cold from the tap so that Kathy could bath the children and wash their hair. Lizzie loved her bath, though in the winter the cellar was freezing. Now that her daddy had got a job, he'd bought an old oil stove which stank like mad but at least made the place warmer.

Lizzie was particularly glad to have her hair washed if she'd had stuff put on it to kill the nits. Every Friday night she had to sit over a newspaper while her mother attacked her with the nit comb, and if any were found, smelly lotion had to be put on her hair, and on Danny's too, and left all the next day, and it stank worse than the oil stove.

That Friday night, nothing had been found in Lizzie's hair, but her mammy gave it a good washing anyway to make it shiny. Then she carried Danny upstairs, and Lizzie's daddy came for her with a towel he'd been warming by the fire while her nightclothes were draped over the guard to air.

Lizzie glanced over at the communion dress hanging from the picture rail. She knew her mother had washed it and starched it before ironing it to take some of the limpness out, and it looked quite pretty really. Kathy knew something of her daughter's feelings; she'd been the eldest in her family and had had a new communion dress that later had to do for both her sisters – Maggie, who was six years younger than her, and Carmel, the baby of the family – and the same with the confirmation dress a few years later. It would have been nice to get Lizzie a new one, but such a waste with Sheelagh's just lying there. It wasn't as if they had another girl in the family to pass it on to either, though there would be one more O'Malley before Christmas, for since her sex life with Barry had resumed in February, she'd not had a period.

18

'Do you like it, pet?' she asked Lizzie.

'Yes, yes, I do, I just wish it hadn't been our Sheelagh's.'

'Now, Lizzie.' But Kathy, though she rebuked her daughter, knew what she meant for, God forgive her, she didn't like the child either, and was less than keen on her mother, Bridie.

She often wished Pat wasn't quite so easy-going, for he'd allowed himself to be led down the aisle by that Bridie Mulligan, and everyone knew what she was. Sheelagh was one in the same mould, and yet Pat was the gentlest, most considerate and pleasant man you could wish to meet.

There would be no more children in that family, if you could go by what Bridie had told her. After Matthew was born, three years after Sheelagh, she'd said Pat would have to tie a knot in it, for he was not getting near her again. Kathy had been shocked, because even though she and Barry were having their own problems, those were connected with Barry having no job. Yet Pat had been steadily employed, and Kathy was sure it was wrong to be cold-bloodedly planning your family that way; it might even be a sin. Still, Bridie could well look after her own immortal soul; Kathy had enough worries of her own.

Lizzie felt like a princess, and as she glanced along the row, she knew her dress was just as nice as all the other communicants'. She'd discovered that most girls with older sisters or cousins had handed-down dresses like hers, and not all the mothers had done such a good job as Kathy at making them look like new. And it was far better than having a dress loaned to you by the school, as some did if their families were really poor. Lizzie would have hated that.

Really, she thought, no one would have known her whole outfit wasn't new, for the dress and veil were sparkling white and her daddy had put white stuff on the sandals to cover any scuff marks. Her mammy had bought new white socks in the end, for she said Sheelagh's had gone a bit grey, and that morning she'd given Lizzie a missal with a white leather cover that was so beautiful to look at it was almost a shame to use it. Her grandma had given her a new rosary as she entered the church, and now she played it through her fingers and attempted to pray.

But she was too excited to concentrate and couldn't help feeling sorry for the boys sitting the other side of the church, for all they had were the white sashes loaned to them by the school. Their shirts were white, of course, and she guessed a fair few were new, but they looked very drab next to the girls in all their finery.

Lizzie's tummy rumbled as she'd known it would, for she'd not been able to have anything to eat or drink that morning as she was taking communion. It was only right, for she knew the little round tablet was not bread but the body and blood of Jesus Christ. It was a miracle, the priests said, that happened in the mass. It always made her feel a bit sick, that thought, but she never told anyone, they'd think her awful. She felt sick now too, waiting to take communion for the first time. Probably, she thought, it was because she was hungry, and she'd feel better when she had her breakfast in the school afterwards.

Lizzie knew the family would all be there for her that Sunday morning. In one way she was glad, but on the other hand, she knew that if she fidgeted too much, or looked round, or dropped her collection pennies, she'd catch it later. She knew where they all were, for out of the corner of her eye she'd seen her Auntie Maggie and Mammy and Daddy arrive with Danny between them, and all the others behind them. She glanced round once to smile, but her mammy made an impatient gesture with her hand that Lizzie knew meant for her to turn round and face the front. She did, but not before she saw Michael and Carmel, who Lizzie felt were too young to be called Uncle and Auntie, grinning back at her. Carmel was only twelve and could remember her own first communion; she knew how Lizzie would be feeling, and how her empty stomach would be churning at the enormity of it all.

Kathy watched all the earnest young communicants and hoped that it was a safe world they were growing up in. The news she listened to on the wireless at her parents' house was disturbing, as it was in the newspaper Barry had taken to bringing home in the evening. She knew that there was great trouble in Germany. Barry had explained that Hitler seemed to want to own the whole of Europe, and they weren't making guns in the quantities Barry said they were making them just to put in some vast storehouse. She said a fervent prayer for the safety of her family, especially Barry, Lizzie, Danny and the unborn child she was carrying, and as the strains of the organ filled the church and she stumbled to her feet for the first hymn, a chill of foreboding ran through her body.

TWO

Lizzie wasn't sure exactly when she became aware over the summer holidays that something wasn't right and that all the adults were worried. In the main, it was a holiday like any other; when the kids in the street got fed up of skipping and playing hopscotch and hide and seek and other street games, they would start to complain and fight and get under their mothers' feet. Then Carmel and girls of similar age would be pressed into service to take the children off to Cannon Hill, or Calthorpe Park, with a couple of bottles of tea and jam sandwiches to stave off hunger till teatime. It had been Carmel's lot to look after her cousins and their friends since she'd been nine years old, and much as she loved them, she often resented it. Sometimes she thought it was no good having a holiday if all you did all day was mind weans. She also knew it was no good saying anything about it and that lots of girls were in the same boat, so she usually went without complaining.

Lizzie thought at first that everyone was worried about her Auntie Rose, who was on her time again and little Pete only just two and Grandma said she was not having it easy. Then she thought it might be the row going on because her Auntie Maggie wanted to marry Con Murray and Grandma and Grandad wouldn't have it. Not only was he just a bookie's runner and not good enough, in their opinion, for Maggie, but he'd been put in prison for it too, and Grandad said no daughter of his would marry a jail bird.

Later, at home, she heard her parents discussing it. Barry said Con wasn't a jail bird really; all he did was place bets, and he at least felt sorry for him, he only did it because he couldn't get a decent job.

'It doesn't matter what you say, Daddy won't let her marry him,' Kathy said. 'He can't provide for her properly as a bookie's runner.'

'I couldn't provide for you for many years,' Barry reminded her.

'Aye, but you could when I married you,' Kathy said. 'And you'd never been inside.'

'No, but I can't blame the man, not totally,' Barry said. 'Anyway, so I hear it, when the men are put away, the firm, the people he places bets for, see to his family.'

'Oh, I'll tell Daddy that,' Kathy said sarcastically. 'I'm sure it will make all the difference! He'd have a fit if he thought his daughter, and possibly grandchildren, was being kept from starvation by people he'd consider not far removed from gangsters. Couldn't you ask round at your place?' she appealed. 'Maybe Con could get set on there?'

Barry shook his head. 'I doubt it, but I'll ask. In the meantime they'll have to wait. After all, once Maggie is twenty-one, she can do as she pleases.'

Kathy wondered if her headstrong young sister would be prepared to wait, for she was just nineteen, and two years seemed a lifetime away. Only the other day, she'd said to Kathy in a voice laced with a veiled threat, 'I could always force their hand, you know.'

'Don't be a bloody fool,' Kathy had snapped. 'Don't suggest bringing a child into this mess till you have something sorted.' She looked at her sister and asked, tentatively, 'You haven't . . . you don't . . .'

Maggie had tossed her mane of black hair so like her elder sister's, flashed her eyes that had a greenish tinge to them and snapped, 'That's my business.'

'Maggie, you'll get your name up.'

'Don't be such a fool. Con loves me.'

'You're the fool! If he loved you, he'd wait.'

'Till when? Till we're drawing the old age pension?'

'Oh, Maggie,' Kathy cried. 'Be careful.'

'I am careful,' Maggie said. 'I'm just saying that if Mammy and Daddy keep being awkward, then I might not be so careful, that's all. We're not made of stone, we can't wait forever.'

Lizzie knew that her family were worried about Maggie and Con, who went arm-in-arm down the street together. But she also knew that it wasn't just these ordinary worries that gave everyone the serious look to their faces; it was something more. They'd gather at Grandma Sullivan's to hear the news on the wireless broadcasts and talk about someone called Hitler, Chamberlain and Czechoslovakia. It was a while before Lizzie realised Czechoslovakia was a country and not a person's name, and that Hitler wanted to dominate it.

Her daddy, who seemed to know more about the situation than the others from the reading he'd done during his time of unemployment, feared that war, at least between Czechoslovakia and Germany, was inevitable. 'Whether we'll just stand by and watch this time is the question,' he said.

'Like we did when he marched into Austria, you mean?' Pat asked.

'Right,' her daddy said. 'The Anschluss he called it, but whatever name he puts on it, Austria ceased to exist from March this year. It's become another part of Germany, and

24

Czechoslovakia will be next, and if Britain do what they've done so far, it will be bugger all.'

'He won't be finished till he has the whole of Europe,' Eamonn commented.

'Aye, you're right,' Lizzie heard her daddy say. 'And we're allowing him to. That's not all, though. Some desperate tales are coming from those places about the terrible things he's doing to the Jews. I think the man has a screw loose and is a sadistic sod into the bargain.'

Lizzie felt her eyes widen. Her daddy had said two bad words, and it seemed to be catching, for she heard her Uncle Pat ask angrily, 'What the hell do you expect us to do, Barry? Go over there and bloody well stop the whole of the German army?'

'It might come to that, aye, it might.'

Mary said quietly, 'You mean war?'

'I mean just that.'

'Dear God!'

Suddenly the room was very quiet. Everyone was looking at Barry, and even Kathy was viewing her husband with new eyes. He spoke with some authority, as if he knew what he was talking about, though the subject of the talk chilled her to the marrow.

'Look,' Barry said, 'we can either let this bugger Hitler march into country after country, killing Jews and anyone else who disagrees with him on the way, or we've got to stop him. I think those are the only two choices.'

No one disagreed, but everyone hoped he might be wrong, that something would happen to avert the war Barry could see them heading straight for.

For a time, it seemed hopeful, for the prime minister, Chamberlain, took a hand in proceedings to promote peace at any price, and everyone was optimistic again. Barry, though, wasn't convinced. He read the papers avidly, and

25

even suggested to Kathy that they buy a wireless set, but she didn't give out to him and said they had plenty of other things to buy before that. Instead, she said he should keep his eye out for a second-hand one.

The day Barry brought a wireless home, just a week or so later, was one of great excitement. It was even bigger than their grandad's, Lizzie noticed, and there was hardly room for it in the fireplace alcove by the door down to the cellar. The accumulator, which Barry would have to have charged up at the garage in Bristol Street, sat beside it, and Lizzie and Danny and all the neighbours who had crowded in to see couldn't wait to hear something come out of the polished wooden box.

The children soon had their favourites. Both enjoyed *Children's Hour*, where Uncle Mac told them the stories of Toytown. They particularly liked Larry the Lamb and Denis the Dachshund and the tricks they got up to together, and they booed enthusiastically when the villain, Mr Crowser, came into the story. Uncle Peter read stories and poems and played the piano, but Lizzie preferred Uncle Mac and was always sorry when she heard him say, 'Goodnight, children everywhere.'

But then there was always Radio Normandy, which told the tale of Flossie, a naughty girl who went to Dr Whacken's School, which made everyone laugh. The very best of all, though, was Radio Luxemburg and the Ovaltineys. Lizzie, Danny, Maura Mahon and others would settle down on Sunday evening to listen to it. Many of the children in the street joined the club, and got a badge and a rule book, and on the programme they used to give out a message in code that the children had to break. Maura and Lizzie would puzzle over it and then help Danny, who hadn't a clue what a code was.

It became one of their favourite games, sending messages in code, and they all knew the Ovaltineys' song and sang it together every time the programme came on.

26

Kathy and Barry were pleased the children enjoyed the wireless so much, but its only value to them was to find out what was happening in the world, and they really only listened to the news. Lizzie couldn't understand it. 'Why don't you listen to music like Grandma?' she said. 'She likes the BBC Variety Orchestra and Victor Sylvester, but Carmel likes *Tune In* from Radio Luxemburg with Jack Payne and his band better. They're good, Mammy.'

'I haven't time to listen to music,' Kathy said dismissively.

Lizzie knew she made time to listen to the news all right and that was deadly boring. It was very puzzling altogether.

What wasn't puzzling was when her cousin Sheelagh, catty as normal, attacked her one day as the children were playing in the street together.

'My mammy says your daddy's a warmonger,' she said.

'He is not.' Lizzie didn't know what a warmonger was, but it didn't sound very nice.

'He is. She says he likes going round scaring people.'

'He doesn't, and anyway he doesn't scare people.'

'He might, going round saying there's going to be a war all the time,' Sheelagh said. 'My mammy says people like him should be locked up.'

Lizzie bounced on the pavement in temper. 'Don't you dare say that about my daddy.'

'I can say what I like, it's a free country.'

'I hate you, Sheelagh Sullivan.'

'I've always hated you, Lizzie up-the-pole O'Malley, and you're stupid and so's your precious daddy.'

The slap took Sheelagh by surprise, and she staggered back holding her hand to her face, where the mark of Lizzie's fingers showed scarlet streaks on her pale cheek. 'You! You . . . !' she screamed, as angry tears spouted out of her eyes. 'I'm telling me mammy about you.'

Aunt Bridie came round later, shouting about it. Lizzie had slunk home and was buried in a chair with a book, but was yanked out of it by her mother to stand before her furious aunt. 'Auntie Bridie says you slapped Sheelagh across the face,' Kathy accused her.

Lizzie was silent, and Bridie said angrily, 'Insolent little sod. Answer when you're spoken to.'

'I'll deal with this,' Kathy snapped, tight-lipped, and then she went for Lizzie herself. 'Well, did you, or didn't you?'

Lizzie, knowing denial was useless, said, 'Yes, I did, but she said—'

Her attempt at an explanation was thwarted, for Bridie leapt in. 'There, what did I tell you? You should see the mark on my Sheelagh's face. Child should be walloped for that.'

'How many times have I told you not to fight with Sheelagh?' Kathy shouted, ignoring Bridie. 'How many times?'

Lizzie shook her head dumbly, and Kathy grasped her shoulders and shook her soundly. 'Well,' she said, 'maybe this will remind you.' And she delivered two ringing slaps to the back of Lizzie's legs. Tears sprang to Lizzie's eyes, but she wouldn't let them fall. She looked defiantly at her Auntie Bridie, but said nothing until Kathy, terrified lest she say anything that would cause her to be punished again, grabbed her and ordered harshly, 'Go and get into bed. Go on! Before I give you another one, and there'll be no supper for you tonight.'

Much later, after Lizzie had cried so much her pillow was damp, her father came in with a mug of cocoa and a hunk of bread and jam. 'I couldn't have you hungry,' he said, and though he must have noticed the red-rimmed eyes, he made no comment about them. 'Want to tell me about it, pet?'

Lizzie nodded and recounted the row to her father, and at the end of it he said, 'Well, don't tell your mother, let it be a secret between us two, but I don't blame you one bit.'

'You don't?'

'No, but next time don't let her get to you. What is she anyway but a bag of wind?'

'Oh, Daddy.' The tears were falling again, and Barry said, 'No more of that now. Eat up your supper. Danny will be up in a wee while and I'll tell your mammy you're sorry, shall I?'

'You can tell her,' Lizzie said flatly. 'But I'm not really.'

Barry winked and said, 'We'll keep that a secret too, I think.'

Lizzie wished the priests were like her father, for she imagined that when she told it in confession – because she knew she'd have to tell – they'd take a very dim view of it altogether.

Downstairs, Barry explained to Kathy what the row had been about.

'Oh, how I hated to smack her,' Kathy said, 'and in front of that woman too, but I had to do something. Lizzie admitted hitting the child. If it had been anyone else it wouldn't have mattered so much.'

'It wouldn't happen to anyone else. No one gets our Lizzie going like Sheelagh,' Barry said. 'And the child's got a tongue on her like her mother, but our Lizzie's sorry now.'

A little later, when Kathy took Danny to bed, she said to Lizzie, 'Daddy's told me all about it and we'll say no more. I'm pleased you're sorry for what you did. I want you to try not to be such a bold girl in future, will you do that?'

'Yes, Mammy,' Lizzie said, and was glad of the dimness of the room that hid her smile.

Czechoslovakia was suddenly the name on everyone's lips, and some of the family and neighbours came round to the O'Malley house each evening now to listen to the news. Even easy-going Pat and his father, Eamonn, had begun to realise there was reason for concern, as had Michael, now a good friend of Barry's. Sean was the last of the men in the family to become aware that things were serious, but then his energies and worries were with his wife, Rose, who'd given birth to a little girl in mid-August but hadn't seemed to pick up as she should have done.

The children were back at school when the news came through about Hitler demanding control of the Sudeten area of Czechoslovakia. He claimed that three and half million German-speaking people there were being discriminated against by the Czech government. Kathy and Barry were by themselves early one evening, and Barry read the news out of the paper as Kathy sat knitting for the new baby, due in November.

'He might be satisfied with that, then?' Kathy asked hopefully, but she sensed Barry's unease.

He gave a grunt of disgust. 'Satisfied?' he repeated. 'He'll not be happy till he has the whole of Europe. I don't believe a thing the bugger says, Kathy, and neither should anyone with any sense.'

Chamberlain didn't share Barry's views and prevailed on the Czech government to make concessions to prevent a German invasion. When Chamberlain and the French prime minister, Daladier, met with Hitler in Munich on 29 September 1938, they agreed to Germany occupying the Sudetenland after guaranteeing the rest of Czechoslovakia safe from attack.

As Chamberlain arrived back waving his piece of paper and declaring, 'I believe it is peace for our time,' many were lulled into a false sense of security that war had been averted. Barry was not one of them.

However, he hadn't time to worry about it much, for in October, six weeks early, Kathy gave birth to a little boy. He was baptised Seamus and lived only for four days. Kathy was inconsolable for some time and her mother took over caring for her and Barry, as well as the children.

Mary, worried as she was about Kathy, was worried still further by Sean and Rose and their wee girl, Nuala. Then there was Maggie, who, seeing the advantage of her mother's time and energy being diverted elsewhere, was out till all hours and probably up to God alone knows what mischief with Con Murray.

Only Bridie seemed unaffected by anything. 'You'd think she'd help a bit,' Mary complained angrily to Eamonn one night. 'After all, the weans are off her hands at school all day, and yet never a hand's turn does she do for anybody.'

'Ah well, sure, that's Bridie for you.'

And that *was* Bridie, that was the trouble, concerned only for her own welfare and that of her children. She was jealous of Kathy and Barry and always had been, and it was all because of their house. Pat and Bridie lived in a communal courtyard, criss-crossed with washing lines. The yard also housed the dustbins, shared toilets and the brew or wash house. Kathy and Barry's house, on the other hand, opened on to the street, and had two doors, the second one on to the entry that led to the yard Bridie lived in. It had a large cellar lit with gas mantles and a huge white sink underneath a grating with a cold water tap. That tap meant Kathy could do her own washing in her own house. She even had a gas boiler beside the sink to boil the whites, and there was still plenty of room to get the bath down from the hook on the back of the door and fill it up for the children's weekly bath.

Mary thought them lucky to have the house, but she imagined they'd more than earned it. After their marriage they had lodged there with Barry's gran, who was the tenant. No sooner were they in than the old lady, seeing someone there to fetch and carry for her, took to her bed, and Kathy had a time of it, especially when she was expecting Lizzie.

Then the old lady became senile and began accusing Kathy of trying to poison her, and yet Kathy didn't lose patience, telling Mary she was just an old lady terrified of being put in the workhouse. When they got the house afterwards, Mary was pleased for them and Kathy said that in many ways she missed the old lady. Bridie, though, could never be happy for someone else's good fortune.

Mary sighed. Pat really deserved a medal for putting up with it all the way he did, but just now her energies had to go to Kathy, for the baby's death had knocked her badly and it was beginning to affect the whole family.

Kathy wouldn't even go to the bonfire down the yard on Guy Fawkes night, but sat huddled over the fire as if she were cold. She said she didn't feel up to it. In the end Eamonn went out and bought fireworks for the weans and Mary cooked the sausages to share, as was the custom, and Barry went down to keep an eye on the weans and let off the fireworks.

When they returned, they were sticky, smoke-grimed and tired, but happier than they'd been since their little brother had died. Mary, who'd been keeping Kathy company, decided the time had come for a straight talk with her daughter. When the weans were tucked in bed and Barry dispatched to the pub with the men, she began. 'Kathy, you can't grieve forever, love. God knows it's hard, pet, but you have two other weans to see to.'

'Lord, don't I know it!' Kathy cried. 'But Mammy, I can't.'

'You can and you must,' Mary said firmly. 'The weans miss you.'

'Sure, they have me.' But they hadn't, and Kathy knew that as well as her mother. They had a shadow of their old mammy, one with no substance and no life. And as for Barry, as far as Kathy was concerned, he might as well not have existed.

Kathy did try, but it was not until after the start of 1939 that she began to feel anything like herself. Even then she avoided Rose, as looking at the chubby, smiling Nuala was like a dagger in her heart. Danny began school in January, although he wasn't five until March. She'd hadn't even to leave him at the school, or collect him. 'Lizzie's well able to take him,' Mary said firmly, and she was right. Lizzie, now turned seven and a half, was proud to take her young brother along Bristol Street and into Bow Street, where the school was.

While the O'Malleys were coming to terms with the loss of their child, the Czechs were just beginning to realise that in agreeing to Hitler's demands, they had lost seventy per cent of their heavy industry. Slovakia, feeling let down by their government, demanded semi-independence. Fearing a revolt, and with the country in total disarray, President Hacha requested Germany's help 'to restore order'. German troops took possession of Czechoslovakia in March 1939. Britain and France complained, but did nothing; Hitler claimed he'd not invaded but been invited in, and turned his attention to Poland and, in particular, the city of Danzig.

Every night Barry would listen to the news reports, usually with Pat, often with young Michael and occasionally with Sean too. For a long time they'd discuss the news items together before dispersing.

No one now tried to convince themselves that the world wasn't at crisis point. Barry and Michael had been making anti-tank rifles, and now they'd been put on to making Browning 303 machine guns. No one objected to the long hours put in; everyone seemed to realise it was a race against time, and there was a sense of inevitability during the spring and summer of that year.

The summer holidays dawned wet, miserable and dull, but when July gave way to August there was a heat wave and the temperatures were sometimes the highest they'd been for thirty years. 'I wish we could go to the seaside,' Lizzie complained one day to Carmel, who agreed. They'd never been but had heard it was grand.

The pavements seemed to radiate the heat, so that it shimmered above them and they were dustier than ever. Lizzie sat on the step and watched three little boys building dust castles, which they then destroyed with their toy cars, making a great deal of noise about it. Others huddled in groups over piles of marbles. One little girl, younger than Lizzie, pushed a pram with a fractious baby inside, while a bit further down the street, two older girls wielded a long, heavy rope while another girl skipped inside the loop. Lizzie wondered how they could be so energetic. She was so hot, her clothes were sticking to her body. 'If we went to Cannon Hill Park, we could paddle at the sides of the lake,' she suggested. 'If Mammy would let us.'

'We'd have to take Sheelagh and Matt too, at least,' Carmel said.

'Couldn't we go on our own just once?'

'You know full well we couldn't.' Carmel was older and wiser than her niece. 'Sure, Bridie would play war if she found out.'

Suddenly Lizzie wasn't sure if she wanted to go, and have Sheelagh goading and sneering at her. She wasn't sure whether it wasn't a better prospect to stay in the hot street and swelter. But in the end she went, and her mammy and Auntie Rose went too.

Kathy was also feeling restless and unsettled and a day out with the children was maybe just what she needed. Also she thought she'd ignored Rose's baby daughter long enough; sure, it wasn't Rose or Sean's fault her baby had died.

They sat on a grassy incline overlooking the lake and watched the ducks and swans swimming between the

34

circling rowing boats. The children had stripped to the bare minimum, as had many others, and were squealing and giggling as they played together. Nuala was practising the new art of walking and now and again would tumble over and chuckle to herself.

'It's hard to believe dreadful things are going on in other parts of the world on a day like this,' Kathy remarked.

'I know Sean's really worried. Is Barry?'

'Everyone's worried. God, Rose, what if war comes and our husbands are called up and there are enemy planes in the sky?'

'You don't think it can be averted?'

'Not now, it's too late,' Kathy said. 'We heard it on the news, Hitler wants the town of Danzig, and if it's given up to German control he has a corridor straight through to Prussia, cutting off Poland's access to the sea. I don't see them agreeing to it, do you?'

Rose shook her head sadly. She looked at her little boy Pete, now a sturdy three-year-old, and Nuala still a baby, and shivered, and yet she believed her sister-in-law. Sean said Barry had a better grasp of the world situation than many of the politicians, which came from all the reading he'd done while he was on the dole.

It was as the women and children made their way home that they came upon men digging trenches. 'What are they doing?' Danny asked.

Rose and Kathy exchanged glances. Everyone was aware of the policy of digging trenches in parks and other open spaces; it had been on the news, but to actually see it being done was dreadful.

'What will they have us do? Cower in the mud like rats?' Bridie had said scathingly.

'Well, it will surely be better than nothing if you're caught in a raid,' Pat had retorted.

Kathy knew her brother was right and, as war was inevitable, and everyone knew that this time civilians everywhere would be targeted too, she should have felt reassured seeing the trenches being dug. Instead it filled her with dread. But she had to answer her small son. 'They're just digging,' she said shortly.

Danny walked to the rim of the trench to look in. The two men digging were stripped to the waist, their backs gleaming with sweat. One of them grinned up at him and all the children began edging forward to see.

'Come on now,' Kathy snapped.

The children, even wee Pete, took no notice and edged closer to look in.

'Pete,' Rose called warningly. 'Come on.'

Pete turned and looked but didn't move, and when Carmel attempted to pull him towards his mother, he began to shout and struggle.

'Come away out of that, the lot of you,' Kathy yelled impatiently, and the children came reluctantly, all except Danny. He continued to stare at one of the men, who suddenly rubbed his dirty hand across his brow. Danny was very envious. He thought it would be great to do work like that – fancy being able to dig all day long!

'Danny!'

Danny ignored his mother and rubbed his hand across his brow, imitating the man, who leant on his shovel and gave a bellow of laughter.

'Just a minute, Mammy.'

'I will not "just a minute", my lad,' Kathy said, marching over and grabbing her son by the arm. 'For once in your life you'll do as you're bloody well told.'

'Ah, missus,' said the man in the trench, understanding Kathy's mood far better than Danny did. 'Let's hope they're not needed.'

'Yes indeed,' said Kathy, dragging her protesting son away. She couldn't wait to get them home.

'Mr Brady came from the school,' Bridie told Kathy later that night. 'While you were away at the park.'

'They're on holiday, what did he want anyway?' she asked, surprised. The headmaster had called round: he'd never done such a thing before.

'He was talking about the evacuation programme.'

'They're not being evacuated,' Kathy said firmly. 'I talked it over with Barry. I've got the cellar and I'm not sending my weans to live with strangers.'

'Me neither. I told him I'd come into your cellar if there were air raids.'

Kathy knew she would, and however she felt about her sister-in-law, she couldn't deny her shelter if the bombs came. 'What did he say?' she asked.

'Well, he wasn't pleased. He said the government wanted to empty the cities of children, but it had to be our decision.'

'I wonder how many will go,' Kathy said. 'I mean, I wonder if they'll close the school.'

'Surely to God they can't do that, they can't leave our children running mad through the streets.'

'We'll have to wait and see,' Kathy said.

It was Lizzie who brought it up next. 'Mammy, Maura's going to the country.'

'I know.'

'Can I go?'

'No you can't.'

'Why not?'

'Because, that's why,' Kathy snapped.

'That's not a proper answer, Mammy.'

'Lizzie, do you want a slap?'

Lizzie looked at her mother reproachfully and Kathy reddened. She'd overreacted, surely. 'Look,' she said, 'I don't want you away with strangers. You're only eight, and Danny's just five.'

Lizzie looked at her mother and saw her fear, but didn't fully understand it. She didn't know what the country was, she'd never been, but Maura had made it sound fun, and she said that if Lizzie stayed at home, she'd be blown up. Lizzie wouldn't have minded going away for a while – well, as long as it wasn't for too long and she could look after Danny.

Suddenly she remembered her little brother Seamus; how her mammy had lost him and how ill she'd been over it, and she thought that must be it – she and Danny couldn't leave their mammy because their baby brother had died. She was even more convinced of it when her mammy put an arm around her and said, 'I don't know what I'd do without the pair of you, and that's God's truth, especially if your daddy gets called up.'

Then Lizzie knew she had to stay with her mother, and she'd explain it to Danny, and if they were blown up at least they'd be blown up together.

The priest thought that was the reason too. Father Cunningham had been a regular visitor after Seamus died and had eventually encouraged Kathy back to mass. Father Flaherty was a different kind of man altogether, and he sat in the easy chair as if he owned the place, while Kathy ran round feeding him tea and biscuits.

'I'm glad to see you're over that other business at last,' he said.

That other business! He was my son, Kathy thought, but the years of having manners drummed into her held firm, so she said nothing.

'Now,' Father Flaherty went on, 'you must protect the children you have.'

'I intend to, Father.'

'Oh, then you've changed your mind about evacuation? I was talking to Mr Brady, and he . . .'

'No, Father, no I haven't,' Kathy said. 'But you see, I don't understand how sending them off to live with strangers is any way to be looking after them.'

'And if the bombs come, what then?'

'At least we'll be together, Father, and my weans will have their mammy beside them, not some stranger, however safe the place.'

'They won't be alone. Many have chosen to send their children away.'

'That's their choice, Father. This is mine and Barry's.'

'It's because of the wee one you lost,' Father Flaherty said with authority. 'You're overprotective of the two you have left. It's understandable, but you must think of the children, not of yourselves.'

Kathy's eyes flashed. 'Father, it really is our business, and why I don't want them to go is just between me and Barry.'

'That's your final word?'

'It is.'

When the priest had gone, Kathy had set down on a chair, her legs trembling, for she'd never stood up to the man before. She knew he was a priest, but God forgive her, she couldn't like him, there was something about him that made her skin crawl.

Almost a week later, the lovely weather broke in Birmingham. Thick black clouds had rolled in and the air was heavy. 'Going to be a storm,' people said. 'We need one to clear the air.' Kathy looked at the purple-tinged sky and agreed. Her head felt muzzy and she knew she'd probably end up with a headache.

But when the storm came, the ferocity and intensity of it shocked everyone. For three hours the lightning flashed

39

and the thunder roared and rumbled. Rain hammered and bounced on the dusty pavements till they gleamed and streamed with water. The newscaster said Staffordshire had had the worst of it, and Kathy looked out at the depth of water outside, far too much for the gurgling gutters to cope with, and felt sorry for those worse off.

The news that night, though, wiped out worries about the weather, for there had been heavy troop movement from Austria to Slovakia and fanning out along the Polish border. Seventy Polish Jewish children arrived in Britain, where they would stay with foster parents until they were eighteen.

'Poor little devils,' Kathy said. 'They're coming to strange people, strange language and strange ways. It must have been a wrench for the parents, for they might never see them again.'

'At least this way they've got a chance,' Barry said. 'Hitler's record with Jewish people is not good. Oh, and thinking about children reminds me, have you picked up the gas masks yet?'

Kathy flushed. The very thought of putting one of those strange contraptions on her children terrified her. But then she remembered what had happened to her father, his lungs permanently damaged with the mustard gas he'd inhaled in the Great War. She knew she'd have to overcome her fear if there was gas about – to protect her children, at least. 'In this downpour?' she said indignantly to cover her unease, and added, 'I'll go up tomorrow.'

'See you do,' Barry said. 'It's as well to be prepared.'

It seemed everyone was getting prepared, for on the news the next day they heard that Paris had begun evacuating people, children first, and the Poles had issued a call-up to all men under forty. At home, the government issued guidelines on what to do in an air raid, black-out restrictions were about to come into force and Kathy and her neighbours were kept busy making shutters and curtains for their windows.

By Thursday, the navy had been mobilised, and working on the assumption that fire could cause as much damage as bombs, people were urged to clear their lofts and attics of junk and keep a bucket of sand or dirt on every landing.

On Friday the children who were being evacuated left from the school. Lizzie went with her mother and Danny to watch them marching out of the playground. In the event there were not many of them, twenty or twenty-five or so, Kathy thought, together with two teachers. The children had haversacks on their backs, or suitcases or carriers in their hands, gas masks in cardboard boxes slung around their necks and labels pinned to their coats. They were singing 'Run, Rabbit, Run' and waving and shouting like mad as they got into the waiting buses to take them to Moor Street Station. It all looked tremendous fun. Lizzie wished, just for a moment, that she was going too. But she knew her mammy needed her.

On the news that night, they learnt that German tanks had invaded Poland. The towns of Krakow, Teschan and Katowice were bombed before dawn, and Warsaw suffered a heavy bombardment and had many, many casualties. Chamberlain issued an ultimatum to Hitler to pull out of Poland or face the consequences, but Hitler had not replied.

'This is it,' Barry said, and indeed it was. The call-up of men under forty-one would begin immediately and the black-out became law.

'Bloody right,' Pat said. 'They can't back down now.'

'Well, why don't they declare war and be done with it?' Sean said. 'Rather than all this pussy-footing around, we should have taken Hitler out long ago.'

'Oh, listen to the big boys,' Bridie sneered. 'Jesus, when they have you all in uniform, you can go over there and show the others how it's done.'

'Be quiet, Bridie,' Pat said quietly.

41

Bridie bristled. 'Oh well, if I can't express an opinion, I'll be away home.'

'Ah, stay a while,' Kathy said. Really she wished Bridie far enough away, but fearing Pat would get the rough edge of her tongue later, she said, 'Have a drop of tea before you go.'

'No,' Bridie said. 'I've got Sadie next door giving an ear to the weans and she likes me to pop in with the news, so I'll be off now.' She looked across at Pat and said sharply, 'And you be in at a reasonable hour.'

'Yes, ma'am,' said Pat in a fake American accent, and gave her a salute.

Bridie glared at him and slammed the entry door, and Pat remarked to no one in particular, 'Should have her in the bloody army, if you ask me. She'd make a good general.'

Kathy spluttered over her tea, but she said nothing. She had wondered if Pat ever got fed up of his wife's constant carping, but he'd never said anything about her before. Pat met his sister's eyes over the wireless and smiled at her as he reached for his coat.

'Are you away?' Barry asked.

'Aye, but not home,' Pat said. 'Bridie can order all she likes, but I'll go home when I'm ready. I'm away to The Bell.'

'Wait,' Barry said. 'I'll come along with you.' He glanced over at Kathy and said, 'OK?'

'Fine, but I'll likely be in bed when you get in,' Kathy said. 'I'm beat.'

'You on, Sean?'

'You bet, lead the way.'

When they'd left, Kathy sat thinking. She wasn't tired really, but she was depressed. She faced the fact that in a day, two days, bombs could be raining down on England's cities, killing, destroying and maiming. Her husband and brothers would be there in the thick of it, and she began to shake with a fear deeper than any she'd experienced so far.

Saturday's news bulletin depressed Kathy further. Poland was fighting for its life. Many towns and cities had been attacked, with heavy civilian casualties, and even an evacuation train carrying women and children had been blown up. It seemed no one could stop the German monster sweeping Europe, and Kathy wondered if Britain would be strong enough. The only cheering news was that the Empire was on their side: Australian troops had arrived in Britain, New Zealand had promised support and Canadian forces were being mobilised. A report from the prime minister was promised in the morning.

That night in bed, Barry said, 'This is it, old girl, you know. After tomorrow, life will never be the same again.'

'I know.'

'I knew it was coming, but I wish to God I'd been wrong.'

'I know that too.' Kathy gave a sniff.

'You're not crying, are you?'

'A bit,' Kathy answered with another sniff. 'Isn't a war worth crying over?'

Barry gave a laugh. 'I'm damned if you ain't right,' he said. 'But for now, what are you going to give your husband to make up for the fact he'll not be sharing your bed for much longer?'

Kathy smiled and said, 'I'm sure I'll think of something.'

THREE

After all the storms, Sunday 3 September 1939 dawned sunny and warm, a perfect late summer's day. Kathy was up early and got breakfast just for Danny, as everyone else would be taking communion. 'The broadcast is at eleven, isn't it?' she asked Barry.

'Aye, and you can bet every person in this land will be listening in, and we'll be no exception.'

The church was fuller than usual and Kathy wondered if they were all praying as fervently as she was. Peace was out of the window now, and Kathy sat head in hands, almost overcome with sadness at it all. There was little chattering in the porch that day, everyone wanted to be away home to get the dinner on so they could listen to the broadcast.

Just before it began, Kathy was startled by how still it had become outside. She glanced out of the window. The streets were deserted, no baby cried, no toddler shrieked or chuckled, and no dog barked. Even the children seemed to know what an historic moment it was, for they'd picked up the atmosphere from the seriousness of the adults. So many people were crowded into the O'Malleys' house that Lizzie and Danny, as usual, had crawled under the table, but even amongst such a mass of people there was an uneasy silence, and Kathy realised she could hear no tram rattling along Bristol Street, nor the drone of the occasional car or the clop of horses' hooves. It was as if the world was holding its breath, waiting, and then they heard the dreaded words.

'I am speaking to you from the cabinet room of Ten Downing Street. This morning the British Ambassador in Berlin handed the German government a final note stating that unless we heard from them by eleven o'clock that they were prepared at once to withdraw their troops from Poland, a state of war would exist between us. I have to tell you now, no such undertaking has been received, and that consequently, this country is at war with Germany.'

For a moment there was silence, and then everyone began speaking at once, saying that it was only to be expected and that the Jerries needed teaching a lesson. Underneath the table, Lizzie told Danny, 'We're at war.'

'What's that?'

Lizzie wasn't sure, but no way was she going to admit it. 'Oh, it means there are lots of soldiers about,' she said. 'And guns and bombs and things, and Daddy might have to go away and fight bad people.'

'Oh,' said Danny, mightily impressed.

People were dispersing back to their own homes, Lizzie noticed, peeping out from between the chair legs, until there was just Auntie Bridie and Uncle Pat with Sheelagh and Matt between them.

'Well,' Pat said, looking across at Barry, 'I'm away for a pint.'

They exchanged a look that Kathy didn't really understand then, and Bridie snapped scornfully, 'Away for a pint? Any excuse for a drink, you. It's nothing to bloody well celebrate.'

'Oh, let them go,' Kathy said despondently. 'I'm away to Mammy's anyway. She'll feel it badly, and Daddy too, with them both remembering the Great War so well. Are you coming?'

Bridie shrugged. 'Might as well. We won't see the pair of them till closing time.'

We might, Kathy thought, if you moaned less about it, but she said nothing.

Rose was already at the Sullivans' house when Kathy arrived with Bridie and the children, Sean having gone with the other men. 'They called for Michael,' Mary said. 'And that bloody Maggie's slipped out somewhere.'

Only Carmel was left, and she suddenly looked very young and vulnerable. 'All right?' Kathy said.

'I suppose,' Carmel said uncertainly, with a slight shrug, and then she asked, 'What's it all mean, Kathy, will there be bombs and things?'

'Maybe,' Kathy said. 'But don't worry, you've got a stout cellar like ours. We'll be fine.'

How easy it was, thought Kathy, to reassure children. Not so easy to reassure adults, and she noticed for the first time that her mother's jet-black hair that she'd passed on to her three daughters and her youngest son was liberally streaked with grey, and deep lines scored her face.

There were tears in Mary's eyes and Kathy was shocked, for she'd never seen her mother cry before. 'Ah, Mammy, don't upset yourself.'

'What's the use of crying over it at all?' Eamonn said, almost roughly. 'Wasn't the last one supposed to be the war to end all wars, and what did I get out of it but buggered-up lungs and a partitioned Ireland?'

Kathy felt a lump in her throat. She'd heard this before, but it had never seemed to mean that much. All men of her father's time would probably feel betrayed, she thought, all those who had fought through the carnage, the blood and the mud of the trenches to make a land fit for heroes. As for the Irish, who had fought in order to obtain home rule for their country, it was even worse, because at the end of it all they'd only gained control of twenty-six of the thirty-two counties.

Disillusioned, and with no wish to return to his native soil, for his home in Beleek, Fermanagh, was still under British rule, Eamonn Sullivan and his wife Mary had settled with their two sons and one daughter in Edgbaston, Birmingham. His chest had a constant wheeze and rattle and he could do little without getting breathless. Kathy had never worried much about it; it had been like that all the years of her growing up. Once she'd asked her mother what was wrong with her daddy and had been told that the unit he was in had been gassed in the war, and that it had wrecked his lungs.

Mary knew that Eamonn, fit only for light duties, would have found it hard getting a job in that bleak time if it hadn't been for the fact that he'd saved an officer's life in France in 1915 by dragging him across the sludge of Flanders to the relative safety of a dugout. The injured officer had proved to be the son of the owner of a small button factory, based in Duddeston, a Mr Charles Sallenger.

Sallenger had sent five sons to the front, and one by one they'd all died, except for the youngest, Henry, saved by the young Irishman. The man's gratitude was sincere and touching, and when Henry explained about Eamonn's lungs, eaten away with gas, he was given a light job and knew he was set for life, and all because he'd been in the right place at the right time.

Now, however, Eamonn felt old and tired, and he looked it. Kathy was quite worried about him. Like Mary, his hair – or at least the bits he still had at the sides – was grey; the only trouble was, his face was the same colour, and he had deep pouches under his eyes, while the skin on his cheeks and around his mouth had begun to sag.

'Didn't you fancy a pint, Daddy?' she asked softly.

'No, child, I'd be no company for anyone this day,' Eamonn said sadly. 'I let the young ones go.'

'Don't need much of an excuse, do they?' Bridie said with a nod at Kathy. 'Any excuse for a drink.'

'They'll be talking over the declaration from this morning,' Kathy said. 'It's what they always do, you know that.'

'Talking, my arse. Tipping it down their necks, more like.'

'Oh, Bridie, give over,' Kathy said. 'We've a lot to be thankful for in our husbands.'

'Speak for your bloody self.'

Stung at the implied criticism of her favourite brother, Kathy snapped, 'Pat's a good man and a good provider. I don't know why you're always on at him.'

'Oh, of course, you won't hear a bloody word against him, will you?' Bridie said. 'Bloody saint, your Pat.'

'That will do!' Eamonn said. 'Haven't we enough troubles facing us without turning on one another?'

'I'll make a drop of tea,' Mary said. 'Sure, the news is enough to make anyone a bit edgy.'

Kathy glared at her sister-in-law, but didn't reply. She wished Maggie was in, and wondered where she'd gone, for between them they could have lightened the atmosphere that grew stiffer and stiffer as they sat together, almost in silence. Carmel was too young and her father too saddened by the news.

None of the children had spoken, and Lizzie had sidled up to Carmel. She liked to have someone at her back when Sheelagh was in the room, or in fact anywhere near her at all. Sheelagh put out her tongue as she passed and Lizzie elected not to see it, though her hands tightened into fists. If she ever hit Sheelagh again, she thought, she'd make a better job of it and really hurt her, and she reckoned it would be worth having the legs smacked off her afterwards.

Mary had just come up the cellar steps with the tray when the front door opened and the men almost fell into the room. At first Kathy thought they were drunk, but there was no smell of alcohol and she realised it was a forced gaiety, and yet she could also feel the exhilaration flowing through them all. Suddenly she knew what they'd done and understood the look that had passed between Barry and Pat earlier that day. Yet still she asked, 'What is it?'

'We've enlisted.'

'You have, begod!' The exclamation was torn from Eamonn. Mary stood with the tray in her hands, staring at them.

'We wanted to be together,' Barry exclaimed, and crossed to Kathy. 'I'm sorry, love, we agreed between ourselves to say nothing till it was done.'

Kathy felt the tears in her eyes, but held them back. She knew they didn't have to join up at all, being Irish citizens, but all she said was, 'It's probably better this way.'

'Not Michael,' Mary said, and she turned to her youngest son. 'Not you?'

'Aye, me and all, Ma.'

'But you're not eighteen yet, you're too young.' Mary's complaint was almost a moan.

'I'll be eighteen in January, Ma,' Michael said. 'Ah, don't cry, I had to do it.' He crossed to his mother, took the tray from her and placed it on a table, then put his arm around her shaking shoulders.

'We'll look after him, Ma,' Pat promised. 'We're all in the Royal Warwickshire Fusiliers and we can look out for one another.'

'You knew what they'd do,' Eamonn said. 'They made no secret of it.'

'Course they didn't,' Bridie snapped. 'They couldn't wait to get into uniform and be given guns to play with.'

49

'Shut your mouth,' Eamonn snapped, and the family was shocked into silence, but it was to Bridie he spoke. 'You know nothing about it,' he said, 'and I hope you never will, but there's no playing in war.'

Bridie said nothing. Eamonn had never spoken to her like that before and she was shaken. Perhaps she might have retaliated, but before she had a chance Pat said, 'Someone else enlisted with us today too. He's waiting outside.' He opened the door and Maggie came in, leading Con Murray by the hand.

'He enlisted, Daddy, like he said he would,' Maggie cried. 'Like he would have got a decent job if there had been any to be had. Now will you let us bloody well get married?'

Eamonn looked at the man before him whom he'd previously dismissed and refused even to talk to, and liked what he saw. Con's face wasn't exactly a handsome one, but it was open and, for all his shady dealings, looked trustworthy and honest. His eyes were clear blue and his hair was almost blond, he had a wide mouth and a determined set to his jaw, and one hand was holding Maggie's as if it belonged there. Certainly, Eamonn thought, the fact that the lad had enlisted put a different complexion on matters. 'Well, young man?' he said.

Con stepped forward and grasped Eamonn's hand. 'I'm very pleased to meet you, sir, and I hope you will allow Maggie to become my wife.'

Mary had tears in her eyes again, and the room was so blurred she couldn't see, but she knew from Eamonn's voice that he was moved, as he said gruffly, 'Well now, I see no reason why not, but it will have to be done speedily. We must remember that your time is not your own any more, so we'll have to see about it without delay.'

Con swept Maggie into his arms and a cheer went up from the men. 'Stupid bloody sod,' Bridie said, but only

Kathy heard; everyone else was too busy congratulating the young couple and welcoming Con to the family, while Maggie was kissing her parents and expressing her thanks.

Eventually Eamonn said, 'I have a bottle of ten-year-old malt put away for just such an occasion, and we'll drink a toast to the young couple and a speedy outcome to the God-awful mess the world is in.'

'I have tea,' Mary said.

'Ach, tea, what good's that, woman?' Eamonn said. 'Sure, this is a celebration.'

As the glasses were raised a little later, Kathy's silent prayer was, 'Keep them safe, God, please, bring them all home safe,' and she caught her mother's eye and knew her sentiments would be exactly the same.

Lizzie missed her father greatly, and the man who came home on a week's leave in October didn't seem like her daddy at all. He was dressed all in khaki that was rough against her legs when he pulled her against him. 'How's my little girl then?' he said, and she wanted to put her arms around his neck and sob into his shoulder because she was scared that everything had changed in her young life, and yet she said nothing, knowing without being told that she shouldn't spoil her daddy's leave with a list of complaints.

The second day of the leave was Con and Maggie's wedding day, which both were anxious to have finalised before Con went overseas. Lizzie was quite disappointed in the sober cream suit Maggie wore, though she had to admit it looked good on her as she walked down the aisle of St Catherine's Church on Eamonn's arm. She'd expected a long, flowing white dress, but her mother said there wasn't time to go to so much trouble and anyway it wasn't right in wartime.

It seemed the war affected everything. The local pub, The Bell, put on a spread for the few friends and family who called to wish the couple well, and the landlord Johnny McEvoy said it was the least he could do.

No one could deny Maggie's happiness, Kathy thought; it shone out of her and affected everyone, even Mary and Eamonn, who'd have liked their girl to have had a better send-off. Con went round with a proud smile on his face and his eyes followed Maggie's every move.

There was no time or money for a honeymoon, but the newly-weds had one night together in a hotel. After that, it was back to Mary and Eamonn's, for all had agreed there was no point in Maggie looking for her own place until the war should be over and Con discharged. However, for the duration of the rest of his leave, Michael and Carmel lodged with Kathy so that Con and Maggie could have the attic bedroom to themselves.

Lizzie loved having Carmel share her room and wished she could do it all the time; it was like having an older sister. Carmel was thirteen now and anxious to be leaving school in the spring. 'What will you do?' Lizzie asked, and Carmel shrugged.

'I'm not sure, but anything has got to be better than school, hasn't it?'

Lizzie liked school, but answered, 'Oh, yes.'

'Since the war's been declared there's more choice,' Carmel said.

'Is there?' That was the first Lizzie had heard of the war being good news for anyone.

'You bet,' Carmel said emphatically. 'My friend's sister is making munitions, that's where the money is. She's making a packet.'

'Gosh.'

'Shame you're so young, really,' Carmel said a little disparagingly. 'The war will be over before you grow up.'

Lizzie remembered all the men going off to fight and thought she hoped it would, but said nothing. 'March next year I'm off,' Carmel went on. 'I'll be fourteen then.' She sat up in the bed she was sharing with her niece and squeezed her knees tight in excitement as she said, 'Just over four months. Ooh, I can hardly wait.'

They heard the footsteps on the stairs and quickly lay down in the bed again, thinking it was Kathy or Barry come to scold, but it was only Michael, who was also sharing the bedroom. 'You two still awake?' he said quietly, to avoid waking the sleeping Danny.

The two girls kept their eyes closed and pretended to be asleep, and Michael chuckled. 'Don't be codding on,' he said. 'We could hear you talking and giggling downstairs. Kathy was for coming up, she thought you'd wake Danny.'

Lizzie opened her eyes and looked at her uncle. 'Danny never wakes,' she said. 'He'd sleep through an earthquake; he's boring.'

'Maybe he thinks bed's the place for sleeping,' Michael said, his voice muffled by the curtain Barry had set up for him to change behind.

'That's what I mean, he's boring,' Lizzie said.

Carmel put in, 'You can't expect our Michael to understand that, he's just a man,' and Michael's throaty chuckle was the last thing Lizzie remembered about Maggie's wedding day.

The five-day leave was almost over before Barry talked to Kathy about the war, not wanting to spoil their time together before. They were by themselves for once. Carmel had returned home; Sean and Pat were with their own wives and children; Con, Maggie and Michael were about their own concerns, and Barry was grateful for it. 'I think it's the big push for us when we go back,' he said.

'You mean overseas? France?'

'I can't be sure, but it's odd to have a week's leave like this, and rumours are flying about everywhere,' Barry said.

'It's so soon,' Kathy said.

'Hitler's hardly likely to wait around while we go through a six-month training period.'

'I know that.'

'And they've been putting us through it, I can tell you,' Barry said.

'You're looking forward to it,' Kathy said accusingly, looking at Barry's excited face.

'Partly,' Barry admitted. 'After all, it's what I joined up for, and it's nice we'll be going together, wherever we end up.'

'Pat seems a bit quiet,' Kathy said. 'Is he all right?'

'That's Bridie, I think,' Barry said. 'Putting him down all the time. He's different at the barracks, life and soul. Very popular bloke.'

Something in Barry's tone alarmed Kathy, and she asked, 'He isn't . . . you know . . . like, cheating on her or anything?'

Barry didn't answer. Instead he dropped his eyes from Kathy's and said, 'She hasn't let him near her for years, you know, not since she had Matt. Many a man would have insisted, a bloke can be too easy-going. Well now, if he is seeking comfort elsewhere, Bridie only has herself to blame. He's flesh and blood same as the rest of us. Mind,' he went on, 'I don't know that he is, not for certain, and I don't ask, but there's plenty of girls who would be only too happy to . . . well, you know. Like I said, he's popular. You'd have to go a long way to find another like Pat.'

Didn't Kathy know it; she couldn't blame him, and God alone knew he needed a medal for putting up with Bridie. Barry was right, a man could be too easy-going; another man would have given Bridie many a clout for half the things Kathy had heard her say to Pat. She didn't doubt what Barry had told her about Pat and Bridie's sex life, for hadn't Bridie said the same to her? But God, wasn't she a stupid fool denying her husband, and it was a sin too. Many would have had the priest to see her by now, but Pat likely wouldn't want to embarrass her like that. Suddenly she gave a huge sigh.

'Come on,' Barry said, pulling her to her feet. 'Stop worrying about Pat. Worry about me for a change. I'll be away in the morning, so I want something to remember in the weeks ahead.'

'Oh, maybe I'll say I'm not in the mood, like Bridie,' Kathy said with a smile.

'Try it, my girl, and I'll have you across my shoulder and carry you to bed, where I'll insist you carry out your wifely duty,' Barry told her with mock severity. 'I'm no Pat Sullivan.'

Lizzie heard them later, going laughing up the stairs. She was glad they were friends, but somehow it made her feel more lonely than ever. She knew her father would be gone in the morning and she hadn't told him how she felt, and she'd not get the chance again.

With Maura Mahon and a couple of Lizzie's other friends either evacuated with the school or sent away privately to relations and friends, Sheelagh was the only one near Lizzie's age in the road, and so they were always being grouped together. Sheelagh never seemed to mind, and Lizzie thought she derived malicious pleasure from having someone to taunt and make fun of all the way to school in the morning and back in the evening. She'd go round in the playground with gangs whose aim in life was to harass Lizzie O'Malley. They thought her fair game, being a year younger, and singled her out mercilessly.

Lizzie, depressed and miserable, considered complaining to her mother, but she'd probably think she was making something out of nothing and say Sheelagh was just having a game, and it wasn't as if they ever did anything.

Anyway, she knew that she couldn't worry her mother, however bad it got; she already had enough on her plate, without Lizzie adding to it. Barry had asked Kathy to keep an eye on his own mother, Molly O'Malley. She was a widow with no daughters, and none of Barry's three brothers were married, but all of them were overseas, so Kathy felt in some way responsible for her. She didn't live far from the O'Malley home, just at the top end of Grant Street, and Kathy had no objections to looking out for her.

'She's bound to feel it,' Barry had said. 'Especially with us all gone,' and she did, for Kathy said she was a bag of nerves worrying about them all and she made a point of going up to Grant Street a couple of times a week. Kathy's father was fire-watching too, and that was another cause for concern, for Lizzie knew her grandad's chest was terrible.

Then there was the black-out, which had to be fixed to every window before the gas could be lit and the ARP wardens parading outside to see it was done properly. Lizzie hated the black drapes at the living-room windows and the black shutters on the bedrooms. They made her feel closed in and uneasy, but her mammy said it had to be done.

And in addition to all this, October had been particularly cold and dismal, and after a warm September it was hard to take. Then November proved to be the same, with biting winds driving the sharp spears of rain bouncing on to the grey pavements. And in the cold and the rain the Royal Warwickshire Fusiliers were part of the British Expeditionary Force that headed for France.

Then December was upon them, and there was also talk of rationing being introduced just after Christmas. Kathy was worried about how they'd cope. 'Same as everyone else, I suppose,' Bridie said gloomily one day, and added, 'I suppose our soldiers will be fed all right and it won't matter if the rest of us starve.'

'I don't think it will come to that,' Kathy said. 'And at least with rationing it will be fair; rich or poor will all have the same.'

'Huh, we'll see.'

Kathy couldn't make Bridie out; she never seemed happy about anything or anyone. She decided to change the subject. 'Have you heard from Pat at all?' she said.

'Aye, though he never has much to say.'

'Their letters are censored, I suppose,' Kathy said. 'Though Barry is usually able to drag up something to amuse the weans.'

'He writes to the weans?'

'Aye, he always includes a wee note, you know. They miss him so much, especially Lizzie.'

Bridie gave a snort of disgust and said, 'If you ask me, he spoils that girl.'

'I didn't ask you.'

'Well, if I can't express an opinion . . .' said Bridie, rising to her feet.

'I'm sorry,' said Kathy. 'I'm all on edge, worry I suppose, and with Christmas nearly on us and hardly anything in the shops it'll be a lean one this year, and strange without Barry.'

The conversation was cut short by the children bursting through the door, Lizzie dragging Maura Mahon after her. 'Maura,' said Kathy, addressing the child in surprise, 'I thought you were away?'

'I was, Mrs O'Malley,' Maura replied. 'Mammy came to fetch me home. She said there was no point in it.'

'Your mammy told me you were staying just outside Stratford.'

'Aye, a tiny wee place called Preston upon Stour.'

'And did you like it?'

'No, I didn't, no one likes it, not even the teachers,' Maura said vehemently. 'It was cold and damp all the time and there was nowhere to go and nothing to do.'

'So the country isn't nice then?' Lizzie asked.

'No it ain't, it's blooming awful,' Maura declared. 'Mammy says I haven't to go back.'

Lizzie didn't care why or how Maura had come back; she was here and that was all that mattered. Her prayers had been answered. Life was almost back to normal again and if only her daddy was home, it would be nearly perfect.

The rationing of basic foodstuffs began on Monday 8 January that year, with every person allowed four ounces each of bacon, sugar and butter per week. Kathy knew it was only the beginning, and she wondered how she would stretch it all to last. She herself was allowed extras like orange juice, cod liver oil and vitamins, because she was pregnant again. She was glad in a way because she still pined for the baby she'd lost, but her pleasure in a new life beginning inside her was tinged with trepidation. She thought back to her last pregnancy, which had been trouble free at first. There had been no reason at all for her little son Seamus to be born so prematurely. 'Just one of those things,' the doctors had told her, which was no help at all. She was terrified of it happening again and this time Barry wouldn't be there beside her either. But then it was no use worrying. Weren't they all in God's hand at the end of all? And yet another mouth to feed on army pay would not be easy. Barry had earned good money making guns at BSA, especially with the overtime he was almost forced to work, but now, as a serving soldier, his pay was substantially reduced and Kathy was glad she'd been prudent enough to save some of his earnings in the post office. Eamonn said it was scandalous that men fighting for their country were so undervalued, but nothing could be done.

Kathy was amazed and pleased to find that both Rose and Maggie were pregnant too, all three babies due in late July.

Sharing their pregnancy pulled them closer together, but Bridie, as soon as she discovered it, would be ready with the cutting remarks Kathy knew only too well. She found out one day in late January when they were all together in Mary's house and she overheard Kathy discussing morning sickness with Rose.

'God in heaven!' she exclaimed. 'Are you on again?'

Kathy stared at her sister-in-law. Though she'd told Rose and Maggie and her parents, she'd dreaded telling Bridie. 'Aye, aye I am,' she said, almost defiantly.

'Well, what kind of a bloody fool are you?' Bridie burst out. 'Christ, as if you haven't enough on your plate.'

'I'm only having a baby, for heaven's sake, like plenty more.'

'Aye, and there's a war on, in case you haven't noticed.'

'Leave her be,' Rose said. 'Like Kathy said, she's not the only one.'

'Not you and all,' Bridie exclaimed. 'Mother of God, what's the matter with the pair of you? And as for you,' she said, addressing Rose directly, 'what are you trying to do, populate the whole of the bleeding earth by yourself? I mean, Pete's only three and Nuala just a baby herself.' She shrugged and went on. 'Well, if you want to go through life with a clutch of children hanging on to your skirt, that's your look-out.'

'That's right, it's our business,' Maggie broke in. 'You live your life and we'll live ours. And you might as well know, I'm expecting as well, so what are you going to say to me?'

Bridie gave a mirthless laugh and said, 'Well, all I'll say is that your old man must have plenty of lead in his pencil.'

'Bridie!' Mary cried. 'Less of that talk.'

But Bridie wasn't finished. 'Unless, of course, the wedding was rushed forward for a reason.'

'You malicious cow!' Maggie cried. 'You'd like that, wouldn't you? Well, let me tell you, my baby is due on the thirtieth of July. Not everyone's the same as you, you know.'

'What d'you mean?' Bridie snapped.

'Well you didn't wait till the ring was on your finger, did you?'

Bridie was white with fury. The reason for her rushed marriage had been covered up and Maggie had only been a child then, so it must have been discussed by them all since. She glared over at Kathy and Maggie cried, 'Don't be blaming anyone, Bridie. No one said a word to me, but I'm not stupid. I was eleven years old and well able to count to nine, but you'd only been married six months when Sheelagh appeared. Now treat me like a bloody simpleton why don't you, and tell me she was premature?'

'Come on now,' Mary said, flustered by the way the whole conversation was going. 'Let's not have all this snapping and snarling at one another, but save our bad temper for the enemy.'

Bridie for once had nothing to say. She threw them all a look of pure hatred and flounced out of the room and slammed the door behind her.

Later, Mary said to Kathy, 'I wonder if she's jealous of you all. I mean, there's been no sign since young Matt. Maybe she wants one herself and that's what makes her so crabby at times.'

'I think she was just born that way, Mammy,' Kathy said. She thought over what Barry had told her before he left and went on, 'and I don't think she wants any more but the two she has, not really.'

A few months later, the three expectant mothers listened, horrified, to the news that Hitler had invaded France, not through the Maginot Line that the French had thought impregnable, but through Belgium. German paratroopers had blasted their way through the Belgian defences, and the road through the country lay wide open.

It soon became clear that many soldiers of the British Expeditionary Force were trapped on the shores of France, and when the news finally broke on 31 May, Operation Dynamo was revealed. Many small, privately owned boats of all shapes and sizes were pressed into service to run a shuttle service from the beaches of Dunkirk to the ships forced to lie offshore in deeper water, battling under heavy bombardment to lift as many men as possible to safety.

Kathy listened to every news report and scoured the papers, and prayed like she'd never prayed before. Her prayers were partially answered, for in early June she got a letter saying that Barry was in a military hospital on the south coast. Her relief was short-lived though, for only minutes later Bridie arrived wailing at the door, waving a telegram in her hand and crying that Pat was missing, presumed dead.

Kathy, though bitterly upset over the news about Pat, was nevertheless determined to see Barry and check he was all right. Her parents thought it was the last thing on earth she should do. 'They'll transfer him nearer later,' Mary said.

'I don't want to wait till later. I must see him now and at least know he's all right. Maybe he has some news of the others.'

'Cutie, dear, think about it,' Mary said. 'Traipsing the country in your condition isn't wise or sensible. God above, look what happened to wee Seamus.'

'You're taking a big risk, Kathy,' Eamonn said, agreeing with his wife.

Kathy knew she was taking a big risk and her parents were justified in their concern – and she knew this headlong dash she was determined on could bring about the very thing she dreaded: a premature birth. But the urge to see Barry and reassure herself overrode her other fears. 'I can't just sit here fretting over him. I'll go mad,' she cried. 'One way or the other, I'm going to make it to that south coast hospital as soon as is humanly possible. And what if he has news of Con, or Michael or Sean,' she went on. 'Don't tell me you're not as worried sick about them as I am?' She looked at her parents, their faces creased and lined with anxiety and said more gently, 'I'm going. Sensible or not, I'm going. Will you mind the weans for me?'

'Aye, surely we will,' Mary said. 'You don't have to ask, if you're determined to go.'

'I'm determined well enough,' Kathy said. 'And I'm away now to tell his mother, give her the good news that Barry is alive.'

'Aye, poor soul,' said Mary with feeling. 'She'll need something to hang on to, with the telegrams she had the other day. Lord, to hear of two sons killed in one day is hard to take.'

'Och, woman, don't be so daft,' snapped Eamonn. 'It doesn't matter a damn when you hear it; to lose two sons would rip the heart out of you.'

The room fell silent and all had the same thought. The only one of the family they were sure about was Barry, and he was in hospital with God alone knew what injuries. Pat was missing, and of Sean, Michael or Con there was no news. They could all be casualties of this war, Kathy thought.

But Barry was alive, she told herself, and she held on to that thought. Nothing else mattered at that moment. She knew she wouldn't rest until she saw him for herself. She needed to hold him close and tell herself that he was alive and going to stay that way.

FOUR

Long before Kathy reached her destination she was feeling hungry and exhausted. Her journey had been subject to unexplained delays and stoppages, and the carriages were full of troops. Posters demanded, *Is Your Journey Really Necessary?* and she thought wearily that if it wasn't, the way her trek had gone so far, she wouldn't have made the effort.

Kathy could never remember travelling on a train before. She knew she must have done when she left Ireland with her parents, but she'd been just a child then and she had little recollection of her life before that of the back-to-back houses of Birmingham's inner ring.

Since then she'd never once ventured out of the city, and was totally unprepared for the clamour, noise and bustle of New Street station. The clatter of trains, slamming of doors and shrill whistles of the porters mixed with the shouts and cries of the people thronging the platform – many in khaki, Kathy noticed – made her nervous.

A train clattered to a stop behind her with a squeal of brakes and a hiss of steam that seeped along its wheels. Suddenly there was a terrifying loud shriek from a train opposite and Kathy saw billows of steam emerging from a brass funnel. She could smell soot and smoke in the air, and the place was so draughty, her teeth began to chatter.

She glanced at the large clock hung above the station platform, wondering where her train was. The clock said ten twenty, and yet the train should have left at five past. When it eventually arrived, with a deafening rumble, she was quite unnerved, but the mass of people surged forward and she was swept along in the flow.

Once inside, everyone but Kathy seemed to know what to do. She trailed up and down the corridor looking for an empty, or near-empty, compartment, but the train was cram-packed.

Eventually a young soldier, seeing her pass back along the corridor again, stepped out of a compartment and said, 'There's room for you in here, missus, we'll all budge up a bit.'

Kathy knew it would have to do and sat down thankfully, but as the train hurtled south, she realised she didn't know where she was going to get off, for all the station names had been blacked out. She found it very unnerving and worried that she wouldn't know when they reached Plymouth.

In the event, the soldiers helped her. Despite having three brothers, she hadn't been used to meeting strange men in such numbers, and at first she found them intimidating. However, most were kindness itself, especially when they knew the purpose of her visit. 'I didn't realise it was so far away or that it would take so long to get here,' she confided to a soldier who'd told her Plymouth was the next station.

'Every journey takes hours in this war, missus,' the soldier said. 'Half our lives we spend waiting.'

Kathy looked at her watch – four o'clock – and knew it was doubtful she'd get home that night. She remembered Lizzie's anxious face pressed to the window pane, watching her walk away. She'd wanted to come and see her daddy, and any other time Kathy might have taken her, but she knew wartime was not the time to haul children about the country, so she'd explained that Lizzie had to be very adult and grown-up and not make a fuss about things. The child was disappointed, but she said not a word and instead sat with a set, worried face waiting for her mother to return and tell her how her daddy was. The stoicism of it tore at Kathy's heart.

'Have you any more children?' the soldier asked. 'I can see you're expecting, like my own wife back home.'

'I have two,' Kathy said. 'A boy and a girl. Lizzie is nearly nine and Danny is six, and this one,' Kathy said, indicating her stomach, 'is due in July.'

'It's our first, Brenda's and mine,' the soldier said. 'Due any day – can't help wondering and hoping that she'll be all right, you know?'

'I'm sure she will,' Kathy assured him. 'After all, women have been doing it for years.'

'Yes, I know, it's just not being there with her . . . I worry a bit.'

'I bet she worries more about you,' Kathy said with feeling. 'Barry was hardly ever out of my thoughts for long, and when I heard he'd been injured, my heart stopped beating for a minute or two.'

'You don't know how bad it is?'

'No, they didn't say.'

'Well, if they've transferred him, he can't be that bad.'

'You think so?' Kathy grasped the lifeline hopefully.

'It's what they say.'

At that moment the train gave a sudden lurch and the soldier turned to Kathy and said, 'We're coming in to Plymouth now. Wait for the crush to pass and I'll get you a taxi.'

'Oh, I don't think . . .'

'You'll never find it on your own.' And Kathy knew he was right and just nodded.

'Have you a bag?' he asked, looking around the compartment.

'Only my handbag,' Kathy said.

'But you'll not get back tonight,' the soldier said. 'Have you a place to stay?'

'No, no, I never thought.'

'You'd be welcome at the barracks,' the soldier said with a smile. 'Well, at least the men would welcome you, but the sergeant might have something to say.'

Kathy smiled. 'I think I'll pass on that,' she said.

'Maybe the taxi driver knows of somewhere. I should check it out before you get to the hospital.'

Kathy thanked him, but once in the taxi she knew she had to see Barry right away. The problem of where she was to spend the night could wait. She'd passed through the countryside in the train without really taking it in, but in the taxi she was surprised by the sea, calm and sparkling in the mid-June afternoon. There were many couples strolling arm-in-arm as if they hadn't a care in the world, and yet the men, almost without exception, were in uniform, and Kathy knew the reality was quite different.

She lost no time when the taxi stopped outside the hospital, but hurried inside to find someone who could tell her where Barry was and when she could see him. Shortly after she entered the building she was confronted by a nurse whose name tag identified her as Sister Hopkins. 'Mrs O'Malley?' she said, when Kathy had introduced herself.

'Yes, I'm Barry's wife,' Kathy said, nervous before the stern-faced woman and almost frightened now she'd got this far. 'Can, can I see him?'

'Well, it's most irregular.'

'Oh, please,' Kathy said. 'I've come all the way from Birmingham. My family are desperate for news of him and I've left behind two very worried weans.'

Sister Hopkins stared at the woman in front of her. She was startling to look at, with her raven-black hair and deep-brown eyes, but her face was pasty white and there were black rings circling the eyes. She was far advanced in pregnancy and yet had come halfway across the country to see her man. 'Maybe you can see him for a little while,' she said.

'Is . . . is he badly injured?'

'No, not really,' the nurse said. 'He has shrapnel wounds to his head and abdomen and his left arm is badly lacerated – we thought at one point he might lose it, but the doctor has managed to save it, at least so far. We have to keep an eye on it in case of infection, and of course only time will tell if he'll ever regain full use of it.' She looked at Kathy's startled face and said, 'Believe me, Mrs O'Malley, your husband was one of the lucky ones.'

Kathy stared open-mouthed, amazed that someone could talk with so little emotion of removing a limb. Sister Hopkins caught her look and said, 'You should see some of the poor beggars lifted from the beaches of Dunkirk.'

Not to mention those left behind. Neither woman said it, but both thought it.

Barry lay staring at the ceiling, a bandage swathed about his head and his face as white as the pillow he lay on. Kathy said nothing till she stood beside the bed and then she whispered, 'Barry.'

He turned his head, and though Kathy could tell that he was pleased to see her, his enthusiasm was slightly forced. There was something lurking behind his eyes. 'Kath!' he cried. 'God, when did you . . . how did you?'

'We were informed you were here,' Kathy said. 'I had to come and see you, the weans were asking for you.' She spread her empty hands and said, 'I couldn't stop to buy anything, not indeed that there's much in the shops.'

'No, no, it's all right,' Barry quickly reassured her. 'To see you is enough.' He passed his unbandaged hand across his eyes and said, 'You've heard about Pat, I suppose?'

'Just before I left, yes,' Kathy said. '"Missing presumed dead", the telegram said.'

'Oh, he's dead all right,' Barry said, almost harshly, and then, catching sight of Kathy's stricken face, went on, 'I'm sorry, that was bloody clumsy.' He took Kathy's hand and said, 'I know you loved him, and I did too, funny that coming from a bloke, but he was the best mate I ever had. I'd known him from the day we started school together and that was that really, it was always us together against the world. I met you through knowing your Pat, and even after our marriages we were mates. God!' he cried. 'What a bloody waste.'

'What happened?' Kathy said. 'Do you want to talk about it?'

'Oh, aye, I'll talk about it. Like lambs to the bleeding slaughter we were,' Barry said bitterly. 'It was bedlam, the Jerries advancing and we had orders to retreat to the beaches. We got separated from our company, Pat and I, as he copped it early on.'

'Copped it?'

'Bullets,' Barry said. 'One shattered his knee and the other was in his chest. By the time I'd strapped him up and turned round, the rest had gone on and it was just the two of us. We met up with others on the way, stragglers like us who'd got separated from their units for one reason or another. I half carried Pat to the beach where I thought we might have a chance, not much of a bloody chance, but the only chance we had.

'There was constant bombing and the Stukas screaming above us, raining down bullets. It was hell on earth, Kath,' Barry said. 'The bombs fell that thick and fast, you couldn't think straight with the noise of them and the screaming and yelling all around. You'd see men fall into the craters from a bomb directly in front of you and then the next blast would cover them up. It was a massacre. I could see some blokes had pushed jeeps into the sea to make a sort of jetty. The destroyers were way out, not able to come in any nearer, and there were all these boats, not military things, yachts, cruisers. Kath, you've never seen anything like it.'

'We heard on the news and read about it,' Kathy said.

'Aye, but nothing could describe the sight of those little pleasure cruisers shuttling between the jetty and the larger ships put out in deeper water,' Barry said. 'They were under constant fire and yet they just carried on as if they were on a pleasure trip. It was a bloody miracle. Me and Pat were starving hungry, thick with mud and dog tired, soaked to the skin and shaking with cold, but these little boats brought a smile even to my lips.

'But I could see Pat was sinking fast and the blood was seeping through the bandaging I'd put on. Then people who'd stood on the jetty for hours for rescue, just as tired, scared and miserable as us, made way for Pat, seeing that he was injured. I put him into a dinghy that came alongside,' Barry went on. 'He wanted me along with him, but it was wounded first. Not yet, I said, I'll see you later in good old Blighty.

'"Hold you to it, mate," Pat said, "we'll have a pint together."

'I watched him sail away and saw them haul him onto the destroyer. I remember thinking how that must have hurt him, but now at least he had a chance; they'd have medical people on board and maybe he could get out of his wet things, and they'd certainly be able to find him something to eat. I wanted to cheer. And then I saw the Messerschmitts, flying in low. I started to scream, stupid really, but I wasn't the only one. When the first bombs fell, I jumped in the water. Didn't know really what I was hoping to do. There I was, thrashing about and getting nowhere. Then the grey foamy water closed over my head and I thought this is it, and then I felt hands clawing at me. Two blokes had lain full stretch across the jeeps to reach me, with others holding their legs to stop them toppling in. They were yelling, "Grab on, mate, Grab on," and d'you know, Kath, I nearly didn't bother, and then I thought of you and the weans and I reached out for their hands. God, it seemed to take hours. I was tired and so was every other bugger and I was weighed down by my clothes. People reached out and caught my tunic and pulled me up on to the jetty. I lay for a minute getting my breath back and spluttering and coughing. By the time I was able to look up again the ship was gone, blown to kingdom come and nothing to show for it but a few dead bodies and debris littering the water.

'I was so stunned, I wasn't ready for the Stukas that seemed to come from nowhere. That's how I copped for all this,' said Barry, touching the bandage on his head. 'And they got my belly and nearly sheared my arm clean off. And you know the other sad thing, Kath? The two blokes that pulled me out of the water and were so concerned with me, they didn't take cover themselves and both were killed beside me.'

'Oh, Barry.' Tears were raining down Kathy's face and, she realised with shock, down her husband's too.

'You know what tortures me?' Barry said brokenly. 'I keep thinking that if we'd stayed where we were when Pat was first hit, the Germans would have picked us up. They'd have seen to Pat's leg and chest and he'd be bloody alive by now, even if he was a prisoner.'

Kathy shook her head. 'He couldn't stand being locked up,' she said, and then added, 'I don't suppose there was a chance Pat might have made it? I mean, he couldn't have been in the water and been picked up by a boat somewhere?'

Barry shook his head. 'Not a chance,' he said. 'He wasn't only tired and starving like the rest of us, but badly wounded too, and very weak. He'd never have survived. They did look; two or three boats diverted and cruised around for a bit when the ship went down. Like I said, it was just dead bodies. I was out of it by then, with my arm near hanging off, and bleeding from my head and guts. I was on the next boat out, not that I knew much about it. Most of the time I was raving. We put in at Dover where they patched me up and sent me here as a non-urgent case. They were run off their feet down there, and you should have seen the poor buggers . . .' Barry stopped and wiped at his eyes before saying, 'Kath, Pat was the greatest mate I ever had, or am likely to have. There'll never be another like him, but he's gone and we've all got to accept it.'

Kathy wiped her own face with a small handkerchief she drew from her bag, then said, 'What about Michael and the others?'

'They were all alive when last I saw them,' Barry said. 'That's all I know. The beaches were chaos, there was no chance of seeing anyone there.'

'You really must leave now, Mrs O'Malley,' said Sister Hopkins' voice at Kathy's elbow. Neither of them had heard her approach in her soft-soled shoes.

'Not yet,' protested Barry.

'I'm sorry, Mr O'Malley, but your wife has been here some time and she shouldn't really have got in at all.'

'When will you come again?' Barry cried.

'Maybe tomorrow,' Kathy said, eyeing the nurse. 'I'll not get back to Birmingham today with trains the way they are. I'll look for somewhere to stay for tonight and, if Sister agrees, come and see you tomorrow before I go back.'

'It's most irregular, Mrs O'Malley,' Sister Hopkins said again.

'I know, but it will have to last Barry a long time,' Kathy said.

'And it will help me get better, Sister, honest,' Barry put in. 'Then I'll be out of your hair altogether.'

Sister Hopkins pursed her lips and said to Kathy as she bent to kiss Barry goodbye, 'You'll have to work it out with the times of your trains, but the doctors are usually finished by ten o'clock.'

Just as Kathy was about to answer, the man in the next bed shouted, 'Good on you, Sister. He's a bleeding hero, Barry. Got to look after us heroes, they'll need us all before this lot's over.'

Kathy glanced at him. She saw there were seven other men besides Barry in the ward, but on her way in she hadn't noticed any of them. She'd had eyes only for her husband. She saw all the men watching her now with interest. Sister Hopkins glanced sternly at the man who had spoken and said, 'Really, Mr Stoddard, we look after everyone well here.'

Mr Stoddard looked not a bit abashed and instead winked at Kathy. She found herself smiling back at him. 'Good-bye,' she said, and there was a chorus of farewells from the other beds.

She stopped at the door to wave to Barry and the other men and hurried after Sister Hopkins. 'Is there a café locally?' Kathy asked the nurse, when they were out of earshot of the ward.

'I believe you need a place to stay too,' Sister Hopkins said. 'I did hear you say that, didn't I?'

'Oh, aye, do you know of one?' Kathy asked eagerly.

'Mrs O'Malley, the town is heaving with soldiers. I think it would be very difficult to find a place tonight.'

'Oh, I see.'

'And if you don't mind me saying so, you look all in.'

'I am rather tired. It's the emotion and everything.'

'I suggest, then, that you come home with me tonight.'

'Oh, I couldn't . . .'

'You can hardly sleep on a park bench, my dear,' Sister Hopkins said with a smile, and Kathy realised that behind the frosty exterior was a very kind woman. 'I'm sure my sofa will be quite comfortable,' she went on. 'And though there are many cafés around, the nurse's canteen is cheaper and I can take you in as a guest. I'm off duty at six, if you could just wait a while.'

'Oh, aye, oh, thank you,' Kathy cried.

The nurse went on: 'There's a reception area where you could sit. I'll show you. Oh, and by the way, when we are away from the hospital, my name is Peggy.'

Oh, thought Kathy, how kind people were, and if only she could get over this feeling of sadness at the death of her beloved brother . . . She'd sort of faced it before she'd left home, but when he was said to be missing she'd felt there was always a chance that he'd be found. Now that chance was gone. She knew she'd never see Pat again, and that hurt. The way Barry had described the hell-hole of Dunkirk, it was amazing that anyone had got out of it alive, but Barry had, and she must latch on to that and hope that with God's help, Sean, Michael and Con were all safe too.

She was surprised how much better she felt with a meal inside her, and while she ate she found herself telling Sister Hopkins about all her family. 'They'll be worried,' she said. 'Mammy and Daddy especially, and my little girl Lizzie.'

'Can you phone?'

Kathy looked at the nurse in amazement. 'We haven't a phone,' she said.

Sister Hopkins realised she'd made an error. 'Of course not,' she said. 'Has anyone else, a shop perhaps?'

'Pickering's have, I believe,' Kathy said.

'Are they far away?'

'No, not far, and they'd pass on a message.'

'Well then, there's a phone in the hospital,' Sister Hopkins said. 'You can tell them you're safe at least, and will be home tomorrow.'

73

'I . . . I don't know how to use a phone. I've never had to,' Kathy confessed.

'That's all right. I'll show you,' said the nurse.

A short time later, Kathy found herself talking to Mrs Pickering, who owned the shop just up from the O'Malleys'. She shouted a bit, unable to believe that sound could travel from one instrument to another so effectively unless she bawled her head off, and though Mrs Pickering might have been rendered deaf in one ear for a time, she reassured Kathy and promised to pass the news on to her parents. Then Kathy went home with Peggy Hopkins and spent a very comfortable night on her sofa.

It was over breakfast that Kathy faced up to the fact that she hadn't told Barry about the deaths of his brothers. There hadn't been time the previous day, and anyway she'd hesitated to load him down with more sadness. She hoped he was feeling stronger this morning, for she'd have to talk to him.

When Kathy walked into the ward, the men greeted her as if they'd known her forever. 'You did them a power of good yesterday, Mrs O'Malley,' a young nurse told Kathy as she passed. 'They all spruced themselves up this morning when they heard you were coming back. Some who hadn't had a shave for a week were asking for razors this morning.'

Kathy laughed and said, 'If they'd do that for someone my shape, they'd be standing on their heads for some of the young lasses in the town.'

'They would that, and it's a sight I wouldn't like to miss.'

But the young nurse was right. Barry was propped up, looking far more cheerful, with his hair brushed and the stubble gone from his cheeks and chin. Kathy was delighted to see him looking so well and was pleased he seemed to be coming to terms with Pat's death and accepting it for the tragic accident it was. She dredged up little incidents about the family, things she couldn't remember writing in her letters, and funny things the weans had said, trying desperately to amuse him.

But Barry was no fool. He knew Kathy was holding something back and he only waited till she stopped to draw breath before saying, 'What is it?'

Kathy was taken aback. 'What's what? Nothing. What do you mean?' she stammered, confused.

Barry studied her, more sure than ever that she was hiding something. 'How's Ma?' he said.

'Great, so she is, great,' Kathy said. 'I go up a couple of times a week and she comes down sometimes . . .' Her voice trailed away as she remembered the last time she'd seen Molly O'Malley, and at once Barry knew there was something wrong at home.

'What is it, Kathy?' he said. 'I know something is bothering you, and if you don't tell me, I'll only worry when you've gone.'

He put out his good hand but Kathy pulled away and said, almost angrily, 'Nothing I tell you. Your ma's fine.'

'My brothers then? Something's damn well wrong,' Barry burst out.

Kathy couldn't prevent the shadow from passing over her face and Barry just asked, 'Who?'

Kathy's voice was barely above a whisper as she answered, 'Phil and Donal.'

'The two of them, dear Christ,' Barry moaned, and after a slight pause asked, 'Are they both . . . dead?'

Kathy just nodded, and Barry shut his eyes against the pain of it. Suddenly his hand shot out and grabbed Kathy's. 'Kath, I want you out of that place.'

'What place?'

'Birmingham.'

'Don't be daft, Barry.'

'I'm not being daft. Pregnant women can be evacuated, with their children.'

'I can't just run away, Barry. What about your ma – she's got to rely on me a lot now – and Bridie and Mammy and Daddy coming to terms with the loss of Pat? And what if Michael, Sean or Con are gone too, that will break Mammy's heart altogether, not to mention Maggie and Rose. I can't just go somewhere safe and pretend they're nothing to me.'

Barry considered this and knew she had a point. 'Well, the children then,' he said.

Kathy made an impatient movement on the bed. 'We've discussed this already,' she said. 'I wasn't keen on the weans going to strangers and you agreed with me.'

'Yes,' Barry said, 'I did, but . . . look, everyone knows Hitler is working towards invasion. However you look at it, Dunkirk was a defeat, and he'll think we're crushed and now is the time to attack the cities. Then, when we're demoralised and depressed, as he thinks, he'll invade.'

'How d'you know all this?'

'It stands to reason, Kath,' Barry said.

'But why Birmingham?'

'Oh, use your loaf,' Barry cried impatiently. 'Birmingham is crucial to the war effort and is bound to be targeted.'

Kathy thought a little and knew that Barry had a point. Everyone was aware of Birmingham's contribution to the war effort. There was the Vickers factory which made Spitfires then pushed them across the road to Castle Bromwich aerodrome to be flown south; and the BSA factory turning out military motorbikes and guns. Even Cadbury's had drastically cut their production of chocolate, and much of the workforce was packing cordite into rockets, while Dunlop made most of the tyres for the planes and military vehicles, and the car factories were busy making tanks.

'Hitler will want to flatten Birmingham,' Barry said. 'You must see that.'

'I can see he'd want to, but we're two hundred miles from the coast.'

'And what d'you think that is in a plane?' Barry demanded angrily.

'We've got the cellar, we'll be all right.'

'Oh, fine,' Barry said sarcastically. 'That's all right then. And who's to see to our weans when you have the baby? Rose or Maggie, who'll have their own hands full, or your ma, who'll be run off her feet looking after you all? And what about when the weans are at school?' Barry went on. 'Or out playing in the streets somewhere, or down the park? Can you protect them then?'

'I won't send my weans to strangers,' Kathy said stubbornly.

Barry sighed in exasperation and said, 'Look, Kathy, the chap in the last bed goes by the name of Barraclough – Chris Barraclough. They're monied people, or were, but their father died some years ago. There's just Chris and a younger brother, David – he's away at school – and the mother wants to do her bit and open her home up to people from the cities who may need to escape for a while. She had evacuees before, in nineteen thirty-nine, but they went back when no bombs fell.'

'Very nice of her, I'm sure,' Kathy put in sarcastically. 'But to me, they're still strangers.'

'Talk to Chris, he can put it better than me.'

To humour Barry, Kathy went to find Chris Barraclough. He was due to be discharged in a day or so and was sitting in a wheelchair with a rug over his knees, reading the paper. Kathy was surprised at how young he was. He had an open, honest kind of face, one you could trust somehow. He was a handsome boy too, with regular features, a full mouth, a firm chin and deep-blue eyes with dark lashes. His hair, regulation short, was blond, but the Brylcreem made it look darker. At Kathy's approach he put aside his paper and gave her such a beautiful smile, her heart flipped in surprise.

'Hello,' he said. 'I don't need to ask who you are. Barry has a photograph of you; he's shown it to everyone in the ward, I think. I feel as if I know you already, and may I say, Mrs O'Malley, the photograph does not do you justice.'

Kathy flushed, not used to gallantry and unable to deal with it. 'Mr . . . Mr Barraclough,' she stammered.

'Oh, Chris, please,' the young man said. 'And may I call you Kathy?'

Kathy gave a shrug and a smile. 'Everyone else does,' she said.

'Well then, so will I.' He regarded the woman in front of him and thought her very beautiful, and Barry a lucky chap. Her pregnancy had lent a bloom to her skin, and her eyes were so large and dark brown you felt you could drown in them. It seemed criminal to him that war would be waged on such as the woman before him in all the industrial cities of Britain; judging by the atrocities in Poland, none were too young, old or infirm to experience Nazi brutality.

'My mother has a house in a small village in Herefordshire,' he began, when Kathy explained what she'd come to see him about. 'It's a rambling old place, far too big for Mother now she's on her own, but she loves it. You would love it too, I know, even if only for a week or two. It has rolling hillsides dotted with sheep, forest land and the River Wye and its tributaries. It truly is idyllic, and once you're there, you'll forget there's a war being waged anywhere.' He smiled and went on. 'I'm off myself soon for a week of pampering and spoiling from my dear mother before I report for active service again.'

'And what makes you think your mother would welcome my weans?' Kathy asked quite sharply.

'She likes children,' Chris said disarmingly. 'Apparently she wanted a houseful, but my father was an officer in the Great War and was badly injured internally and externally. Over the years the old wounds gave him much trouble – in fact, I can never remember him as a fit, well man; he always seemed to be an invalid. He died when my young brother David was a year old.'

'How old is your brother now?'

'Thirteen,' Chris said. 'And I'm twenty. I went from boarding school to the army. Mother was a bit upset, she thought I'd go to university first – keep me safe, as it were – but I didn't want to skulk at home, you know. Now she's worried for David, who is keeping his fingers crossed that the war won't be over before he's through school.'

'You say your mother wanted lots of children,' Kathy said, 'but both you and your brother went away to school. What can she know about having children around her all day?'

'We didn't go away till we were turned eleven,' Chris explained. 'David has only been boarding for just over two years, and unfortunately that coincided more or less with me joining up. Mother is so lonely now, though she seldom complains. All her life she's longed for a daughter; she'd love yours.'

'Maybe,' Kathy said. 'But I don't like my children going to people I don't know, however kind and well-off they are.'

'Oh, but you will go with them, surely?'

'No, I've explained to Barry,' Kathy said. 'There's no way I can go.'

'Then send your children before the bombs come,' Chris pleaded. 'I can vouch for their happiness there.'

'No one can do that, Mr Barraclough,' Kathy said, but she accepted the address that he scribbled down, and promised to think about it.

79

FIVE

Back home, the place was in uproar, and Kathy was delighted to hear that Sean, Michael and Con had been in touch. They were all safe and sound and would be home for a week's leave as soon as they were allowed, but it was nearly ten days before they arrived. It was wonderful to have them back and they were all interested in hearing about Barry, but terribly upset about Pat being missing. Not wishing to depress them still further, Kathy kept from them Barry's revelations about what had really happened to Pat and confided only in Mary. 'Shall I tell Bridie, Mammy?' she asked. 'Do you think it will help her to know the truth?'

Mary shook her head. 'It would serve no purpose,' she said at last. 'She's coming to terms with it in her own way, leave it so.'

The men were amazed that so many had escaped the beaches, and said so. 'We were badly equipped,' Sean complained. 'One bloody tin hat, rifle and bayonet was all we had to combat the German panzer division. Bloody ridiculous it was.'

'And then we had the order to retreat to the beaches,' Con put in. 'And that was just madness too. No one knew what was what, or where to go, or any damn thing.'

'That had us by the balls right enough,' Michael said.

'Michael,' warned Mary automatically. Sean and Con were convulsed with laughter, and even Eamonn had a twinkle in his eye. Mary rounded on them all. 'You're no help, any of youse.'

'Ma,' said Sean, wiping his eyes, 'don't be giving out. Michael's a man now and he's earned the right to say what he likes.'

'Begorra he has,' Mary said, but she knew Sean was right. The adolescent Michael who'd joined up in a fever of patriotism had shed his youth's skin and had stepped over into the man's world. Sean had also changed, and Mary supposed that the experiences they'd lived through would have affected anyone. He also seemed very worried about Rose, as her pregnancy seemed to be taking it out of her. He knew she had a lot to do with the little ones.

'I don't think she's that strong,' Mary confided one day to Kathy. 'And she's so thin, you'd hardly know she was pregnant.'

It was true. While Kathy and Maggie had ballooned out and had little to fit them, Rose had seemed not to change shape much at all. She tried to put on a brave face for Sean, but the lines of strain were visible to everyone and Sean was not fooled. 'I'm not wishing anything against Sean, mind,' Mary said one day to Kathy, 'but it would help if he was sent overseas for a wee while, give her time to get over this one before he's at her again.'

'Mammy!'

'Well, I'm only saying what I'm thinking, and it doesn't have to go any further.'

'Well, I shan't say anything, and I do feel sorry for Rose,' Kathy said. 'I'm also glad Maggie gave up at the factory at the beginning of Con's leave. I was beginning to think she'd have her baby on the factory floor.' She looked at her mother and said, 'Daddy seems all right with Con now.'

'Oh, sure, that's your father. He thinks him a fine fellow of a man now, so he does. Sure, it's Carmel we have the problems with these days.'

Kathy knew a little about that. Carmel was turned fourteen now and was working in Cadbury's. She loved her workmates and her new-found freedom, and the money she'd never had before, and she had become pert and cheeky in Mary's opinion. 'You should see how she dresses up to go to the cinema or dancing with the other girls; the skirts are positively indecent,' Mary said.

'You know the government have said skirts must be above the knee now,' Kathy reminded her, but with a smile.

Mary sniffed. 'There's above the knee and there's well above the knee, and don't think it's patriotism that decides Carmel's skirt length. They chop and change with their friends to have different outfits. I told her there will be clothes rationing soon and I don't know what she'll do then.'

'What did she say?'

'She said she'd worry about it when it happens.'

'She's right in a way, Mammy. I mean, why worry before you have to?'

'You don't see her plastered to the eyeballs with make-up, with gravy browning on her legs to make them look like stockings, and trotting off on high heels.'

'Where does she find to go?'

'Cinema, she says, or dancing. I'm sure she's meeting boys. Your da would go mad if he thought that.'

'You can't stop her, Mammy, they're probably all the same, you know, just having fun.'

'She says they are, and the other mothers aren't always giving out to them,' Mary said wearily, and gave a sigh. 'She often sneaks away when I go round to Rose's to give her a hand with the weans. Eamonn caught her smoking a cigarette the other day and she wasn't even ashamed. She said they all did on the line and what was the harm. She had a packet of ten Woodbines half gone and she had the nerve to offer her dad one.'

Kathy had to laugh at the sheer cheek of it. 'Did he take it?' she asked, and Mary pushed at her and shook her head as she said, 'You're as much help as our Maggie. She tells me to stop giving out or I'll make her worse, but God, Kathy, the place is full of soldiers. What if she has a lad?'

'What if she has?'

'You know your da and you can say that?' Mary said. 'Dear God, if he caught her arm-in-arm with some soldier out for all he could get, he'd take his belt off to her.'

'Mammy, she has to sometime,' Kathy said. 'She's not a little girl any more. She's mixing with older women, it's bound to have an effect, but in the long run it will do no harm.'

'You don't think she'll get herself into trouble?'

'Why should she?' Kathy said, and pushed away the revelations Maggie had made about sleeping with Con before they were married. They'd been older than Carmel and wanted to marry; this was entirely different. 'She'll be all right, Mammy,' she told Mary confidently. 'She's a good girl and she knows right from wrong.'

'Humph,' said Mary, 'I just hope you're right,' and Kathy hoped she was too.

It was almost the end of the men's week's leave and Lizzie's birthday had been and gone days before, but her very best present of all was hearing that her dad had been transferred to the General Hospital in Birmingham. Her mam had been to see him often, but alone, because children weren't usually allowed in the wards. But Mammy had worked something of a miracle with the nursing staff, because they allowed Lizzie to visit her daddy once in the hospital, together with her mammy and her uncles.

The rules said only two visitors to a bed, but the Sullivan clan disregarded the rule, as no one was about to enforce it, and clustered around the bed. Con, Sean and Michael ribbed Barry, mercilessly.

'Nothing much wrong with him that I can see,' Sean said.

'Not a thing,' agreed Con.

'Amazing what a man will do to get out of fighting,' Michael put in.

'Be quiet, you lot,' Kathy said, though she was glad to see Barry cheered up. He needed something to take his mind off the terrible events in Dunkirk. 'Shut up now or we'll be thrown out.'

Soon they were anyway, for the nurse came back and hustled the three men out into the corridor, and then there was just Lizzie and Kathy beside Barry's bed, and Lizzie's eyes were shining in her head.

'Have you a kiss for your daddy now you're a big girl of nine years old?' Barry asked.

'Daddy!' Lizzie cried, and threw her arms around her father's neck.

'Here, here, you're not crying, are you?'

'No,' Lizzie said untruthfully, scrubbing at her eyes.

'I should think not,' Barry said in mock severity, and then his voice dropped and with a sad expression on his face he said, 'I'm afraid I couldn't get out to get you a present.'

'I don't care, Daddy. I just want you better.'

'Mind you,' Barry said with a wink at Kathy, who was in on the joke, 'I might have some old thing lying around.'

'It doesn't matter, Daddy.'

'No, no, let me see now,' Barry said, and reaching over to his locker he withdrew a rag doll so beautiful that Lizzie's eyes nearly popped out. She had golden plaits sewn to the top of her head, her eyes were the most brilliant blue and her mouth was rosy red, with two crimson cheeks as well. She wore a dress

84

of plum velvet trimmed with lace at the cuffs and the hem, which nearly reached the top of her soft black leather boots.

'Oh, Daddy, oh, she's beautiful, thank you, thank you.'

'It's OK, princess, cheap at the price,' Barry said, winking at Kathy again. 'Three packets of fags and half a pound of bull's-eyes.'

Kathy had been told about the present in a letter Barry had sent her just after her visit to Plymouth, in which he explained about the dolls made by a relative of Sister Hopkins. 'Where does she get the clothes from, and the material?' Kathy asked, fingering the plush velvet.

'Odds and ends, I think,' Barry said. 'I know she buys very little, and she sends the fags and sweets overseas to men who have no doting wives to make their lives more bearable.'

'Some odds and ends,' said Kathy incredulously. 'She must have rich connections.'

'Anyway, it's for you now, Lizzie,' Barry said. 'Something to remember your daddy by when you go off to the country.'

Lizzie stared at her father, not sure if she'd heard right. She remembered the children going to the country nine months ago, and nothing had happened. No bombs had fallen, and all the children who'd been evacuated had come back. Most of them had been glad to return. Lizzie didn't want to go to any country, it sounded awful. Maura had said as much.

Beside her, she knew her mother was angry, bristling with it. She saw her open her mouth to speak, but Barry forestalled her by adding, 'Surely your mammy has told you about it?'

Before Lizzie had time to speak, Kathy burst out, 'Stop it, Barry, you have no right.'

'No right,' Barry exploded. 'She's my bloody child too, her and Danny, and I want them safe. Is that so wrong? I think I have a perfect right.'

'Not to spring it on us, on Lizzie, like this.'

'You told Chris Barraclough?'

'I told him I'd think about it.'

'Well?'

'I'm still thinking about it.'

'Well, I hope you're still able to think when you're buried under a landmine,' Barry snapped.

'Barry!' Kathy was shocked, and Barry, catching sight of the faces of his wife and daughter, was ashamed of his outburst. 'You're upsetting the child,' Kathy said, and Barry could not deny it, because tears were squeezing out of Lizzie's eyes and dribbling down her cheeks. But she wasn't upset about what her daddy had said about bombs; it was her mammy and daddy arguing that she didn't like.

'I'm sorry,' Barry said. 'Don't mind me, Lizzie. I get fed up waiting around for my head and stomach to heal, so I can get out of here.'

Kathy, glad to change the subject, said, 'Have they given you any idea?'

'Next couple of days they said last time I asked,' Barry said. 'I'll have to go back in for physio on the arm, but I'll be home for a while.'

'That's wonderful,' Kathy said. 'It would be great, so it would.'

'Then I'll have to see what I can do,' Barry said with a smile. 'Now, about that other business . . .'

'Leave it till you get home,' Kathy said. 'Then we'll talk, promise.' She kissed him on the cheek and added, 'We'd better be on our way and let the other hooligans in before they wreck the hospital.'

Barry knew she was anxious to get away and was sorry he'd soured Lizzie's visit, but he said nothing. He'd be home soon, and then he'd make Kathy see sense.

On 22 June, France finally surrendered. The so-called impregnable Maginot Line had provided little opposition to the seemingly unstoppable German army. People were only too well aware that just a small stretch of water separated Britain from the Nazi-dominated Europe. Defeat seemed probable, invasion imminent. The government realised the seriousness of the situation and mustered the Home Guard, and an information sheet went out to all householders entitled 'If the Invader Comes'. People were encouraged to disable cars not in use, and hide maps and so on to confuse enemy spies, who many were sure were behind every lamp post.

Barry was due home the next day, and he was still there two days later when the first bombs fell in West Bromwich. 'You see,' he cried to Kathy as they clustered around the wireless. 'That will happen here.'

'No,' Kathy snapped back. 'It might not, but what will happen is invasion, everyone says so, and if we're going to be invaded, my children stay here with me.'

Barry slammed out of the house angrily. There was no budging Kathy. He'd been working on her ever since he came out of the hospital, but she wouldn't agree to the children being evacuated. He might have stood a chance if the children had been for it, but they weren't. Lizzie, in particular, was dead against going anywhere in the country.

Barry was an impatient man anyway; his arm wasn't healing as quickly as he'd hoped and he was missing his mates. Only the other day, Kathy, hurt by his attitude, had cried, 'You can't wait to get back, can you?'

And he'd replied, 'No, I can't, out of the bleeding road. You live your life quite well without me.'

The point was, Kathy had lived her life without Barry because she'd had to do it, and she had responsibilities to the family she couldn't just drop. Much worse for Barry was Bridie, who never seemed to be away from the house for five minutes, and who went on and on about Pat and how she missed him, as if Barry didn't feel bad enough already.

He was uncomfortably aware that had he and Pat stayed where they were and surrendered, they might both have survived. As it was, he was alive and Pat wasn't, and even the fact that Con had told him he'd heard the SS had taken few prisoners but gunned down many who'd surrendered only made him feel moderately better – and guilt made him lash out, even at the children.

Also, Kathy was easily tired and heavily pregnant, and though she lay beside him in bed every night, he could hardly take her in his arms and love her as he wanted – he wasn't that selfish. But God, it didn't help his frustration. He knew that Kathy was worried he would want to make love, so she was nervous even as she enjoyed his kisses and closeness, and that made him crosser than ever with her. Did she think he was some sort of animal with no self-control? All in all, the visit was not the happy time Kathy, Barry and the children had expected it to be.

At his mother's he was hailed as a conquering hero. She was coming to terms with the death of her two sons and was aware that Hitler had still to be beaten or they would have died in vain. But for now Barry, her eldest and favourite son, was home, and it was a pleasure to fuss over him. Barry enjoyed the spoiling and cosseting and couldn't help comparing it with Kathy's attitude. She had always to give Rose a hand, or mind her weans, or sit with Bridie a while, or pop to her mother's. Everyone had a higher priority in Kathy's life than her husband, Barry thought, and he was bloody sick and tired of it.

Kathy herself was often bone weary, and yet she tried to help her family as she'd always done and keep a demanding husband happy. It was exhausting for her, and an additional worry was Barry's appetite. It had always been healthy, but now boredom and inactivity – which had never sat easily on Barry's shoulders – caused him to eat more. Meat rationing had been introduced in March, and early July found tea rationed to two ounces per person. The allowance of fats had changed too, and now each person was allowed two ounces of cooking fat and four of margarine but only two butter. Barry, being a serving soldier, had had none of these restrictions on his food and found it irksome when he couldn't have a cup of tea whenever he wanted. Even the foods not yet rationed, like eggs and cheese, were in short supply, and luxury foods like biscuits and cakes were very hard to get hold of at all. Barry refused to acknowledge how difficult it was for Kathy to prepare nourishing meals every day. He accused her of moaning and complaining all the time, and Lizzie and Danny often heard their parents arguing.

Eventually Barry talked the doctor into signing him off before he was fully fit. Kathy watched him go with a mixture of feelings, including relief, because although she would worry about him away fighting, he'd been difficult to live with, like a bear with a sore head, and she knew life would be more peaceful once he was gone.

As for Lizzie, though she was sorry to see her daddy leave again, she hadn't understood what had made him so cross and scratchy, even with her and Danny. She was almost ashamed that she felt relief to match her mother's as she watched him walk away, his kit bag on his shoulder.

But she was glad, after Barry left, that she had the doll, the last present her daddy had bought her. She called her Daisy, not for any reason she could think of except that she looked like a Daisy. Every night she cuddled her tight and told her all her worries and fears, and imagined she was talking to her daddy about it all.

She had a big problem of her own at this time, for her mammy had told her to be nice to Sheelagh. 'She's lost her daddy,' Mammy had said. 'He isn't ever coming back. She'll never see him again; think how awful that would be if it was your daddy.'

Lizzie did, but not for long; it was too terrible a thought to hold in her mind. Sheelagh was hard to be nice to, but she told herself she'd try.

The Saturday after Barry left, Bridie and Kathy sent the two girls outside out of the way, while they talked. Lizzie sat down on the step beside her cousin and watched Danny and Matt, who were playing marbles with a crowd of other young boys further up the street. It was hot and dusty, and Lizzie felt sticky with it, and though both girls had their skipping ropes with them, it was far too warm to skip. Lizzie felt uncomfortable with her cousin because she'd said nothing to her yet about Uncle Pat's death, and so eventually she said, 'I'm sorry about your daddy.'

'No you ain't.'

Whatever Lizzie had expected Sheelagh to say, it wasn't those words that she spat out so bitterly. 'Course I am,' she said. 'Everyone is.'

'No you ain't. No one cares, and my mammy knows it.'

'How can you say that? I loved my Uncle Pat,' Lizzie declared. 'And my daddy did. Everyone did.'

'Then why didn't they look after him?'

'What d'you mean?'

'They were supposed to look out for one another. That's what they said when they joined up,' Sheelagh said.

Lizzie remembered it, but she didn't know if you could always do that in battles. She knew that lots of others had been killed at Dunkirk as well as her Uncle Pat, and she said so to Sheelagh. 'My daddy said it was such a mess at Dunkirk, it was a wonder anyone got out alive.'

'But he did though, didn't he?' Sheelagh snapped. 'And all the others did. Only my daddy was killed, and that wouldn't have happened if they'd all looked after each other.'

Lizzie was puzzled, unsure of how to argue that point with her cousin. While she was still thinking of a reply, Sheelagh said, 'Anyway, my mammy said it won't matter soon. We're going to lose the war.'

'No we're not.'

'Yes we are. You don't know anything, you're only a baby.'

'I am not.'

'Oh yes you are, and everyone knows we're losing,' Sheelagh said. 'There'll be an invasion and we'll be overrun with Germans, then you'll see.'

Lizzie didn't ask what she'd see; she was too frightened by what Sheelagh had said.

'Then you'll be sorry,' Sheelagh went on, ''cos do you know what they do to the men in the countries they rule?'

'No,' said Lizzie in a scared little voice.

'They shoot them,' Sheelagh said in grim satisfaction. 'They stand them against the wall and shoot them, and then you won't have a daddy either.'

Lizzie gasped in horror. 'It's not true,' she said. 'It isn't. They don't do that.'

'Yes they do,' Sheelagh said, delighted she'd managed to terrify her cousin. 'They've done it already in France, and my mammy told me they do it everywhere.'

'But they won't invade us, our air force will stop them,' Lizzie burst in.

'They won't be able to do anything,' Sheelagh said dismissively.

Both girls knew the war was going badly; everyone knew. It was all that was talked about and it made the adults bad-tempered. Since the evacuation of Dunkirk, the Luftwaffe had been making sporadic raids on coastal towns in an effort to smash their defences and destroy ships, and everyone knew that was just the beginning. Invasion was the word on everyone's lips. 'Do you think we'll be invaded, Mammy?' Lizzie asked her mother later, desperate for reassurance after her cousin's revelations.

Kathy sighed. 'I don't know, pet. I hope not.'

It wasn't what Lizzie wanted to hear. 'We're not going to lose the war, are we?' she asked desperately.

'It's in God's hands, pet,' Kathy said. 'We must pray about it.'

Lizzie didn't want it to be just in God's hands. She thought he'd made a bad enough fist of it already, and she didn't understand about praying either. The priests and teachers urged them to pray for peace, but what sort of peace? The sort where Hitler did what he wanted, for she couldn't see him just giving up, and especially now, when most people thought he was winning. She could pray for Britain to win the war, but they couldn't do that without killing German people, and surely that was wrong too. Anyway, she thought, if God was everywhere, like the priests said, and if he knew everything, why did she have to pray at all? Her mother was no good, Lizzie realised. She was as scared of defeat as Lizzie herself.

The schools broke up and the Battle of Britain began in earnest, and Lizzie found she could go nowhere without having Sheelagh in tow.

'Don't be selfish,' Kathy admonished when Lizzie complained. 'Think of poor Sheelagh, who has no daddy.'

Lizzie did think of her, but she didn't see how trailing after her would make her cousin get over her loss quicker. They'd never got on, and in the past Sheelagh had always tried to make Lizzie look small and scorn her ideas. Now she seemed to hold her almost personally responsible for her father's death, and Lizzie found her constant verbal attacks hard to take. She didn't bother complaining, for she knew it would get her nowhere. Grown-up decisions, she knew, often made little sense, but there was no point arguing with them.

But there was no skipping off now to play with Maura Mahon, for Kathy was firm. Sheelagh, she said, needed her cousin. Maura didn't understand Lizzie's sudden devotion to a girl she'd always professed to detest and so thought she was being huffy with her, and Lizzie could have been upset about it if she'd had time.

But the point was, her free time was limited, for her mammy and Aunt Rose and Aunt Maggie, all heavily pregnant, needed her to give a hand. And then there was Auntie Bridie at the door: could Lizzie go a message or help turn the mangle for her, or scrub the step or wash the pots? Poor wee Sheelagh wasn't able to give her a hand at all, she was too upset, but Lizzie was a grand girl altogether and Bridie was sure she didn't mind and she must be a fine help to her mother, and Lizzie was pig sick about the whole thing.

Rose's pains started in the early hours of Friday morning, just five days after the beginning of the summer holidays. The first Lizzie and her mother knew of it was when Mary walked in the entry door just as they'd finished breakfast holding Nuala and Peter by the hand. 'Has she started then?' Kathy said.

'This long while, and no sign yet,' Mary said. 'I've been over there half the night. We could do with you if you can come. Bella Amis is after fetching the doctor.'

'The doctor?' Kathy echoed, hardly able to believe it. Bella Amis was the midwife, and all most women needed. To have a doctor usually meant trouble. Lizzie's eyes had opened wide in surprise and noticing them, Kathy, with a glance at Rose's two bemused children, asked quietly, 'Is she bad?'

'Bad enough,' Mary answered shortly. 'I must get back. I wondered, could Lizzie mind the weans?'

'Of course,' Kathy said, answering for her daughter.

There was a click as the entry door opened again and Sheelagh slunk into the room. Lizzie's heart sank.

'And here's Sheelagh to help you,' Mary said, handing Lizzie a list, ration books and a purse. 'You can fetch your aunt's rations first, and I've put an extra sixpence in the purse so you can get a wee treat for yourself.' She passed over the shopping bags to Lizzie and added, 'When you've done that, take them out for the day. To the park or some-where, to get them out of the way for now.'

'Can I take them down the Bull Ring?'

'Aye, that's a good idea,' Mary said. 'Anywhere will do, and there's plenty to see in the Bull Ring.'

As the door closed on the two women, Nuala began to cry and Peter's eyes were very bright and shiny, and Lizzie realised they were both very frightened without knowing why. She bent down and put her arms around them. 'Don't cry,' she said. 'Soon you'll have a wee baby brother or sister, and that's nothing to cry over.'

The children looked at her in astonishment, and Lizzie realised they probably hadn't even known their mother was expecting. She certainly didn't look as though she was; whereas Lizzie's own mother and her Aunt Maggie resembled a couple of huge whales, Rose hadn't changed her shape that much at all. She thought they might have picked up something in the adults' conversation, but it was obvious from their amazement at what she said that they hadn't.

'Baby?' Nuala said, her tears forgotten.

'A baby,' Peter said. 'Is Mammy having a baby?'

'She surely is,' Lizzie answered. 'D'you want a wee boy or a wee girl?'

'A boy,' Peter said stoutly. 'Girls are stupid.' He glanced over at his sister and added, 'Nuala's stupid.'

'No she isn't,' Lizzie said, but she laughed at the deter-mined look on Peter's face. 'She's just wee. You were much the same at her age.'

Peter looked as if he might dispute that, so before he was able to, Lizzie said, 'Come on, let's get the rations fetched and then we can have the rest of the day.'

She picked Nuala up to dump her in the pram that her grandma had left outside the door, and said to Sheelagh, 'You coming?'

'I don't think so,' Sheelagh said. 'Shopping with weans is not my idea of fun, but I'll go down to the Bull Ring with you later.'

'Oh, please yourself,' Lizzie said in exasperation.

She strapped Nuala in her pram and stuck her tongue out at Sheelagh before going off down the road.

Pickering's grocery store lay one side of the O'Malley home, and Morcroft's the other, and people went to whichever one they were registered at. As Rose was registered at Morcroft's, that was where Lizzie went. There was a queue as always, Lizzie noticed. She parked Nuala's pram outside and went in, holding Peter by the hand.

She saw Maura Mahon just in front of her and smiled at her, but Maura pretended not to see her, so she sidled up alongside. 'Hello, Maura,' she said.

'Oh, hello,' Maura said, and then, letting her eyes scan the shop, remarked sarcastically, 'Sheelagh's not with you?'

Lizzie flushed. 'Don't be like that. I told you how it is. My mammy makes me take her about with me.'

'Well, where is she today, then?'

'She wouldn't come. I was sent to fetch Aunt Rose's rations, but only to get the weans out of the way, 'cos my aunt's started,' Lizzie said. 'After that I'm to take them down the Bull Ring, and you can bet our Sheelagh wants to come there.'

'Oh, I'd love to go down the Bull Ring,' Maura said. Maura, like Lizzie, often went down there with her mother, usually late on Saturday afternoon to catch the bargains in

95

meat and vegetables, and it was always entertaining. Lately, though, Kathy had been too tired for the trek, so Lizzie herself hadn't been for a few weeks. Suddenly a spirit of mischief seized her. Why shouldn't she go now, just her and Maura? If she didn't go back to the house, Sheelagh would never know.

'Let's go together,' she said. 'Now.'

'Just us?'

'And the weans,' Lizzie said. 'I must take them, but they'll be no trouble.'

'What about the rations?' Maura said. 'And your Sheelagh?'

'Grandma's not waiting on the rations, I know,' Lizzie said, and added rudely, 'As for Sheelagh, she can . . . she can go to the devil, for all I care.'

'Och, Lizzie, what would Father Flaherty say?' Maura said, and the girls' spluttering laughter caught the attention of Mr Morcroft.

'Now then, you two, what's to do?' he said.

Lizzie handed over the list, the ration books and the shopping bags, and Mrs Morcroft, looking over her husband's shoulder, said, 'Is your aunt bad again, pet?'

'She's having the baby, I think,' Lizzie said. 'Only it's taking a while. I have to keep the weans away from the house.'

'God, but hasn't she had a tough time of it?' Mrs Morcroft said. 'And you're a grand girl, Lizzie, to be minding the children. Leave the bags and list here and we'll make them up for you.' She leant into the till, extracted a threepenny bit and gave it to Lizzie. 'And that's for yourself,' she said, 'for being such a good girl.'

Lizzie smiled and thanked her, and added it to the sixpence her gran had given her, then waited while Maura collected her purchases. They had to go back to Maura's house to deliver the groceries and ask Mrs Mahon if Maura could go to the Bull Ring with Lizzie. This suited Lizzie, for Maura lived just off Bell Barn Road in Spring Street, which was the opposite way from the O'Malley house. From there they could go along Sun Street and out on to Bristol Street without anyone in her house or Rose's knowing anything about it.

Mrs Mahon gave Maura one and sixpence to get kippers if there were any cheap, and Lizzie realised with a jolt that it was Friday and possibly she too would have been asked to bring back kippers or fish pieces for tea, as they couldn't eat meat on Fridays. Eggs used to be a good standby, but even they were hard to come by these days. She knew she'd catch it when she got home, but she didn't care. Even if she was going to be killed at the end of it, she might as well enjoy herself. It was ages since she'd been out somewhere with Maura as they used to, before the war changed everything.

Lizzie did have a few pangs of guilt as they made their way along Sun Street. She was acting totally out of character, for she'd been trained from when she was little to be helpful to others, and it was in her nature to be considerate too, but the last few weeks had been very trying, and made more so by Sheelagh tagging behind her everywhere. Surely I can have one day off? Lizzie thought to herself, and I'm not going just on my own, I've got Pete and Nuala with me. She knew in her heart of hearts that her mother wouldn't see it the same way, but she gave a defiant lift to her head and smiled across to Maura, and Maura, who knew some of Lizzie's train of thought, said, 'It'll be grand, you'll see.'

SIX

It was a tidy step to the Bull Ring, but the girls had done it many a time. Trams cost money, and neither Kathy nor Mrs Mahon were keen on throwing their money about. They set a brisk pace along Bristol Street while Nuala bounced about in her pram and laughed and waved her arms and Peter trotted along beside them holding the pram handle.

'Isn't this great?' Lizzie said. 'Just the two of us, without my moaning cousin spoiling anything.'

'She is awful,' Maura agreed. 'Why does your mammy make you take her around with you all the time?'

'Och, who can understand mothers?' Lizzie said with a shrug. 'Mammy says it's because she's lost her daddy, but I don't see that hanging on to me helps. I mean, I don't like her and I never have, and she doesn't like me.' She stopped a minute and then went on, 'I think she sticks to me to be spiteful, because she knows I hate it. She's always either giving out or moaning at me, and when she's with her friends at school, she makes fun of me all the time.'

'Poor you,' Maura sympathised. 'How long d'you think your mammy will make you take her about?'

'I don't know,' Lizzie said, turning the pram into

Bromsgrove Street, and added gloomily, 'I hope it doesn't last till the war ends.'

'That might not be long, though, mightn't it?' Maura said almost in a whisper. She looked about to see if anyone was listening and then said, 'Some people think we're going to lose, and soon.'

Hearing Maura say the same thing as Sheelagh caused Lizzie to snap, 'Don't be stupid, that's a crazy thing to say.'

'No it isn't,' Maura said. 'Everyone thinks there will be an invasion.'

Lizzie couldn't deny that. 'It doesn't mean we'll lose, though,' she said obstinately.

She was so upset by Maura unknowingly backing Sheelagh's theories on the progress of the war that she'd increased the speed she was pushing the pram and was unaware of it until suddenly Pete, unable to take the pace, tripped and pitched forward. He'd skinned both knees and was bawling loud enough to wake the dead. Lizzie bent down and pulled him to his feet, putting her arms around him while she examined his injuries. 'Don't cry,' she said, spitting on the hem of her dress and rubbing the grime gently from his knees with it. 'It isn't much. Look.'

Pete looked. He'd stopped crying, but the tears were still visible on his cheeks and lurked on his eyelashes, and Lizzie knew he was liable to start again any minute. 'They sting,' he whined.

'I know,' Lizzie sympathised. 'Tell you what, I'll lift you up on to the pram and you can have a ride, how's that?'

Pete looked at the pram and then at the length of Bromsgrove Street stretching before them. 'How much further is it?' he asked.

'Still a fair bit,' Maura told him, and added to Lizzie, 'But you don't have to go on as if you were in some sort of race. No wonder Pete fell over. It's too hot to rush about like that, I'm boiling already myself.'

'I'll ride,' Pete said suddenly, and Lizzie lifted him up on to the pram, thankful he wasn't going to make more of a fuss. Maura was right, she realised, because as the morning wore on it had become hotter and she was feeling prickly with it already. So with Peter settled at the bottom of the pram opposite his sister, the two girls went at a more leisurely pace.

Lizzie didn't want to discuss the war any more, so she said to Maura, 'Tell me about when you was evacuated.'

'What about it?'

'Well, why didn't you like it?' Lizzie asked. ''Cos I haven't ever been to the countryside. What's it like?'

'Well, when I was there, everything was always dripping wet,' Maura said. 'There weren't proper pavements, just muddy lanes and soaking wet fields. There were great big cows and smelly pigs and dogs that barked all the time.'

'Was she nice, the woman you were sent to?'

Maura shrugged. 'She was all right,' she said. ''Cept she made me take my shoes off at the door, 'cos they were always muddy. She said I needed wellingtons, but I didn't have none. It was freezing on her lino and kitchen tiles in my socks. It was all right for her, she had big fluffy slippers, but I didn't.'

Lizzie nodded. She knew her mother had no money for slippers either.

'Mammy was mad,' Maura went on. 'She said I'd catch my death of cold, and it was cold, everything was blinking cold.'

'What about your brothers?'

'Oh, Harry and Gerry went to someone else,' Maura said. 'It was on a farm and they wanted big strapping boys and they quite liked it, but Mammy took us all back at Christmas.'

'I'm glad I didn't go,' Lizzie said. 'It sounds horrible.'

'Well, you didn't miss much,' Maura said. 'And there's never been any bombs falling either, has there?'

'No,' Lizzie said uncertainly. 'But Daddy said that there will be.'

'Och, my mammy said if they were going to bomb Birmingham, they'd have done it already,' Maura said airily. 'She said we're safe enough two hundred miles from the coast.'

'Daddy said something about a landmine flattening the house.'

'I don't think that will happen, do you?'

'I don't know,' Lizzie admitted. 'But I hope not.'

They turned into Jamaica Row as they talked and could see the spire of the Bull Ring's church and Times Furnishing on the corner of High Street. The crowds had increased around them as they neared the Bull Ring, and Lizzie felt the familiar excitement as she turned the pram and looked for a moment at the teeming mass of people on the hill running down towards the Bull Ring proper.

The statue of Nelson surrounded by railings was in the centre, with the barrows selling their wares to the right of it stretching from Bell Street down past Woolworth's to Edgbaston Street. Smithfield Market and Rag Alley were to the left, and towering above it all was St Martin's in the Field Church, with all the flower sellers around it.

Lizzie had a job to hold the pram on the steep incline down to the market, and she lifted Pete out to make it easier and he held the pram handle. The cobbled streets gave Nuala a bumpy ride and she seemed to enjoy it, for she squealed in delight.

Once among the thronging crowds, Lizzie was afraid of losing Pete and warned him to stay close with no wandering off, but there were such interesting things to see and hear, he was very tempted. All around traders plied their wares, fruit, vegetables, fish and meat interspersed with stalls selling curtain material, bedding, antiques and cheap crockery in baskets.

The cries of the vendors, mixed with the voices of those bartering with customers and the general crush of people, made a clamorous noise everywhere, but there was a buzz about the whole place that most of the shoppers seemed to feel. It had a special smell too, as the aromas of all the different things for sale rose on the air. Over all the bustle, one voice rang out loud and clear, and that was the bag lady chanting ''Andy carriers, 'andy carriers.' She was very old, toothless and blind, and had a label round her neck saying so and she'd been there as long as Lizzie and Maura could remember, selling her paper carrier bags in all weathers.

Maura was holding Pete's hand tightly as he'd made more than one dash for freedom as they looked around the stalls. 'Hello, ducks, what you after then?' the stall holders would enquire, but Maura and Lizzie would just smile and shake their heads. They passed Solly's fish cart and greeted him, but he hadn't reduced the fish yet so Maura kept her money in her pocket.

Peacock's store beckoned, and they took the children to gaze in wonder at the wide array of toys. There were dolls of all shapes and sizes from the cheap to the dear, and beautiful prams and cribs for them like those for a real baby, but Lizzie noted with satisfaction that none of the dolls was as beautiful as her dear Daisy. Pete was more interested in the railway made of tin, and the metal cars, and the little lead soldiers in the fort. None of the children had toys like these and to them it was like an Aladdin's cave. Eventually Lizzie turned the pram and they went on to Woolworth's, where nothing cost more than sixpence. Maura said, 'Bit of a swizz, though, my mammy says.'

'Why?'

''Cos they sell a teapot for sixpence and then the lid for another sixpence. I mean, a lid's no good on its own, is it?'

'Well, no,' Lizzie agreed, but added, 'Though it's useful to be able to buy another lid if you break one, and anyway Woolworth's sells lots of other things.'

Maura couldn't argue with that. The two girls particularly liked the counters with the jewellery, rings with sparkling diamonds, or red glass stones that shone like rubies. There were necklaces of pearl, and a wide variety of brooches, earrings and bracelets, and all for sixpence. 'I'm going to buy some of this jewellery when I'm working,' Maura said, and Lizzie thought she might too. Then there was the counter with the pretty hairslides and bands and silver-backed brushes and matching combs, and all manner of other items to make their hair beautiful. Lizzie sighed and said, 'I wish I had bands like this, don't you?'

'Oh aye, and some pretty ribbons,' Maura said wistfully.

'Let me see,' Pete demanded.

Lizzie laughed at him. 'What do you need to see for, Pete? Choosing a ribbon for your own hair, are you?'

Pete stuck out his bottom lip obstinately. He hated being made fun of and he aimed a kick at Lizzie's shins, which she side-stepped neatly. She grasped her young cousin by the shoulders and gave him a shake. 'If you don't behave, I won't take you to see the clock.'

'What clock?'

'You'll never know unless you're good.'

'Put him back up on the pram,' Maura suggested. 'He'll see all he wants then.'

Lizzie saw the sense of that and dumped Pete at the bottom end of the pram again, and they all stopped to drool longingly over the sweet counter. 'How much have we got altogether?' Maura asked.

'Eleven pence,' Lizzie said. 'Sixpence from Gran, three-pence from Mrs Morcroft and tuppence from your mammy.'

'Not enough, is it?'

'It might be, but we'd better save it, 'cos we'll be hungry later,' Lizzie said.

Regretfully they turned away from the beautiful array of sweets, out into the thronging market again. Next door to Woolworth's was the plywood model shop, Hobbies, and they stood for a minute to let the little ones see the model yachts, trains and cars arranged in the window before crossing the market to the bottom of the steps leading to the Market Hall.

To one side of the steps stood an ex-serviceman from the Great War selling razor blades from a tray around his neck, and on the other side another ex-army man, who was also blind, sold shoelaces. 'Black or brown, best in town!' he'd cry, over and over. Lizzie always felt sorry for the old soldiers – her daddy said there were many like them, just thrown on to the scrap heap – but she hadn't money spare to buy things she didn't need, so she averted her eyes and brought her mind back to the problem in hand.

'How we going to get up there?' Maura asked.

'I suppose if our Pete walks up we could carry the pram,' Lizzie suggested.

'Are you kidding?' Maura said. She thought a minute and said, 'You could leave the pram at the bottom.'

'I'd have to carry Nuala everywhere then,' Lizzie complained. 'And what if someone walked off with the pram while we're inside?'

'What's up, duck?' said a man at a nearby stall. 'You want to go up the market?'

'Um, yes,' Lizzie said. 'Yes please, but the pram . . .'

'No trouble,' the man said. He lifted Pete off the pram and called to his mate. 'Come on, Fred, these two lasses want to get up the steps with the pram and the babby. Give us a hand.'

They lifted the pram, Nuala and all, and carried the whole lot up the steps, while Pete ran up alongside holding Maura and Lizzie's hands. Once inside the Market Hall he stood and stared wide-eyed. The ceilings were high and criss-crossed with beams, and long metal poles led down from the beams to hold up the roof. High arched windows lined the sides of the hall, with lower ones at the ends, and stalls of every description lay before them. The noise was incredible.

They hadn't gone very far when the clock began to strike. Until that moment, neither Pete nor Nuala had noticed the clock, but now they watched it spellbound. Lizzie noticed that most people did, even grown-ups, and the hubbub around them died down as the figures of three knights and a lady struck the bell twelve times. 'Is that the clock you said about?' Pete asked when it was all over.

'That's it,' Lizzie said, 'and if you keep being a good boy, I'll take you to see the animals.'

Pete beamed. 'There's animals?' he cried disbelievingly.

Maura laughed at the little boy's amazed face. 'You wait and see,' she said. 'My mammy used to bring me here for a treat when I was about your age.'

There were stalls for everything in the Market Hall, and although the smell of fish lingered, it didn't seem to matter and even added a little to the atmosphere of the place. There were flower stalls, clothes stalls and material stalls, and the junk stalls sold a wide array of interesting objects. There were stalls selling fruit and vegetables, fresh fish and meat and cheese. There were people setting pots and pans and other kitchen utensils, and there were stalls piled with sweets, toys, haberdashery and knick-knacks.

Pimm's pet shop drew the children like a magnet, for none of them owned pets of their own. The canaries twittered around them in their cages as the children stared, and even Nuala clamoured to be let down. There were mewing kittens and boisterous puppies that nipped their fingers playfully as they tumbled about the large box that held them. They saw fish swimming endlessly around their bowls, and baby rabbits and guinea pigs in their cages, and they stopped by the budgies to try and teach them to talk. Pete didn't believe they could, and although Maura and Lizzie repeated over and over, 'Who's a pretty boy then?' none of the birds co-operated and copied them. In the end they gave up and Pete said triumphantly, 'See, told you they couldn't talk. You must think I'm stupid.'

Lizzie laughed and cuffed Pete lightly around the head, and he yelled, 'Gerroff!' but any further protests were stopped by the clock striking again.

'Two o'clock,' Maura exclaimed in disbelief. We'd better get going. I'm starving, aren't you?'

'Not half,' Lizzie agreed, bouncing the pram back to the Market Hall entrance.

Willing customers carried the pram down the steps for them, and once on the cobbles Maura said, 'Sniff that.'

Lizzie didn't have to; she could already smell the joints of meat roasting in Mountford's shop window, and it made her mouth water. 'Come on,' she said, 'my stomach thinks my throat's cut.'

They couldn't afford a meat sandwich because it cost sixpence, and anyway it was Friday, so instead they bought a cone of baked potatoes for a penny each, with a slice of bread dipped in gravy for Nuala. 'Are you sure she should be eating that?' Maura asked.

Lizzie wasn't really certain, but she shrugged and said, 'Surely eating meat doesn't count when you're only a baby?'

'I don't know,' Maura said. 'But then, sure, she has to eat something.'

Nuala certainly seemed to enjoy her slice of dipped bread. She ate every bit and all told didn't make much mess at all. Pete finished his cone of potatoes and licked his fingers and said, 'I'm thirsty now,' and Lizzie realised she was too.

'Have we enough for drinks?' Maura asked.

'Not if we want sweets,' Lizzie said. 'But we can get threepence worth of over-ripe fruit that might cure the thirst, and still have money for some sweets too.'

Everyone agreed with that suggestion and they wandered down to the bottom where the cheaper barrows were and got some bruised apples, soft oranges and bananas going brown. They demolished them in quick order, sitting on a bench by the horse trough near St Martin's, where Pete was entertained by the trams that came rattling up Moor Street.

Then they made their way to the sweet stall, where they pored over the goodly selection on sale. Gobstoppers lasted forever, but pear drops tasted better, and toffee was nice but would make them thirsty again. Eventually they bought a stick of liquorice at a halfpenny each, and two penn'orth of pear drops. Nuala had fallen asleep in the pram with her thumb in her mouth, so she didn't have to be considered as they shared the sweets out among themselves.

'We'll have to be off soon,' Lizzie said. 'It's a tidy step home and time must be getting on.'

'Aye, I'll have to get Mammy's fish,' Maura said. 'If it's gone down enough in price.'

Before that, though, Pete was enchanted by the day-old chicks a man had for sale by Nelson's Square. They did look sweet, like little yellow fluff balls, and Pete was all for taking one home. Lizzie and Maura had a hard job to convince him that the chick would grow to a hen, and hens couldn't be kept in a back-to-back house with no garden.

Pete had reached the mutinous stage when Maura spotted the man walking round with the tray of mechanical toys and successfully distracted his attention. He watched the toys jumping around the tray in open-mouthed astonishment, and Lizzie stayed with him while Maura got a huge parcel of kippers for her mother for one and six. She stored it at the bottom of the pram and they set off home. Pete's legs were tired, and Lizzie tucked him in beside the fish, and even though the hill up to High Street was steep and she was puffed at the top of it, she left Pete where he was. It was a long way home, she thought, for legs as short as his.

All the way back, while Nuala slumbered, the two girls told Peter tales about the Bull Ring on a Saturday. 'It's better then,' Maura said. 'Late afternoon and evening's the best time, and the food is nearly given away, my mammy says.'

'Aye, but that's not all,' Lizzie said. 'They have stilt walkers and a man in chains – all tied up, he is, and you wouldn't think how he'd get out of it, but he always does.'

'Aye, when the money in the hat is a pound or more,' Maura reminded her. 'And there's a fire-eater and a man that lies on a bed of nails and lets other people walk on him.'

'And others play music and sing,' Lizzie said. 'And a feller called Jimmy Jesus preaches from the Bible. He's got long white hair and a beard and that's why he's called Jesus.'

Pete's mouth dropped open in astonishment as he drank in all the two girls told him, scarcely able to believe it was true. 'We'll take you one day, Pete,' Lizzie promised. 'If your mammy says it's all right, you can come with me and Maura. We'll stay till the Sally Army brass band comes marching down Corporation Street. Later they give all the tramps soup at the Citadel. Jimmy Jesus too, so my daddy said anyway.'

'Oh, they do,' Maura said. 'It's great down the Bull Ring, isn't it?'

'Nowhere like it,' Lizzie agreed. 'And it was worth it today, even if I'm never allowed out again for a whole year.'

'Och, course you will be,' Maura said confidently. 'They'll just shout a bit, that's all.'

Lizzie didn't answer, for Maura didn't know how her Mammy could go on, not to mention her Auntie Bridie, and whatever Maura said, she knew she was going to catch it.

She said goodbye to Maura at her door and went along Bell Barn Road to collect the rations before she dared go home. 'How's your aunt, dear?' Mrs Morcroft asked, and Lizzie realised with a jolt she hadn't thought about Auntie Rose and the reason for her jaunt to the Bull Ring all day. She wasn't terribly worried – after all, women had babies all the time, and even though her gran said she'd had to have the doctor, it didn't really mean she was deadly sick – so she said quite cheerfully, 'All right, I suppose, Mrs Morcroft, but I don't know, we've been out all day.'

She was more concerned when she got to Rose's house and found no one in. She left the children in the pram outside and pounded upstairs. The bed was stripped and had a big stain across it, and there was bed linen soiled with blood thrown into a corner. Alarmed, Lizzie ran downstairs and pushed the pram across the road to her own house, but that was also empty, so then she ran, pushing the pram before her, past Pickering's to her grandma's.

She lifted Pete down and hauled Nuala from her straps, suddenly aware that not only was the little girl sopping wet, but that something was seeping from her nappy on to Lizzie's dress as she balanced Nuala on her hip to open the entry door.

They were all there, Kathy, Maggie and Carmel, and they all turned at her entrance. 'Where in the name of God have you been?' Kathy demanded.

'D-down the Bull Ring. Grandma told me to take the weans.'

'She meant you to take them all,' Kathy said. 'Dear God, girl, you're not stupid, and I'd keep out of Bridie's way if I were you. She's been spitting feathers all day, and Sheelagh's done nothing but moan.'

'Aye, as if we hadn't enough on our plate,' Maggie said bitterly. 'It wouldn't have hurt Bridie to look to her own weans the once, for she was worse than useless here, and Lizzie at least kept the wee ones away for the day.'

'What d'you mean?' Lizzie cried, suddenly frightened. 'What's happened?'

Kathy glanced at her sisters and then at her daughter, and said, 'Rose has been sent to the hospital, the doctor thought it best.'

'Will she . . . she will be all right, won't she?'

'Course she will,' Kathy said, but she didn't meet Lizzie's eyes as she said it.

Lizzie knew her mother was worried and wasn't sure if Rose was going to be all right at all, and she hoped Peter and Nuala weren't aware of it. But both had picked up on the tension, and Nuala said, 'Mammy, want Mammy,' and began to wail.

'Och, there's no need to cry,' Kathy said, lifting Nuala into her arms. 'Your mammy will be as right as rain, you'll see. Grandma Sullivan has gone with her, so there's no need to fret at all, and you're both to come home with me tonight.'

She set Nuala on her feet again, wiped her hand down her apron and asked Lizzie, 'Hasn't that child been changed all day?'

'No,' Lizzie said. 'I didn't come back for a change for her.'

'You didn't come back because you didn't want Sheelagh with you, if we're telling the truth,' Kathy said.

'You can't blame her,' Maggie said.

'Maybe you can't, but I can,' Kathy snapped. 'She knows she has to be understanding to Sheelagh just at the minute.'

'It's like being understanding to a rattlesnake.' Carmel said it under her breath so Kathy didn't hear, but Lizzie did, and grinned at her young aunt.

'And you can take that silly smile off your face,' Kathy said. 'I'm sure I never said anything to laugh at. You can come across to Rose's with me to get a few things for the weans for tonight and tomorrow. Bring Nuala and you can change her and make her more comfortable.'

'We'll rustle up something to eat,' Maggie said. 'We might as well eat together tonight, and Daddy will be in any minute.'

'Aye,' Kathy said. 'Life goes on, and Lord knows when we'll see Mammy.'

Bridie went for Lizzie that night as she'd known she would, and she stood and took it without a word, feeling it was just punishment, for she felt guilty to be out enjoying herself while her Aunt Rose lay so ill. 'I'm sorry, Aunt Bridie,' she said, when eventually the tirade had stopped.

Bridie looked at Lizzie through narrowed eyes, not at all sure that she wasn't being sarcastic, but she thought she looked suitably chastened. 'Yes, well,' she said, 'I mean, being sorry is all very well, but it was a terrible thing to do. Poor wee Sheelagh cried her eyes out and then—'

Kathy cut in then, deciding enough was enough. 'The child has said sorry, Bridie,' she said. 'Let that be the end of it now. What do you want her to do? Grovel on the floor?'

Lizzie looked at her mother in amazement and Bridie snapped, 'You just encourage her with that attitude.'

'Encourage her?' Kathy exclaimed. 'It was hardly the crime of the century, Bridie. She went for a wee jaunt to the Bull Ring with a friend, that's all.'

'She was supposed to come back for Sheelagh.'

'There was nothing to stop Sheelagh going along to the Bull Ring on her own,' Kathy said sharply. 'She said Lizzie had told her where they were going. Anyway she's sorry now.' She looked across to Lizzie and said, 'You won't do it again, sure you won't?'

And Lizzie was certain sure her mammy gave her a huge wink. 'No, Mammy,' she said.

Bridie glared at the two of them, but no one cared for that and when she left just afterwards, Lizzie felt she could breathe more easily. Kathy gave a smile and said, 'Phew! I'm glad that's over with. Now don't be forgetting Aunt Rose in your prayers tonight.'

'I won't,' Lizzie promised but she smiled because she knew her mammy wasn't cross with her any more and she disliked Bridie and her way of going on as much as she did herself.

Rose didn't die, as had been feared, and neither did her tiny baby girl, whom she called Josephine after her mother, but the pair of them were very ill and were still in hospital a week later when Maggie and Kathy both gave birth to baby boys on 30 July. Kathy called her son Padraic, after her beloved brother Pat, and Maggie named her baby Tim, and by the middle of August Lizzie had forgotten there was such a thing as a holiday, for she was run off her feet.

Eventually Kathy and Maggie were both up and about again. Their two boys were placid and good sleepers. In contrast, little Josie, tinier by far than her plump, healthy-looking cousins, still cried often, wouldn't settle and refused to suckle. She had to be put on the bottle, which made Rose feel a failure on top of everything else. She was very weak herself, and often tired, and a demanding baby as well as the other two little ones made things harder for her.

Kathy was unable to do much for Rose, for she had her own family to see to, Bridie never off the doorstep and Barry's mother Molly to visit, but Maggie and Mary both tried to help. All the family were worried about Rose and wee Josie and took Pete and Nuala off her hands as often as they could.

The first bombs fell in Birmingham on the night of 8 August, leaving one person dead and five injured. Many thought the lone German bomber was actually looking for Fort Dunlop, but was unable to find it in the black-out and dropped his load in Erdington instead. Kathy knew that the battle was on now and the phoney war was over, and she prepared her cellar as if for a siege, while sporadic bombing raids took place in various parts of the city throughout August. She lugged mattresses down the stone steps, and told the astonished children that in future they would sleep with her in her bed. If they were woken by a raid, they were to put on their shoes and their outdoor coats, which Kathy would leave at the end of the bed. If they could drag their eiderdowns after them without tripping themselves up, so much the better. Danny was in charge of the torch, and Lizzie was responsible for Kathy's box containing the ration books, identity cards and post office savings book. Kathy would follow with the baby in the large wicker basket that she was using for a cradle just now, and she assured the children they'd be as safe as houses.

On the night of 25 August, the children hadn't been in bed long when the siren went off. Kathy wasn't too worried, though she urged them to hurry. They'd had plenty of these skirmishes that had turned out to be nothing, and she crept down behind the children, carrying the sleeping Padraic, and hoping it would be over soon.

She met Bridie coming in through the cellar door – she'd given her sister-in-law a key as it saved time – and they settled the children on the mattresses, cuddled up with the eiderdowns. Kathy made tea and produced biscuits, and it began to take on the air of a picnic.

When the droning planes came so near that they could hear the whine and whistle of the bombs and the shuddering crashes as they descended on the city centre, the children's eyes opened wider with fear. Kathy's blood seemed to freeze in her veins, and she looked at Bridie and saw stark terror in her face as the ack-ack guns began the attack.

Matt, Danny and Sheelagh began to howl. Lizzie wanted to cry too – she'd never in all her life been as scared – but she noticed that her mammy wasn't crying, so she decided she wouldn't either. She held herself so rigid on the mattress, with her hands balled into fists beside her, that she shook slightly, but no tears slid down her cheeks.

The noise was incredible, the ferocious blasts and crashes hurt Lizzie's ears, and in the middle of it came a furious knocking at the entry door at the top of the cellar steps. Kathy's startled eyes met those of Bridie. Who would knock at the door in the middle of a raid? But whoever it was, it must be trouble, and with a feeling of dread she crossed the room.

As Kathy was about to open the cellar door, Lizzie threw herself at her mother. 'No, Mammy!' It was almost a scream, and Lizzie's eyes looked wild as she pleaded, 'Don't, don't go up there.'

Kathy understood how Lizzie felt; God, she felt it herself. She took her daughter's protesting hands in her own and said gently, 'I must see who it is, Lizzie.' Then she gave her a little push away and added, 'Go on now, be a good girl. I'll be back in a minute.' Lizzie said nothing more, but stood watching her mother go up the cellar steps.

Kathy swung open the entry door. In the dim light she could just make out the figures of two ARP wardens. One cradled little Josie in a blanket and the other had Nuala in her arms and was supporting Rose, who held tight to Pete's hand.

'What in God's name . . .?' The words were almost lost in the deafening crash terrifyingly near. Kathy tasted dust in her mouth, and there was an acrid smell in her nose.

'Found her in the street, missus,' said one of the wardens, as Kathy pulled her sister-in-law inside and took Josie from the woman's arms. 'Trying to get to her ma's with the children. Your place was closer, so we brought her here.'

'Yes, of course, you did right,' Kathy said.

114

'We'll leave you to it, then, missus,' the other warden said, setting little Nuala on her feet.

'Yes, thank you. Thank you for bringing her.'

Rose had not uttered a word. Kathy closed the door and turned to the trembling woman. 'Can you manage the steps?' she asked in a loud voice, as if she had to rouse her in some way. Rose nodded, and Lizzie ran up to help her mother bring the little ones down to the comparative safety of the cellar, while the pounding went on all around them.

It was a little while later before Rose could begin to explain. At first Kathy was involved with practicalities, such as dealing with the shivering children and the restless baby, who'd begun to wail in a cross, tired voice. Kathy soothed Josie while Lizzie tucked the little ones under the eiderdown with Danny, Matt and Sheelagh and wondered why her Auntie Bridie didn't get off her behind and give a hand.

Lizzie marvelled that her mother seemed not even to hear the clamour around her, while Lizzie herself could hardly bear it. The German engines had a sort of intermittent burring sound that you'd hear sometimes between the almost incessant ack-ack guns peppering the night. But most terrifying of all was the shrill and whistle of the bombs, and the crash and boom of them landing that often seemed to shake the walls of the cellar.

Rose, sitting beside Bridie on the mattress, began suddenly to cry. Kathy put a cup of tea in her hands, but they shook so much Lizzie thought most of it would be spilt. 'I'm sorry,' she said to Kathy. 'I tried to get to Mam's, but I, I . . .' She gave a shudder and said, 'I was so scared.'

'Hush,' Kathy said, putting an arm around her. 'You'll wake the weans. You're not alone; sure, we're all bloody scared.'

'Aye, but you don't understand. I can't do it,' Rose cried. 'I can't get the three of them up and dressed and off in the middle of the night to Ma's.'

Kathy was smitten with guilt. Of course she couldn't. Lizzie and Danny were of an age to see to themselves a bit, and were even a help to Kathy, but Rose's three were still wee. Why hadn't she thought about it? Bridie could help, but Kathy knew it was no good asking her, and Maggie had her own little one to see to. 'You need someone with you,' she said. 'What about our Carmel?'

Rose looked up with the deep-brown eyes her children had inherited, but hers seemed sunk in her head and ringed with black, and Kathy realised she was so thin her cheek-bones stuck out. 'Your ma said your Carmel's gone a bit wild, she's never in nights. She'd be just another to look after and worry about.'

'Your sisters?'

'They're all away,' Rose said. 'Mammy sent them at the beginning of the holidays to our people in Ireland. There's only Catrin, and she's living in Lozell's near her chap's people.'

'Mammy?'

'She has enough on her plate with her worries about your da.'

'What about him?' Kathy said, alarmed.

'With his chest playing up again.'

Mary had said nothing to Kathy, and for a moment she was a little upset that she'd confided in Rose, but that wasn't the issue at the moment. She said suddenly and decisively, 'You must come to us.'

'How can she?' Bridie put in, the first time she'd spoken in ages. 'We have little enough room as it is.'

'Well, what we have, we'll share,' Kathy snapped. To Rose she said, 'You and the weans can bed down in my attic night-times. I'll be on hand to help you then, and you can share the cellar.'

Rose's eyes showed her gratitude, and yet she said, 'I wanted to stay in my own place, you know, to have a nice home for Sean to come back to.'

Hitler might see you have no home at all, Kathy thought, but aloud she said, 'Sure, you'll be in your own home in the daytime, it's only nights you'll be here.'

Lizzie gave a yawn and suddenly realised how weary she was. Her eyelids felt heavy and she blinked to keep them open. Kathy and Rose were still talking softly, with a sharp rejoinder now and then from Bridie, but she was too tired to take it in. She leant sleepily against her mother, and Kathy smiled down at her. Her hands were full – one arm cradled Josie, thankfully asleep again, and the other was round the distressed Rose – but she saw the exhaustion in her daughter's face. 'Lie down for a wee while,' she said. 'You'll be tired out tomorrow.'

Doubting she would sleep in the noise all about them, Lizzie crawled under the eiderdowns with her brother and cousins. Danny, Matt and Pete were fast asleep already at the other end, and Sheelagh stirred as Lizzie moved in between her and Nuala, but didn't wake. The murmur of the women's voices was comforting amid the din coming from above the cellar, Lizzie thought as she closed her eyes.

She slept deeply and didn't wake, not even when the baby cried for a feed and Matt and Danny both needed the toilet and had to be stood on the draining board to wee in the big sink. Neither did a nearby explosion cause her to do little more than turn over. Kathy, lying on the other mattress, envied the slumber Lizzie was enjoying. Though her eyes felt gritty with tiredness, she knew she'd be unable to rest until the raid was over.

She felt Rose sag beside her as the night wore on, and Bridie had already slipped under the eiderdowns with the children. Kathy laid the sleeping Josie at the other end of Padraic's basket and tried to close her smarting eyes, but each crash brought them shooting open again, and in the end she gave up and waited for the morning, wondering fearfully if any of them would still be alive to see it.

SEVEN

The next morning they stumbled stiff-legged up the cellar steps as the all-clear blasted out its reassuring sound over the city. In the streets people were pointing and looking and chattering to each other, as Lizzie opened the door and stepped out.

A sour smell of burning hit her, and black smoke rose in a column from an orange glow on the skyline. Later, they found out that it was the Bull Ring that had borne the brunt of the attack. Many homes around the city centre were destroyed, and Mary said they had a lot to be thankful for that they were all safe, though she'd been worried all night about Rose and her weans and would have gone to look for her if Eamonn had let her.

'I told her she can come to us at night,' Kathy said. 'She needs help, with them all so little and wee Josie so demanding.'

'Dear Lord, where will it all end?' Mary said wearily.

'Let's just be thankful none of ours were hurt,' Kathy said impatiently, tiredness making her tetchy, and added, 'I need to go across and check on Molly. Will you mind the weans for me?'

'I'll come round,' Maggie offered. 'Ma's tired and Da's bad this morning.'

'You mean he's not at work?'

'He's in bed,' Mary said. 'His chest's been playing up lately. Being out in all weathers fire-watching didn't help, but at least he's giving that up now. He knew himself it was no good for him.'

'But still, he must be feeling bad if he's in bed,' Kathy said, for she'd never known her dad lie in before.

'I don't think the worry of it all helps,' Mary said. 'But whatever it is, as soon as he steps outside he starts to cough and can't catch his breath.'

'Oh, Mammy, I'm sorry.'

'I'm sorry too, lass, but there's nothing anyone can do. And I'm one of the lucky ones, for Molly is on her own with two sons dead and two to fret over. You're right to go and see her.'

'I'll come over as soon as I've had a bite to eat,' Maggie promised, and Kathy returned home, where Rose was still trying to wash and dress her children and giving an eye to Kathy's too, glad that Lizzie was such a help.

Maggie had barely arrived when there was a knock at the door. Kathy opened it, Padraic in her arms, to find Molly standing there with an ARP warden. She had a huge bruise on one cheek, her grey hair was frizzed out about her face and she was covered in a layer of brick and plaster dust.

'Oh, Kathy,' she said as she saw her daughter-in-law, and burst into helpless sobs. Kathy drew them all in from the pavement and the eyes of the gawping children playing in the street. 'What's happened?' she said, and as Molly continued to sob, it was the warden who replied.

'Mrs O'Malley was sheltering with her neighbours, the Sutcliffes, in their cellar when a bomb fell in the next street. Their homes were caught in the blast.'

119

'Went down like a bleeding house of cards, they did,' Molly wailed from the armchair. 'And we were trapped underneath.'

'God,' breathed Kathy, knowing it could just as easily have been her place. 'How are the other family, the Sutcliffes? Are they all right?'

'The parents and two elder kids have just cuts and bruises and are a bit shook up, but the youngest child, Charlie, was crushed by one of the cellar walls collapsing on him.' The warden shook his head sadly and said, I believe he's in a bad way. The whole family's gone to hospital to be checked over. Mrs O'Malley wouldn't go, insisted on coming here, said you're her daughter-in-law.'

'Aye, I am,' Kathy said. 'She'll be all right with me.'

Kathy felt very sorry for Molly. To have two sons killed in the war was enough for anyone, but then having your house blown up and being trapped in a cellar must have been a terrifying experience.

Later, drinking a cup of tea, Molly confessed to Kathy and Maggie, 'I never thought I'd see the light of day again, I'll tell you straight. We could hear them working on getting us out, but as they moved things above us, so more fell down, and there was brick dust and rubble trickling through all the time. And little Charlie was in the corner groaning, and of course it was so bleeding dark. We tried to pull him out but he was stuck fast and then he began to scream.'

She shook her head. 'God, Kathy, it was awful. We could do nothing to ease the pain he must have been in, not even budge the bricks and timber pinning him down. Christ, what a war, fighting women and weans, eh?'

Kathy could only imagine the terror of the little boy, who she knew was only a year or two older than her Danny. Later, when the Sutcliffes called, she was struck with pity for them all. The hospital had cleaned them up and done what they could with their clothes, but they still looked bedraggled. The parents, Sid and Enid, were white with shock, while the children's faces were tear-stained. They all looked utterly exhausted, and the news from the hospital on Charlie's condition was not good. Kathy could have cried for them.

'Come in,' she said. 'Please.' And afterwards she asked her mother helplessly, 'What else could I have done?'

The authorities had not organised alternative accommodation for the bombed-out families, and though Eamonn was able to bully them into giving him mattresses and blankets, there were no clothes banks either. The clothes they had were filthy and dust-laden as well as ripped and torn from their ordeal, and the family had to get together to do what they could for them.

It was obvious that Molly and the Sutcliffes would stay with Kathy, although Sid and Enid said they wanted to make arrangements for the children to go somewhere safer eventually. For the time being, though, they lodged at Kathy's, so Rose had to put her children to bed at Mary's place instead.

When the sirens went off the following night, Kathy groaned. She needed to sleep, she couldn't go on night after night like this. The Sutcliffes were too afraid to use the cellar after their recent experience, and Molly too was reluctant. Kathy was too tired to argue with them. 'You must please yourselves,' she said. 'But Bridie and me and the children will; it must be safer than staying in the house.'

The raid that night was mainly in the Tyburn Road, Ward End area of the city, they found out later, although the Bull Ring got it again too, and some bombs fell uncomfortably close. Kathy dozed from sheer exhaustion, but kept jerking awake and checking on her sleeping children, and by the morning she'd made a decision.

'You're mad,' Bridie said flatly. 'You always said you'd not send them away to strangers.'

'I still don't want to,' Kathy said, 'but after seeing what happened to the Sutcliffes, I feel they will be safer. And I did talk to Chris Barraclough in the hospital, I have the address and telephone number.' She looked across at Bridie and said, 'You wouldn't consider it for yours?'

'Hasn't the war robbed me of enough already?' Bridie said tartly.

Kathy made no answer, but she'd made her decision and that was that.

Everyone was talking about what had happened in the Bull Ring, and rumours were flying about all over the place. Lizzie wanted to go and see for herself, but Kathy wouldn't let her. In fact, with Barry's words about protecting them in her head, she hardly let either Danny or Lizzie out of her sight.

But Lizzie had to know. After the second raid, the following night was quiet, and Lizzie woke on the mattress she shared with Danny in the bedroom very early the next morning. She lay for a moment in the semi-darkness, dimmed by the black-out curtains at the window.

Her mother's alarm clock read six o'clock. Lizzie knew that soon the house would be astir, and if she was going to go to the Bull Ring, this was about her only chance. She slid from under the eiderdown, careful not to disturb Danny, and crept past her sleeping mother, grandmother and Padraic snuffling in his cradle and carrying her clothes in her hands, crept out of the room.

Once downstairs, she dressed quickly and left the house by the entry door. Outside the sun shone despite the early hour, and Lizzie hurried along Bell Barn Road and down Bristol Passage into Bristol Street. As she turned into Bromsgrove Street, she breathed a little easier.

Around her the city was coming to life. The first trams had trundled past her virtually empty in Bristol Street, but in Bromsgrove Street they were noticeably fuller and there was more traffic generally on the road. As she turned into Jamaica Row, she realised she'd never seen the place so quiet, and when she came to Times Furnishings on the corner of High Street and looked down she could hardly believe her eyes. Many shops were mere shells; unsupported walls leant drunkenly against their neighbour, while inside they were filled with rubble, broken bricks, plasterboard, charred wood and jagged splinters of glass. Much of the same sort of debris filled the cobbled streets outside.

Lizzie walked slowly down into the empty market, and was able to see for herself the damage that had been done. Even St Martin's hadn't escaped, she noticed, but it was the Market Hall, or what was left of it, that drew her in horrified fascination.

Only the walls still stood; the Market Hall was open to the sky. She peered through the dusty windows, but it was hard to see in. A hole had been blasted in the side wall, and a barrier had been put across to prevent people entering the building, but Lizzie could see all that was left of the place, and that was a mass of rubble. Blackened beams lay among bricks and pieces of iron, while some of the battered utensils that had been on sale littered the ground. Many of the buckled iron frames of the stalls were still there, and some of the name plaques. 'Albert Pope' was one; another was 'Yates', and beside that name was their new address with the message 'Burnt but not broke'.

Funny that such a thing should bring tears to Lizzie's eyes, but it did, like the little Union Jack flags stuck defiantly in the rubble piles. She didn't understand herself, for she knew people had been killed in the raids, and yet the wanton devastation around her seemed to have affected her more. It was as if the German bombers had struck at the heart of the city and torn it out. The Bull Ring would never be the same, and she realised she could never take Peter on his promised return trip to Market Hall, for it was no more. There were no animals now inside that shattered building, and the magnificent clock had been wrenched from the wall and lay in pieces.

She turned from the sight, unable to bear it any longer, and watched the first barrows rushing past her to set up opposite Woolworth's. 'Chin up, ducks,' a man said to her. He was pulling the canvas awning over his barrow while his wife arranged the fruit on the stall. 'What's the sad face for?'

Lizzie stared at him, surprised that he'd had to ask. 'Look at it,' she said.

'That's nowt,' the man said, 'a bit bashed about, that's all. Take more than Hitler to kill the old Bull Ring.'

Lizzie looked disbelieving for a moment, and then she noticed the people bustling all around her and realised the market was coming to life again. 'The Bull Ring's the people, ducks,' the man said. 'We'll soon replace buildings, so don't you fret.'

Suddenly Lizzie realised he was right. Hitler had tried and failed. He'd smashed shops and stalls and injured and killed people, but the Brummie spirit was alive and well.

She went home in better heart, though when Kathy heard what she'd done, she gave out to her good and proper. She would have smacked her too, if it hadn't been for Molly. 'Leave the girl be,' she said. 'It's obvious she had to see it for herself. God, I took a gander up there myself yesterday when I had Padraic out for a walk.'

Kathy stared at her mother-in-law in amazement. 'Did you? You never said anything.'

'I was shook up, to tell you the truth,' Molly said, 'and I didn't want to upset you, but everyone was talking about it and I had to go and have a look. It's a bloody shambles and no mistake, and I doubt it will ever be put right again.

But it's my city and Lizzie's, and she was bound to be as curious as I was.'

'It was the sneaking out without a word I was so cross about,' Kathy said in defence.

'And what was the girl to do?' Molly said. 'I heard her ask you yesterday, but lately you won't let either of them move from the street.'

Kathy knew her mother-in-law had a point; she couldn't keep tying them down the way she had been trying to do. At the same time she realised Barry was right; he'd known she'd be unable to protect them all the time. They'd be better out of it for a while, she acknowledged, for life was stressful enough in the small house, cramped as they were with the Sutcliffe family now occupying the attic.

Kathy felt very sorry for the Sutcliffes, as Charlie continued to deteriorate. Enid spent her days by his hospital bed, and though there was little chance that he'd survive, Kathy thought she probably prayed for a miracle like any mother would. None of them was left unscathed, for eleven-year-old Barbara had suffered nightmares since the night they'd been trapped, and her screams and sobs had the ability to raise the house. Kenny was thirteen and tried to assume the duties of the man of the house, since his father had never fully recovered from the TB that he'd had the previous year. Sid was still easily tired and had little strength, and often felt useless as a father as he watched his son deliver papers morning and evening, chop wood and haul coal for the fire and generally help in any way he could.

Kathy couldn't help but be affected by the Sutcliffes and knew that each one of them would never forget the terrible night when they must have thought they'd been buried alive. Charlie's name was seldom mentioned, but he was in everyone's thoughts, and Enid's dejected figure returning each day from the hospital could give them no good news.

'I'll be glad when the school opens,' Kathy confided to Mary one day. 'It will be better for the children, and they'll have a school dinner, thank God, so that's one meal I won't have to juggle money and coupons for.'

'And with the weans off her hands, maybe Bridie will get a grip on herself,' Mary commented grimly.

'Ah, who knows, Mammy?' Kathy said. Secretly she thought Bridie was almost enjoying her widowhood and the sympathy it evoked in people when she lamented her loss. It made Kathy cross, because to hear her one would think her marriage to Pat had been the love match of the century, and yet she'd never had a kind word for Pat when he was alive.

'And I wish she would give over going on about it,' Kathy said. 'It doesn't help.'

'Nothing helps, cutie dear,' Mary said. 'Nothing but time.'

Kathy missed her eldest brother so much it was like a gigantic hole. It was still hard to accept he'd not be there any more for her and she'd never talk to him again, or hear his ready laugh. She often cried at the waste, and it hurt her so much to think of him at all. She knew her parents still grieved for him just as much, but they too had to accept that they'd never see him again and get on with their lives, as Bridie seemed either unable or unwilling to do.

And Mary did grieve. Pat was her first-born and a son, the light of her life, and though he'd been full of mischief as a child, he was never malicious. He grew up to be a hard-working youth and a fine young man, and she couldn't understand it when he took up with Bridie Mulligan. She was pretty enough, Mary knew, with her trim little figure and her wavy brown curls and the eyes that looked green rather than brown. But Mary had seen the nose pinched in and the thin line of her lips and knew she'd have a mean streak in her. The Mulligans were a rough lot, everyone

126

knew, and it was said the young scallion Bridie could rip you to pieces with her tongue.

'Leave him be,' Eamonn had said when Mary expressed concern. 'Sure, he has to sow his wild oats.'

Pat had sown them well, but not wisely. Mary knew she'd never forget the evening he'd faced his parents just after tea and told them. 'It's mine and I mean to marry her,' he'd said firmly, and without a hint of shame about it all.

Mary felt as if her heart was breaking. She wanted no Bridie Mulligan for her son. 'Are you sure it's yours?' Eamonn had asked, and Mary was glad he had, because it was what she wanted to say but couldn't bring herself to.

'I'm sure,' Pat said firmly. 'She was a virgin before that and now she's carrying my child. We're to be married as soon as it can be arranged. She's telling her parents tonight.'

'You're only nineteen,' Mary had cried. 'You're not old enough to be a father.'

'Be quiet, woman,' Eamonn had snapped. 'If he's old enough to do the deed, he's old enough to take the consequences. You'd best see the priest in the morning.'

There was no more to be said. Mary knew Pat would be tied to Bridie for life and she'd have to get on with her, for her son's sake, despite her feelings.

Later that evening, there'd been a loud hammering on the door and Mary had opened it to old Owen Mulligan, Bridie's father, with three of his sons to give a thrashing to the young cub who'd taken his daughter down.

'Let them try,' said Sean, moving closer to his brother.

'No,' said Mary firmly. 'I'll have no fighting around my door. The two both did wrong, but fighting won't make it better. I'm seeing the priest tomorrow and we'll see if they can be respectably married, before Bridie is showing too much.'

Owen Mulligan was not easily mollified. His way of settling most things in his life was with his fists, or his belt. All his children had had more than a taste of it over the years, and his wife often sported black eyes. He'd come spoiling for a fight with Pat Sullivan. He'd already leathered his daughter when she told him and her mother about her condition, despite her crying that they were to be married. No one was to take his lass down and get away with it, he thought, and calling to his sons, he left his wife tending to the weals on his young daughter's body and set out to settle the score.

Eamonn knew his two boys would be no match for the Mulligans, and with his bad chest, he'd be worse than useless. He had no rime for Owen Mulligan – he considered him a bully, and he disliked bullies – but for his son's sake he'd have to act as if the man was his bosom friend.

'What's this talk of fighting, man?' he said. 'What's done's done and we have a wedding to celebrate. Put away your fists and let's away to The Bell and drink the couple's good health.'

Owen Mulligan wavered and Eamonn cut in again. 'Come on, we're wasting drinking time standing here.'

'Come on, Da,' one of the sons said, and Owen swung round angrily.

'Shut it, you,' he snapped. 'I'll say whether we go or not.' He turned to Eamonn and said, 'Aye, I suppose as you say the damage is done.' Then he clapped Pat on the shoulder and said, 'You've had a lucky escape, for I'd a mind to beat you to pulp, and you can thank your father for saving your skin. He's a man after my own heart and I'll drink the lot of you under the table.'

Mary had breathed a sigh of relief when they'd gone, for she'd not been sure until that moment that Eamonn would be able to head off the man bent on violence, though she'd been aware what he was trying to do. The house was quiet with the lads gone, for seventeen-year-old Kathy was out with Barry O'Malley, and the three younger ones, Maggie, Michael and Carmel, were in bed. She made a cup of tea in the hope it would still her shaking limbs, and hoped that Kathy would be in early that night, for she knew she'd be too restless to sleep for hours.

However, both she and Kathy were asleep when the men returned, more drunk than Mary had ever seen any of them. She went down, woken by their noise, to see them staggering about, laughing and hardly able to stand. She helped them to bed and said not a word of censure, not then, or the next day, when they went about with sore heads and snapped the head off everyone. It was, she considered, a small price to pay, for she was only too well aware that had it not been for Eamonn's invitation to Owen to accompany them to the pub, she might have been visiting them all in hospital.

A few weeks later, she'd watched Pat marry Bridie Mulligan and hoped he wouldn't live to regret it. And he didn't really live that long after all, she thought now sadly, and she'd seldom known Bridie give him a kind word during their marriage. Once, listening to her give out to him in Kathy's house, Molly O'Malley, who was visiting at the time, waited until Bridie had flounced out and then remarked to Pat, 'My Dan was the gentlest man in the world, God rest his soul, but if I'd ever spoken to him like that, he'd have punched me in the gob.'

'She's had enough of that the whole of her bloody life,' Pat had said angrily. 'She'll never get it from me.'

And she hadn't, though Mary knew she'd asked for it time and again, and not many would have stayed their hand. And now where was her beloved son? All she knew was that his broken body lay somewhere under a murky grey sea. He hadn't even had a funeral, and there was no grave to tend in his memory. God, she thought, life was hard, too bloody hard at times to understand.

Mind, none were safe. It wasn't only the serving man at risk in this war, with the bombs and incendiaries and land mines; every minute might be your last, and now the Bull Ring was near destroyed.

She'd been as curious as Lizzie as to whether the rumours about the devastation were true or not, and had gone down one day to see for herself without telling a soul. The sight had totally depressed her. As she'd looked at the rubble-littered streets, the roofless Market Hall and the shells of shops the only reminder of how it used to be, her spirits had sunk.

Years before, after 'the war to end all wars', she'd come to England with three weans and an ailing and embittered husband, his health broken by the country now happy to see him thrown on the scrapheap. Many of those unfortunates who'd fought alongside him were to be found in the Bull Ring, where she searched for bargains to feed and clothe her family for next to nothing. As she scoured the rag market, she'd pass the ex-soldiers eking out a living of sorts selling boot laces, matches, hair grips, safety pins and razor blades. Often they'd be blind or have limbs missing, and Mary would wish she had the money to buy the things they had for sale, but she never had any spare cash. She felt sorriest of all for the old soldier who'd had both legs blown away in some trench in a French field. The sight of him wedged into a box fixed on pram wheels always saddened her.

Even after Eamonn had met up with the officer whose life he'd saved, and a job was secured for him, money was tight. In those days, Saturday nights in the Bull Ring were entertainment nights. Despite the sight of the destitute old soldiers, musicians, acrobats and many other performers were there to amuse the crowds, and the Sally Army band would be belting out hymns. The stalls were open till nine or ten o'clock at night, lit by great gas flares, and Mary would wait almost till the end to get meat, fish and vegetables for next to nothing, for everything had to be got rid of.

She loved the Bull Ring. It seemed to be at the heart of Birmingham, her adopted city, and it had life and vitality like nowhere else, a magic all its own. She hated the war. It should never have happened again in her lifetime, and it threatened not only her sons, but her daughters and grandchildren as well. She felt old and useless. Life had changed in ways she'd never thought to see, and like Lizzie, she thought the Bull Ring would never be quite the same again.

She had much on her plate at that time. With Eamonn's chest so bad, he often found it hard to breathe. Then Carmel was off gallivanting each night, and wee Josie was still giving cause for concern. She seemed to cry a lot and be difficult to settle, and was tiring Rose out. Mary tried to help where she could, but all the extra work tended to make her bad-tempered. She vented her spleen on poor Maggie, and particularly on how she was bringing up young Tim, and the two were often at loggerheads.

Kathy felt sorry for Maggie, knowing her mother was often unfair, but she tried to pour oil on troubled waters and side with neither of them. She had problems of her own too, with Bridie nearly resident in the house. 'I mean,' she said to Rose, whom she'd called to see one day, 'it isn't as if she ever comes in for anything definite, and she wants a cup of tea every five minutes and never does a hand's turn to help anyone. I try to hold my tongue, but oh, Rose, she gets on my nerves, and after all it's our tea ration she's drinking; she'd never bring a spoonful of her own. Molly, Sid and Enid never say a word, but it's hardly fair.'

'Maybe she's lonely?'

'Aye, maybe she is,' Kathy said grimly. 'Maybe I'd feel lonely too if I had the time. God, Rose, I know Pat's gone, no one feels it more than me, but all the men are away, and we all miss them.'

"That's true enough,' Rose said. 'Not a day goes past when I don't think of them and say a wee prayer.'

Kathy knew exactly what she meant. She herself listened avidly to the wireless and scoured the newspaper with a sick dread inside her, aware that the report of battles meant lives lost on both sides. 'And,' she said to Rose, 'I don't think Hitler is finished with us yet. He's playing a sort of cat-and-mouse game. Lull us into a false sense of security and then he'll be at it again, you'll see.'

But even though Kathy said that, she was surprised by a raid towards the end of September because it was in the daytime, the first of the daytime raids that attacked industrial targets. Kathy, cowering in the cellar with the baby and Molly – for the Sutcliffes still refused to go below ground – was petrified for the safety of her children at school.

'They'll have taken cover,' Molly assured her, but Kathy kept hearing Barry's words from the hospital, and she determined to write to Mrs Barraclough without delay. There could be no harm in asking her if the children could go there; she wasn't committing herself to anything.

Before Kathy could receive any answer to her letter, little Charlie Sutcliffe relinquished his hold on life and slipped away. His parents were with him at his bedside, and when they returned to the house, Kathy was moved by the sight of them. A deep sadness settled over everyone, even the children. It was the first time Lizzie had come into contact with death, for though her Uncle Pat had died, she'd not seen the body, or even missed him any more than her own daddy she'd not seen for months. But Charlie had only been eight years old, a year younger than her, and she felt sorry for all the family, especially Barbara, whom she'd become fond of. She wondered how she'd feel if anything happened

132

to Padraic, or Danny, and remembered how ill her mammy had been after baby Seamus had died, and she understood the tears Barbara and her mother often shed in the days following Charlie's funeral.

During this time there were a few more daylight raids. Lizzie told Kathy that they had to shelter from these in the cloakroom at the school. 'It must be reinforced,' Molly said when Kathy told her. 'They couldn't use it otherwise.'

Kathy wondered how it would stand up to a direct hit, or even a blast from a bomb landing close by, but felt she could do nothing about it.

Since Charlie's death, the Sutcliffes had changed their minds about letting Kenny and Barbara go away. Kathy could understand their reluctance. Kenny was aghast that it had even been considered. 'I'm thirteen,' he said, 'not a baby to be ferried away somewhere safe. I want to stay here. I'm leaving school next year and I don't want to go to no blooming countryside.'

'And I'm not going, if our Kenny's not,' Barbara stated.

Enid wasn't displeased; she needed the presence of her two remaining children with her, and Kathy felt she couldn't try and persuade her otherwise, but she'd received a reply from Sophie Barraclough, who said she would be delighted to look after her children, for as long as she liked.

'We'll have to take a train to Hereford. Mrs Barraclough will meet us there and drive us to Millover, the village she lives in,' Kathy told her mother.

Mary pursed her lips. She didn't wholly approve of what Kathy intended to do, as she thought children were best left with their mothers, but these were dreadful times altogether and normal rules didn't apply anymore. Sporadic night raids had begun again, and Lord knew how long it would go on for. What if Lizzie or Danny were to be crushed by the cellar walls collapsing, like the wee Sutcliffe boy? That would be

133

desperate altogether. So she swallowed her misgivings and told Kathy she must do what she thought best, and even offered to take the children down on the train to save Kathy the journey.

Lizzie couldn't understand her mother. She'd said her children would never be sent away, but now she'd changed her mind. Lizzie begged and pleaded with her not to send them to some horrible, strange place, but Kathy held firm. Danny screamed and stamped his feet and said he wouldn't go, and Kathy gave him a smack on the legs and said like it or lump it, he was going and that was that.

Even Kenny and Barbara were no help. 'Look what happened to our little Charlie,' Barbara said.

'But you're not going.'

'We're older than you,' Kenny said patronisingly.

'Barbara's not much older,' Lizzie protested.

'But you have to look after your little brother,' Barbara said patiently. 'Your mom can hardly send him on his own.' And Lizzie knew she couldn't, and she had to go to look after their Danny and that was that, and she gave over crying and protesting, knowing it would make no difference. She poured her heart out only to Daisy in the semi-privacy of bed, and was suddenly glad that her father had given her the doll, though she knew he would have agreed with her mother sending her and Danny off to the country because he'd been for it ever since Dunkirk.

On 23 October, Mary took a resigned Lizzie and a reluctant Danny off to New Street station to catch the train to Hereford, and though both children were excited by the thought of the train journey, Lizzie had serious misgivings about what they'd find at their journey's end.

EIGHT

Lizzie thought Millover village one of the prettiest places she'd ever seen. She saw it first bathed in the golden light of an autumn day, so warm it could easily have been summer. It was situated in a valley about five miles from Hereford, in rolling countryside dotted here and there with sheep

The village shops were grouped around a green. They were low buildings generally, made of beige-orange stone, and they looked as though they'd taken root in the place and would be there for many more years to come. There was a pub at either end of the green, the Queen's Head and the Plough and Harrow, and between them the butcher, the greengrocer and fishmonger on one side of the street, while the general store, sweet shop, post office and paper shop were on the other. Lizzie and Danny soon made friends with the shopkeepers, but particularly Mrs Bell who owned the general store, which sold practically anything, Miss Cavendish at the sweet shop and Mr and Mrs Carr who ran the post office and paper shop.

At first the villagers had been quite scornful of Sophie Barraclough taking in more evacuees. They'd all had their share of them in 1939 and for their trouble many had

had wet beds, head lice, children sewn into clothes for the winter and almost all of them totally inadequately dressed for the elements. The homesick children had moaned about the food, the weather and the dullness of the place. Most had wanted a chip shop on the corner, the flicks and their mams, and had returned to the cities by Christmas. Now Sophie Barraclough was doing it again, and they thought she needed her head examined.

Millie put them right about that, and they all acknowledged that she would know, because she'd worked for Sophie Barraclough for years, taken on when the poor woman was struggling to cope with a young son, a baby and a demanding, terminally ill husband. Mind you, they said that Mrs Barraclough was always one to give credit where it was due. She often said she didn't know what she'd have done all those years without Millie, who'd become a friend rather than just an employee. Millie was a farmer's daughter and when war was imminent, she'd prophesied that food would be scarce, just as it had been during the first war. Together, the two women had tilled and cultivated most of the back garden long before 'Dig for Victory' was considered patriotic. It was also Millie who'd got a young clutch of hens from her father's place and a young piglet to fatten, so now they had more than enough food for themselves with enough left over to trade for other things, so they lived quite well.

Yet Millie never got uppity and put airs and graces on because she was working for quality and everyone recognised that Sophie Barraclough was quality, a nice woman for all that. They didn't want to see her run ragged by ungrateful little evacuees and told Millie so as she did the shopping a couple of days after their arrival.

Millie told them the children were from Birmingham and were nothing like the cockney sparrows they'd all had experience of in the past. She said they were well dressed and polite and spoke with a slight Brummie accent with an Irish lilt in it that was quite attractive to the ear. Added to that, neither child had head lice and that far from being sewn into their clothes, they had a case full of things, including many changes of underwear. She said they came from honest, hardworking parents and that their father had been hurt at Dunkirk, along with Master Christopher.

That settled it for the villagers; if their father was a friend of nice Master Christopher, that immediately raised their status in everyone's eyes. Miss Cavendish said she might have known Mrs Barraclough would not take in riff-raff and she was glad she would not have to watch them like a hawk when they came into the shop. She was getting on a bit in years and couldn't see so well, and had been no match for the evacuees from London, who'd enter the shop in a gang. One or two would engage her in conversation and purchase a couple of items, while behind them their friends would be filling their pockets. It distressed Miss Cavendish greatly that children would do such things, and in the end she had to ban them from the shop.

But Lizzie and Danny were welcome. Sophie gave them money to spend every weekend, and they would pore for hours over the counter. Miss Cavendish made the toffee herself, and there was ordinary, treacle or walnut toffee set out in silver trays with a little hammer. Miss Cavendish never minded weighing you out a halfpenny's worth. Then there were pear drops, bull's-eyes, aniseed balls, pineapple rock and boiled sweets, all different colours. Kayli and sherbert dabs tickled the tongue, and everlasting strips really did last a long time, like gobstoppers, but then there were liquorice bootlaces and ju-jubs, and two penn'orth of monkey nuts could last all day if you chewed slowly. They often took a long time spending their Saturday pennies.

Apart from the pubs and shops in the village, there were houses straggling out from it in all directions, with the village school on the far side and the parish church of St Peter on the near side. It was a nice church, built in the same mellowed stone as the rest of the village. It had a steeple and was approached through a lych gate, and all around it were well-tended graves.

Lizzie and Danny, of course, could not go to that church. Sophie drove them to the outskirts of Hereford every Sunday to attend mass at St Luke's Catholic church, and every other Saturday she also took Lizzie to confession. She said she didn't mind this in the least. It had been explained to her by their grandmother, but Lizzie often thought it would have been much simpler if they could have gone to the parish church. She liked the parson, Reverend Phillips, very much. She'd spoken to him a few times when he'd come upon her reading the names on the gravestones on her way home from school.

The school took Lizzie by surprise, because there seemed to be so few children in it compared with St Catherine's in Edgbaston. There were just three classrooms and three teachers and a headmaster. The children aged five to seven were in one room, under an old lady called Mrs Carruthers, who'd been brought out of retirement and as far as Lizzie could see let the children do what they liked. Miss Adams, Lizzie's teacher, was much stricter, though Lizzie liked her. She had the children till they were ten, when they went into Mr Donnelly's class until the age of fourteen, unless they were clever enough to go to grammar school. Mr Donnelly was lovely, young, handsome and very kind, and Lizzie was dying to go into his class, but she did wonder why he wasn't away fighting like every other man seemed to be. 'He has a false leg,' one of the children told her. 'From a motorbike accident before the war.'

Lizzie was sorry for him, but rather glad for herself. Mr Donnelly would never be called up. He would be able to teach her until the war was over and she could go home, and she couldn't help feeling happy about it.

Of course all this wasn't apparent on that awful first day when they'd arrived at Hereford station. It had been a long and monotonous journey; often the train would stop for an interminable time for seemingly no reason at all. There were many troops on the train too, and Lizzie was rather nervous of their loud voices and raucous laughter, and far too shy to do anything other than smile when they spoke to her.

After two or three hours, though, nobody was smiling much at anyone. Lizzie and Danny were hungry, thirsty and bored enough to be quarrelsome, and they'd grown tired of the miles and miles of green fields that they'd first been so astonished by. They'd never seen so much grass except at a park, and were further amazed by the animals: the cows that leant over farm gates, contentedly chewing the cud and placidly watching the trains pass, the horses galloping away from the noise, and the sheep tirelessly tugging the grass as if their lives depended on it, seemingly scarcely aware of the train at all.

But even this had begun to pall after a time, and Mary was beginning to wish she'd not been so willing to come in Kathy's stead, when the train began to pull into Hereford. Not that Mary was sure it was Hereford, of course, because all the stations had their names blacked out, but most of the troops were getting off here, and they were able to advise Mary.

Everyone was glad to leave the stuffy train, but the station was draughty and it had begun to get dusky and cold, and Mary hoped they hadn't got long to wait for Sophie Barraclough. In fact she was waiting in the station car park, and both Danny and Lizzie were pop-eyed with excitement at their first ride in a car.

It was disappointing that it had got so dark and they were not really able to see where they were going, just vague trees and bushes, greyish in the darkening night, positioned on either side of the country lane that Sophie drove along. She was talking to their grandmother, but neither child could hear what was being said, and the movement of the car eventually lulled them both to sleep, leaning against one another and taking no notice of the rumblings of their empty stomachs.

Suddenly Lizzie was jerked awake. The car had stopped in front of a house looming in the dark. There was another woman silhouetted in the doorway whom Sophie Barraclough introduced as Millie. Later, they got to know her very well but it was all confusing that first evening. Lizzie was aware of gravel under her feet, and then she was following her grandmother into the house, with a sleepy Danny stumbling along beside her.

The hall was large, and once the door was shut it was lit with a gentle light. 'The cloakroom's here for your coats,' Sophie said, opening a door to her right.

It was almost the size of a room, Lizzie realised, with hooks all round and racks with shoes and slippers on, and a longish tube thing with umbrellas sticking out of it. She took off her coat and helped Danny with his, all the time amazed that anyone should have a huge big space like this just to put coats in.

A wide corridor stretched before them with numerous closed doors off it, but Sophie walked past them all, explaining, 'Not much point in opening up the whole house; after all, coal's a price and hard to get, and it seems unpatriotic to have all the rooms heated for just Millie and me. I'm afraid we tend to live in the kitchen these days.'

But what a kitchen! It ran the width of the house, and one side of it was undoubtedly a kitchen, with a sink and stove and cupboards and a table. Everything shone, and though Lizzie didn't know the wood was pine, she knew it was warm and friendly. A dresser displayed plates, and cups hung from hooks beneath a wall cupboard, while gleaming pans were fastened to the wall.

Lizzie sniffed the air appreciatively. A gorgeous smell was coming from somewhere, so delicious it was making her feel faint. The room was warm, because the oven was on and two pans bubbled on the cooker top, but also because of the fire at the other end of the room. This other half had a carpet square laid on it, and a three-piece suite was drawn up in front of the fire round a white sheepskin rug. It was all so comforting that Lizzie let out a huge sigh.

'Come on, Lizzie, are you half asleep?' Mary chided, and Lizzie realised Millie had taken a huge casserole dish out of the oven and set the table for them all, and that Mary and Danny were already seated.

Lizzie never forgot that first meal she had in Sophie Barraclough's kitchen. It was chicken casserole, and she'd tasted chicken only at Christmas before and then not much of it. Now her plate was piled high. One of the pans from the cooker contained potatoes, which Millie tipped into a dish, while a smaller dish held the peas from the other pan, and both had a large knob of butter melting over them.

Never had Lizzie tasted food like it, and as she attacked her plate with relish, Millie commented, 'I'd guessed you'd be starving. I bet it's been a terrible journey.'

'I don't know about the weans,' Mary said, 'but my stomach thought my throat was cut. And this is a wonderful meal. We don't set eyes on food like this much, isn't that right, you two?'

'No, Gran,' Lizzie said happily, still eating, but Danny didn't answer and Mary noticed he was nearly falling off his chair with weariness, now that his appetite had been somewhat satisfied.

'We do all right most of the time,' Sophie said. 'We keep hens for the eggs, and this one had got too old for laying.'

Lizzie fortunately did not understand what Sophie meant – she'd never associated the small ration of meat she got from their butcher with a living, breathing animal – but Mary knew. She'd wrung the neck of many a chicken in her native Ireland, but she chose not to enlighten her grandchildren. Instead she said, 'I think these two could do with bed. It's been a long day.'

It had, but Lizzie had no desire to leave this warm kitchen and go out into the long hall again. 'I'm not tired, Gran,' she said.

'Well I am,' Mary said. 'I'll be seeking my bed soon, I can tell you, so no arguing.'

That made Lizzie feel better. She knew her grandmother was staying the night and imagined they would all sleep together in the one room, and so she followed Sophie willingly enough as her grandmother began to help Millie wash the dirty dishes. Lizzie just hoped Gran would be up before too long.

Sophie picked up the children's bags from the bottom of the stairs as if they weighed no more than a feather and led the way to the bedrooms. In the dim light of the landing Lizzie saw another long, dark corridor stretching away into the darkness, and amazingly yet another staircase leading to what she presumed to be another floor like this one.

'I've put you in adjoining rooms,' Sophie said. 'I thought you'd like to be close. You share a bathroom and lavatory between you and you can leave the connecting doors open if you like.'

Connecting doors! Like to be close! Lizzie and Danny had never been more than a hair's breadth from each other, and now they were to be in different rooms. Lizzie paled at the thought, though her room was lovely, she had to admit.

There was a carpet on the floor, and the curtains that fluttered against the black-out shutters matched the bedspread. The bed itself was huge, even bigger than the mattress she shared with Danny on her mother's bedroom floor, and all of a sudden she wished her mother was there with them. 'There's a wardrobe and chest of drawers for your things,' Sophie was saying, 'and a dressing table so you can see to do your hair in the morning.' It was, Lizzie thought, a great improvement on the cracked mirror balanced on the stone sink in the cellar.

Danny's room was much the same as Lizzie's, and between them was a bathroom with a hand basin, a bath with claw feet and a lavatory – oh, what luxury! No chamber pots under these beds, Lizzie thought, and no stumbling down in the dark to the lavvy in the yard with only the wavering light of a torch to light the way, and that was when there were batteries to be had.

Danny's eyes were wide with excitement, and Lizzie guessed he couldn't wait to try the lavvy out. 'Maybe you can have a bath before bed tomorrow?' Sophie suggested, hiding a smile at the look of astonishment and indignation on the two faces.

'Tomorrow? That would only be Thursday. Me and Danny have a bath on Saturdays,' Lizzie said firmly.

Sophie smiled. Though she had no experience of the enamel bath hung on the door, she knew that many cottagers washed that way and guessed that for these children, a bath was a major undertaking. No matter, she thought, they'll learn. Aloud she said, 'Oh yes, of course.'

She didn't kiss them goodnight, and Lizzie was glad of it. Her mammy wouldn't like her to be kissing strangers, and that was what Sophie Barraclough was, however kind she might be.

She lay in bed listening to the quietness, and realised she'd never known silence before and she found it unnerving. She had on a brand-new nightie and lay in a warm and comfortable bed, and her stomach was full. She should have been asleep in minutes, but she wasn't. She pulled Daisy out of the bag she'd packed her in and hugged her tight, and yet it didn't make her feel any better.

Suddenly she realised she hadn't said her prayers. Her mammy or granny would have had her kneel down to pray, but even lying in bed she should say something, so she closed her eyes and said three Hail Marys, and then for good measure she added a Glory Be. '. . . As it was in the beginning, is now and ever shall be, world without end, Amen.'

'Lizzie!'

Lizzie opened her eyes to see Danny standing before her. His new pyjamas were too big for him so he could grow into them, and the sleeves hung over his hands and the trouser legs trailed on the floor. 'What's the matter?' Lizzie said.

'I'm lonely, Liz.'

And me, Lizzie thought, but she didn't say it. She was there to look after Dan, not admit to being a bit frightened herself. She threw the covers back. 'Come in here,' she said. 'There's plenty of room,' and as Danny clambered in beside her and she felt his warm body next to hers, she felt a measure of contentment and was soon fast asleep.

Later, Mary, on her way to bed with Sophie to direct her, looked in on the sleeping children, and when she saw them entwined together she smiled and envied them slightly. It's a big house to be lying all alone in a strange bedroom, she thought, and I'm damned if I don't wish I had Eamonn beside me this minute. For all the rooms this place has, I'll be glad to get home in the morning.

By the morning, Lizzie had decided that, despite the indoor lavvy, the chicken casserole of the previous night and the big bowl of porridge with treacle and warm creamy milk she'd enjoyed that morning, she wanted to go back to Birmingham with her gran. She already missed her mother, and all her family, even carping Auntie Bridie. She missed her school and her friends and the life she knew and she didn't want to be left in a strange place with people she didn't know at all.

Danny, who'd remained stoical through breakfast, burst into tears when he realised his gran's departure was imminent. 'I want to go home,' he cried. 'Please, Gran, let us come home.' Mary looked at him and had an urge to grab them both, bundle them into the car and return with them. But then she remembered wee Charlie Sutcliffe. Could she live with herself if she took Lizzie and Danny back and one, or both, was injured in some way? No, she decided, she couldn't.

Regretfully she pushed Danny away. 'Come on now, caddie,' she said soothingly. 'Sure, it will be no time at all till you're back with us all. Till then, sure, won't you be just fine here?' She looked across Danny's bent head and saw Lizzie's sad, troubled eyes and strained face. 'And haven't you Lizzie to mind you?' she went on. 'She's not crying now, is she?'

No, but I'd like to be, Lizzie thought. I'd like to be falling on your neck and wailing like Danny, but instead she held tight to her brother's shoulders when he would have thrown himself into the car alongside his grandmother. 'Come on, Dan,' she said impatiently. 'That's enough now. You know we have to stay here till the bombing's over.'

Mary waved until she could see the pair no more, and when the car was out of sight, Millie took them both inside and gave them a big plate of toast and a large pot of plum jam for them to help themselves.

Later Kathy asked her mother, 'Were they nice people, Mammy? Will they be good to the weans? Will they like it there, d'you think?'

'Kathy, Kathy,' Mary said. 'Sure, they'd be hard to please if they don't like the place. They'll live like kings and Mrs Barraclough and that Millie are kindness itself.' Inside her head a little voice was asking if they would ever fit back in their own home if they got used to the affluent luxury of the Barraclough house, but these doubts she didn't share with her daughter.

'Oh God, Maggie, I miss them so much,' Kathy said to her sister. 'It doesn't get easier like I thought it would, and I only ever feel justified in sending the weans away when there's a raid on.'

'Well, there's plenty of those,' Maggie said. 'What about that bad one just a few days after Mammy got back from leaving the weans in Hereford? And the one the following night where nineteen people were killed at the Carlton cinema?'

'I know, I know,' Kathy said resignedly. 'And then there was the raid on the Austin factory that killed six and injured twenty-six the night before Coventry was virtually razed to the ground. I think it's only a matter of time till Hitler tries the same thing here.'

Maggie didn't answer her sister. She had no need to; everyone knew what had happened in Coventry on 14 November. The intensity of the night's bombing was such that it couldn't be hushed up or glossed over.

'I mean,' Kathy went on, 'Lewis's and Ansell's basements are only two of the places I know of that are going to be used as emergency casualty centres. Christ, Maggie, how many casualties do they think we'll be having?'

'Stop it, Kath, you don't help going on this way. At least your weans are out of it.'

'But the rest of us aren't.'

'It isn't your job to try and keep the whole world safe. We've just all got to do our bit,' Maggie said. She knew, though, what was upsetting her sister. Bridie had been going on about one thing or another ever since she'd begun to use Kathy's cellar, and Kathy usually took little notice, for that was just Bridie's way, but in early October, before Danny and Lizzie left, she started on about the gas pipes.

'I mean,' she said to Kathy, 'if they were broken or cracked in a raid, we'd all be gassed to death. Have you thought of that?'

Kathy hadn't, and wished Bridie hadn't either, for she'd seen stark terror in the eyes of the children, and in Molly, who had at last given in to Kathy's urging and was using the cellar when a raid was on. She had begun to tremble, while outside the thuds and crashes of a raid in progress continued unabated.

She wondered at the stupidity of her sister-in-law. Hadn't they all enough to worry about? 'Will you whist?' she hissed in a low voice. 'Stop putting the fear of God into the weans.'

Bridie had been offended by Kathy's tone and elected not to speak at all, which Kathy thought preferable to her doom-laden prophecies.

Then, a couple of weeks later, just before the two O'Malley children had been evacuated out of it, Bridie had arrived at Kathy's door waving a copy of the *Evening Mail* almost triumphantly. Kathy had taken the paper from her and read of the bravery of Home Guard officer George Inwood, who'd lost his life crawling into a gas-filled cellar in Bishop's Street on the night of 15 October. He'd rescued two people before he was overcome himself and died from gas poisoning.

'See, what did I tell you?' Bridie had cried. 'That will happen to you one of these fine nights. Well, I've had enough. You can keep your bloody cellar, me and the weans will be up to the communal one from now on.'

'Oh, please yourself,' Kathy said wearily, but the report had shaken her. What was she to do? Go out into the raw

147

autumn nights, which were swiftly turning to winter, with a wee baby and Molly who, with her bulk and bad legs, could hardly hurry? No, she thought she'd take her chance in the cellar, and was relieved that the older children would soon be safe from yet another danger.

'If it's got your number on it, that's it,' Molly said. 'Don't you worry, lass. I reckon lightning don't strike the same place twice and I've been near buried alive once. I don't believe I was rescued so I could be gassed to death.'

'Oh, Molly,' Kathy said, putting her arms around the woman's ample waist while tears ran down her cheeks.

'Now, now, don't you upset yourself. We'll be better off without the silly besom,' Molly said, for she'd never had any time for Bridie and thought Kathy had the patience of a saint. 'Miserable old cow she is, and no mistake. Pat should have given her a good hiding in the early days of that marriage and she might be better for it today.'

'Aye,' Kathy had said. 'Maybe you're right, but that was never Pat's way. Anyway, Bridie's not coming in any more and that's that.'

It was ironic that at the time Bridie decided to go to the communal shelters, the Sutcliffes asked Kathy if they could use her cellar again, as they thought the reinforced surface shelters were little better than a house. 'You have to be safer underground,' Sid said. 'And we'll take our chance with the gas.'

Kathy had been glad of their company, for Sid and Enid, and especially Kenny, could lighten the atmosphere some-what, where Bridie had successfully dampened it.

'You get on well with the Sutcliffes, don't you?' Maggie said now, hoping to stop Kathy carrying the worries of the entire family on her shoulders.

'Oh, aye,' Kathy said. 'And especially the children, but life's difficult with three women in one little house. I mean, we're all used to our own kitchen and our own way of doing things, and we're tripping over one another to look after one wee baby, not that any of us gets a look-in when Molly's around.'

'I have noticed that,' Maggie said.

'Well, she's lost so much, and if caring for Padraic helps her, all well and good.'

'Yes,' Maggie said. 'But don't forget he's yours, will you?'

'Good God, Maggie, what would you have me do, snatch him out of her arms?' Kathy cried. 'She has no husband, no home, two sons dead and two others away fighting. If she wants to share in the care of my son, I haven't the heart to stop her.'

Aye, but share is one thing, Maggie thought, because she'd seen the jealous, possessive way Molly had taken over Padraic. No one got a look-in, least of all his own mother, and Maggie guessed she'd be the loser one day. But she had troubles enough of her own.

'Anyway,' Kathy said, 'thanks be to God, Sid's got set on now. The doctor's signed him off for light duties. It was getting to him hanging around the house with the women. He was beginning to feel useless.'

'Where's he working?' Maggie asked.

'Lucas's, in Chester Street.'

'Doing what?'

'It's all war-related stuff. He's in inspection and says there's jobs for all of us, and we'll be needed before it's all over. Enid's thinking of it, and to be honest I'd be glad if she went, for with the two of them eating in the canteen it'll help the rations go further for everyone else.'

'And Kenny will be leaving school soon, won't he?'

'Aye, next year,' Kathy said. 'Mind, he does his bit now, delivering the papers the way he does. He often gets first choice in the shop for old newspapers or even cardboard occasionally, and the odd wooden box he chops up in the cellar, and it all helps get the fires going. He's a good lad, Kenny.' She gave a sudden smile and went on, 'He reads the women's magazines and titbits out of the paper as he walks along, and he's always coming up with some tip or other.'

'Like what?'

'Oh, you know. Recipes that show you a hundred and one ways of serving potatoes, turnip or carrots, which is about the only thing most people have a lot of.'

'Are they any good?'

'Some,' Kathy admitted. 'It's the monotony gets you down more than anything else, and trying Kenny's recipes at least gives me something to do while Molly's spoiling my son. Then there's his tips for saving fuel.'

'Oh, tell me those,' Maggie said. 'And for once I might be in Mammy's good books.'

'Well,' said Kathy with a laugh, 'one is to save all the dead matches and put them back in the box and use them in place of wood to start the fire.'

'Does it work?'

'How would I know? I only use matches for the gas stove and gas mantles, and the fire, of course. None of us smoke and it would take me a year to fill a box with spent matches.'

'Might do me some good, though,' Maggie said. 'Daddy uses half a box to light his pipe.'

'Aye, it does his chest a power of good,' Kathy said grimly, and added, 'But it would be no good, Mag, he never lets the match go till it's burning the ends of his fingers. There'd be nothing but ash to put in your box.'

'Aye, you're right there,' Maggie agreed.

'There's another one he came up with the other day. You keep a few cinders back from the day before and soak them with paraffin to help light the fire the following day to save on wood. It's not a bad idea, except paraffin's not so easy to get either. Mind you,' Kathy added, 'he did have one good idea that I have started to use. You mix coal dust with damp tea leaves and put it into small cartons or bags, and put them on the fire when you have to go out. That way it burns slowly and saves the precious coal and you only have to poke it into life and throw a few lumps of coal on when you come home and the house is warm again.'

'So at least Kenny's useful.'

'Aye, and not least for making us laugh. He's a great kid. Wee Charlie was supposed to be very like him, God rest his soul, and Barbara's a good girl, but quieter. She says she misses our Lizzie, and God's truth, she's not the only one.'

'At least you haven't Mammy to put up with,' Maggie said. 'She won't let me help cook anything, in fact she won't let me near the kitchen at all, unless to wash the pots afterwards, and then she's not always satisfied with the way I do it. And as for our Carmel – well, Mammy gives out about her clothes, her friends and where she spends her evenings, but she doesn't try to stop her doing anything. She gets away with murder and isn't expected to help at all. I tell you, Kath, it gets me down, and when I think what we were expected to do at her age . . . Then of course there's Tim.'

'Don't say you're having trouble with him,' Kathy said. 'I won't believe it – he's never been a bother.'

'He isn't,' Maggie said fiercely. 'It's Mammy again. God, she's aggravating. If I pick him up I'm spoiling him, if I let him cry I'm neglecting him. I'm feeding him too often, or not enough. I've too many clothes on him, or too little. I tell you, Kath, she'd argue with the devil himself and win, so she would, and between the two of us the child will be ruined.'

'Molly has Padraic that way,' Kathy said. 'If this war drags on much longer, the pair of us will have a couple of spoiled brats on our hands.'

'Aye, if I'm not tempted to kill Mammy first,' Maggie said, and though they laughed, Kathy knew her sister was near the end of her tether. 'If I hadn't come out today I would have screamed,' she went on. 'Course, you could always ask Sid to get me set on at the factory with him and Enid and I'll leave the child totally to Mammy then.'

Kathy glanced at her sister, not sure if she was joking or not, but before she could ask, they heard the entry door open.

'Are you home?'

'Oh God, it's Bridie,' Kathy said under her breath. 'Bloody hell, I've left some washing soaking in the boiler and I thought I'd get it done while Molly took Padraic out.'

'And I've kept you talking,' Maggie said, getting to her feet. 'But I'll be away now.'

'There's no need to go.'

'There is,' Maggie said softly. 'I can't stand that one, and Mammy will give out to me as it is when I get back, for trying to take a minute or two for myself.'

'Is this all you two do all day, chat and drink tea?' Bridie said, coming into the room.

Kathy, as usual, bit her lip, and said nothing.

'Are you away, Maggie?' Bridie continued. 'Your mother was looking for you this long while. She had the wee one in her arms and he was wailing his head off.'

'Oh God!' Maggie said, casting her eyes to the ceiling. 'Now I'm for it.'

The smile that slid on to Bridie's face maddened Kathy, and she wondered at the pleasure the woman took at the misfortune of others. She said sharply, 'If you're here for a natter, Bridie, you'll have to come down the cellar. I've a lot of washing to get through before they all get in. Maggie's only been in a few minutes and she was just going anyway.'

Bridie bristled at once. 'I was only making a comment,' she said crossly.

'Well, you've made it,' Kathy put in. 'Now come and brew us both a drop of tea while I pound the clothes.'

When the door had closed behind Maggie, Bridie said, 'No need to get shirty with me. I was only saying what others think. It's as if the pair of you had no weans at all, for you've sent two of yours away and the one you have left is being brought up by Molly, and everyone knows who's rearing Tim.'

They'd been walking towards the cellar steps as Bridie spoke, and Kathy stopped dead and, glaring at her sister-in-law, said, 'Who spreads malicious tales like that?'

Bridie shrugged. 'It's said, that's all. Someone had to tell you.'

'Why?' Kathy demanded. 'What purpose did it serve? You know well why I sent my weans away, and they weren't the only ones. You saw what happened to wee Charlie Sutcliffe, and that's what decided me in the end.'

'I'm only saying what I heard.'

'And enjoyed repeating it,' Kathy snapped. 'Sometimes, Bridie, I don't understand you.'

'No need to get on your bleeding high horse,' Bridie said. 'And no good biting my head off either. Even if we leave Lizzie and Dan out of it altogether, everyone knows you and Maggie have little enough time for your own wee sons.'

'Bridie, that's a wicked thing to say.'

'Well, you know it's true. You never see Molly but she has Padraic in her arms or pushing him in the pram.'

Kathy felt her fingers curl into fists as she swung away from Bridie's accusing face and led the way down into the

153

cellar. Tears stung her eyes, but she'd not let Bridie see how she'd hurt her. She had her own reasons for allowing Molly an active part in her son's life, and would justify herself to no one, least of all Bridie.

She filled the kettle at the sink and had put it on the stove before she could trust herself to speak without her voice trembling. Then she changed the subject. 'What about you, now the nights are getting colder, isn't it a trek to the communal shelter all the time?'

'It's all right,' said Bridie. 'And it's warm inside with that many people. We have a bit of a sing sometimes to cover up the noise for the weans.' She laughed and went on, 'An Irish fellow comes in some nights when he's not fire-watching and brings chocolate for the weans. He works at Cadbury's and buys all the mis-shapes. His name is Johnnie and he seems to love weans, and sometimes he brings his gramophone and records – jigs and reels and Irish songs we all know. Johnnie makes everyone laugh. You want to come down, Kath.'

Kathy didn't answer. She hardly heard what Bridie had said, for her earlier accusations kept going around and around in her head. She pounded the clothes in the sink viciously and wished it was her sister-in-law in the tub. Eventually she glanced over at her sharply and snapped impatiently, 'Are you ever going to make that tea, Bridie, or they'll all be in on top of me and I won't have a thing done.'

With a sigh, Bridie got to her feet while thoughts continued to career round Kathy's head. It was obvious that some people thought she was a neglectful mother who just wanted her weans out of the way, and yet it wasn't like that at all.

Bridie watched Kathy out of the corner of her eye as she poured water onto the tea leaves. She saw the frown puckering her sister-in-law's forehead and knew she'd rattled her with her words, and she was glad. She was sick and tired of everyone going on about how wonderful Kathy was. Well, she'd made her think, and she wouldn't be at all surprised if she didn't up and fetch her weans home.

But Kathy didn't, because the events of the night of 19 November put paid to that.

NINE

Every week Kathy wrote to Lizzie and Danny, but when she took up her pen on 21 November she wondered what she could tell them. Certainly not about the worst raid of the war so far, when 350 bombers had attacked the city on the evening of the 19th. She couldn't tell how she cowered in abject terror in the cellar with the Sutcliffe family, Molly and wee Padraic, and listened to the constant drone as wave after wave of planes bringing death and destruction flew over. Nothing seemed to deter them, neither the ack-ack guns nor the barrage balloons, as they released their lethal loads of bombs, land mines and incendiaries.

Too scared to cry, Kathy had the urge to grasp herself tight around the middle and howl like an animal in distress. But it was a luxury she couldn't allow herself, for the petrified eyes of Kenny and Barbara were looking to her for reassurance. Padraic was wailing, Molly was trembling from head to foot and Sid Sutcliffe seemed to be having trouble drawing breath.

Hour after hour they sat there, thinking every moment might be their last as the juddering crashes and bangs and the sickening thuds of explosion after explosion went on above them. The screams of the people were answered by the emergency services they heard streaking through the night. Time after time the cellar walls shook and shuddered, but they did not fall, and when the all-clear eventually sounded, the adults looked at each other wearily over the heads of the children, who'd eventually fallen asleep, as if they couldn't quite believe they'd survived the night.

Upstairs, there was a pile of soot in the grate, and a film of grey dust covered everything, but total devastation met Kathy's eyes when she opened her door. The other side of Bell Barn Road and the bottom end of Grant Street was gone, and in front of her, in the half-light of a November morning, was a sea of rubble. Oh God, our Rose, she thought, for Rose's house across the road was no longer there, and she hoped and prayed she'd gone in with Mary and Eamonn that night. Pockets of fire were still burning everywhere and other people were emerging from cellars and shelters, as dazed and distressed as Kathy.

But she could tell Lizzie little of this, nor could she tell her of the news that filtered through later of well over a thousand people killed or injured that night, including fifty-three at the BSA factory buried under tons of rubble. She had to tell her about Rose's house, and Rose's subsequent decision that now that there was no home for Sean to return to, she'd go to her mother's people in Ireland, as her sisters had. But she couldn't bring herself to break the news that Carmel was missing.

However, Lizzie knew that something was wrong, because the tone of the letter was different. Kathy hadn't been able to overcome the misery she'd felt at the desolation around her and the worry of her missing youngest sister to write a light-hearted letter to her daughter. 'Don't worry,' Aunt Sophie said when Lizzie brought her concerns to her. She'd been listening to the news and, reading between the lines

157

of what they were allowed to say, guessed that Birmingham was having a time of it. 'She's likely tired at nights and she'll be worried about your aunt's house being bombed. Is her house close to yours?'

'It's across the road and down a bit, that's all,' said Lizzie. 'We all sort of live together.' She shivered suddenly. What if it had been their house? Where would they all go? They had no people in Ireland to speak of. Not people they knew well enough to land on, anyway.

She shook her head, for she had few answers to the questions. She wished the war was over and things were back to the way they'd been before, although she knew in her heart of hearts it could never be the same. Hereford and the Barraclough house was changing her, slowly, so slowly she was almost unaware of it herself, and yet the changes were there.

She was almost ashamed that she was enjoying herself so much when it was obvious that her mother, and everyone else, was going through it. She tried not to let on what a good time she was having but it was hard for it not to come over in her letters back home.

Her own life was full, and she couldn't understand Maura, who'd said the countryside was boring and awful, for she found it was anything but. At first, admittedly, both she and Danny had been the subject of frank curiosity at the village school. The school children had had their share of evacuees in 1939 but they'd not stayed long and had never really settled, and they wondered if Danny and Lizzie O'Malley would be any different . . .

Lizzie was put beside a plumpish girl called Alice Buxton. Her brown hair was scraped back into plaits with such severity that they stuck out from her head as if they had a life of their own. Her face was round, her eyes were a sort of wishy-washy blue and her nose was freckled. She was awed by the raven-haired beauty of Lizzie O'Malley who sat down beside her, so awed she didn't know whether she'd ever have the nerve to talk to her.

Fortunately, Lizzie wasn't given to such misapprehension, and by the end of the day she knew that Alice Buxton's father owned a farm and that she had three older brothers, the two younger ones away fighting, despite the exemption farmers could have. She also had a little brother, Frankie, who was a pain in the neck. Lizzie had also told Alice about her own family left behind in Birmingham and about life at Sophie Barraclough's, and soon she and Alice Buxton were the best of friends.

That was only the beginning, and since then she'd been asked to tea a few times at the Buxton farm. Lizzie had been a little nervous of Mrs Buxton, who was a large woman in every sense of the word. She always had a huge apron tied around her waist, and arms bare to the elbow that bulged like two large pink hams and went down to fat fingers on the end of big hands. Those hands could smack the life out of you, Alice told Lizzie, and Lizzie, watching the power of them kneading bread, or pounding the dolly tub, and observing the stern expression usually resident on Mrs Buxton's face, could well believe it.

Laziness annoyed Mrs Buxton before anything else, Alice said, and to be fair, she had a lot to do, for there were two land girls to cook and clean for, as well as Mr Buxton, their eldest son Colin, Alice and Frankie. She also did most of the work in the dairy and helped out generally on the farm, and Alice, the only girl in the family, was expected to lend a hand too. 'She hates to see me reading,' said Alice gloomily, who loved to read at school. 'She can't see the point of it, and in the past she's got so angry she's thrown books in the fire.'

'Gosh!' said Lizzie. Her own love of books had been started by her father and further encouraged by Aunt

Sophie, who'd had both children join the public lending library in Hereford. Now Lizzie and Danny got out two books every fortnight.

After this conversation with Alice, Lizzie would loan her friend her library books one at a time. They were easy enough to smuggle in and out in their school bags. 'Don't let your mammy see,' she cautioned Alice, not knowing how she'd be able to explain to the librarian that one of their books had been burnt to cinders.

'It's all right,' Alice assured her. 'I read in bed. I used to do it by the flashlight I found in my brother's room when he left, but the batteries gave out and now there's none to be got. But we've got a stack of candles and I smuggle one or two upstairs.'

It seemed an awful way to go on. Lizzie could read wherever and whenever she wanted, but Alice was just pleased to get new books. 'I've read all the ones I've got . . . oh, so many times, I don't have to read some of them at all, I know the stories word for word. And,' she added, 'I'll never forget what you've done, you're a true friend.'

Lizzie glowed. No one had ever told her that before, and she decided Alice was one of the nicest people in the world.

As well as the time spent with Alice, or at school, or reading, there was so much to do at Aunt Sophie's, the days simply flew past. Millie was always glad of a hand to do a bit of weeding or dig up potatoes and carrots or whatever else happened to be growing at the time. There were also hens kept in a large coop that Sophie or Millie would let out in the morning to scratch amongst the cobbles by the back door, and both Danny and Lizzie loved to scatter the corn for them and collect the eggs, often still warm from their nesting boxes.

Lizzie was less impressed with the fat pink and black pig in a sty at the end of the garden and held her nose as she went past, but Millie seemed ridiculously proud of it. 'We'll have some fine bacon from this,' she said one day as she sat on the wall with Lizzie and watched the pig tuck into the bucket of swill she had tipped into the trough.

'Bacon?' Lizzie said. She'd had bacon for breakfast that morning and suddenly felt rather sick.

'Sure, bacon,' Millie said. 'And ham and joints of pork, and that means lots of dripping. There's a great deal you can get out of a pig.' She caught sight of Lizzie's horrified face and said, 'They're not pets, Lizzie. There's a war on, and keeping hens and a pig helps our food stocks. What we can't use, we'll trade for other things, that's how things are managed.'

Lizzie looked at the pig. She had no particular liking for the animal, but it didn't seem fair somehow.

'You can't deny that was good bacon you had on your plate this morning?' Millie said. Lizzie couldn't, and didn't try. 'Well then, how d'you think we get it as often as we do with the rations as they are?'

Lizzie shook her head. 'I don't know, I never thought of killing things. Do you do it?'

'No I do not,' Millie said emphatically. 'She'll go up to the farm when it's time, and we'll get a wee piglet to fatten up again. Our pig will be shared out and we have a portion of other people's when they're ready. Come on,' she said, jumping from the wall and pulling Lizzie by the hand. 'Stop worrying about one fat porker. Come into the kitchen and I'll show you how to make a casserole that we can have for tea.'

Millie never minded showing Lizzie how to cook things; she said she'd have to do it someday and it was the best way to learn. It was Lizzie's first attempt at making meals and she was so good and enjoyed it so much that Millie said she was a natural.

Aunt Sophie also taught her to knit, and under her direction she'd knitted a balaclava for Danny and was now attempting socks. 'When you've mastered that, you can try knitting for the troops,' Sophie said. 'They'll be glad of it, I'll tell you. And I've been collecting scrap wool and knitting squares to be sewn into blankets. Apparently the cities have great need of them for the bombed-out families.'

'They do,' Lizzie said. 'My grandad had to bully the people in charge to get mattresses and blankets for everyone when Granny O'Malley and the Sutcliffe family came to live with us.' She threw herself into the knitting every evening, feeling that at least she was doing her bit to help by sending things to the fighting men, or the poor families who'd lost their homes.

So all in all, Lizzie had much to occupy her when she wasn't at school. And school itself wasn't bad at all.

The following September, Lizzie and Alice would go up into Mr Donnelly's class. Lizzie couldn't wait.

'He might not be teaching you for long,' Millie said, as Lizzie told them at tea that night how she was looking forward to being in his class. 'After all, the bombs might have stopped by next September and your mammy might want you back home.'

'Oh,' said Lizzie. 'Oh yes, of course.' She was horrified to think she'd almost forgotten that this house in Hereford was not her home, that her real home was in the back streets of Birmingham with her family. There would be no Sophie or Millie, no Alice, no Mr Donnelly, no Millover, and worst of all no space, and she was ashamed of herself for thinking that way.

Sophie and Millie felt the same. In the relatively short time the children had been there, they'd settled so well that neither of the women really wanted to think about them going home again so soon. Sophie in particular, never having had a daughter, loved the company and chatter of Lizzie.

But Lizzie could not wish for the war to go on, for already it had done so much to tear her family apart.

She didn't allow herself to think of any of them being injured, though she knew that bombs which could reduce buildings to rubble could also kill and maim and hurt people. So she closed her eyes that night and prayed for a speedy end to the war, and asked God to keep everyone safe.

Carmel was found in the early hours of 22 November. She and the young soldier she was with had been caught in the blast of a bomb landing near them as they hurried towards a shelter. A building had collapsed on top of them, and it was only the young man throwing himself across Carmel that saved her life. She had cuts and bruises, her legs were in a dreadful mess and broken in places and she had internal injuries, but she was alive and in no imminent danger. The young soldier, though, was dead, crushed by the roof beams.

But although she'd been located, it took hours for her to be released, as the rubble around and above her was so unstable. It was painstakingly slow work to get her out without causing further damage. The news was relayed to the family in the early evening, but before Mary and Eamonn could go and see her, the sirens wailed out again.

'Bloody hell,' Maggie said. 'Don't they ever let up?'

'Bombs or no, I'm away to see my girl,' Mary said.

'You are not,' Eamonn said firmly. 'What good will you do, risking your life in the raid? Do you want to end up as a casualty in the next bed, or what?'

Mary bit her lip. She wanted to be with her daughter with every fibre of her being, and yet she knew Eamonn had a point, for she could hear distant thuds even before the siren's drone had finished.

Part of Mary was annoyed that it was Carmel's own refusal to take the war seriously that had brought this tragic accident about. Night after night she went out, raid or not; it

163

was as if she believed she was immortal, and nothing Mary could say would stop her.

But then that hardly mattered now, she thought. Who cares whose fault it is, for she's little more than a child herself, my youngest, my baby, and I'll not rest easy till I see her. But the raid was so intense that she knew that to go out in it would be worse than foolhardy, and she allowed herself to be persuaded to go down into the cellar until it was all over.

By the time the all-clear had sounded the next morning, more than six hundred fires had been started by the incendiary bombs that had rained from the planes the previous night. Added to that, the water mains had been severely damaged. Many families were without water and the fire services were unable to fight most of the blazes, which just had to be left to burn. Black smoke hung over everything.

Kathy felt depressed as she looked out that morning. She was going to the hospital with her mother, as Eamonn had had to go to work, and as they picked their way through the rubble-strewn streets awash with water, she felt her spirits sink and thanked God her two older children were safe and out of it.

Kathy had to snap out of her despondency and put a brave face on when she reached the hospital, for Carmel was in very low spirits. 'If you could cheer her up it would help,' the matron told them. 'The doctor is quite concerned about her. Of course, she was incarcerated for some time, and with the young man dead beside her it's bound to have had a great effect on her mind.'

Something had certainly had an effect on Carmel all right, Kathy thought, looking at her young sister lying in the hospital bed. Her face was almost as white as the sheets, and her black-ringed eyes had a dead, hopeless look about them. Her hair, still grey with dust, was plastered to her head and her mouth had a sullen, unhappy droop to it. Kathy saw the large blanket-covered box at the bottom of the bed that she knew was there to protect Carmel's legs from further damage, and her heart was filled with pity for her sister.

Conversation was hard work, and Carmel didn't try to help. Any answers to their questions were monosyllabic and terse. No, she wasn't in much pain, she said; the food was all right, the nurses were fine, there was nothing she wanted. She listened without any response to the things they told her about the family, and eventually Mary, wearied and saddened by it all, left Kathy alone with Carmel, making the excuse that she needed the toilet.

She'd barely left the ward when Carmel's hand shot out and grasped Kathy's. 'He's dead, isn't he?' she said. 'Andy, the boy who was with me. I've asked and asked and they just say not to worry and everything's all right.'

Kathy looked at her sister and realised she had to be told the truth. 'Yes,' she said. 'He is.'

Tears brimmed in Carmel's eyes, but she didn't cry. Instead she said, 'I knew he was dead. I heard the rescuers talking, they said he'd saved my life, but it should have been me that died.'

'Don't talk like that.'

'No, listen,' Carmel said. 'Andy wanted to go to the shelter early on, when the raid started. It was me that held back. We'd gone dancing and I didn't want to stop. Then all of a sudden the power lines were hit and all the lights went out and everyone was bumbling about and the management were shouting about finding candles and not to panic. Andy said we were going to find a shelter and no more messing about. He said it was his job to look after me, because we were going to be married.'

'Married!'

'Ssh,' Carmel warned. 'I don't want Mammy to hear. You know how she'll give out.'

165

'But you're only . . .'

'Fourteen and three-quarters, I know. We were going to wait until I was sixteen and ask Daddy,' Carmel said. 'I'd known Andy ages, he's my friend Carol's brother, we'd been seeing each other for six months.'

Kathy recalled her mother saying how Eamonn would take his belt to Carmel if he was to find out about her seeing boys, and her heart went out to her sister. She knew her father would never have allowed her to get married at sixteen, and yet people did that sort of thing in wartime, not sure how much time they had together. So Kathy didn't pooh-pooh her sister. Instead she said, 'Tell me about him.'

Carmel gulped and tried to swallow the lump in her throat. 'I don't think I can,' she said.

'It might help,' Kathy said.

Carmel sighed. 'He was Carol's brother, like I told you, and until recently, when he joined up, he worked in Cadbury's with me. We'd come home together and plan what we'd do that evening.' She looked at Kathy and said, almost defiantly, 'I loved him, Kath, and he loved me, but . . . but I never did anything wrong.'

'I know, love,' Kathy said, hoping the relief she felt at that reassurance was not showing on her face.

'And he said when I was sixteen we'd get married,' Carmel went on. 'But he turned eighteen in September and joined up. He just had forty-eight hours' leave. That's why I didn't want to spend any of it cooped up in an air-raid shelter, but if I had done, he'd be alive now. As it was . . . as it was, he died saving me. Oh, Kath,' she wailed, 'I feel I've killed him.'

'Now that's nonsense,' Kathy said. 'You listen to me, Carmel, only one thing killed Andy and that's war, and in this type of war that means dropping bombs on innocent people who've never done anyone any harm. Andy did try to save you, because he loved you, but you didn't get by unscathed either, don't forget. And don't be too hard on Mammy. She nearly went demented when you were missing. She went to the police and the hospital and saw all your friends that she knew – of course, she doesn't know where they all live and some she did know the address of had been bombed out.'

'It wasn't any picnic for me either,' Carmel said. 'I thought I'd go mad down there, unable to move. I wanted to scream, but I couldn't. My throat was full of dust and I was afraid of choking to death. It was worse when Andy went quiet, for he didn't die straight away. He moaned so I knew he was in pain, but I couldn't help him and it was pitch black, of course, but at least while he moaned I knew he was alive. When he stopped, I thought I'd go mad. It was so quiet, Kath, like you'd imagine a tomb to be. I kept thinking I hope I die quick because I never thought I'd get out.' She gave a sudden shiver. 'I tell you, the nicest sound in all the world was to hear people moving bricks and stuff above me and asking if anyone was there. I couldn't answer, my throat was so dry, and my eyes smarted with the dust they'd disturbed trickling down into them, but inside my head I was shouting and laughing.'

'Oh, Carmel,' Kathy said, looking at her sister's face and realising how frightened she must have been. Her own face was wet and tears were running down Carmel's cheeks as Kathy gathered her in a hug. 'You must get better quickly now,' she said. 'It's what Andy would want, I'm sure. He saved you, and you must be grateful for that and work on getting well again.' After that Carmel did begin to improve, though all the family knew her injuries would take time to heal. The next evening at home, Kathy took up her pen to write to Barry. She'd already written to him to tell him of Rose's house being demolished, but all the family had decided to tell the men nothing of Carmel's disappearance, thinking they all had enough to worry about. Even in the letter she eventually sent, she didn't stress how long Carmel lay buried, nor the extent of her injuries, but said only that she'd been hurt in a raid and was in hospital.

She missed Barry very much. She wanted his arms around her to reassure her and tell her everything would be all right, but she could hardly write that down. She had to work hard not to turn the letter into a litany of self-pity and complaint because there was little cheery news to be had, but eventually it was finished and she posted it on her way to the hospital to see her sister.

There had been a bit of a lull in the bombing in Birmingham, and while the Brummies were glad of a respite, they learnt that the mass of the German air force had been directed to Southampton. There was a second evacuation of schoolchildren and pregnant women, most of them going to Mardy, a small town in South Wales. Kathy felt she had been right to send her children away, and she wrote to tell them about recent events. She enclosed a letter thanking Sophie Barraclough for her kind offer of accommodation over Christmas, but saying that it would be difficult for her to get away.

Birmingham was attacked again on the night of 3 December, just as people were beginning to sleep easier in their beds, and then again on the 9th. Then the city was left alone while the ports took a hammering, although people still went to bed each night waiting in fear and trepidation for the air-raid sirens to wail across the skies. All in all, everyone was war-weary and few looked forward with any enthusiasm to Christmas, or the new year of 1941.

TEN

Lizzie was upset to hear of Carmel's ordeal because she loved her young aunt, who had always seemed more like a cousin or older sister. To be buried alive for three days was one of the worst things Lizzie could think of, and she really felt she'd go completely mad if it had happened to her. Kathy had written and told her that Carmel's legs were so badly mangled it would be some time before she'd leave the hospital. Lizzie wrote Carmel a long letter saying how sorry she was to hear of her accident and telling her all about her new life.

Lizzie wasn't afraid to tell Carmel how much she was enjoying herself at the Barracloughs', and in the countryside generally, things which she tried not to say in any of her letters home. The things she wrote made Carmel laugh and cheered her enormously, but though she told Kathy of the existence of the letters she didn't show any of them to her, knowing that the contents might hurt her feelings.

Lizzie felt almost ashamed that she didn't miss her family so much as Christmas loomed closer. 'I'd like the chance to miss mine,' Alice said. 'I'll spend the holiday bent over hot saucepans, or up to my elbows in greasy washing-up water after the hordes have eaten.'

'Don't you enjoy any of it?'

'Not really. It's just one long round of eating and drinking, isn't it?'

Lizzie was shocked. Christmas had never seemed that way to her, even when it was celebrated in the little back-to-back house in Edgbaston. She'd never before spent a Christmas with Millie and Sophie, but they seemed as excited as she and Danny were.

Lizzie was also looking forward to meeting David Barraclough. She knew what he looked like already, for there were photographs of both Sophie's sons all over the house, from babyhood and all through the stages of their growing-up, and Lizzie had had plenty of time to study them. She had had less opportunity to study Rosamund Harrington, Sophie's niece, whom she'd also meet at Christmas, for there weren't quite as many photographs of her.

She'd learnt about Rosamund's history from Millie, that fount of knowledge of all things that mattered. She'd told her that Rosamund's mother Marjorie was Sophie's half-sister. It was hard to believe, for in the two months Lizzie had been resident in the Barracloughs' house, Marjorie had visited a number of times and Lizzie had not taken to her at all. She'd treated Lizzie with a patronising air, and though Lizzie couldn't have put her finger on what it was that had made her feel uncomfortable, she just hadn't liked her at all, and confessed to Daisy that she thought her a stuck-up cow.

Marjorie had the same father as Sophie, but a different mother, and was Sophie's junior by almost nine years. She was married to Gerald, who was a general in the army, and lived at the Grange, which had been the family house where both women had grown up. It was known in the village as the Big House, as it was easily the largest residence there, a fact that Marjorie revelled in.

Rosamund was born when Marjorie and Gerald had been married some time, and was a total shock to Marjorie, who'd never included motherhood in her plan of life and was resentful of the small bundle of dependent humanity handed to her in the nursing home. Gerald was besotted with his daughter, but away a lot, and before she left the nursing home, Marjorie had decided that someone else had to care for the child.

Nanny Townsend was a treasure. She'd lost her young husband to TB in 1925 and her daughter to influenza two years later. In 1928 she was engaged to look after the infant daughter of Marjorie and Gerald Harrington. When she was five Rosamund had a governess, who lasted two years until the girl was sent away to boarding school. Nanny Townsend, however, was retained, to entertain Rosamund in the holidays. Nanny, who'd grown extremely fond of Rosamund, was only too happy to look after the child, who lacked nothing all her life but love and attention, while Marjorie continued in her role as the general's wife, a life she'd grown accustomed to.

And then came the war. Nanny Townsend heard of the number of casualties expected when the cities were bombed, as it seemed inevitable that they would be, and her conscience smote her. She was a qualified nurse, playing nanny to a privileged and pampered girl at a time when the nation needed qualified medical staff, and she gave in her notice.

Marjorie couldn't believe it. How, she demanded, would she cope without her, to which Nanny Townsend replied that everyone had to do their bit and Mrs Harrington had to remember there was a war on. Stubborn and stalwart in the pursuit of her duty, Nanny bade a tearful farewell to Rosamund and, with a promise to write, went off to the East End of London for a period of training before taking up a position in a London hospital.

Marjorie still had little time for her daughter, whose care during the holidays was left to indifferent servants. Not wishing to take in evacuees, Marjorie offered the Grange to the military, though officers only, of course. Mindful of soldiers' careless ways, she had her paintings, expensive ornaments and antique furniture removed to other rooms or the basement for safe-keeping during the occupation, but certainly found the officers sharing her home a much better alternative to city brats. She was amazed at Sophie, who'd offered to look after the children of some soldier who just happened to be in the same hospital as Chris. She was of the opinion that people were better off left in their own environment. After all, the children who'd come in 1939 weren't in the least grateful to be safe in Millover, or appreciative of the people who'd taken them in, and couldn't wait to get back to the slums they came from. It all went to show, she thought.

She'd been surprised by the O'Malley children, especially Lizzie, who she recognised would be a stunner when she grew up. She'd always thought of her Rosamund as pretty, with her ash-blonde hair and vivid-blue eyes, but Elizabeth O'Malley's beauty was too vibrant to be described as just pretty. 'You have a looker there,' she commented to her sister.

'You think so?' Sophie said, only too aware of her sister's love of beauty. She assumed a sadness she didn't really feel and went on, 'Pity she hasn't got any really pretty clothes. I mean, I'm sure her mother does her best, and she has plenty of sturdy everyday things, but nothing to show off her true beauty, you know?'

'Oh, that's a tragedy!' Marjorie cried. 'Rosamund has more clothes than she knows what to do with. I'll sort out the things she's outgrown and I'm sure between us we'll be able to clothe your little evacuee properly.'

'That's very kind of you, Marjorie,' said Sophie, trying not to let her smile of satisfaction show, thankful that her sister had eventually agreed to part with Rosamund's things which, despite the national call from the cities for clothes to help the bombed-out families, had been gathering dust in wardrobes in one of the spare bedrooms of the Grange.

Lizzie, of course, knew nothing of this conversation between the sisters; she only knew that liking Sophie, she was looking forward to meeting David, and disliking Marjorie, she was anxious about making Rosamund's acquaintance. In the event, her anxieties were justified.

They still had a week to go at the village school when David's term finished. Sophie had driven up to fetch him while Lizzie and Danny were at school. He was standing in the kitchen doorway when the children tore through the back gate, and Lizzie drew up so sharply when she saw him that Dan cannoned into her.

Despite the photographs, she was unprepared for the handsomeness of the boy before her, and she just stood and stared at him. She'd never seen hair so light before, or eyes such a vivid blue, with black lashes so long. His skin was flawless and his mouth large and generous-looking. It was turned up in a smile at her arrival, and the light danced in his eyes, and Lizzie's heart seemed to stop and the breath catch in her throat at that devastating smile.

'You must be Elizabeth and Daniel O'Malley,' David said. He'd given Elizabeth her full title for the first time, and she wondered as she gazed at the young man in front of her why she hadn't realised before that her name was Elizabeth. Elizabeth O'Malley had class, while Lizzie . . . well, Lizzie was just Lizzie. She'd be Lizzie no longer, she decided. Elizabeth was her name and that was what she'd insist on being called from now on.

For David's part, he was impressed by the girl before him, with her jet-black hair and deep-brown eyes. She looked nice and friendly, he thought, and was quite pretty too.

Lizzie was so stunned, she hadn't spoken a word, and Millie, coming into the kitchen, tutted. 'Come in, come in, and don't be letting the warmth out,' she cried. Bustling Danny and Lizzie inside, she helped them take off their coats, scarves and hats damp from the misty December afternoon and hung them to steam over the guard before the kitchen fire.

'Well, Lizzie, this must be a record,' Sophie said, coming into the kitchen at that moment. 'I've never known you this quiet before.' She'd seen that the child had been bowled over by David and was as pleased as any mother would be.

'Why d'you call her Lizzie, Mother?' David asked. 'It's such an ugly name, and Elizabeth is much nicer.'

'Well, she told me her name was Lizzie when she came, didn't you?' Sophie asked.

Lizzie nodded. 'That's what I'd always been called,' she said. 'But now I think I like Elizabeth better.'

'Elizabeth it shall be then,' Sophie declared. 'And now that that important point has been decided, do you think, Elizabeth O'Malley, we could sit up to the table and have something to eat?'

Lizzie's cheeks were scarlet, but everybody was laughing, so she laughed too and looked forward to the Christmas holidays with all her heart and soul.

'I've had a letter from our Lizzie and she's signed it "Elizabeth",' Kathy said later to Maggie.

'Aye, Mam had one too, it fair amused her,' Maggie said.

It didn't amuse Kathy, for Elizabeth O'Malley for some reason didn't seem the same person as Lizzie O'Malley. She waved the letter in front of her sister and said, 'It's all about this David, Mrs Barraclough's son that's home for Christmas. I'd say she's taken a shine to him.'

'Where's the harm?' Maggie said. 'She's only a child.'

'I know,' Kathy snapped. 'Oh, I don't know, I'm out of sorts I suppose. There's nothing in the shops for me to send the weans for Christmas. Barry's parcel will be better than theirs this year. I've packed him some cigarettes and the two pairs of socks I've knitted, and a bar of chocolate, and then Mrs Pickering threw in a quarter of bull's-eyes free when she knew the chocolate and cigarettes were for Barry. Molly's made him a cake, and even Mammy has knitted him some gloves, while all I've got for the weans is scarves and mittens. It's what they need all right, but not much fun for weans, is it?'

'Everyone's the same,' Maggie reminded her. 'They're not the only ones to be having few toys this year.'

'I know, but that hardly makes me feel better,' Kathy said. She scanned the letter again and remarked with a wry smile, 'One person she's not keen on is a girl called Rosamund Harrington, who she says is a niece of Mrs Barraclough and just a year younger than David. Her parents own a big house, and reading between the lines, this Rosamund is an uppity bitch.'

'Bit like our Sheelagh, eh, and she's nothing to get uppity about.'

'Huh, she will have if Bridie has her way and gets her into that convent in Erdington,' Kathy said. 'Went up there crowing on about being a poor war widow and all.'

'D'you think they'll take her?'

'Oh, aye. Have you ever known Bridie not get what she wants?' Kathy said. 'She'll have to pass an exam, but I don't think that will be a problem. One thing that girl isn't is stupid.'

'So she'll go on scholarship?'

'Yes, but they don't have many scholarship places,' Kathy said. 'Most of the other girls will come from homes with money.' She shook her head sadly. 'It will do Sheelagh no good and affect her more than most, for after all, she already thinks she's better than the rest of us put together.'

'I know,' Maggie said. 'Where does she get her fine ideas from?'

'Her bloody mother, where else,' Kathy retorted. 'Lizzie couldn't stand either of them and I couldn't blame her, for neither could I. I thought Pat a bloody fool to get trapped that way, and I know Barry did too.'

'Ah well, he's out of it now, God rest his soul,' Maggie said. 'Maybe when Elizabeth O'Malley returns to her roots, she'll be able to get on with her Aunt Bridie and be best friends with her cousin Sheelagh.'

"That'll be the day,' Kathy said with a laugh. 'Aye, indeed it would. But she won't be Elizabeth, not to me she won't. She's been Lizzie O'Malley for nine and a half years and Lizzie she'll stay, and I'll write a letter telling her so.'

Lizzie wasn't upset to get her mother's letter. Somehow she didn't want her mother to call her Elizabeth, because Elizabeth seemed to exist only in the Barracloughs' home. To everyone else she'd still be Lizzie. Danny wouldn't call her Elizabeth and hooted with laughter when she suggested it. Alice was the same. 'You've always been Lizzie to me up until now,' she said. 'I can't just change to call you Elizabeth. I'd never remember. Anyway, I think Lizzie is friendlier somehow, and some of the other kids might think you were getting too big for your boots if you just announced your name was Elizabeth O'Malley.'

Lizzie knew Alice had a point. They might see it as swank. She'd hate her new-found friends to think she was getting all snobby. That was the sort of thing her cousin Sheelagh would have done, and enjoyed doing too. 'Oh, let's not bother then,' she said, linking arms with her friend. 'To you and everyone else I'll stay Lizzie.'

'Good,' said Alice. 'That Elizabeth O'Malley sounds much too posh a person to be friends with me.'

'Oh, Alice, you are a fool,' Lizzie said, giggling. She thought Alice was a special person, the very best friend she'd ever had, and if she wanted to call her Lizzie, then she didn't mind in the least.

Really, Lizzie thought that Christmas Eve, this was the sort of house where you could almost believe in Father Christmas, though she'd had her doubts about his existence for some time. Certainly the Father Christmas who had appeared at their Christmas party, despite the white moustache and beard, bore a strong resemblance to Abel Potter the postman, who brought weekly letters to Lizzie and Dan and had a cup of tea with Millie in the kitchen.

In the event it was the nicest Christmas Lizzie and Dan had ever had. They had stockings full of goodies: yo-yos, colouring pencils, glove puppets, mouth organs, bars of chocolate and shiny sixpences. Elsewhere in their rooms, Santa had been very busy indeed. Danny had a fort with a box of lead soldiers by his bed, and a clockwork train set laid out on a board that wove between little hills and trees and houses. Both were much better than the ones Lizzie had shown Pete in Peacock's the day she'd escaped to the Bull Ring with Maura. Neither child knew the toys were not new and had once been David's, carried down from the attic in the dead of night.

Lizzie had a doll dressed in a beautiful ball gown. It had a china head and a soft body and eyes that opened and shut. It had once been Rosamund's, and though Lizzie didn't know that, she thought it far too grand to play with and sat it up on her windowsill while she opened the rest of her things. There was a beautiful paintbox and a sketch pad and set of proper artist's brushes, a fountain pen and matching propelling pencil, a large compendium of games and two books, *Black Beauty* and *Arabian Nights*.

The children also had the very first dressing gowns and slippers they'd ever owned, from Millie and Sophie, who came with their parcels to wish them happy Christmas. Sophie urged Lizzie to change quickly for early mass and pulled from the wardrobe the most beautiful dress Lizzie had ever seen.

The top was soft tartan wool in red and grey, and the flared black velvet skirt had layers and layers of petticoats so that it stuck out. There was a velvet waistcoat trimmed with tartan to go over the bodice and in her hands Sophie had socks and black shiny shoes to complete the outfit.

'Is it really mine?' Lizzie asked.

'Why, of course it's yours,' Sophie said. 'It's not new, but it's seen little enough wear. It's Rosamund's, but I wrote to your mother and she said she didn't mind. We have to be sensible in these times.'

It was like Sheelagh's communion dress over again, Lizzie thought, and vowed she'd never, ever have second-hand clothes when she grew up. Yet it wasn't the clothes them-selves, but the sort of people they came from, because Dan had an outgrown suit of David's, complete with shirt and tie, and David would not make Dan feel bad about it.

Yet Lizzie could hardly refuse the dress, and nor did she want to. When she looked at herself in a full-length mirror, she was amazed by the difference clothes made. Sophie brushed her hair till it shone and tied it back with a red ribbon, and when she came into the kitchen, she thought David looked very handsome in his first grown-up suit with long trousers, and his tie matched the handkerchief in his pocket. He was rendered speechless as he saw Lizzie in all her finery, while Millie declared, 'You look a treat, Elizabeth, you do really.'

It began to go wrong just before lunch. Millie had chased them from the kitchen as she wanted to lay the table and cook the dinner in peace, and the children went into the small sitting room where in honour of the occasion the fire was blazing brightly. They played snap first, and were into a game of dominoes when Rosamund came into the room. Lizzie immediately felt the chill in the air, but she knew she had to be polite. Rosamund was David's cousin and a guest in Sophie Barraclough's house, and though Lizzie recognised her as another Sheelagh, she knew she'd have to curb her temper.

Rosamund looked at Lizzie in her new clothes and said with a sneer, 'Oh, it all fits then?' She gave a sniff and went on, 'I'd hate to wear cast-offs myself, but I suppose the likes of you have to be grateful for what you can get.'

The dress was spoiled now for Lizzie, and she had the urge to strip it off and throw it back at Rosamund. David saw the angry flush on Lizzie's face, and her tight pursed lips, and said, 'Not very patriotic, you know, Ros. The government are always on about making do and mending, and if your clothes no longer fit you, it's better to let someone else have them than throw them away.'

Lizzie's heart soared. David was protecting her. But Rosamund was furious, Lizzie could see, so angry that two spots of colour appeared on her cheeks and her lips were set in a thin, tight line across her face. Just then Sophie called them through for dinner and Lizzie, going ahead of Rosamund, heard her hiss to David, 'You're wasting your time trying to tame the city dwellers.'

Lizzie's face burnt with indignation. Who the hell was she to talk in such a way about her and Dan? For two pins she'd turn round and smack her face. But she was a guest and it was Christmas Day, and she knew she could do nothing, and so with her face set, she went into the kitchen to take her place at the table.

'Darling, these officers with me can get anything. You name it, cigarettes, nylons, booze, the odd joint of beef or pork, eggs, sugar. We don't go short at the Grange, I tell you,' Marjorie said.

Lizzie knew Sophie was annoyed by what her half-sister said. Lizzie was just fed up of her, full stop. Marjorie had talked incessantly since they'd sat down at the table, and was still at it. And how she talked, in that high, false voice, and the loud laughter that never touched her eyes.

'They'd better watch out,' Millie said. 'The stuff must be black market and against the law. Even the army don't protect you from that.'

Marjorie looked with disdain at Millie. Her face was long, rather like a horse, Lizzie thought, and her nose was large, and now she lifted it even higher. She seldom spoke to Millie, and Lizzie knew she didn't think the other woman should be sitting at the table with the family. Millie was a servant and shouldn't be there aping her betters, so now Marjorie said scornfully, 'I shouldn't think I would have any trouble with the officers who lodge with me. They are *gentlemen*, I mean *real* gentlemen, and would never do anything underhand.'

Lizzie was the only one who heard the muffled 'Huh' Millie made to this reply, but Sophie, Lizzie could see, was cross. She didn't like Millie being spoken to that way and never considered her a servant. 'I don't see how you can say that, Marjorie,' she said. 'Rationing is supposed to be fair for everyone, so how can they have such large amounts of things forbidden to others in the legal way?'

"They're officers, Sophie, not ordinary fighting men.'

'It makes little difference.'

'Well, if it doesn't, it should do,' Marjorie said. 'You can hardly expect men of breeding to exist on the meagre rations allowed. Cook would be distracted if the officers were not able to slip her the odd thing now and again.'

Sophie sighed. 'You are a terrible snob, Marjorie,' she said. 'And perhaps it's escaped your notice, but there is a war on.'

'Oh, isn't that the constant cry when anyone wants to do anything remotely interesting these days?' Marjorie said. 'But darling, really, you can't accuse me of not being patriotic. Who was it that brought order to the decrepit Home Guard, organised knitting bees and established collection points for pig swill and another for salvaged metal to make Spitfires? I'm working as hard as anyone.'

Sophie hid a smile, for in reality Marjorie delegated others to do the work then took the credit herself. She doubted her half-sister was even aware of it and despaired of ever making her see it.

Sophie's mother had died when she was just an infant, and she was brought up by a strict but loving nanny and had learnt self-reliance at an early age. Her father, George, always a remote figure, had met and married Marjorie's mother Evelyn in the space of three months when he was on one of his frequent trips away from home. The first Sophie knew of her new mother was when she arrived with George to meet his daughter and the staff of the Grange.

Evelyn bullied the servants unmercifully and many left, so she engaged her own staff. Even Sophie's nanny eventually decided enough was enough and left too. Sophie clung to her and cried bitterly at her departure, and was inclined to blame Evelyn.

Evelyn complained to her husband of Sophie's sullenness and said she would be unable to cope with her and the new baby too. A boarding school with a great emphasis on discipline was decided upon, and Sophie was dispatched with haste, aged eight years old.

Marjorie was born while she was away from home, and from the moment she opened her eyes and let out her first cry, her doting parents had given in to her every whim. Sophie, on her holidays from school, could hardly recognise the father she'd barely known as the one who cuddled his new daughter.

A night nurse and day nurse were engaged for the baby, and in time she bullied the servants worse than her mother did. Yet on her infrequent visits home, Sophie felt an affection for her little half-sister, despite the favouritism displayed. Marjorie, in her turn, adored the big sister who would descend every so often and play with her for hours.

But Marjorie, brought up in indulged isolation, had never learnt to consider others, and had a spiteful streak. Stunningly beautiful, she liked to be the centre of attention everywhere. During her season in London – an advantage denied to Sophie – she met Gerald Harrington, who was entranced by her loveliness, and they were swiftly married.

Sophie was married herself by then and the mother of a baby son, Christopher, but Marjorie noticed the attention the new infant got and decided motherhood was not for her. By then their father was old and frail, and he died before Christopher's sixth birthday.

Sophie found herself feeling sorry for the stepmother she'd once disliked, because Evelyn pined for her late husband and the spirit seemed to go out of her. She died just as Sophie realised, to her intense joy, that she was pregnant again.

Sophie had expected Marjorie to be devastated by the loss of her parents, especially her mother, but she didn't appear to be. She was interested, however, in the will, which left the Grange and the bulk of the estate to her. Though many thought Sophie should contest it, she refused to do so. She was settled by then in her own house, a little way from the Grange in the Hereford countryside she loved, but was grateful for the money she'd been left. It enabled her to have improvements done on the house, ensure her sons had a first-rate education and make the last years of her ailing husband's life easier and less stressful.

Really, Sophie often reflected, she was a much happier person than Marjorie, despite the fact that her upbringing had been harsh, for it had enabled her to show fortitude at her early widowhood. Marjorie, on the other hand, had been brought up ill equipped to deal with not only hardship, but even life's realities, and it was probably too late for her to change now.

'It's Christmas,' Sophie said now. 'Let's not argue. Millie has done us proud with this dinner, we shouldn't spoil it by quarrelling.'

Marjorie said, with a sniff, 'Well, I'm sure I never meant to quarrel. I just made a comment, it was you and Millie who made something of it.'

'Let's forget it now,' Sophie said, 'and talk about something more pleasant.'

Marjorie, placated, launched immediately into the pre-Christmas ball she'd attended with Colonel Sotherby. 'Everybody who was anyone was there, darling,' she enthused. 'My, you should have seen the dresses, they were divine. I suppose you'd like to know where they got them from when there's precious little in the shops, but if you have the money you can buy anything, and why not, I say. And these people had money, honestly, darling, some of them were dripping with diamonds, literally dripping, and the food . . .'

Lizzie tried to shut out Marjorie's voice droning on and instead looked across at the Christmas tree she'd helped David decorate. She remembered how amazed she had been when it had been delivered, though of course she'd seen Christmas trees before. They'd had one in the school hall and the church, and the larger stores in Birmingham had them, but she'd never seen a real one, and such a big one, in a house. 'Where are we going to put it?' she said in a high, surprised voice.

183

'Where it always goes, to the right side of the fire by the window,' David said, and Lizzie watched amazed as he sank the tree into a bucket of soil and then brought down the decorations that were stored in the attic for use year after year. There were wooden figures, imitation parcels and home-made snowmen and Father Christmases, made, Lizzie guessed, by David when he was much younger, and maybe even by his brother Chris. There were tinsel strands and lots of shiny balls that spun in the heat from the fire and shimmered in a myriad of colours caught by the dancing flames. Then, on the top branch, David placed a large silver star.

It was a truly beautiful tree, and Lizzie would never get tired of looking at it, but her preoccupation had been noticed. 'What are you smiling about, Elizabeth?' Sophie asked.

'Oh, nothing,' Lizzie said. 'I was just admiring the tree.' And then, as Marjorie began her monologue again, Lizzie's eyes met the resigned ones of Sophie, and she thought that Sophie must be one of the kindest people in the world, putting up with Marjorie like she did.

ELEVEN

Lizzie looked up from the letter she was reading at the breakfast table one morning in early March and said, 'Mammy and Aunt Maggie have got themselves jobs.'

She was surprised her mother had never said anything about taking a job before. Sophie looked up from her boiled egg and said, 'Many women have to work these days. What are your mother and aunt doing?'

'She can't say,' Lizzie said. 'Careless talk and all that. She just says people came round the doors asking for women to go back to work and so she went. Granny O'Malley's looking after Padraic, and now Carmel's able to get about a bit, Granny Sullivan is caring for Tim.'

'Well, it's working out very well then,' Sophie said.

Lizzie read a bit more of her letter and said, 'She's coming to see us! She can't say when, now she's working, but she'll try and wangle a Friday when she's been there a wee while longer and come for the weekend. She says she's almost forgotten what we look like.'

'I hope she isn't coming to try and fetch us home,' Danny said. 'I like it here better than Brum, don't you, Liz?'

Lizzie bit her lip, but didn't answer her brother directly.

Instead she said, 'Don't be daft, Dan, there isn't room for us at home any more, with Granny O'Malley and the Sutcliffe family, and now Mammy's got a job, she'd have no time to look after us. We're better off where we are.'

Sophie and Millie exchanged glances, but said nothing. Lizzie tucked the letter behind the clock on the mantelpiece and didn't think about it much again. She'd like to see her mother and would enjoy her visit, but she didn't want to leave this lovely house in the beautiful countryside where the sky was bigger than it had ever been in her home town, and there even seemed to be more air to breathe. Already outside Sophie's front door there were snowdrops and crocuses pushing up through the cold, hard earth of the flowerbeds, a sign that spring was in the air despite the frost that rimmed everything in the garden in the early morning. She gave a little shiver of excitement and hoped her mother would come fairly soon.

Back in Birmingham, Kathy was also counting the days. Christmas had been hard without the weans there to open their stockings, and she felt their loss keenly. She was better now she was at work, for it filled her days. Really, there hadn't been enough to occupy two women in that small house. And then their labour in the workplace was necessary, she knew, with all the men away and so many things needed to help them win the war, as they must.

Sid, as promised, had got both Kathy and Maggie jobs straight away; they were crying out for people, he said. Enid seemed to enjoy the work too, and always had tales to tell of what went on at the factory, or the lives of some of the girls. It had made Kathy very wistful listening to her at the tea table, for her own day seemed very boring in comparison.

But in the end the pay packet was the real draw, as it was becoming harder and harder to stretch the money and

Kathy dreaded going back to the pre-war poverty she'd endured. After Barry had eventually got a job at the BSA in 1938, she'd managed to put away a tidy nest egg in the post office, but that account was virtually empty now because she'd kitted the children out before they went off to the Barracloughs' place – she'd have no one saying her children were dressed in rags. The worrying thing was that on army pay she was seldom able to put anything away again, and was grateful to Sophie Barraclough for helping to clothe Lizzie and Danny.

She was frightened, too, that after the war was over, Barry would be unable to find employment and there would be a slump like there had been after the first war. She didn't want to go down that road again – she needed savings to guard against it and make her feel secure. There was a further knot of anxiety that gnawed at her in bed at night, that Barry might not come back at all. It seemed that almost daily she was hearing of someone else reported missing or worse, and everyone dreaded the sight of the telegraph boy on his motorbike. She hated the thought of Barry never coming home – she'd loved him for many years and still did – but facts had to be faced, and hard as it was to manage on army pay, it would be harder still to manage without it, and then however would she provide for her family?

When Kathy asked Molly for advice, her mother-in-law urged her to go to work. She said she could look after the house well enough and cook for them all coming home in the evening, and this way, too, Molly got Padraic to herself. She adored her grandchildren, and with Lizzie and Danny out of harm's way in the countryside, all her attention was levelled at Padraic, who she wished belonged totally to her. She knew Kathy disapproved of her softness with him, but she could never bring herself to smack or discipline the child. With Kathy out at work, she'd have a free hand.

Only Bridie said she'd never heard anything so ridiculous in all her life as married women with children and babies going to work. She said she'd given her husband to help win the war and that was sacrifice enough for anyone. Kathy, who found Bridie's constant carping presence very irksome, said she must do what she saw fit.

But in reality Bridie at that time only had her mind on one thing, and that was the exam that Sheelagh would take at Easter to enable her to enter the convent of St Agnes in Erdington as a scholarship girl. 'She has no father to watch out for her,' Bridie had explained to the family, who'd looked at her in astonishment when she'd first announced her plans. 'She must make her own way in the world, and if I can give her a leg-up, why not?'

Kathy wasn't about to argue. She had troubles of her own, and the thing she was working on now was how to wangle a day off to visit the children. Production was at full stretch and Kathy didn't think the foreman would take kindly to her skipping off. 'There's rules and things about mothers visiting their evacuated children,' Maggie said. 'I'm sure there are; find out about it.'

'I will when we're less busy,' Kathy promised.

But then the raids began again. Most of Birmingham was stunned because they'd had a lull of three months. A lot of people thought that the city had been given a pasting and now they'd be left alone, so the March raids were a shock, despite the fact that they were usually light and fairly infrequent.

Then Kathy had a visit from Father Flaherty, who wanted to know what she was doing about Danny's spiritual welfare. 'He is now seven,' he said. 'It's time he was making his first holy communion. All the children in his class, including his cousin Matthew, will be going to the rails for the first time in June. Daniel should be with them.'

'But, Father, you see how I'm placed,' Kathy said. 'The house is already crowded out with Molly, the Sutcliffes and little Padraic, and then there's my job . . .'

'We are talking about a child's immortal soul here,' Father Flaherty said sternly. 'Communion is one of the sacraments, and I'm surprised you even hesitate. The child should be brought home now.'

'But the raids . . .'

'Have eased considerably,' Father Flaherty said. 'Most evacuated children are home now.'

Kathy knew that was true and wondered if she were an unnatural mother not to want to bring her children back where they belonged. God knew she missed them terribly, but their safety was her first concern. Barry too was urging her to leave the children where they were. His letters had begun to arrive regularly at last, much to Kathy's relief. There had been a dreadful worrying period in December when none came at all, and then a large parcel of letters arrived together just before Christmas. Now, though he couldn't tell her where he was, he was in a position to have his letters and parcels posted on more regularly. He was pleased that Kathy had decided to send the children away and had written to both of them, and even Danny was now writing little replies. From the tone of Lizzie's letters, he knew she was having the time of her life, and he told Kathy so.

Kathy knew Barry would go mad if she was to bring the children home on the say-so of a priest, but then he wasn't the one who had to face the man. Funny that Father Flaherty had been all for the children being sent out of the cities once, and had been mad because she'd opposed him. 'Seems I can't bloody win whatever I do,' Kathy said to herself.

'Tell him to mind his own business,' Maggie said when Kathy told her of the priest's visit.

'But it is his business really, isn't it?' Kathy said.

'No it isn't. What does it matter what age Dan makes his first communion? You say they go to mass every Sunday and Lizzie is taken to confession every other week; that's what's important.'

'Oh, Maggie, I don't know.'

'Go and see them,' Maggie advised. 'See the set-up for yourself, talk to the priest down there and make your own decision. They're your children, not Father Flaherty's.'

'You're right, Maggie,' Kathy said. "That's what I'll do. I'll write today and tell them I'm on my way down.'

But she didn't go straight away, because as March made way for April the raids intensified. Mary and Eamonn again began to use their cellar. With Eamonn's bad chest and the blustery March days that turned bitter at night, Mary had decided he was safer in bed than coughing his lungs up in the damp cellar, but once or twice, bombs had got too close for comfort. Now that the nights had lost their intense chill and Eamonn had got some colour back in his cheeks and coughed a little less, Mary decided they'd all be better off in the cellar.

Kathy, Molly and the Sutcliffes had begun to use their cellar again too, as the raids got worse in early April. Padraic was not so easy to transport now he was nine months old, nor, once woken from his slumbers, did he go off again so easily. As far as he was concerned he was up and it was time to play. He didn't want to sit on anyone's knee unless they were entertaining him, and his dearest wish was to get down on the floor and crawl around the cellar, a fascinating place he wasn't usually allowed in. Barbara Sutcliffe proved a boon here, as she had a seemingly endless store of funny songs with which to amuse Padraic while she jiggled him on her knee. Her energy was inexhaustible, and even Molly was glad to hand the squirming baby to her in the end.

They were all there together in the cellar on 9 April and heard the planes overhead as the strains of the siren died

190

away. It was the sort of day when you knew spring wasn't far away. The weather had been warm, with a mild breeze, and Kathy realised she didn't want the summer to slip by with the weans in someone else's house. She would fetch them back, not just because Father Flaherty said she must, but because she wanted to. She missed them, and Padraic was growing up with the idea that Kenny and Barbara were his brother and sister. It wasn't right, and tomorrow she'd make arrangements for the train down.

The crash brought Kathy out of her reverie, but before she was fully recovered there was another whine of a descending bomb and another shuddering crash. They heard the sound of ack-ack guns searing the sky and the cellar walls shook with the blast of yet another bomb close by.

Padraic began to scream in terror, and Kathy didn't blame him; nor did she blame Molly, who dropped to her knees and began the rosary, playing the beads through her hands as she muttered to herself with her eyes tight shut. That night Birmingham families took shelter wherever they could find it as 650 bombs and 170 sets of incendiaries dropped by 250 bombers set light to the city.

As the shocked, frightened people crept from their hiding places the next morning, the scale of the damage was not immediately fully apparent. The news filtered in throughout the day that the city centre had copped it again. A fire had begun at the corner of High and New Street and had soon blazed out of control. As the firemen fought to control it, it destroyed many other buildings in its wake. The east side of the Bull Ring caught the full force, and one of the city's theatres, the Prince of Wales, was completely destroyed. Over a thousand people were killed or injured that night.

Among the injured, Kathy found out later, were Bridie and her son, Matthew, who lay buried under the rubble of the public shelter they'd been in when it suffered a direct hit. Kathy stood with Padraic in her arms and watched as body after body was brought out. She had little hope for the survival of the sister-in-law she'd never liked, and she hoped God would forgive her, but Bridie's poor wee son was only months older than Dan, and he now lay entombed in this mound of crumbled bricks and timbers and burst sandbags. Sheelagh, badly shocked and distressed, was safe with her grandmother, but Kathy had to see, to be there, and she didn't even mind Padraic's struggles to be let down and his protests when he wasn't, for at least it showed he was alive and well.

Matthew's small body was so still and his dusty face so pale when he was carried out on a stretcher that Kathy felt tears raining down her face. She was surprised no one had covered his face but then, as he was being placed in the ambulance, she heard one ambulanceman say to the driver, 'Step on it, Paula. This little lad is alive, but only just.'

'Please,' Kathy cried. 'Where are you taking him? He's my nephew.'

'We'll try the General first,' the driver told her. 'But there's been heavy casualties, we may be diverted.'

'Thank you,' Kathy remembered to say before running home to tell the family and to leave Padraic with Molly. Eamonn accompanied her to the hospital, for her mother had her hands full with Sheelagh, while Carmel was dispatched to Bridie's family to tell them.

They found Matthew eventually in Lewis's basement, which had been set up as an emergency casualty centre. Bridie was there too. She'd been one of the first brought in, before Kathy had arrived on the scene, and was not too seriously injured. Matthew's life, however, hung in the balance for several days, and as Kathy watched her nephew suffer, she reversed her decision made in the cellar. She didn't mind what happened, or who tried to force her, or how quiet it was; her two older children would stay in the countryside until the war ended, however long it took.

Kathy travelled to Hereford on Friday 22 April, needing to see and hold Lizzie and Danny in her arms after the days of sadness, and often despair, she'd gone through. She knew before she left that both Bridie and Matthew would survive, but no one could say they were fully recovered. Mary and Maggie had urged her to get away for a few days; they'd seen she'd been near the end of her tether. She'd toyed with the idea of taking Padraic with her, for the children hadn't seen him since he was a wee baby, but then she remembered the frequent delays on the trains, and Mary's description of the Barraclough house, which was probably not at all suitable for an inquisitive crawling baby, and left him instead in Molly's capable hands.

Sophie drove into Hereford to fetch Kathy, recognising her at once as an older replica of Lizzie, and just as nervous as Lizzie had been that first evening. She was glad the countryside looked at its best, with the hedgerows full of wild flowers and the trees bursting with blossom.

Even forewarned by Mary of the splendour of Sophie's house, it still took Kathy's breath away to see it. She was nervous of entering it, and even more nervous of the woman who owned it, who'd driven a car as if it were nothing and talked all the way. Kathy had given short answers while she worried at the speed they were travelling at, and wondered how Sophie could concentrate on the road and talk as well. Now that they'd arrived, Kathy was almost too scared to get out of the car. 'Elizabeth and Dan will be home at half four,' Sophie said. 'That gives us plenty of time to have a bite to eat, and then I'll show you round the house before they burst in on us.'

'Thank you, you're very kind.'

'Not at all. We're enjoying looking after your children, and really, you seem to be going through it in Birmingham.' She noticed Kathy's pasty face and the blue smudges under her eyes, and thought that things were probably getting on top of her. And suddenly, all the worries that Kathy had previously kept to herself came spilling out as she followed Sophie into the house. She was surprised at herself, for she wasn't one to lumber people outside of the family with her problems, and Sophie Barraclough was a stranger, however kind she might be. But so much had happened lately, Kathy was like a coiled spring, and Sophie's sympathy for the plight of those in Birmingham had been like the flame to light the spark of her deep concern.

When Sophie opened the door to the kitchen, though, Kathy's eyes opened wide with astonishment and she fell silent. 'I could murder someone for a kitchen like that,' she was to say later to Maggie, but for that moment there at the threshold, she could say nothing at all.

It didn't matter, for Sophie was saying, 'You poor dear, it must be so upsetting for you all. We're so lucky here, it's almost as if there's no war on at all, although of course we've had our share of tragedies. Some of our neighbours here have had the dreaded telegrams delivered. It's a terrible war, and it isn't as if it gets any better.'

The genuine sympathy in Sophie's voice was like a balm to Kathy's bruised soul. At home everyone loaded on to her, and while Kathy knew they all had genuine worries, sometimes she felt like a wrung-out sponge.

By the time Lizzie and Dan burst through the door – early, for they'd run all the way – Kathy felt as if she'd known both Sophie and Millie for years. She'd been on a tour of the house and the garden, but went around the garden again to please the children. They pointed out the potatoes and carrots and onions still growing in their furrows and the peas and beans climbing up the canes. They showed her the tomatoes and lettuces that Millie was attempting to cultivate for the first time under the home-made cloches she'd devised from scrap wood and glass. She admired the barrels of damp earth filled with mushroom spores, and the enclosure where the hens constantly pecked at the ground, and the growing piglet, though she agreed with Lizzie that it was smelly.

All through tea, Lizzie watched her mother and realised how much she'd missed her. She didn't long to be back in Birmingham, she realised; it was the people she missed, not the place. She tried hard to be sorry her aunt and cousin had been hurt. It was easy to feel sorry for Matthew and pray fervently for him every night, but it wasn't so easy to feel sorry for Bridie, though she tried.

Kathy knew how Lizzie was feeling, because she'd felt it herself and confessed it. She was glad that it had been Father Cunningham who listened to her stumbling explanation in the confessional box, and not the judgemental Father Flaherty. Recognising Lizzie's dilemma, she veered away from the subject of the raid and its effects and told them instead funny tales of the job she and Maggie did, making distress lamps for air crews.

Lizzie told her mother all about Alice and the farm, and said they'd been invited to tea at the farmhouse the following day. Both land girls were from the Midlands, she said, and would probably welcome news of the place they still considered their home.

First, though, on Saturday morning, the children took their mother around the village and introduced her to the shopkeepers. Lizzie was proud of her pretty, trim mother and her attractive lilting accent. Kathy, for her part, saw that they all had a cheery greeting for her children, especially Mr and Mrs Carr who ran the paper shop, Mrs Bell at the general store and Miss Cavendish in the sweet shop, who gave them a big bag of sweets to share with their 'dear mother'.

Everyone loved Kathy, as Lizzie knew they would, wondering how she'd got on without her mother for so long. She even charmed the frightening Mrs Buxton so that Lizzie was able to enjoy the tea she and Alice had prepared. But all the way home from the farm, Kathy wrestled with her misgivings. She wouldn't go back on her word and take the children back to Birmingham, to destruction and possibly death. She could never live with herself if anything happened to either of them, and she knew she'd have to resign herself to them growing up apart from her. That was hard enough to cope with, but harder still was the knowledge that while it would be difficult for them to settle back home if she took them away now, how much worse would it be if they'd had years of living in the Barracloughs' house?

But what was the alternative? After the massive raid of 9 April, going home was out of the question. Who knew when that madman Hitler might plan another raid that was quite as severe? So should she go to the authorities and complain that her children were being looked after too well? Should she say the food was too good and too appetising, and the fresh air they enjoyed was damaging and they were having too good a time altogether and she wanted it stopped?

She gave a wry smile at the thought as her chattering daughter ran by her side, talking about David Barraclough. That was another thing. She wondered if Lizzie was aware how often she mentioned Sophie's son's name, and thought probably not. She was sorry she hadn't met him herself, because he'd returned to school for the summer term a few days before her visit.

'He showed us how to colour boiled eggs,' Lizzie said. 'And we drew faces on them before we ate them.'

Colouring boiled eggs, Kathy thought. And drawing faces on them, when those in the city would be lucky to see one egg a week. And she learnt how David had taken them for a walk and showed Lizzie how to pick and press wild flowers, and how they'd gone on a picnic to the banks of the Wye and Lizzie had plodged in the icy water with her dress tucked into her knickers and got it all wet. On and on Lizzie talked, and Kathy knew she had a crush on David Barraclough, providing an added incentive for her to stay in Hereford, and her heart ached for her daughter.

'The priest thought there would be no problem,' Kathy said to Maggie the following Monday dinnertime as the two sat over their meal. 'Apparently there is a Catholic preparatory school from London in Hereford and all the boys aged seven to eight are making their first communion in June. He runs classes for them after confession on Saturday and he's offered to have Danny in them. Lizzie was going in every other week anyway, and Sophie says she's well old enough now to take the bus and her wee brother every week instead, wait for him to finish his lessons and fetch him home again.'

'Well, so she is,' Maggie said.

'I know,' Kathy said. 'And Lizzie doesn't mind. She says it will give her a chance to look round the library.'

'So you can tell Father Flaherty that Danny's immortal soul will be saved,' Maggie said.

'I suppose so,' Kathy said miserably.

'What's the matter with you?' Maggie snapped irritably. 'You say the weans are fine and healthy and the people they stay with are kindness itself. You tell me you enjoyed yourself, and now you've sorted out Danny's first communion, and yet you're as miserable as sin.'

'Oh, I don't know,' Kathy said resignedly. 'It makes me feel . . . well, a bit of a failure, I suppose. I mean, my two older weans are living as far from me as if they belonged to someone else, and that someone else feeds them, looks after them, even gets bloody clothes for them, and as for Padraic . . .'

Maggie knew what was the matter with Padraic; everyone in the family was aware of it. But if Kathy was honest, she was often tired enough after being at work all day to be glad of the nights Molly had put him to bed before she got home. And she was away from the house before he was up, so it was only natural he would turn to Molly when he was hurt or upset, even if Kathy was home at the weekend. He loved Molly dearly, but he was slightly wary of Kathy, who sometimes told him 'no' and tapped his hand for some misdemeanour. However, it had shocked her to the core when she'd overheard him calling Molly 'Mammy' and realised Molly hadn't corrected him.

'My young son thinks Molly is his mother,' she said now to her sister. 'And Molly is quite happy to allow him to do so.'

'You should put your foot down there,' Maggie said. Her own son was being raised by Mary with the same loving discipline with which she had brought up her own children. Mary also had Eamonn to think of, and Carmel, although she was now thankfully fully recovered from her ordeal. And now there was Sheelagh, who was enjoying her status as the poor wee child whose mammy and brother were badly injured, just as Bridie had appeared to enjoy her widow's weeds.

It had been hard not to feel sorry for the poor girl, badly shocked and racked with sobs, who'd been taken in to her grandmother's house that first terrible night, and for days afterwards, allowances had been made for Sheelagh's delicate state of mind. She could not be expected to help in the house, but had to rest with her legs up on the couch, listening to the wireless, or reading the comics her grandmother bought. The choicest things to eat, the cherished egg or bit of under-the-counter sausage, were for Sheelagh, and Mary would often buy her a little treat from the shop. Tim during this time was rather neglected, and although Maggie thought that would do him no harm, she was disturbed by the fact that she'd seen a calculating look in her young niece's face. She knew that Sheelagh didn't want the pampering she was enjoying to cease, and so prolonged her woebegone expression, heavy sighs and ready tears even after her mother and Matthew were pronounced out of danger. As the weeks passed, there was little improvement in Sheelagh, and yet when Mary was not around, she seemed to recover miraculously and was as snappy as she'd ever been before, and twice as nasty.

In the end Carmel had been taken on to train as a telephonist in the GPO. 'The job came just in time to stop me stringing Sheelagh up by her knicker elastic,' she said to Kathy and Maggie, making them both laugh, although sympathetically, for they knew just what she meant.

Kenny had also got a job at the GPO, as a delivery boy. 'I get my own motorbike, Auntie Kathy,' he said excitedly. 'And I can pay something for my keep.'

Kathy smiled at the young boy she'd become so fond of and wondered, as she often had, how he seemed to put no fat on his bones when he was always eating. He was so pleased with the job, she hadn't the heart to tell him that the telegrams he'd be delivering would, in the main, probably be unwelcome ones.

In late June, Maggie and Kathy travelled down to Hereford together and arrived on Saturday afternoon. Maggie was glad to eventually see the place her sister and mother appeared overawed with and she was impressed by it. No one could doubt the warmth of the welcome of the two women, and the children were ecstatic. The next day at nine o'clock mass, Kathy watched her small son receive his first communion from a strange priest, in a strange church, amongst people he hardly knew. He was dressed in nearly new grey serge trousers that had once been David's, a new white shirt that Kathy had searched Birmingham for, a white satin sash, grey socks knitted by Millie and David's old black shoes polished so they shone to look like new. His sun-tanned face was scrubbed clean and his unruly hair tamed down with Brylcreem and he looked as unlike Danny as Kathy had ever seen him.

It was harder than ever to part with the children that time, and Kathy cried halfway back to Birmingham while Maggie tried to comfort her. For weeks afterwards she was dispirited and depressed. She was glad of the work and the overtime that ensured she got home late enough and tired enough to sleep, and was grateful for the cheerful banter that went on amongst the women. Most had husbands and children, and some of their children were evacuated too and knew what Kathy was going through.

When she'd first gone to work, Kathy had been slightly shocked by the things the women discussed, the ribald jokes told and the free and easy manner they had with the men working there. It had been way out of Kathy's understanding and she wasn't at all surprised that her young sister Carmel had had her head turned by such talk, if the women on her factory line had been the same. 'It's just their way of coping,' Maggie said in defence when Kathy expressed her concerns.

Their way of coping also included dating others while their men were away, and they seemed to have no shame about it, nor any guilt either. 'Go on,' said one when Kathy expressed shock. 'What my old man don't see won't hurt him, now will it?'

'Yeah,' said another. 'When the cat's away, you know . . .'

Kathy pursed her lips and wondered if she was growing old. She certainly seemed to have lost her sense of fun.

She'd almost forgotten what it was like to laugh and joke and hang the consequences, and she didn't know whether that was being sensible or mature or just dull. Either way, she wasn't happy. Life and all its problems seemed drab and uninteresting, and the war unending, the only difference being that on 22 June Germany had invaded Russia, breaking the non-aggression pact, though Kathy didn't know whether that was good news or bad. Eamonn told her the invasion fear was less because with half of Hitler's forces deployed in Russia, he hadn't enough power to attack Britain, and that had to be grand for them all. Kathy was not so sure.

Maggie said she needed taking out of herself. 'I don't suppose you'd consider going out somewhere, just you and me?' she suggested cautiously. 'You know, like some of the others, to . . . to a dance, for example?'

'A dance?' Kathy snapped.

'Lots of the other girls go,' Maggie said.

Kathy tossed her head, hardly able to believe her ears. 'Maggie, don't be talking like that. Whatever do you mean?'

'I mean nothing but the possibility of a little fun,' Maggie hit back. 'God, Kathy, doesn't it get you down, the drabness everywhere and the sameness of every day?' She caught sight of Kathy's disapproving face and cried, 'It's not a sin to have a bit of fun.'

'Fun!' Kathy almost spat out, as if it was the dirtiest word she'd ever heard. 'Well, I'll write to your husband and mine fighting for their country and ask them how much fun they're having.'

'Oh, for God's sake,' Maggie said, exasperated. 'I'm not suggesting making love to someone, just dancing together. Come on, it can't be that bad, and surely to God we haven't to sit in night after night looking at the same four bloody walls?'

'You have a husband and son,' Kathy said stiffly.

'I know that, but it doesn't mean life stops,' Maggie said, and added wearily, 'I have a husband I had a few short days with before he left, who sometimes I don't hear from for weeks, and a son I'm not allowed to rear myself. I live a sort of half-life, in my mother's house, where she treats me midway between a child and a skivvy.'

Kathy knew that what Maggie said was true, she did have a time of it – they all did now Bridie was never away from the house and constantly moaning and complaining. Kathy knew Mary felt heart-sorry for her and Sheelagh, and worried for wee Matthew still ill in hospital, but she was worn out looking after them all and Maggie often bore the brunt of her bad humour. Kathy looked at her sister's face and noted the strain, and thought that maybe a little relaxation wouldn't come amiss.

But no dancing; she instinctively knew that dancing in another man's arms when your own had been away for months was a bad idea. After all, women had their needs too, and natural instincts. Not that she believed in discussing it at all – she deplored all this frankness in talking of intimate things that many people indulged in these days. The war had seemingly changed people's morals too, but Maggie couldn't be allowed to go down the same road.

'Maybe,' she said tentatively, 'if Molly and Mammy would be willing to mind the weans, we might go to the pictures a time or two?'

Maggie looked at her sister, and knowing what was going through her mind, she laughed as she said, 'Aye, maybe we could, only it wouldn't do to sit too near the back row watching the courting couples, for it might put ideas into our sex-starved minds and bodies.'

'Maggie!' cried Kathy, shocked. 'There's no need for such talk.'

'What talk?' Maggie asked mockingly. 'Sex talk?'

'Och, will you whist, Maggie?' Kathy pleaded, glancing anxiously round the canteen. 'Sure, someone will hear.'

'Kath, no one is interested enough to listen,' Maggie said wearily, and added with a sigh, 'They all have their own lives and concerns and aren't a whit bothered about ours.'

'I don't know what's got into you, really I don't,' Kathy burst out, confused. 'All I did was suggest going to the pictures one evening, and it's got to be better than nothing, hasn't it?'

And Maggie knew then that her sister would sooner run naked down Bristol Street than accompany her to a dance, so she sighed again and said, 'Aye, Kath, as you say, it's better than nothing. I'll talk to Mammy about it when I get in this evening.'

Kathy looked at her sister's dejected face. She didn't seem very happy, but it was the best she could do. No way could she go along to a dance with her, nor condone her going alone. 'Aye, that's best,' she said. 'It will be a treat for us to go out now and again, and sure, we work hard enough.'

Maggie said nothing more and in time they began to really enjoy their weekly visits to the cinema, and though Maggie still listened wistfully when the other women chatted at work about this dance or that they'd attended, she never mentioned going again herself.

TWELVE

Kathy wrote to the children religiously every week and told them what was happening in the family. It was her way of reminding them of where they really belonged, and that their stay in Hereford would eventually come to an end.

Lizzie, who missed her mother greatly, looked forward to her letters, although sometimes the things she wrote about seemed as remote as those in her father's letters. She felt removed from it all.

As the summer of 1941 drew on and every day appeared wonderful, Lizzie realised that she recognised the seasons here more than she ever had done in Birmingham. They seemed more denned somehow, and she liked each one in its own special way.

Summer days seemed to be always fine and the holidays not long enough for all she wanted to do. She learnt to swim that summer in the torpid river that encircled the village, and David unearthed his old cricket set and gave it to Dan, who then suddenly became one of the most popular boys in the place.

Lizzie was happy and content, and though she'd not grown much, she was healthier than she'd been for a long time. Her skin had a golden glow to it, while Danny, who was not much smaller than his sister now, had a definite tan and hair bleached blond by the summer sun.

David had never met anyone quite like Lizzie. The only other girl he knew was Rosamund, and she never seemed satisfied about anything. Comparing her with Lizzie, he had begun to realise how selfish and grasping she was. He'd always given in to her in the past and thought most girls acted as she did. Lizzie O'Malley showed that this was not so.

Since the evacuees had arrived, Rosamund had become worse, David thought, and seemed to want to spend every minute of the holidays with him. He'd found it stifling. He'd already broached with his mother the subject of asking a couple of friends to stay for part of the Christmas holidays, and Sophie was glad he had such good friends. 'Their parents will probably want them home for Christmas,' she said, 'but they can certainly come for the new year.'

Sophie knew Chris would be relieved too. He'd already suggested to her that David needed more male company in the holidays, and that it was unhealthy for his constant companion to be a girl a year younger than himself, whether they were related or not.

David was so irritated by Rosamund and her scorn at his attempts to teach the O'Malley children to swim, that he heartily wished he'd invited his friends that summer. Philip Bletchley and John Carruthers had been his friends from their first days at school, and they didn't scream at him for nothing or go off in a sulk at the drop of a hat. He was soon heartily sick of his cousin and decided it was time she realised he had a life of his own to live.

In August, Kathy wrote to Lizzie about Matthew leaving hospital, and though she explained about the calliper on his left leg, which he still dragged, and his left side appearing stiff, she didn't tell the whole story. She didn't say she hardly knew the silent, serious child who seemed to have forgotten how to laugh and who shook uncontrollably at any sudden noise and stuttered when he tried to talk.

Eamonn had been furious that Matthew had been released from hospital before he was completely better. 'The child's shell-shocked,' he said. 'I saw lots of poor sods like him in the first war.'

'Maybe they think he'll recover better at home,' Mary suggested.

Maybe they did, but Kathy knew it would be unlikely to happen, for Bridie was short-tempered with her son and Kathy was sure that would only compound the problem. She didn't tell her daughter any of this, but instead wrote about the whale and horse meat now on sale at the Bull Ring, as meat and cheese were both on ration and eggs near unobtainable.

'Ugh,' Lizzie said. 'Whale and horse meat.'

'Well, they can hardly catch rabbits like we can,' Millie said.

'Yes, and horse has been eaten in France for years, I believe,' Sophie said.

'Yes, and frogs' legs and snails if all tales are to be believed,' Millie said grimly, and everyone burst out laughing. Lizzie was glad she didn't have to eat horse meat, however edible it was supposed to be, and whale meat sounded even worse.

Kathy's heart went out to little Matt. He'd have been content to skulk at home, but Bridie would drive him out and he'd slouch miserably up the entry and usually position himself on Kathy's step. From there he'd watch the children playing in the street, or among the ruins of the buildings that had once stood across the road. Kathy sometimes saw him there, a look of abject sadness on his face as he watched and envied the others. He'd have his good leg pulled up to his chin and his callipered one stretched out stiffly before him, so that nearly everyone that passed would trip over it.

Not, of course, that Kathy saw him often, as she was out at work, but Molly did. 'What that child needs is plenty of love,' she said to Kathy one day. 'Poor little bugger, starved of it he is.'

Though Bridie had been hurt too, her injuries had not been serious. She'd been near the door when the blast came and was blown into the street. In that way she was tended to straight away and not left buried under tons of masonry as Matthew had been. Yet she had little sympathy for her son and seemed constantly cross with him for one thing or another, and more than anxious to leave him with others while she went into Birmingham to buy things Sheelagh needed. Kathy didn't know how she did it now that clothes rationing was in and the points system introduced, but Molly said she used Mart's points too. 'The poor child's in rags,' she said angrily. 'Enid said she'll alter some of Kenny's clothes for him.'

And though Kenny had been quite hard on his things, especially his trousers, Molly and Enid worked on them to make Matt more respectable. Bridie never seemed grateful, and Kathy wondered if she even noticed Matt that much. Sheelagh was the light of her life during that time, and Molly remarked grimly that they deserved each other.

Lizzie hadn't a care about Sheelagh beginning at the convent in September. Her mother wrote and told her, and she thought her cousin was welcome to it.

Alice was more interested. 'Don't you mind her going to a convent school?' she asked one dinnertime in early October.

'Why on earth should I?' Lizzie asked in genuine amazement. 'It sounds awfully strict, according to what Mammy says.'

'Wouldn't you like to go to something like that, though?' Alice persisted. 'You know, grammar school or something?'

Lizzie shrugged. 'Never thought about it,' she said. 'Would you?'

'Oh yes,' Alice said. 'I'd like to do something with myself, and I like learning things.'

Lizzie knew she did. Alice was quick at picking things up and only needed to be told how to do something once. 'You'd pass for grammar school,' she said. 'Why not ask Mr Donnelly, and he may talk to your mother for you?'

'Wouldn't be any point,' Alice said miserably. 'Mam was married at seventeen and says she can't see any reason why I shouldn't do the same.'

'What, get married?'

'Yes, to some burly farmer or other,' Alice said. 'She's probably got someone in mind already.'

Lizzie thought it sounded awful. 'What d'you want to do?' she asked.

Alice pondered for a while and then said, 'If I can't go to grammar school, I'd like to work in Hereford in a shop or an office. I'd like to have money in my pocket so I could go to the pictures, or dancing, enough to buy nice clothes. I'd like . . . oh, I don't know, to be able to please myself before I have to please anyone else, and if I marry I want to choose who it will be to.'

Lizzie nodded. 'And me, I suppose,' she said, but the future had never really bothered her. 'I mean,' she went on, 'I want to get married. I suppose everyone does.'

'Yes, but not when they've barely left school,' Alice pointed out. 'Anyway, with so many men being killed in the war, lots of girls might be left on the shelf.'

'Gosh, that would be awful.'

Alice tossed her plaits back impatiently and said, 'No it wouldn't, I wouldn't care. I want to travel and see places and do things, be somebody, and I will, whatever my mother has lined up for me.'

'I don't blame you,' Lizzie said.

'D'you know what gets me about this exam, this eleven-plus thing?' Alice said. 'If it had been one of my brothers, my parents would have given them the chance, but none of them liked school and they used to play the wag all the time. I'd love to have the chance, but because I'm a girl, no one has even thought of it.'

'Oh, Alice, don't worry about it,' cried Lizzie. 'What if you'd been allowed to sit and I hadn't? How would I manage without you?'

'That would be awful,' Alice agreed, for the girls had become bosom friends.

'Then let's not talk about it again,' Lizzie said. 'This way we'll be in Mr Donnelly's class till we leave school.' Or until I leave Hereford, Lizzie thought, but she kept that disquieting thought to herself.

In fact, both Alice's parents and Sophie Barraclough had been approached without the girls' knowledge for their permission to allow them to sit the exam. Mr Buxton didn't say a word either way, but Mrs Buxton told Mr Donnelly firmly that it was pointless educating girls. 'I teach her what she needs to know, how to cook and clean and keep house, and that's all the learning a girl needs.'

Mr Donnelly tried to remonstrate, but Mrs Buxton was having none of it. 'Our Alice's future will be talked over by her father and me when the time is right,' she said. 'A place at grammar school is not part of it. She's not taking any exam and that's that.'

Mr Donnelly had to admit defeat and went to visit Sophie Barraclough, who seemed more amenable to the whole thing but said the decision didn't rest with her but with Lizzie's mother. Mr Donnelly said he hoped Mrs O'Malley would prove more open-minded than Alice's mother, and Sophie promised to write to Kathy O'Malley without delay.

Kathy read Sophie's letter in amazement. At first, she was pleased that her daughter had been considered clever, and then she remembered Sheelagh and the swank of her up and down the road and the lah-de-dah accent she was trying to perfect to fit in with her posh friends, and she was afraid.

Already her daughter had suggested calling herself Elizabeth and she'd had to nip that firmly in the bud. What if she was now to sit and pass this exam and go to some grammar school and give herself airs and graces and look down on her own people when she did come home? And what if the war ended next year? Would she be able to transfer to a Birmingham grammar school? Kathy didn't know but thought probably not, and then where would her fancy ideas get her? No, she decided she'd have no grammar school place for her daughter.

She told no one but Maggie of the letter from Sophie. They were alone walking home, for Sid and Enid had gone dancing straight after work. Maggie listened without a word as Kathy described what Sophie had suggested, and what she'd done in response, and when the silence between them had stretched to be uncomfortable, Kathy began to try and explain and justify her actions. 'I mean,' she said, 'what in God's name is the point of putting such ideas in her head?'

'Have you written back already?' Maggie asked.

'Aye, straight off.'

'You didn't think of asking Barry's opinion?'

'Och, for God's sake,' Kathy snapped irritably. 'No one knows where our men are, or any other damn thing either. I don't know when he'd even get my letter, never mind when I'd get an answer from him. You know we sometimes get nothing for weeks and then a batch of letters together. These days women have to take the decisions, and anyway Barry would agree with me.'

But would he? A small niggle of doubt began in her mind. He was all for the weans doing their best and getting on, and would probably want Lizzie to have the chance and with no idea on God's earth how it was going to be afforded. In that case, Kathy thought, it was better he knew nothing about it.

'D'you think she'll be disappointed at all?' Maggie asked.

'She doesn't know,' Kathy said. 'Mrs Barraclough said the teacher came to see her and she told him she had to get my permission before saying anything to Lizzie – or Elizabeth, as she calls her. Now she's not to take it, there's no need for her to know anything at all.'

'I can't help feeling it's a shame.'

'Oh, Maggie,' Kathy cried wearily. 'You've seen the place they're at. Compared to our house it's a little palace. Inside lavatory just off the bedroom, proper bath and that lovely kitchen. I'm scared Lizzie and Danny will not fit in when they come back home as it is. What happens if I let Lizzie take this exam and send her to grammar school if she passes? Then, just as she's beginning to believe she's someone special, the war ends and I haul her back here, to no grammar school, just a line in a factory like ours, or behind a counter in Woolworth's.'

Kathy had a point, Maggie knew, for those were all the employment prospects open to Lizzie when she was fourteen. Taking it all round, it wasn't a bad life – a job was a job and a pay packet at the end of the week made the dullest work worthwhile – yet for all that, Maggie couldn't rid herself of the feeling that that wasn't the whole reason for Kathy's refusal. She thought she'd refused partly because she had the power to do so, because Lizzie was her child and by saying she was not allowing her to take the examination, she was reminding Sophie of that fact.

211

'Come on, Maggie,' Kathy said. 'Mrs Barraclough will say nothing, nor I dare say will the teacher, and it's more than likely our Lizzie won't even know about the examination.'

But though no one said anything directly to Alice or Lizzie, they did know all about the exam. There was one boy in their class, Robert Fairley, who was entered for it – 'A boy, you see,' Alice said knowingly – but Lizzie didn't envy him. He was a quiet, studious boy anyway, with few friends, and now he seemed loaded down with homework every night, and she thought it was a poor way to spend the evenings.

Sophie had been bitterly disappointed by Kathy's reply to her letter. She recognised, as Maggie had, that Kathy's refusal was a stamp of her maternal authority, and that any pleas she made would fall on deaf ears. She considered writing again, but in the end reminded herself that Lizzie was Kathy's child and she had to abide by her decision.

Soon there was a new development in the war that everyone was talking about, because on 7 December, the American fleet based at Pearl Harbor was bombed by the Japanese. Everyone knew now that America was in the war, and many thought it was about time. 'They were prepared to let us stew,' Bridie said. 'Thinking of their own skins, they were.'

'Aye,' said Eamonn. 'But I'd rather fight a German than a Japanese any day.'

Most people were cheered by America's involvement and thought it might shorten the war; only Eamonn sadly shook his head and said it might lengthen the whole procedure.

By spring of 1942 the people of Birmingham, like many other cities, became used to the sight of GIs in their streets. Some found them brusque, while others saw them as interesting and exciting, with their smart uniforms and drawling accents. Girls' heads were completely turned by the dashing

Americans, and when Carmel brought one home to meet her parents, not even Eamonn put up any objection.

Ricky Westwood was a personable young man who called Mary ma'am and Eamonn sir. He talked about his folks back home in Pittsburgh and his kid sister and young brother still in high school, and Carmel listened enthralled. He asked Eamonn formally if he could court his daughter, and on their subsequent dates gave her presents of chocolates, cigarettes or nylons, unheard-of luxuries for so long in Britain. When he was finally asked for tea at the Sullivan house, he produced tins of fruit and meat for Mary to supplement the meagre fare on the table, and more cigarettes for Eamonn.

'Oh, that will do his chest a lot of good,' said Kathy crossly. She felt unreasonably annoyed that she'd not been asked to meet Carmel's young man. Truth to tell, she was afflicted by a depression similar to that Maggie had gone through earlier in the war, caused, or at least not helped, by the sameness and drabness of every day. Not even the weekly cinema trip could always make her feel better, and she was often tetchy and irritable as a result.

The war seemed relentless and never ending and the involvement of the United States seemed to escalate it rather than having the reverse effect. She missed her children more than ever. Bridie still had her poisonous tongue, which she used relentlessly, and every time Kathy saw Sheelagh in the convent uniform, her conscience smote her on account of the opportunity she'd refused for her own daughter.

The American soldiers were often a welcome diversion in those monotonous days. They were not yet war-weary and were smarter and more affluent then most British soldiers. Some complained that the GIs' ways were strange, but it had to be remembered they'd not been fighting a war already for three years, they'd experienced none of the devastation suffered by the British and of course they had no idea of rationing. 'Two of them came in and asked me for an ice,' Mrs Pickering complained to Molly as she waited for her rations one day. 'I didn't understand him at first, turns out he wanted an ice cream. God, I'd almost forgotten what ice cream tastes like and I told him so, and he could scarce believe it.'

The strangest Americans of all were those who were black. They were the first black people most of the residents of Birmingham had ever seen, but generally they were prepared to take them on face value and couldn't understand the attitudes of some of the white Americans towards their own countrymen. 'Two of those coloured people were in my shop the other day,' an outraged Mr Morcroft said to anyone who'd listen. 'And then two of the others came in, white fellows, you know, and ordered the coloured men out. I let them have it, I'll tell you, I told them those coloured blokes were in the queue first and it's my shop and I'll decide who stays in or goes out.'

'Quite right,' one of the customers said. British people were all well used to queuing – they'd had three years of it already – and queue-jumping was not on, certainly not because of the colour of a person's skin.

Colour seemed to matter to some Americans, though. Many of the factory workers told of the dances where black soldiers weren't allowed to partner white girls and were warned off by their white counterparts. That of course annoyed the girls and made the attraction of the black boys the greater, and many a fight ensued. Even Sid and Enid stopped going dancing for a while because of the nasty atmosphere in some dance halls.

In time, though, most people learnt to get along with the American soldiers, and housewives had another reason to be grateful to America, for in June 1942 dried egg was introduced from the States. Although it was nothing like the real thing, it was one more item to make a meal from. However, it was hardly party fare, and Maggie and Kathy were planning a joint second birthday party for Tim and Padraic and scouring the shops for presents and things to make Kathy's house more festive.

But a few days before the party was due to take place, there was another air raid. Kathy could scarcely believe it, but she struggled down to the cellar just in case. It soon became apparent that it was no false alarm, as they heard wave after wave of bombers overhead dropping their deadly loads while they all shivered in fear. Afterwards it was established that many of those killed or injured had not taken shelter. Kathy was glad she'd insisted they spend the time till the all-clear in the cellar, although the next day she was sluggish and worn out from lack of sleep. Yet a day's work had to be got through, and she hoped and prayed that the Blitz wasn't due to start again.

Two days later, the sirens rang out again just after the six o'clock news. It was the day of Padraic's birthday and the alarming wail broke in on the family's rendition of 'Happy Birthday'. Kathy struggled down the stairs with her small son in her arms and a terrifying fear that they were for it again. She dragged an eiderdown and blanket after her, and was followed soon after by Enid, Sid and Barbara Sutcliffe.

That night Bridie also came through the entry door to use the cellar after hearing of the heavy casualties of two nights earlier. Kathy, who'd gone up to carry Matt down the steps, as he was awkward with his calliper, was shocked at the child's weight. He was a year older than Danny and yet she doubted whether he weighed much more than chubby Padraic. But the middle of an air raid was not the place to discuss it. It was obvious that Matt was terrified of the loud blasts, and he shook from head to toe, but Bridie was

215

brusque with him and told him not to be so stupid and babyish. In the end, Kathy handed Padraic to Molly and, risking Bridie's anger, pulled Matt into her arms, where his shudders grew less.

She felt sad suddenly that someone else was bringing up her two oldest weans and comforting them when they needed it. In two days' time she had a joint party to give for the one child who remained with her, and his cousin Tim, and God knew she hadn't the heart for it. Yet it wasn't the wee boys' fault they'd been born into a war, and she'd have to make the best of it. At least so far all her children were fine and healthy; some mothers weren't as lucky.

Despite the shuddering crashes around them, Padraic had fallen asleep on Molly's knee, tucked under the eiderdown. Matt, comforted by his aunt, had grown drowsy, too, and Kathy laid him beside his cousin, while Sheelagh got in the other end with Barbara Sutcliffe. Kenny was fire-watching, and Kathy knew his parents were anxious about him out there in the middle of it all.

Kathy's eyes felt gritty with tiredness, and she closed them and laid her head on Molly's comforting shoulder, and eventually, totally exhausted, fell into a deep sleep.

THIRTEEN

The war went on apace. Lizzie had a bike from Sophie for her eleventh birthday in June 1942. It wasn't new, but one David had grown too big for which she'd had resprayed and cleaned up. Lizzie was absolutely stunned by such a gift and cared not a jot that it had a boy's crossbar. It made going to see Alice easier, and as both land girls had bikes they didn't usually mind loaning out, it opened new horizons for the girls during the holidays, when Lizzie wasn't needed at home and Alice was allowed to escape the farm.

The friendship between the two girls was deeper than ever, which was as well, since every holiday now David either had his friends to stay or went to one of their houses for at least part of the time. Lizzie didn't miss him as much as Sophie appeared to, and Rosamund seemed lost altogether. Lizzie often saw her going for long solitary rides on her pony.

Lizzie found David different now anyway, and by the summer of 1943 his voice had deepened considerably and he sounded like a man. He had dark fuzz above his upper lip and on his chin that he had to shave off. It set him apart somehow from Danny and Lizzie, and he was often moody and argumentative with his mother.

He was sixteen and had taken his school certificate in May of 1943, and he felt it was stupid to return to school for another two years to do his Highers when at any time the war could end and what would he have done? Absolutely nothing but skulk at school, while others like Chris, or Elizabeth and Danny's father, risked their lives daily to protect him.

Sophie couldn't or wouldn't see it, and they squabbled constantly. David was due to return reluctantly to school when Italy surrendered on 8 September. Everyone but David was delighted, and he was so sharp and nasty with his mother that Lizzie, for the first time, was glad to see the back of him.

By 1943, most things were either just very hard to get or totally unobtainable. Even the books and paper needed at school were in short supply. Mr Donnelly encouraged the children to use the public library in Hereford to expand their knowledge.

Alice was ecstatic. 'I told Mom it was unpatriotic not to,' she said. 'It's sort of make-do-and-mend anyway, isn't it, if we haven't enough books and things?'

Lizzie laughed and agreed it was. Make-do-and-mend was the order of the day, and to be a squander-bug was the worst thing in the world. Kathy had written about how difficult it was to keep Padraic clothed when he grew so quickly. She said his outgrown jumpers had to be constantly unravelled and knitted up again, which made for some very oddly patterned woollies, but she said most mothers were in the same boat.

Lizzie didn't think much about clothes really; it was Alice who was clothes-mad. The two girls went into Hereford every Saturday on the bus with Danny, and sometimes they cycled in on their own, if the weather wasn't absolutely foul.

Either way, when they'd finished at church, or in the library, Alice always wanted to look around the clothes shops or mooch around the market – not that there was ever that much to see. 'When this blasted war is over, I'm going to have a dress for every day of the week,' Alice declared one day.

Lizzie thought there were much better ways of spending money, but then she reminded herself of all Rosamund's cast-off dresses she had lining her wardrobe. And for some time to come, she guessed, for she was still small for her age and fine-boned, while Rosamund was much bigger and had a fuller figure. It didn't seem fair that Alice, who loved fashion and pretty clothes, had never worn one thing that had looked newish or had any shape to it all the time Lizzie had known her, so she followed her around the clothes stores and let her have her dreams.

Kathy came down for a few days in the summer holidays of 1943 with Padraic, but it could hardly be judged a success. Lizzie and Danny were keen to see the little boy who'd been just a baby when they'd left home, and were taken at first by the attractive chattering three-year-old. He was not fazed by the children introduced as his brother and sister, nor intimidated by the splendour of the Barraclough house, being too young to understand affluence, but in his short life little had been denied him and he didn't understand the word no. He thought the world revolved around him and everything was his for the taking, and Kathy, who had through necessity allowed Molly to have the rearing of her small son, was not used to dealing with his tantrums.

They left after two days. Kathy was exhausted, Padraic mutinous and Danny and Lizzie embarrassed by Padraic's behaviour and puzzled by Kathy's response to it. Why, Lizzie wondered, hadn't she scooped up the scarlet-faced screaming child with his flailing arms and thrashing legs and spanked him to teach him better manners, like she'd have done to her or Dan if they'd behaved so badly?

Sophie and Millie, who'd looked forward to meeting the youngest O'Malley and had used the entire month's sugar ration to make tempting delicacies for him to enjoy, were disappointed and dismayed. 'A handsome child,' Sophie remarked, returning home after running Kathy back to the station. 'Very like our Elizabeth in looks.'

'Well, handsome is as handsome does,' Millie said grimly. 'That child is spoiled rotten. Spare the rod and spoil the child, they say, and by God, you can see the sense of it.'

Kathy knew what they all thought. The visit had been a failure and she felt a failure too. How was it, she asked herself, that she, a mature adult, was unable to cope with a three-year-old child? The train rumbled on and she had no answers, while Padraic, thumb in his mouth, slept on her knee and looked totally angelic.

A lot of changes happened to Lizzie's body a couple of months after her twelfth birthday, and some of them frightened her. At first she noticed hair growing in the private place between her legs and then in little tufts under her arms, and added to this, there were lumps on her chest where once it had been flat. For all the lack of privacy the family had had in the back-to-back home, Lizzie had never, ever seen a naked adult, neither man nor woman, so she didn't know whether it was normal to have hair on your body or not. And, she thought, it wasn't something you could go round asking, because if it wasn't normal then the person you asked would know you were odd.

For months she worried about things and made sure no one, not even Danny, saw her completely undressed, and then, just as 1943 was drawing to a close, she started to have griping pains in her stomach. They'd last a day or two and then go away, to return a few weeks later. Lizzie couldn't understand it – she'd never suffered from stomach aches before – and when she complained to Millie, she said vaguely it was just her age.

Lizzie couldn't understand why Millie and Sophie were not more concerned, and thought she was probably making a fuss over nothing. She told herself she'd feel much better when the warmer weather came, and she looked forward to the spring of 1944.

Kathy was also looking forward to the warmer weather, as day after day dawned grey and dull and cold. At least she had her weekly visit to the cinema to keep her going. But one evening in mid-February, while she and Maggie were making their way up the aisle in the dim lighting at the end of the film, she was literally knocked to the ground by an American serviceman who'd cannoned into her after falling over his mate's feet. 'Oh, gee, lady, I'm real sorry,' he cried. 'Here, let me help you up. Oh, gee, my folks are always saying how clumsy I am.'

Despite the American accent, the man's voice was deep and warm-sounding, pleasing to the ear, Kathy thought, as she lay in an untidy heap at his feet. He put out an arm to help her up, and as she struggled to her feet, she found herself looking into the darkest-brown eyes she'd ever seen. For a second or two they stood staring at one another. Kathy felt a little dazed. She could never remember being so affected by a man's presence before.

At last he spoke and broke the silence. 'Are you sure you're OK?'

'I'm grand,' Kathy said. 'Really, I didn't hurt myself at all.'

'I love your accent,' the man said. 'Are you Irish?'

'Well, I was born there,' Kathy said. 'I've lived here years, but our parents are Irish.'

221

'Come on, Kath,' Maggie said impatiently. 'We'll be locked in in a minute.'

Kathy tore her gaze from the American and saw that the cinema was emptying fast. Maggie linked her arm and they made their way to the exit. 'Talk about being bowled over by a man, eh, Kath?' Maggie said.

Aye indeed, Kathy thought, but didn't say it aloud.

Her heart was thudding against her ribs and her mouth had suddenly become unaccountably dry, and she told herself not to be so stupid. She was glad when they reached the street, but surprised to find the two Americans still close behind them. 'Let me make it up to you,' the one who'd knocked her over said, looking directly at Kathy. 'My name is Doug Howister, and this is my friend Phil Martin, and we'd sure like to take you two ladies for a drink.'

'There's no need, really. I'm fine. We're both fine,' Kathy said.

'A coffee then?' Doug persisted, remembering the talk they'd all had before they came to England about things to say or not to say to avoid giving offence. He remembered being told that nice English women did not frequent bars. 'Do you have a drug store around here?' he said. 'Maybe you call them coffee bars?'

'No, really, we must go home,' Kathy said firmly.

Maggie couldn't understand her sister. Here was an attractive American serviceman offering to take them for a drink, and she was refusing it. Maggie herself would have loved to have a drink. She'd not been in a pub since Con had left, because women who went in on their own were frowned on, but Kathy never asked her what she wanted. Now here was an invitation to add a little spice to their dull, mundane lives. It wasn't as if the Americans weren't respectable-looking or were trying to pick them up, for heaven's sake. She was sure they were only being friendly, for he'd invited the two of them and anyone could see they both wore wedding rings. Suddenly she was sick of Kathy deciding everything they bloody well did. 'Come on, Kath,' she said. 'Don't be such a stick-in-the-mud.' She smiled at the two men and added, 'I don't know about Kathy, but I'd love a drink.'

'We need to be getting home, we have work tomorrow,' Kathy said testily.

'The night's young,' Doug insisted.

'Just the one drink,' his friend Phil put in. 'And then we'll walk you to your doors.'

'Oh, go on, Kath,' Maggie pleaded.

Kathy looked at them all watching her, waiting for her answer. Then her eyes met those of Doug Howister. He smiled, and her heart turned a somersault and her legs felt suddenly very weak. Oh God, this is madness, she cried to herself, and though she knew it was far from wise, she found herself saying, 'Just one drink then.'

They went to The Trees public house on Bristol Street, not The Bell or the Sun on Bell Barn Road where they might meet people they knew, and while Kathy sipped her sweet sherry she told Doug all about herself. In case he should get the wrong idea, she started with her family: Barry away fighting, her older children evacuated to Hereford and Padraic minded by her mother-in-law while she worked with her sister Maggie at Lucas's.

Doug sipped the watery English beer that was never really cold enough and that he didn't like much, but he said nothing about it and just listened to Kathy talk. It was as if he'd been waiting all his life for this beautiful woman, with her deep-brown eyes and expressive face. He'd had a fair few dalliances in his life, but none of them had meant anything. This time he'd lost his heart, and to a woman already spoken for. Suddenly it got too uncomfortable to sit beside her any longer, feeling as he did, and he got up and went over to the bar. When he returned with a tray of drinks, Kathy said, 'And what about you? All I've done is talk about myself.'

'What do you want to know?'

'Well, where are you from and where are you stationed? Those sort of things, you know,' Kathy said.

Doug met Phil's eyes and said, 'Well, Phil and I are from Texas and we both joined up after Pearl Harbor was bombed.'

'Have you been in England since?' Maggie asked.

'No, ma'am,' Phil said. 'After training we were sent to a place called Guadalcanal.'

'Guadalcanal?' Kathy said, testing the word on her tongue. 'I've never heard of it.'

'Few had till recently,' Doug said. 'The Japs were island-hopping. If they'd got as far as New Guinea and built an airstrip there, they could have attacked the supply routes between Australia and the States. Obviously they had to be stopped.'

'But then how come you're here in England?' Maggie said.

'We were shipped home again at the beginning of forty-four. Guadalcanal was holding out,' Doug said. 'Phil and I both had quite severe bouts of malaria, and anyway they wanted us over here for the big push when it comes.'

'And it can't come early enough for me,' Maggie said fervently. 'Where in Birmingham are you stationed?'

'We're sharing the base at Castle Bromwich aerodrome,' Doug said. 'It's not working at full capacity now and our commanding officers don't expect us to be here long.'

'But Castle Bromwich is miles from Edgbaston,' Maggie cried.

Doug and Phil exchanged an amused glance and then Phil said, 'Not by American standards it isn't. You Brits think a few miles is a distance. We didn't set out to come to Edgbaston, if that's what this place is called. We came into

224

Birmingham to see if we could find better night life than we have around the camp. We found nothing we really fancied and decided to walk around to explore the area a little, and found ourselves outside that cinema where we met you. *Casablanca* was on, and because we'd already seen it while we were convalescing back home, I guess it made us both kinda homesick, and so we went in and, well, here we are.'

Doug sat silent, many thoughts pouring through his head as he let Phil talk without really listening. He was watching Kathy, thinking how he would love to hold her in his arms, but he also knew that she would not be the sort of woman to fool around with other men as many did, using wartime as an excuse.

Kathy felt Doug's eyes upon her, boring into her, and wondered what was the matter with him. She tried to ignore him and concentrate on Phil, who she found very amusing and not a bit disturbing, and yet she couldn't be unaware of the man beside her. 'Do . . . do you and your sister come to the pictures every week?' Doug asked at last, almost tentatively.

Before she had time to voice a denial, Maggie cried, 'You bet, we look forward to it, don't we, Kath?' She didn't wait for her sister's reply, but went on: 'We decided a while ago to give ourselves a treat. After all, we work hard and both of us have resident baby-sitters, so we thought we may as well.'

'Hey, then maybe we'll meet up with you again some time?' suggested Phil.

'You just might,' Maggie said. She was finishing her second sherry and feeling slightly reckless, and she went on, 'We'll look out for you.'

No we won't, Kathy thought, it would be madness. Here's me sitting with a man who stirs me in a way no man but my husband should and, God forgive me, I'm enjoying it. She made some noncommittal remark to her sister and got to her feet quickly. 'We . . . we really must be off now,' she said. 'Thank you so much for the drinks. I've . . . I've enjoyed it and . . . and I'm sure my sister has.'

'Oh, Kathy,' cried Maggie, unwilling to let the night to end. 'Let's just have one more drink.'

'I think you've had enough,' said Kathy. 'And you know we must be up early tomorrow.'

Maggie gave a sigh and got to her feet giggling, for the two sherries had gone to her head, and Kathy went on, 'See, if I let you have another, we'd have to carry you out.'

They were all laughing together as they left the pub. Kathy had been careful to position herself as far from Doug as possible. "We'll see you home,' he said, once they were outside.

'No, no,' Kathy protested. 'There's no need for that.'

'There's every need,' Doug said. 'I always see a lady home, and your sister maybe could do with assistance?'

Maggie certainly was tipsy, Kathy thought, watching her unsteady gait and the silly grin on her face. 'She'll be all right,' she said. 'She's not used to alcohol, that's all. I'll see her home.'

'But I insist.'

'No,' Kathy said firmly. 'If you walked along with us, it could easily be misunderstood. We're only a stop away from home anyway. Thanks again for a really nice evening.'

'Aye, that's right, thanks again,' said Maggie, stumbling over her own feet as she came towards them and laughing at her efforts. Even Kathy had to smile, though she thought her sister would probably have a thick head in the morning. 'Come on,' she said, holding out her arm. 'Catch hold of me before you fall over altogether.'

'Then we might meet again some time?' Doug persisted.

Kathy didn't answer. Instead she said, 'Goodbye, and thanks again. I've enjoyed it,' then gave a slight nod and began walking purposefully away, supporting Maggie as she went.

'Goodnight, ladies,' Kathy heard one of them call, but she didn't turn around or call back, but waved her hand vaguely and carried on up the street.

All their unsteady way home, Maggie talked, and Kathy was glad she needed no answers, because she'd have been too confused to reply.

Later she tried to make sense of it all, but it made no sense at all, and she told herself it was ridiculous to fantasise about the man who had so affected her and make something out of nothing.

She loved Barry – she'd known him all her life and loved him almost as long, and that was real love, not the desire that flowed through her at the American's touch, or the look in his deep-brown eyes. God, even the memory of it made her gasp.

'Carnal desire', the priests would call it, 'sins of the flesh', but unbidden the image came into her mind of Doug holding her fast against him, his lips upon hers, his hands on her body. 'Stop it,' she told herself, shutting out the images.

They'd done nothing wrong, and yet Kathy knew she would have liked for it to have gone further, and so would the American, she'd sensed that. She'd thought that feelings for other men stopped on marriage, and she could honestly say that throughout her courtship and marriage she'd never wanted any other man. But Barry had been away for so long, and she was a sexually healthy woman, and though she'd missed the physical side of the marriage in the beginning, she had such a busy life now, she'd pushed it to the back of her mind.

Maybe that was it. She'd denied the desire she still had for sexual fulfilment, and the first time she met someone who wasn't familiar, related to her, or a workmate or neighbour, she'd felt unnatural urges for him. All she had to do was keep away and that would be that. She knew she'd have to confess, though, to the sin of lust; the thought was as bad as the deed, the Church's teaching was clear, and she couldn't risk such a mortal sin on her soul.

The next week she told Maggie she was too tired to go to the cinema, and the week after that she claimed she had a headache. Maggie was bitterly disappointed and Kathy felt guilty; it was hardly Maggie's fault that she fancied an American soldier. They might not even still be in Britain, she reasoned by the end of the second week, they could easily have been shipped out, and she decided she couldn't spend her life cooped up inside the house. She suggested they try the ABC on Bristol Road as a change, and though Maggie was puzzled she agreed readily. 'Let's get out quick,' she urged as Kathy scurried around getting ready. 'Bridie was in on Mammy today complaining we've never invited her along with us.'

'Why would we?' Kathy asked. 'She's always snapping the head off us both.'

'I know that,' Maggie agreed. 'Mind, she does that with anyone. Anyway, she says Sheelagh's well old enough to give an eye to young Matt now and she never gets past the door.'

Kathy felt a pang of guilt and Maggie, seeing it flit over her face, said sharply, 'Don't you be feeling sorry for her now, our Kath, because if you ask her out with us, I'll not be going.'

Kathy had no real desire to ask Bridie out with them anyway, and she laughed and said, 'OK. It will be just the two of us.'

'Unless we meet the Americans again,' Maggie said with a giggle.

'Why would we?'

'Well, we could, that's all. We did that one time.'

'That was at the Broadway.'

'Aye, well, there's no law saying they couldn't fancy a change too. Or perhaps we might meet other servicemen who might take a shine to us both.'

'Maggie, for goodness' sake!' Kathy snapped.

'I'm only joking,' Maggie said. 'What are you getting all hot and bothered about? We never see many men now except the old or very young, and it was nice to be chatted up and taken for a drink by two GIs. There was no harm in it.'

Guilt made Kathy say, 'Yes there was. We shouldn't have gone.' She stopped suddenly, aware that her face was hot, and probably red, and she was panting as if she were out of breath.

However, Maggie knew her sister well and could recognise guilt when she saw it. So that was it, she thought, Kath was attracted to one of the GIs. She knew which one, it would be Doug Howister and, thinking back, he hadn't been able to keep his eyes off her sister all night. Well, well, well. Aloud she said, 'Don't bite my head off, Kath.'

'Oh, I'm sorry,' Kathy said wearily. 'Let's just go to the pictures if we're going at all.' And Maggie stepped into the street and said nothing more.

Maybe it was the conversation Kathy had with her sister, or maybe the sloppy romance they'd watched at the cinema, but that night Kathy had a dream. She dreamt she lay in a lush green field, such as those she'd seen from the train to Hereford, and the sun shone down and warmed her naked body. Doug Howister lay beside her also naked, and it didn't feel strange, but right. He pressed his lips upon hers and she parted them, and his tongue sent shafts of desire through her body. His hands caressed her all over while they kissed, and then he broke away and kissed her neck, her throat, her breasts. She cried out, calling his name, and he stroked her gently, and then he was kissing her belly while his hands slipped between her legs, and she groaned with pleasure and pulled Doug towards her as a strange ringing began in her ears.

'Kath, Kath, the alarm, girl!' Molly's voice and elbow prodded her awake, and she felt tears of disappointment fill her eyes as she realised she was in bed with Molly and the alarm was heralding the start of another day.

That was only the beginning, and where once the Luftwaffe had disturbed her sleep, now it was strange erotic dreams that upset her slumber. And yet she wondered at them, because the sex she'd enjoyed with Barry had been just that, pure sex. He didn't tantalise, or tease, or send her into a wild frenzy kissing her all over. His fingers seldom caressed her breasts or her stomach or her . . . What in God's name was the matter with her, thinking this way? Barry didn't need to do those things now, she told herself firmly; they were married, and that sort of thing stopped there.

Sex between a married couple was for the procreation of children and that was all, the Church told you that, and Kathy had often felt guilty that she enjoyed it as much as she did. In fact the times when Barry had been too hasty and lay spent and satisfied beside her while she was still unfulfilled and frustrated to the point of tears, she'd told herself it was judgement on her as she wasn't supposed to enjoy it. No woman of her acquaintance ever spoke of enjoying sex.

She'd been having the dreams for almost two weeks when she and Maggie had the afternoon off and went to visit a nursery school in Rea Street, not far from their homes, to see if places could be found for their sons. Tim and Padraic were both getting too much for their grandmothers, for the bombed ruins opposite their houses drew them like a magnet and yet they were far too dangerous for little boys not yet

230

four years old to play on. They were also uncomfortably close to Bristol Street, with all its traffic, and both Kathy and Maggie were worried for their safely.

Kathy was anxious to get a place for Padraic for another reason. She'd tried to talk to Molly about spoiling the child, but it had fallen on deaf ears. Molly could see no wrong in her grandson and no harm in giving in to him. If he had a place at the nursery it would remove him from her influence as well as keeping him safe. Places were limited, but some of the women at the factory had told Kathy that children with mothers on war work had priority. And so it would seem, for both children were promised a place after the Easter holidays, which had already begun.

'That's a load off my mind anyway,' Kathy said as they walked back home, the two boys skipping between them.

'Aye, and it will be good for them too.'

'Molly's just not up to it any more,' Kathy said. 'God, her legs are like balloons some nights, and Padraic has her run ragged.'

'Mammy gets tired too,' Maggie admitted. 'It's worse when Daddy's sick, like he is at the moment. And isn't he the world's worst invalid? God, he's worse than one of the weans.'

'All men are,' Kathy said, and added, 'Are you going straight home now? It's so nice to have some time off. I hardly ever get Padraic on my own. I thought we might take these two to Calthorpe Park for a wee while.'

'I can't,' Maggie said. 'I promised to go straight back. Mammy was up half the night with Daddy and she looks awful. I want to persuade her to have a wee lie-down.' She glanced at her sister and said, 'It would help if you'd take the wee fellow out of the way for an hour or two.'

'I will surely,' Kathy said, and holding her son with one hand and her nephew with the other, she set off.

It was as she was pushing both boys on the swings that she heard the voice in her ear. 'So we meet again, Kathy O'Malley.'

Kathy couldn't believe it. She'd dreamt about this man for almost a fortnight, and now here he was again, miles from his base, as if she was fated to meet him. 'What are you doing here?' she asked.

Looking for you, Doug might have said. After their first meeting he'd dragged Phil out night after night to the Broadway in an effort to see Kathy again. Phil had eventually told him to back off. 'She's married, man, and trying to avoid you I'd say.'

Doug knew Phil was probably right. So why, when he'd had a few hours' leave, had he headed straight for Edgbaston and toured the area looking for a woman with a captivating face and raven-black hair? Then, wearied by walking the streets, he'd slipped into the park to rest for a while before returning to camp, and there she was before him. He shrugged. 'Just walking around,' he said. 'Getting the feel of the place.'

Kathy wondered if he'd been looking for her, but why should he? Anyway, she'd not told him where she lived, and she wasn't going to; it wouldn't be safe. They stood silent, just staring at one another, till suddenly Padraic called, 'Push us again, Mammy,' and she turned her attention to the children, whose swings were now just swaying gently backwards and forwards.

'Here, let me,' Doug said. Stepping forward, he gave Padraic's swing a gigantic shove.

'And Tim,' Padraic said. 'We like to swing together.'

'Tim's my nephew,' Kathy said. 'Maggie's son. We both cadged an afternoon off to try and get the boys into a nursery school after Easter, and it seemed a pity to waste such a lovely spring day.'

232

'I agree,' Doug said, pushing Tim as hard as his cousin. 'Didn't your sister come to the park with you?'

'No, she had to go home, my father's ill.'

And where's home, Kathy? He wanted to ask the question, but knew he had no right to. And then there was no time, for the children were clamouring for attention.

Much later, after Doug had pushed them so high on the swings they'd squealed with delight, spun them so fast on the roundabout they were both dizzy, placed them on the slide their mother had forbidden them to climb on and watched them swoop down at speed, he sat beside Kathy on the grass and watched the two cousins cavorting together. 'They're fine boys,' Doug said rather breathlessly. 'I bet your husband's proud of his son.'

'Barry's never even seen him. Nor has Maggie's husband Con seen Tim,' Kathy said. 'They'd both joined their units after a few weeks' leave to get over Dunkirk before our sons were born and have been away ever since. Barry had a longer leave than the others because he was injured.' She stopped and took a deep breath before she went on. 'My eldest brother Pat was killed.'

Doug's heart turned over at the anguished look on Kathy's face. He gave her hand a squeeze and said, 'I've got two younger brothers back home and I hope this little lot's over before they get sucked in. I don't know how I'd feel if anything happened to them. I've never experienced anyone dying that was close to me. It must have been awful losing your brother.'

Kathy had to swallow the lump in her throat before she was able to say, 'It's hard for all of us, not even to have a grave to visit, you know, and no real funeral or anything.'

'Ah, Kathy, don't cry.'

Kathy hadn't been aware she was crying till Doug spoke, but once she started, she couldn't stop. Doug fought with

233

himself for just a moment or two before his arms went around her shaking shoulders, and she buried her head in his chest and struggled to control herself.

When eventually she was quiet, she lay in the circle of Doug's arm, feeling weak with all the emotion brought to the fore. Then she pulled away slowly and unwillingly, and apologised while she wiped her eyes with a hanky, glad that neither Padraic nor Tim had noticed her tears.

By the time the boys joined them, she was feeling calmer altogether, but still Doug leapt to his feet and began wrestling with them on the grass. Kathy knew he was allowing her time to compose herself, and was grateful. For a little while she watched them, smiling, as they rolled about on the grass, the two young boys attacking Doug again and again until he said, 'We need a ball. Have either of you two got a ball?' The boys shook their heads sadly.

Kathy stared at him, suddenly angry. She wondered how the hell he thought she could get hold of a ball in austere Britain, five years into a world war, when every bit of rubber seemed to be needed for the war effort. 'No,' she said stiffly. 'They haven't.'

Immediately, Doug realised his mistake. 'Okay,' he said. 'I guess I goofed. There's hardly enough food in the shops, and what there is is bloody rationed. I suppose non-essentials like footballs aren't considered important to the nation's survival, right?'

Kathy smiled despite herself. 'Something like that,' she said.

'I'll get one from the camp,' Doug promised. 'We have plenty, and every little boy needs a football.'

'That's very kind of you, but . . .'

'Kind be damned. I'd like a kick-about myself. Come on, when will you be back here?'

'Oh, I don't know.'

'Well, I'm on duty the next two days, but I'm off on Saturday. Do you work Saturdays?'

'We do sometimes, yes, but not this week,' Kathy admitted. She wondered if it were wise to meet him. She wanted to, but was worried because she felt attracted to him. The boys would be thrilled to bits with the football, though, and what harm could it do? She could always bring Maggie with her to be on the safe side. So she smiled at Doug Howister and said, 'Yes, I'd like that. Maggie and I could be here about two o'clock.'

'That would be just about perfect,' Doug said, so happy he felt like a teenager. He leant forward and kissed Kathy on the cheek, and instantly her face flushed again. Doug chuckled, and the sound gave Kathy an excited thrill. She floated home, listening with half an ear to the children's chatter, and remembering how Doug's eyes sparkled and how the skin creased around them, and his sensual mouth and very white teeth, and she knew she longed to see him again.

FOURTEEN

Lizzie had never dreamt she could be so unhappy in Hereford, and it was because David and Aunt Sophie were constantly arguing. They'd been at it since David had come home from school for the Easter vacation. She'd heard them and it had frightened her. 'I'm seventeen years old,' David had said loudly. 'Seventeen, and I've done nothing in this war but skulk away at school.'

'Don't be ridiculous,' Sophie had said. 'You have your education to finish.'

'Education be damned,' David had snapped, and Lizzie's eyes had opened wider. Never had she heard David use a bad word, and certainly not in front of his mother, for whom he had always showed infinite respect.

But that respect seemed to have gone, for David went on, 'I've used my wealth and position to hide away and let others fight for me. How d'you think that makes me feel?'

'You're being ridiculous.'

'I am not, and don't treat me like a bloody child. But then that's how you see me still, isn't it?'

'Don't you dare talk to me like that.'

'Oh, Mother!' David cried, and peeping through the

236

sittingroom door, Lizzie saw him run his fingers through his hair agitatedly. 'There's a war on and you are shocked by how I speak to you. There are worse things, and one of them is how I feel, but does that matter a jot to you?'

'David, how can you say that? You and Chris are my life.'

'I don't want to be your life,' David said. 'I want to be given the chance to live mine.'

'By leaving school?'

'Yes, just that. It would only be a postponement, like Chris's university place.' Sophie was silent, and David went on, 'How d'you think I feel when I meet people in the village who've lost sons or fathers? I mean, I avoid old Sam Purser, I just can't imagine how it feels to have raised three sons and lost them all . . .' He shook his head and then said, 'It's a bloody crying shame. He's a broken man and then he sees me hale and hearty and knows I probably haven't seen hide nor hair of even one bomb. There might as well be no war on as far as I'm concerned.'

Sophie bit her lip and wondered where her compliant child had gone. The angry young man before her bore no resemblance to the David of the previous year. But concern for his safety caused her to snap sarcastically, 'I suppose you think your not returning to school will make Sam Purser and his wife feel better about the loss of their sons? What do you intend to do, pray, learn to milk a cow, collect salvage for making Spitfires, or knit balaclavas for the troops?'

David's face was suffused with rage, and the look he turned on his mother was so full of hate that she took a step backwards, but his words when he spoke were quiet and cold, like drops of ice in the room. 'I've never realised before what a patronising old bugger you are. For your information, Mother, I intend to enlist, and so do John Carruthers and Philip Bletchley.'

237

Sophie was struck dumb. She didn't forbid David to talk to her in that way, or argue that he was too young to enlist, for she knew that neither approach would be of any use. She had a throbbing pain in the side of her head, and suddenly it was all too much for her, and with a glare at David she walked from the room without another word.

Lizzie, who'd been cowering in the hall while the row between Sophie and David had been going on in the small sitting room, had retreated to the kitchen when she saw Sophie cross the room. Now she looked round uncertainly, knowing that if Sophie came in here she'd realise that Lizzie had heard everything. Maybe she'd think she'd come down on purpose to listen, but she hadn't, she'd wanted a hot drink and a couple of aspirins to help her cope with the pains in her stomach.

She crept to the door and peeped out. Sophie, she saw, had mounted the stairs, but David was still in the sitting room. As she watched, half hidden by the door, he came out, strode purposefully along the passage, took a coat from the cloakroom and slammed out of the front door.

Lizzie felt immeasurably sad that two people she loved had quarrelled so badly. She also felt lonely all of a sudden, and the pains in her stomach were the worst yet. Sobbing to herself, she made a cup of tea, took two aspirins from the first-aid box Millie kept in the kitchen and went back upstairs.

In the lavatory, she found things were worse than she'd feared, for her knickers were covered in blood. Thoroughly frightened, she huddled under the blankets in bed and trembled. Something terrible was happening to her and there was no one to tell. Certainly not Aunt Sophie, nursing her hurt feelings in the bedroom; nor David, stamping the bad humour out of him; nor Millie away in Hereford shopping. She wished her mammy was there; she wanted Kathy as she'd never wanted her before, and she felt very sorry for herself indeed.

That was how Millie found her. She'd already had a run-in with David, who'd snapped her head off, and Sophie had retired to bed with a headache, so Millie knew the two had had another row. She'd seen Danny playing cricket in the village, but went in search of Lizzie and found her cocooned in her bed.

'What is it, pet?' she said, catching sight of her white, tear-stained face peeping over the blankets.

'Oh, Millie,' cried Lizzie, 'I think I'm dying.'

Millie laughed, but gently, and put her arms around Lizzie. 'Not yet, I hope,' she said

'But . . . but you don't understand,' Lizzie said, spluttering through her tears. 'I'm bleeding, down below, you know.'

And then Millie understood, and she was annoyed that Sophie had told Lizzie nothing. She'd advised her to when Lizzie began having stomach pains, and had even offered to do it herself, but Sophie said she'd deal with it. However, she'd been too bothered about David since Christmas to notice the changes happening to Lizzie's body, and now it had caused the girl fear and unhappiness.

Millie sat on the bed and told Lizzie that the bleeding would happen once a month and showed that she was becoming a woman, and then brought her the white linen pads that she would fasten to her vest with safety pins and that had to be soaked daily in the bucket Millie would leave ready. Then she made her comfortable and brought her up another cup of tea, feather-light scones with butter and jam and a hot-water bottle for her stomach, and when she looked in an hour later, Lizzie was fast asleep. Millie wished all problems were solved so easily, for once Lizzie knew she wasn't dying and that this sort of thing would happen every month and every woman had to cope with it, she stopped being frightened.

The following day she went over to see Alice, glad to be out of the house, where David and Sophie continued to spit at each other. Eventually David told his mother he wished to go back to school early, and Sophie did not argue. 'Fine,' she said. 'Your things are ready. We'll get you packed and I'll drive you in tomorrow.'

Even Danny and Lizzie didn't care. David hadn't bothered much with them that holiday, and his unpredictable temper and glowering face had meant they hadn't approached him either. As Lizzie watched Sophie and David setting off for the station, she said to Millie, 'I don't think I want to grow up, Millie.'

'Nothing you can do about that, little lass,' Millie said. 'You just enjoy every day that comes and don't fret about growing up, or any other thing, because it happens whether we worry about it or not.'

There was no way Kathy could have kept meeting Doug Howister a secret from her family even had she wanted to, for Padraic had spilled the beans almost before he was through the door. 'He was the American we met that time at the pictures a few weeks ago,' Kathy said. 'The one who knocked me flying. You mind I told you of it at the time?'

'Oh, aye,' Molly said. 'Fancy meeting him again like that.'

'Aye,' said Kathy, hoping and praying she wouldn't blush. 'He made a lot of fuss of the boys. Maggie says she thinks they're homesick.'

'Oh, to be sure, I'm certain many of those over here miss their own fireside.'

'I just met him by chance,' Kathy went on. 'He said he'll try and get a ball for the lads from the camp and if I'm at the park Saturday afternoon he'll give it to me.'

'He must be a kind man, so he must,' Molly said. 'Tim and Padraic would love to have a ball, I know.'

Maggie was a little more discerning than the innocent Molly. 'I think that man fancies you.'

'Don't be so ridiculous. It was the children he paid more attention to,' Kathy said, but she didn't mention the fact that she'd cried in his arms.

'Could be a front,' Maggie said impishly, and then, at the look on her sister's face, added, 'Joke, Kath, it was a joke.'

'A very poor one.'

'Look, all I'm saying is be careful. He's attractive, and whatever you say, he likes you. I saw him looking at you in the pub. I was too tipsy to take it in at the time, but I realised it afterwards.'

'I think you're imagining it,' Kathy said.

'No I'm not,' Maggie said firmly. 'You know I'm not, and . . .' There she hesitated, knowing Kathy might be really cross with her, but it needed to be said. 'And I'm not altogether convinced you're not attracted to him too.'

Now Kathy did blush, and it told its own tale. She wanted to deny what her sister had suggested, but knew that if she was to do so she wouldn't be believed, not now.

'Oh, Kath, it's nothing,' Maggie cried. 'It's just that we've been apart from our menfolk for far too long.'

'I know,' Kathy said miserably. 'But I feel so alive when I'm with him, as if all my body is tingling, you know.'

Maggie knew only too well. 'You need to keep away from him, Kath.'

'He wants us to meet him in the park on Saturday afternoon. He's bringing a ball for the boys to play with.'

'Did he ask for both of us to be there?'

'Well, no, no he didn't, but . . .'

'I can't go, Kathy, I'm expected at Con's parents for the day.'

'Oh, Maggie!'

'It's only fair. They see little enough of me and even less of Tim, and he is their grandson too, and Carmel's here on Saturdays to give Mam a hand.'

'I know, it's just . . .' Kathy spread her hands out helplessly.

'Will you go?' Maggie asked.

'I must,' Kathy said. 'I can't leave him just standing there. Anyway, I'll have Padraic with me; nothing could possibly happen.'

And it really seemed that way. Saturday was fine but with the slight chill of an English spring. Doug was waiting for them at the park entrance, and Padraic was enchanted by the ball. 'Maggie couldn't come,' Kathy explained breathlessly as if she'd been running. 'She had other plans.'

Doug's face showed neither disappointment nor relief. Instead he smiled and said, 'I'm glad you both came.' Then he bent to Padraic. 'Come on then, let's see what you're made of.'

Kath watched them running through the park, dribbling the ball between them, with a smile on her face. They looked so right together, and with their dark-brown eyes, people might even assume they were father and son. When Kathy caught up with them, she heard Doug saying, 'Now, if you were an American boy, I'd be teaching you baseball, or American football, but I must say I've got kinda keen on this soccer since I've been here.'

Padraic listened to every word as if he was bewitched. Doug was the first man who had ever played with him. His grandad and Uncle Sid got too breathless to play boisterous games, and Padraic loved the attention of this strong, tall American who could kick a ball with him one minute and toss him high into the air the next.

Padraic showed none of his sullen side to Doug, and there were no tantrums, and Kathy realised that he needed a father's firm but loving hand. He wasn't the only one;

many of the women complained the children had gone wild, especially the boys. That was another reason why Kathy was glad Lizzie and Danny were out of it.

Suddenly Doug was sitting on the grass beside her. 'Penny for your thoughts,' he said. 'Isn't that what you British say?'

'They're not worth a penny,' Kathy answered. 'I was just thinking of the children – not Padraic, but the two I have in Hereford.'

'I expect you miss them.'

'All the time,' Kathy said. 'I've been to see them, and they're happy and with lovely people, but they're my children and every year they're growing further away from me. I mean, my daughter became a woman the other day, you know?' Kathy said, flustered as she realised she was discussing an intimate and personal subject with a man.

Doug was confused by her embarrassment; after all, she'd had three children, but despite that there was a simplicity, a naivety about Kathy that he found appealing. 'I understand,' he said.

'Well, I hadn't told her,' Kathy said bleakly. 'I mean, when she went away she was nine years old, and it isn't the sort of thing to tell a child of that age, nor yet put in a letter, and the times I've been down it's never occurred to me. Someone else had to deal with it and then write and tell me, her mother.'

Doug felt for Kathy. 'Couldn't you bring them back home now?' he suggested.

'Oh, if only I could,' Kathy cried. 'But how can I?' She looked Doug full in the face and went on, 'I live in a back-to-back house. I don't know if you have such things in America, but my house consists of a cellar kitchen, a living room, one bedroom and an attic room. In nineteen forty, my mother-in-law and her neighbours were bombed out of their houses and have lived with me ever since. Now my mother-in-law sleeps

243

in the bed I once shared with Barry, and we have Padraic on a mattress on the floor. Sid and Enid and their two children sleep in the attic. It was all right while they were all weans, but now Kenny is seventeen and Barbara fifteen, the sleeping pattern has changed. Kenny sleeps with his father in the one bed and Barbara with her mother in the other one.'

She stopped, looked up at Doug and asked, 'How could I fit in my daughter who's going on for thirteen and my ten-year-old son? I don't even know what I'm going to do when Barry eventually comes home. It's a bloody awful war, Doug. I wish it were over, but when it is, and all the men arrive back, it will cause further problems, because I'm not the only woman who has more than one family living with them.'

Doug felt immensely sorry for Kathy and the thousands like her, but knew it wouldn't help to say so. Instead he turned his attention to Padraic. As the proud owner of a football, he was invited to join the older boys on the grass, and as Doug watched him run around, he wished for the time when children like Padraic could grow up in peace. He said to Kathy, 'I hope it's soon over too. I think you've all suffered enough, but it won't be long now; something big's happening. Half the camp has already gone.'

'Gone where?'

'South, I suppose,' Doug said. 'I mean, that's where it will come from.'

'What? Invasion?'

'What else?'

'Oh God, another Dunkirk!'

'No, no,' Doug assured her. 'This time it will be better thought out. They'll have learnt from Dunkirk, they'll be better prepared.'

'And so will the Germans,' Kathy snapped. 'Whichever way you look at it, there will be great loss of life, won't there? I mean, they'll hardly welcome you with open arms.'

'I suppose,' Doug said. 'But it's how it must be. This war can't just limp along year after year, and don't forget, people are dying daily anyway in battles and skirmishes. Better this one massive onslaught.'

Kathy wasn't so sure, and was silent thinking of the other invasion in 1940 that had gone so terribly wrong. She remembered 1939, when the men had gone off in a mood of patriotic optimism. Most had thought the war would be over by Christmas; only Barry, knowing more of the political situation, thought differently, and told Kathy so. But she wondered if even he had imagined a war lasting five years plus, a war where he'd be separated from his home and children for such a long time.

She gave a huge sigh, and Doug covered her hand with his and said, 'Don't be sad, Kathy. I can't bear to think of you sad.'

The electric touch of Doug's hand and his very nearness brought a weakness to Kathy's limbs. She felt tears pricking behind her eyes and forced herself to speak almost harshly as she pulled her hand away. 'Don't waste your pity. I'm only one of many.'

Doug reclaimed her hand and said, firmly, 'It's not pity, just tremendous admiration for you and all those like you. I understand how you get kinda upset at times, but I don't like to see it. I wish I could make things better for you.'

He dropped her hand suddenly, gripped his arms around his knees to stop himself folding Kathy in his arms and looked out across the park.

England in springtime, he thought, good old England, often talked about at home but never visited until the war years. He'd grown fond of the country in the weeks he'd been here, and had developed an admiration for the British people and an anger at what they had suffered. And now he had met Kathy O'Malley, and it mattered even more to him.

Kathy sat near Doug, but was careful not to touch him, and watched his face. Eventually he said, 'I think a lot of you, Kathy, I have done almost from the moment I sent you flying in the cinema, and I know you feel something for me . . .'

'Don't be ridiculous,' Kathy cried. 'That's nonsense, and . . .'

Doug smiled. 'Deny it all you like, but it's there, the love in your eyes and what happens when our eyes meet. When I think of you I go weak at the knees, and I'd like to bet it's the same for you.'

Oh yes, Kathy could have said. Instead she snapped back, 'Doug, for heaven's sake!'

'I know,' Doug said. 'I'm probably out of order saying anything, but I know how you feel and how I feel, and neither of us can deny it. But in a month, a week, who knows, I'll be gone. I'd like to meet you some time.'

'I . . . I can't.'

'Bring your sister with you if you like,' Doug said, taking no notice of Kathy's refusal. 'It would be better for you anyway, safer for the pair of us.'

'Doug, I can't go around meeting other men.'

Doug swung round to face Kathy, and his eyes were darker than ever and seemed full of sadness. She had to stop herself taking his face between her hands. She gasped, ashamed of herself as Doug went on, 'I won't be here much longer, as I said. I promise you, I won't ask anything more of you than your friendship, but give me something to hold dear as I go over to France with my buddies.'

Kathy swallowed deeply, almost swamped by emotion. 'Doug,' she said eventually, 'I will see you, but only when other people are present. I'll never come alone like this again. Mammy would be glad to meet you, she made Carmel's Ricky welcome enough. I'll tell her about you and Phil, and I know she will ask you to the house. That is the only way I can be a friend to you.'

Doug knew that what Kathy said made sense. He could ask nothing further than that of her, and he gave a brief nod. 'Then so be it, Kathy O'Malley.'

'Honestly, Alice, I thought Aunt Sophie was going to kill David,' Lizzie said as they sat one day on a hill overlooking the house. 'Either that or pass out.'

'Ooh, but isn't it romantic,' Alice said, and with a giggle went on, 'I love a man in uniform, don't you, and the Air Force is so . . . I don't know, so sexy?'

'Alice!'

'Well, I don't know how else to describe it,' Alice said, blushing. 'I bet even toffee-nosed Rosamund will fall for David all over again.'

'Maybe,' Lizzie said, though she wasn't thinking of Rosamund and her reaction to the news, but of the moment when David had marched into the kitchen, just days after he'd left to go back to school, wearing the blue uniform of the Royal Air Force. He looked even more handsome in uniform, Lizzie thought; in fact, he was stunning. She had been struck dumb, and Sophie had had to clutch the door post for support.

'Well, Mother,' David had said, in the clipped, cold voice he seemed to reserve for Sophie, 'are you going to ring up the recruitment board and tell them your little lambkin is only seventeen and can't possibly be subjected to the same danger as other people's sons?'

Sophie flashed him a look of contempt, but Lizzie could see the gleam of tears in her eyes too as she turned and walked from the room without a word. Millie had given a sigh, leant her hands heavily on the table and stared at David. 'The uniform looks very fine on you,' she said. 'It's a pity that what comes out of your mouth defiles it.'

David started, and Lizzie guessed Millie had never spoken to him like that before, and in a way she was glad. She saw

247

David flush and knew he was embarrassed. 'Why do you go on at her?' Millie asked. 'Be a man and do your duty if you must, but why must you tear your mother to ribbons in order to do it?'

'I . . . I . . . she wouldn't agree,' David said, stumbling in his effort to explain. 'She wanted to keep me tied to her for ever.'

'Don't be so stupid,' Millie said angrily. 'She wanted to keep you safe, at least until you were of an age to fight. Every mother in the land would do the same thing given half a chance, but men, especially young men, are hotheads and seemingly can't wait to get stuck into the blood and gore of war.' She glared at David, shook her head and said, 'You have no idea – and never will, until you have your own flesh and blood – how your mother suffers daily worrying about Christopher. When he was injured at Dunkirk, she nearly went off her head. You were away at school, you don't know.' She wagged a finger at David and said, 'War took your father too in a way, don't forget, and your mother tended the invalid who returned – and often a crotchety, demanding invalid he was – for years until he died. And now Chris risks his life and has done since nineteen thirty-nine. Is it any wonder your mother wants one of her sons to stay safe when she struggled to bring both of you up single-handed? Tell me, is that so wrong, David Barraclough?'

David's face was brick-red and Lizzie saw him struggling with emotion. In the end he said, 'I'm sorry.'

'You're telling the wrong person,' Millie said, tight-lipped. 'You're man enough to fight. Are you man enough to make a sincere apology to your mother?'

And he must have done, because after that things were better between them. 'She's all right with him now,' Lizzie told Alice. 'Or almost, anyway.'

'Has he seen Rosamund yet?'

'I don't know. He'd have to go to her school to see her, and he didn't say he had,' Lizzie said. 'He saw his Aunt Marjorie though; he called at the Grange.' She thought for a minute and said, 'They're not as pally as they were, Rosamund and David. Ever since David started bringing friends home, it hasn't been the same between them. David was particularly mad with her when she started flirting with his friends.'

'She's sex-mad, that girl,' Alice declared emphatically. 'After anything in trousers.'

'I think she prefers them without any trousers at all,' Lizzie said with an impish grin, and both girls burst out laughing.

But although they laughed, Lizzie knew that if Rosamund's behaviour was to get talked about, there would be ructions at the Grange. They'd both seen Rosamund in action the previous year. Lizzie and Alice had been for a bike ride one day in the summer holidays, and as they'd started home in the evening, Alice's bike had got a puncture. 'Oh bother,' she said. 'That's torn it.' She got off and surveyed the flat tyre with a frown. 'The inner tube's been patched that often, dad said there's not much tube left.'

'You probably need a new one.'

'Yeah, and gold dust would be easier to get right now,' Alice said gloomily. 'The last puncture was mended with a pair of our Frankie's outgrown Wellingtons. I hope there's some left because this bike belongs to one of our land girls.' She'd looked at the long road stretching before them and said, 'How are we to get home now? I can't push the bike all the way. It'll take hours and not do the bike much good.'

'Leave it in the hedge,' Lizzie suggested. 'I'll give you a lift on mine and maybe someone can fetch it tomorrow.'

Alice saw the sense in that, but as she wheeled her bike to the side of the road and rammed it into the hedge, she heard strangled cries coming from the other side. The two girls exchanged glances and then, using the bike as a stepping stone, peered curiously over the unkempt hedge. What they saw made their eyes widen and their mouths drop agape with shock. Rosamund lay before them on the grass, stark naked, and straddled by a man devoid of his army tunic, tie and trousers, which lay on the ground beside him. Rosamund had her eyes closed and in a husky voice that sounded as if she had a sore throat was chanting over and over, 'Oh God! Oh God! Oh God!' She gave a sudden exultant shout and then said, 'Oh, Giles, God, I love you!'

Lizzie and Alice looked at each other again and slid down from the hedge without a word. Still in silence, Lizzie picked up her bike and wheeled it down the road, and Alice, leaving hers stuck in the hedge, followed her. Lizzie was reeling with shock. The facts of life had eventually been passed on to her by Alice, who, as a farmer's daughter and the sister of elder brothers, had picked up a great deal more than Lizzie, although much of it was still sketchy.

But however sketchy it was, it was obvious to both girls what Rosamund was doing – or, to be more precise, what she was allowing someone to do to her. Lizzie felt ashamed, and that was strange, for she was not responsible for Rosamund's behaviour. But she felt she was, because Rosamund was related to Sophie and Lizzie herself was living with Sophie and loved her, and the shame was real.

She knew also that Sophie was worried about her niece, because she'd heard her taking to Millie. She knew Marjorie had gone north to join Gerald, who'd been granted some special leave. Nanny Townsend, on holiday from the London hospital where she was working, had agreed to come and look after Rosamund, but she'd caught shingles and was too ill to come. The only other women at the Grange were the cook and the housekeeper, and neither seemed to keep a check on Rosamund's growing friendships with the officers living there. They seemed not to care where she went, or what time she came in. Concerned, Sophie had asked if Rosamund wanted to live with her while her mother was away. 'No, sorry, Aunt Sophie,' Rosamund had replied. 'I have no desire to play nursemaid to city brats,' and Sophie had been too angry to ask again.

'Never mind,' Lizzie had assured Alice. 'David will be home next week after his camping trip and Rosamund will be all over him then.' Not that she'd tell him what she'd seen, but she was sure David would fix Rosamund somehow.

But he hadn't. Rosamund didn't seem to have time for David any more. She told him he was immature and too young for her, and he'd returned confused, but in some strange way relieved. All through that summer, Lizzie had caught glimpses of Rosamund and a young man – and not always the same one either – slipping through the trees hand in hand, or had almost stumbled upon her lying with a lover in the long grass.

Sometimes Lizzie was alone, sometimes with Alice, and though Lizzie felt disloyal, she knew she had to talk about her worries with someone. 'She's only fifteen,' she'd said one day to Alice as they sat by the side of the river. 'And she's so . . . so shameless about it all.'

'Does Mrs Barraclough know?'

'I don't know. I mean, I haven't told her. But Rosamund's not very . . . well, I mean, she doesn't exactly keep quiet about it,' Lizzie said miserably. 'I think Millie knows, or guesses at any rate.

'I mean,' Lizzie went on, 'what if she has a baby? She could, couldn't she?'

'I suppose so.'

They waited through the summer for Rosamund's stomach to swell and indicate that their fears were justified, but nothing happened. Then one day Alice came with news that cleared up the mystery. 'There's something they can use,' she said. 'When they do . . . well, you know, to stop having babies.'

'Is there? What is it?'

'French letters,' Alice said in a whisper.

Lizzie was mystified. 'How do letters stop it?' she said. 'And why do they have to be French?'

Alice gave a shrug. 'I don't know,' she said. 'I just heard the land girls talking and that's what they said. I could hardly ask them to explain. They'd kill me if they knew I'd been listening.'

Lizzie could well understand that. She overheard many confusing things too that she could ask no one to clarify. Anyway, it certainly seemed as if the French letters, or whatever Rosamund used, worked, because her stomach was as flat as ever by the time they went back to school.

The next time they saw her was the Christmas holidays, and by then Marjorie was back home, but she saw no harm in what she thought of as Rosamund's harmless flirtation with the young officers resident at the Grange.

'Flighty herself, that's why,' Lizzie heard Millie remark almost to herself. 'She's been having many a flirtation since the war began and her man was called up, and not so harmless either, I'd say.'

Sophie was alarmed enough at the name Rosamund was making for herself in the village to mention it to Marjorie at Christmas, but Marjorie pooh-poohed her sister's concern. 'Really, Sophie, it isn't as if she's dating some village yokel. These are officers, gentlemen, and would hardly harm my Rosamund.'

Lizzie hid her wry smile and wondered whether Marjorie would change her opinion if she'd witnessed what she and Alice had the previous summer.

By the Easter holidays, Rosamund was turned sixteen and seemed what Millie termed man-mad. 'Like her mother before her,' she said to Lizzie. 'Set the village alight she did, with her carry-on. Sophie, busy looking after a father who never had time for her and a cantankerous, demanding stepmother, and later an ailing husband, doesn't know the half of it.'

Lizzie hitched herself on to a stool and prepared to listen, but Millie suddenly remembered who she was talking to. 'And it's not for your ears either, miss,' she said. 'Go on, out of my kitchen and let me get on, for goodness' sake.'

But even if Rosamund had run naked down the market square that Easter holidays when David seemed to snarl and snap at everyone, Lizzie doubted if Sophie would have noticed. David and his unhappiness and aggressive attitude seemed to take all her energy. She had little time for Lizzie and Danny, let alone Rosamund and Marjorie, and Millie said that anyway it was time she let them work things out for themselves.

But now David had joined the Air Force, and to Alice that made all the difference. 'When Rosamund sees him,' she declared, 'she'll fall madly in love with him, you'll see.' She gripped her knees and rocked to and fro before she went on, 'Maybe they'll get wed.'

Lizzie didn't like to think of that. 'Don't be so silly,' she said. 'Rosamund's only sixteen.'

'Shakespeare's Juliet was younger,' Alice pointed out. 'Think about it. I know she's not so nice to you just now, but David could change her. Love of a good man and all that.'

'It's love of a good woman, stupid,' Lizzie snapped angrily. 'It doesn't work the other way round. David's too soft for Rosamund, she'd eat him alive. God, she'd devour him.'

And suddenly she had a vision of the future and David tying himself to Rosamund for life because everyone expected him to. She felt angry that David was so malleable, but surely he wouldn't go so far as to actually marry Rosamund just to please other people?' 'Never,' she said decisively. 'Rosamund is not the one for David.' And she closed her eyes and prayed that what she'd said was the truth.

FIFTEEN

Twice over the next two weekends, Doug had taken Kathy
and Maggie and their sons to the Lickey Hills. He'd been
invited with his friend Phil back to Mary's house for tea
afterwards, where they'd met Carmel's Ricky and got on
very well together. Kathy told herself that it was all out
in the open, her friendship with Doug, and that was all it
was, a friendship, and the feelings she had for him were
only because she hadn't Barry to cuddle up to. Mary and
Eamonn, missing their own sons, liked the young men and
made them welcome, and they came fairly often. Bridie
said that the conniving bloody Americans seemed to have
taken over the family. 'Overpaid, over-sexed and over here
is bloody right,' she complained. 'Wouldn't even be in the
damn war unless Japan had forced them into it.'

Kathy took no notice of Bridie. She delighted in being
near Doug. She liked to watch him talk, his white teeth
flashing, his ready smile and near-black eyes twinkling, and
the hair that fell forward on his brow that she longed to
smooth back. She watched his hands, big square hands that
moved constantly while he talked and described things to
the family. She wished she could hold one of those hands

255

in her own, or against her cheek, but she fought the temptation. And although she yearned to be alone with Doug, she never allowed it to happen. She wasn't stupid, and she knew that if they were ever on their own their feelings could easily overpower them.

At the beginning of May, Doug was still around, though almost every day, he said, he awaited orders to move out. Other units had already gone, including that of Carmel's Ricky, who'd kissed her goodbye days ago and left her tearful and bereft. 'Something big is building up on the south coast,' Doug told the family one teatime just a couple of days after Rick's departure.

'Do you want to go?' Kathy asked.

'Sure I do,' Doug said. 'If there's an invasion planned, I want to be part of it; God, it's what I joined up for. I don't want to languish in Britain when my fellow countrymen are over-running Europe.'

After that conversation, Doug and Phil seemed to disappear into thin air. They were due to come to tea the following Tuesday, but never turned up. When Kathy and Maggie took their sons to Cannon Hill Park the following Saturday, neither Doug nor Phil arrived, though they hung about for over an hour, pushing the two lads on the swing and kicking the ball around the grass.

Disappointment made Kathy sharp. 'You'd think if they were being shipped out they would have come to say goodbye,' she said to her parents one day. 'I mean, Ricky managed it.'

'Aye, but he took a risk,' Eamonn said. 'Soldiers can't just please themselves, you know. Maybe they weren't given notice.'

'Maybe,' Kathy said, but she didn't really believe it. Ricky had taken a risk because he cared for Carmel. If Doug cared for her, as Maggie seemed to think, wouldn't he have somehow got a message to her that he was leaving? Oh God, she thought, what's wrong with me? Isn't one man enough? Maybe Doug had chosen not to come and say goodbye because he'd decided himself it wasn't right. Anyway, whichever way it was, she decided, whatever the attraction between them, it was over now. They'd obviously left for the unknown destination down south and she had to get back to her ordinary life.

But ordinary life seemed very boring and dull, and that was why, when Kathy noticed that *Mrs Miniver* was showing at the Broadway cinema, she was determined to go. They'd not been to the Broadway since the night they met Doug and Phil, but Kathy had no hesitation in suggesting it, sure that the two men were no longer in England.

Maggie was just as keen, but that afternoon she was taken ill at work, and later, when Kathy went around to see her, she found her with a raging temperature and a sore throat. 'You'll have to go without me, Kath,' she croaked.

'Away out of that,' Kathy said and tried to keep the disappointment out of her voice. 'I'll not go at all if you can't come too.'

'Don't be silly, everyone's talking about the film and you've been looking forward to it all week.'

Kathy shrugged. 'There'll be another time,' she said. 'Anyway, it's no fun on your own.'

'Maybe Carmel will go with you,' Mary suggested, but Carmel had already made plans for the evening. 'Bridie would jump at the chance,' Mary said, and Kathy made a face.

'No fear, Mammy. If I ask her now, she'll be hanging around us every time,' she said. 'I think I'll just go home.'

She didn't want to go home and knew she wouldn't be welcome there either. Sid and Enid valued the few hours alone they had the nights Kathy went out with Maggie. Molly was always early to bed, and with Kenny and Barbara both out too, Kathy knew they were looking forward to a night to themselves.

'Now why should you go home?' Mary said. 'God knows you work hard enough, and you're sure to see someone in the queue to sit with.'

Kathy wavered and Mary saw it. 'Go on,' she said. 'Go and put on your glad rags and have a few hours to yourself.'

And so Kathy went. She put on her best artificial silk blouse, bought before clothes rationing, and scraped out the last bit of lipstick from the tube with her little finger and smeared it over her full lips. She dabbed a precious few drops of perfume behind her ears and carefully eased her equally precious pair of nylon stockings over her legs. Doug and Phil had bought a couple of pairs for every woman in the family as a thank-you for asking them to tea, and Kathy remembered how they'd gone into raptures at the time. She gave a quick polish to her well-worn shoes, picked up her handbag and was ready to be off.

'I'm away then,' she shouted to Enid and Sid. 'Enjoy yourselves and don't do anything I wouldn't do.'

'Go on,' Enid said. 'I hope the film's as good as everyone says it is.'

'I'll tell you when I come in,' Kathy promised. 'I shouldn't be late.'

She took her jacket off the hook at the back of the stair door and had a look in the mirror as she left the house. She knew she looked good; her dark eyes were sparkling and her hair gleamed as she gave it a final brush. 'You lead an uneventful life,' she said to her reflection, 'when you can get so excited by a visit to a cinema only round the corner.'

But she *was* excited, and she tripped her way down the road and out on to Bristol Street, where she joined the queue outside the cinema. But she hadn't been there above a couple of minutes when she heard a voice in her ear say, 'Hello, Kathy O'Malley.'

258

She jumped as if she'd been shot. She knew before she turned around and faced the deep-brown eyes and the sardonic grin who the voice belonged to, and she shook from head to foot and told herself to stop being so stupid.

'Are you on your own?' Doug asked.

Kathy scanned the crowd desperately. Surely there'd be someone she could say she was with; she'd lived all her life in the area. But although there were people she knew by sight, and perhaps to nod to in the street, there was not one person she could claim a closer acquaintance with, not one person she could declare she was going into the cinema with, as if they'd arranged it earlier.

'Yes,' she said at last. 'At least . . . well . . . Maggie was coming, but she was taken ill.'

'Ah. And Phil was coming, but at the last minute he was put on guard duty,' Doug said.

'We thought you'd left,' Kathy said, and wished her heart would stop jumping about. 'You haven't been to see us for some time.'

'All leave was stopped,' Doug said. 'And so suddenly I was unable to let you know. I'm sorry. Tonight I had a few hours off, but I didn't want to see your folks, I didn't want to see anyone really. I said once I'd almost welcome invasion, that it couldn't come quickly enough, and I still do, but it's scary. Tonight I wanted to relax for a bit and try to forget the war, that's why I'm here.' He lowered his voice to a whisper and went on, 'We're not supposed to know, but we move out in the morning.'

'The morning!'

'Ssh, it's top secret,' Doug said, glancing round to see if anyone had heard Kathy's high, surprised exclamation.

'Sorry,' Kathy said, and then went on, 'Bit stupid coming to see *Mrs Miniver*, though. It's a war film, you'll hardly be able to relax and forget about it in here.'

'Better than sitting in a pub nursing a warm beer by myself. It might have been different if Phil had got off with me,' Doug said and added with a grin, 'Anyway, now I've found you, and you're by yourself too, Kate. Maybe you can make me forget the war for a while.'

Kathy didn't answer, for she was startled by the name he'd called her. No one had ever addressed her as Kate before. Kathy sounded soft and malleable, as she'd been in her childhood and through her courtship and early married years with Barry. Now, partly because of the hardships of living in a country at war, and separated from her man for most of that time, she was harder and more self-sufficient. If Barry came back safe – and she prayed nightly that he would – he'd find a totally different wife to the one he'd left behind, and Kate seemed the right name for such a person.

She was glad that the cinema doors opened and put paid to the thoughts crowding her head. She was suddenly nervous of the man standing beside her, as if it was a proper planned date, and hoped no one she was acquainted with among the waiting crowds was putting the wrong complexion on it. But despite that, she felt a thrill of excitement as Doug took her arm.

Kathy's conflicting emotions kept her silent as Doug bought tickets for them both and escorted her into the cinema, past the back row and the courting couples. When they were seated he turned to Kathy and said, 'OK, Kate, you can relax now. This is me, Doug Howister, and I have no intention of leaping on you.'

Kathy smiled at him and said, 'I'm being silly really. I mean, it isn't as if we don't know one another. It's just that I've never been to the cinema with a man, or at least not for years.' She'd gone with Barry once or twice the first few months after they were married. Then Lizzie was born and money was tighter, and then Barry was out of work and they had less money than ever. And when Barry got the job at BSA, he was working all the hours God sent, and there was little time and less enthusiasm for a night at the cinema.

So it was Doug Howister who now sat beside Kathy and watched the film with her. He behaved like a perfect gentleman, although Kathy tingled with anticipation, wondering if he would put his arm around her, half hoping he would and yet not sure how she should act if he did. But he didn't, and when they rose at the end of the film, she suddenly realised that this was probably the last time she'd see this man who'd been so kind to her parents and her young son and Maggie's. Tears began trickling down her cheeks, though Doug wasn't aware of this until she started to sniff, and then he attributed her tears to the film. 'Don't cry,' he said. 'It ended happily.'

Actually, Kathy had been disappointed by the film, which she thought sickly sweet, unrealistic and made only to raise morale. 'It's not that.'

'Then what is it?'

She could hardly tell him, so she hurried ahead of him, through the milling crowds, to the exit door.

She'd reached the street by the time he'd caught up with her. 'What is it?' he persisted. 'What made you cry?'

She couldn't walk away and leave him like that, and she cried, 'It's you, you daft bugger. It's the thought of you going away that upset me.'

'Ah, Kate.' Doug's arms went around Kathy, and as he spoke his lips descended on hers and she knew that this was what she'd been waiting for since he'd knocked her flying that night weeks earlier. Her lips parted and his tongue probed into her mouth, and Kathy seemed to melt into his arms. He eventually pulled away, although she had the urge to draw him back and go on and on.

'Kate,' he said breathlessly. 'Oh, Kate.'

Kathy smiled at his startled surprise and kissed him gently on the lips. 'You must have known how I felt about you,' she said, amazed at her own daring.

'I thought . . . I wasn't sure.'

'I'm sure.'

'Are you . . . are you still sure now?'

Into Kathy's mind flew a picture of Barry as he'd been when he'd last left, and then at their wedding some years before. She'd promised herself to him forever, till death parted them, and yet she wanted the man holding her in his arms. She'd wanted him for ages, she'd imagined him making love to her, and dreamt about it too, and so had already sinned, for the thought was as bad as the deed, the Church said. Already she'd committed a mortal sin in even considering adultery; now she was going to add another sin to it, for she said, almost in a whisper, 'I'm sure, Doug. But not here. We must get away quickly, we could be seen.'

She knew it was a distinct possibility, because, despite the black-out, while she'd been returning Doug's embrace, people had been streaming past them out of the picture house. Any one of them could have recognised Kathy, and seen her in the arms of an American serviceman. But Kathy didn't care. All that mattered at that moment was letting Doug make love to her. She'd yearned for him long enough; this was her last chance and she was determined to take it.

At the end of Bell Bam Road nearest to Sun Street were some shells of houses popular with courting couples. Stealthily, Kathy drew Doug through the streets by the hand, watching warily for anyone who might recognise her, but they reached the houses without incident.

Here they had to be especially careful in case there were people already there, but again they were in luck. And once inside, the sagging door blocking the entrance to the street afforded a degree of privacy, though the house was open to the sky.

Doug pulled Kathy towards him and kissed her long and hard. 'Oh, Kate, how I've longed for this moment.'

'And I,' Kathy said.

Suddenly Doug held Kathy away from him slightly and looked deep into her eyes. 'I love you, Kate. I've said that to other women in the past, but then I didn't know what love was. Now I do, and that's why I'm going to say what I must. I want to make love to you badly, but I have less to lose than you. I don't want you to do this and feel bad about yourself tomorrow, or regret what we've done in the weeks ahead.'

'Oh, Doug, don't you realise how I ache for you?' Kathy said, aware as she spoke that the one night might have to last her a lifetime.

Doug's kiss set her body tingling and desire coursing through her veins. 'Oh, quickly,' she breathed.

'No rush, honey,' Doug said gently, releasing her. 'We've got all the time in the world.'

He spread his coat on the dusty floor and Kathy began peeling off her clothes as if she'd done this every day of her life.

But even as they lay together, Doug was in no hurry. 'God, you're beautiful, Kate,' he said and Kathy stared back at him, realising that she'd never seen a naked man before. For all the years they'd been married, Barry had always turned the light out before he undressed, and she was always in bed, undressed and under the covers, before he came up, so he'd probably never seen her naked either. So now she looked at Doug's body and saw how aroused he was, and her own desire mounted.

Doug bent over her and gently kissed her eyelids and her lips, and she wriggled beneath him as he moved down to her throat and neck and then her breasts, his kisses mounting in intensity and his lips teasing her body. Kathy moaned and Doug covered her mouth with his, his tongue probing while his hands moved over her body, caressing and stroking until she could hardly bear it.

'Please, oh please,' she begged, and eventually Doug gently entered her. Kathy felt as if she was caught in a spiral of intense pleasure and excitement that went in waves, higher and higher. She was aware of crying aloud and of Doug crying out beside her, and then it was over and they lay spent, satisfied and contented, and still entwined together.

Never, never had Kathy experienced such exquisite joy. She felt wonderful, refreshed, renewed and not at all sorry. 'Kate, Kate, you're beautiful,' Doug said again. 'Wonderful, terrific. God, what a lady.' He kissed her on the lips and said, 'I've never felt this way about a woman before. I love you, Kate O'Malley.'

And Kathy was surprised to hear herself saying, 'I love you too, Doug.'

Doug eased himself from her and leaning on his elbow he gazed at her and said, 'Wow, that was really something. How was it for you, honey?'

Kathy stared at him, surprised at the question, for never had Barry asked if she'd enjoyed sex with him. 'Oh, it was marvellous, so it was,' she said. 'It's never been this good for me either.'

'Oh, Kate,' Doug said again, holding her close. He'd made love to many women in his life, but none had caused such an explosion in his body and his mind as Kate O'Malley.

He drew Kathy to her feet gently, and they clung together, kissing passionately. When eventually they drew apart, Doug said, 'Don't ever feel bad about what happened tonight, Kate, for you've given me a great gift to take with me tomorrow.'

Kathy felt joy flow through her at his words, and suddenly regretted the weeks that she'd known Doug and had dampened down her own desire. Never again would she experience such intense and exquisite pleasure, never again would she be held in his arms and feel his lips upon hers. She could have cried at the desolation she felt. Almost mechanically, and to try to stop the thoughts pouring through her mind, Kathy began to dress. She shivered as she realised that in a few hours Doug would be gone from her.

Doug put his arms around her shoulders. 'You're shivering, honey. Are you cold?'

'No,' Kathy said, and though her teeth chattered she had told the truth.

'Get dressed quickly,' Doug said. 'It's probably late.' He began to dress himself and added, 'Will you get into trouble?'

Kathy shook her head. 'I don't know,' she said, and added recklessly, 'I don't care either.'

She was amazed at herself. It was funny how people's opinion suddenly mattered so little. She wondered what had happened to Kathy O'Malley, devoted wife and dedicated mother to her children. Surely she wasn't the same person Doug Howister called Kate, who'd just rolled naked and shameless with a man she hardly knew, a man who'd set her body on fire?

Suddenly she gave a cry of distress and wrapped her arms around Doug's neck, and as his hands caressed her body she wished she had the ability to stop time. Eventually they drew apart, but they continued to embrace and Doug held Kathy closer as he said, 'Kate, Kate, though I hate to leave you I have to be back at camp by midnight.'

'Oh . . . oh, yes, of course,' Kate said, but still she leant against him. 'When . . . what time do you go tomorrow?'

'Dawn,' Doug said shortly, and added with a sigh, 'I sure hate to leave you, honey. Oh, God.' He pressed her close to him again and Kathy realised how deeply upset he was.

'I'll never forget you,' she said. 'Nor this one night we've had together.'

'Nor will I, baby,' Doug said. He looked at her full of sadness and went on, 'Say goodbye here. It wouldn't be seemly for me to be spotted walking you to your door.'

'No, I suppose not,' Kathy said dully.

'One last kiss,' Doug said. 'To remember you by.'

The kiss was nearly their undoing. Both became aroused again so quickly, it took all Doug's willpower to stop it going further. 'Go on,' he said at last, pulling away from her and attempting a smile. 'Go on home before I risk a court martial and ravish you again.'

Kathy stumbled out of the bombed house, hardly able to see for the tears coursing down her cheeks. No one was still up at home to see the time or the condition she arrived home in, and she was grateful, because she was unable to stop crying. It was as if the floodgates had opened.

She crept inside quietly – she had no desire to wake anyone, particularly Molly – and took herself down to the cellar, where she made a pot of tea to try and still her jangling nerves. She felt she couldn't go to bed. For one thing, she was still upset enough to disturb Molly, and for another, she was too churned up with all that had happened.

She continued to sit at the table and drink tea as the night drew in around her. She expected to feel guilt or shame, but felt neither. She didn't know what was the matter with her. She'd previously had no patience with the women at work who'd had affairs, and particularly those who'd gone with Americans. She wondered what they'd say if they were to find out about her and Doug – not that she would tell them, of course; she couldn't tell anyone. It would have to be her secret.

She remembered with a tingling excitement Doug's hands and lips on her body, and wondered if he was just a good lover and Barry less than perfect, or whether Barry was the norm and Doug extraordinary. She wouldn't know; she'd only ever slept with Barry before Doug and she couldn't speak of it to anyone. Certainly the conversation of other women seemed to suggest that they didn't enjoy it much generally. They talked about letting the old man get his leg over, or his end up, especially when he came in tanked up on a Saturday night.

Kathy felt no guilt that she had slept with a man other than the one she was married to, only extreme sadness that Doug was leaving and she'd probably never see him again. She poured another cup of tea to try to stop the tears flowing at the thought. But it was no good, and eventually she put her head on the table and cried as if her heart was broken.

The next morning Molly found her there fast asleep. Kathy was still groggy when she was woken up, and explained she'd come home with a headache and had made a cup of tea and must have gone to sleep over it. Molly noticed her dishevelled appearance and red-rimmed eyes but said nothing about either. Whether the story of the headache was true or not, she thought, Kathy looked ill, very ill, and she urged her to take the day off work, but it was the last thing Kathy wanted. She needed people around her, and to be able to work till she was tired enough to fall into bed that night and sleep. She brushed Molly's concerns aside and told her not to fuss, and went up to the bedroom to take off her finery and get ready for work. Molly watched her with worried eyes.

'I'm really glad you joined the Air Force, and I think you look grand in your uniform,' Lizzie said to David. It was nearly the end of May now and the days were warmer and the nights longer. Summer was just around the corner, and they were sitting outside in the garden. David was stationed at the nearby Air Force base at Madley, and they'd seen a fair bit of him, which had helped to heal the rift between him and his mother.

'Thank you, Elizabeth,' David said with a little bow. 'I'm glad you approve.'

Lizzie didn't catch the slight sarcasm in his voice and went on, 'I'd love to go up in a plane, it must be so exciting.'

'I suppose it is,' David said. 'I must say, I'm looking forward to it. It's the way the future's going – aviation. One day people will be able to take a plane to anywhere in the world.' Lizzie thought that incredible, but if David said it, she thought, it must be true.

'Is that what you want to do, I mean after the war?' she asked.

'I might,' David said, and gave a grin. 'Provided I survive, of course.'

Lizzie gave a sudden shiver and said sharply, 'Don't say things like that. It's stupid, and you must see how it upsets your mother.'

David looked at the little girl before him and saw that she wasn't such a little girl any more. She was still slender, but had grown taller and very shapely, and he wondered why he'd not noticed before. 'How old are you now, Elizabeth?' he asked.

'Thirteen,' Lizzie said. 'Well, nearly, next month I am.'

'A teenager. My, my,' David said, then asked, 'What d'you want to do when you leave school?'

Lizzie shrugged. 'Work in a shop, I suppose, or a factory. Mammy will probably have some idea.'

'Pity really she didn't let you take the eleven-plus.'

'What?' Lizzie said, startled. 'What do you mean?'

'Didn't she tell you?' David said. 'I thought she might have done, or perhaps my mother. She mentioned it to me.'

'Mentioned what to you?'

'That your teacher wanted you to take the eleven-plus. That Mr Donnelly you're always on about. He thought you and Alice had a good chance of passing.'

Lizzie looked at him, stunned. 'Then . . . then why didn't I take it?' she asked.

'Because your mother didn't want you to,' David said. 'Nor Alice's mother apparently. I'm surprised no one ever told you.'

Lizzie wasn't surprised. Her mammy wouldn't tell her in case she was upset, in case she blamed her. She wondered if she would have liked to go to grammar school. She didn't know really, but it was nice to think Mr Donnelly thought her capable of it.

'Do you mind?' David asked.

'I don't know,' Lizzie said. 'Not really, I suppose. I mean, I never thought about going to grammar school. Alice might be upset, she would have loved the chance.'

'Don't tell her then. It will achieve nothing.'

'I won't,' Lizzie said. 'At least not yet. Her mother wants her to stay at home after she leaves school until she's married off to some farmer when she's about seventeen, the same age as her mother when she married.'

David made a face as he said, 'I can never think of that Mrs Buxton as ever being seventeen.'

Lizzie laughed and said, 'I know what you mean, but doesn't the life she has mapped out for Alice sound awful?'

'Dreadful. Alice should stand up to her.'

'She means to,' Lizzie said. 'That's when the knowledge that her mother stopped her even taking the eleven-plus might work in her favour.'

David was silent for a minute, sorry he'd told Lizzie now. He hoped she really didn't mind as she'd said. He'd hate her to think any less of her mother for refusing to let her take the exam. Maybe, he thought, it would be better to talk about something else and take her mind off the stupid eleven-plus altogether, and so he said, 'Now, let's think about your birthday. After all, it's not every day you're thirteen. Let's see now.' He looked at Lizzie for a minute or two and said, 'Would you like to go for a meal?'

'A meal!' cried Lizzie. 'You mean a real meal, at night, in a real restaurant?'

'Well, it was something like that I had in mind,' David said, amused by the astonished delight on Lizzie's face.

'Oh, David,' she cried, and flung her arms around his neck.

It felt good to be able to please Elizabeth so much with such a little thing, and he gave her a hug back, surprised at the softness of her and the definite waist she had and the small breasts he could feel pressing against him. 'Here, here, don't strangle me,' he said, laughing and slightly embarrassed, and disentangled Lizzie's arms. 'Let's go and ask Mother.'

I love you, David Barraclough, Lizzie thought as they walked side by side towards the house, I always have, but I don't know if I'll ever have the courage to tell you.

SIXTEEN

It wasn't long before the whole of Britain knew that something big had happened on the south coast, and Kathy knew that Doug's invasion theory had been right. Operation Overlord began on June 1944 – D-Day, as it became known.

Most people knew that this was it. A make-or-break time for Britain who, with the Commonwealth troops and America's help, stood alone against a superpower. People tuned into their wirelesses and scoured papers, while many remembered Dunkirk and trembled for the troops sent over to the French beaches again.

They heard that before dawn on 6 June, Allied paratroops and gliders had begun landing behind German lines in northern France, while Bomber Command was pounding the Normandy beaches. By nightfall, 156,000 troops had landed along the French coast from Cherbourg to Le Havre. By the next day they'd liberated Bayeux and established control on all beach-heads, while the American troops had continued to drive north.

It was cheering news, but Kathy knew that such landings and advances could not have been made without severe loss of life, and she doubled her prayers for her loved ones in the thick of it.

A week later, people were hearing of a new threat, known as 'Hitler's revenge', that was attacking the beleaguered southeast coast. These were VI flying bombs. The first fell in Kent on 13 June, and they were particularly dangerous because they were pilotless. They came over with a high-pitched scream, and then the engine would cut out and there would be an ominous silence while the bomb fell through the night, before the explosion. As well as the death and destruction they caused, they also affected people's nerves badly, and as most fell in or around London, it was particularly bad for the people of that city. Within a few days, the bombs had become known as doodlebugs.

By July new evacuees from London were arriving at Birmingham's New Street station, frightened and bewildered. They were trying to get away from this new menace that was killing and injuring people and destroying buildings just as they were beginning to recover from the Blitz.

'You can't help feeling sorry for them,' Maggie said to Kathy one evening as they walked home. Kathy didn't answer, but that wasn't unusual these days. Everyone had noticed her pale, strained face and her preoccupation, which caused her not even to seem to hear when people spoke to her. Molly had urged her to see the doctor, but she just snapped she was all right and told her not to fuss.

'She seems worried about something,' Molly said to Mary.

'Sure, we're all worried,' Mary answered.

And so they were, but Molly was sure it was something else bigger and deeper that was eating at Kathy. She was right, although Kathy could discuss her anxieties with no one, least of all Molly.

At first, after the fateful night when Kathy and Doug had made love, she'd been bereft and terrified for his safety. She was slightly ashamed of herself, for her husband, brothers and brother-in-law had been in danger from the beginning, and yet as she opened her eyes every morning, it was Doug's face she saw and his name in her thoughts. Not that she slept much, and when she did, she began to dream again, only now she didn't see herself and Doug in a passionate embrace, but him lying dying and bleeding on French soil.

Then, as she began listening to reports of the D-Day invasion and its effects as the Allies pressed forward, she realised she hadn't had her period, which had been due at the beginning of June. She told herself periods could stop for many reasons: she was under pressure, worried about D-Day – anything like that could disturb your cycle. But in her heart of hearts, she knew what was the matter with her and wondered why it had never occurred to her that the one passionate night could have produced results.

She was scared to death, and daily she wondered what to do about it. God, how was she to face people? Molly – what would Molly think of her lying with another man while her own was away fighting for freedom for them all? And how could she tell her mother, her sisters? Kathy's appetite dropped and sleep eluded her nightly as she wrestled with the problem. Molly shook her head sadly and told Maggie that Kathy's nerves were shot to pieces, but in fact she was just scared to death and couldn't think where to turn. She knew a few women at work who'd had abortions, though no one was supposed to know about it and it was spoken about in hushed tones. Still, Kathy knew she could find someone to help her if that was what she wanted. Others claimed that the pills they obtained at a high price from some old woman they knew worked a treat at 'clearing them out'.

Kathy shied away from both alternatives, though to continue with the pregnancy was almost as unthinkable. And yet she couldn't just take away a child's right to live;

it was a mortal sin so grave she dared not risk it, or she was sure she'd roast forever in hell's flames. It was also a hazardous procedure with these back-street people; everyone had heard the horror stories of women seriously ill afterwards, or even bleeding to death. In her blackest moments, Kathy thought she wouldn't mind dying; it might be preferable to the alternative.

Doug had told her never to be disgusted or ashamed of the night when they'd eventually given in to their need and longing for each other, and she hadn't. That was, until she realised she was pregnant, and then she felt shame for the disgrace she'd bring not just on herself alone, but on the whole family. 'Oh God,' she cried silently, 'God help me.'

So, barely eating or sleeping, she stumbled mechanically through the days, interested only in the news from wireless or newspaper about how the invasion was progressing, while the constant knot of worry tightened inside her till it was like a lead weight. She took little notice of anyone else, even Padraic, and felt guilty even writing to her older children. In fact, she didn't know how she was going to break the news to them at all.

In Hereford, news of the invasion was the topic of conversation on everyone's lips. It was plotted out in school with the large map of Europe and little flags, and people talked of 'after the war' now with more optimism.

They listened with horror to news of the doodlebug attacks being endured by the people in the south-east and particularly London. 'It isn't fair, is it, Aunt Sophie?' Lizzie said. 'They've been through so much already.'

'War is seldom fair, Elizabeth, surely you've learnt that,' Aunt Sophie said quite sharply. 'Just be grateful these wretched things don't seem able to reach Birmingham, so your family at least are safe.'

274

Lizzie knew what was making Sophie tetchy, and that was the fact that David was now on active service as a fighter pilot. Gone were the Battle of Britain days when the country lost so many young men that airmen had a bare two weeks' training before they were thrown to the wolves. David's training had been longer and more thorough, but as the invasion bit deeper, the call for fighter pilots grew.

'Will you miss him?' Alice asked.

'Not really,' Lizzie said. 'I'm used to him being away really, aren't I? I'll worry about him, but then I worry about all my family too and pray for them every night.'

'I like your David,' Alice said.

'He is nice,' Lizzie agreed, unaware of the blush that turned her face crimson as she thought of him. 'But he isn't *my* David.'

'It was his idea to take you on that birthday meal.'

'Well, I know, but you came too, and his mother, so it was hardly a date.'

It had been rather special, though. They'd all gone to a posh restaurant in Hereford. Lizzie's feet had sunk into the pile of the deep carpet and she'd been dazzled by the crystal chandeliers and more cutlery than she'd seen in her life laid on the white-clothed tables.

A waiter showed them to their table, where a sparkling glass stood beside each place with a red serviettes folded inside like a fan. He gave Lizzie a menu as if she dined like that every day, and she gazed at it, not able to understand how it all worked. 'You have a starter, then the main meal, followed by the sweet,' David whispered to her. 'Rationing doesn't exist in places like this.'

She read the menu, and was further confused because a lot of the things were so foreign to her. What on earth was pâté or egg mayonnaise, or prawn cocktail? She knew what soup was, but it felt dull just to start with soup.

In the end both girls allowed themselves to be guided by David and ordered pâté to start with. It came with salad and crispy thin toast and it was so tasty Lizzie could have made a meal of it alone. But then she saw the main course David had ordered for them: succulent roast beef and crispy Yorkshire puddings, with baby carrots, deliciously sweet peas, roast potatoes and plenty of gravy to pour over it all.

'Is it all right?' David asked.

All right? Fabulous, Lizzie's eyes said, but she could only nod her head, for her mouth was full.

David even let them try the wine he'd ordered, though Sophie protested. 'They're both growing up, Mother,' he said. 'And it is Elizabeth's birthday.'

It was a shame after that, Lizzie thought, that she found she didn't like the taste of wine at all, not even when David diluted it with water from the jug on the table, but she drank it anyway to please him.

Both Lizzie and Alice were almost too full for gâteau, though they struggled to finish it, but neither could face the cheese and biscuits. Lizzie felt as if she could burst, and was glad of the coffee, despite its slightly bitter taste, but she did wonder why they served it in such small cups.

Both girls agreed it had been a very special evening and David had been kindness himself. 'I probably won't see him for ages now,' Lizzie told Alice. 'I hope he looks after himself.'

But David wasn't away that long, for in mid-August he was back home nursing a broken arm. 'The old kite had been shot up a fair bit,' he told the family. 'I had to make a bit of a crash landing, and that's how I crocked up my arm.'

David was patient with his mother, who was glad to have her son home and safe for a few weeks. He knew she'd suffered badly as reports came in of pilots shot down, some losing limbs and others quite horrifically burnt and disfigured, and she'd be glad that this time his injury was relatively minor.

Lizzie was in her element, fetching and carrying and doing things for David he couldn't do himself. She even put up with Rosamund, who rode over from the Grange with a basket of fruit for the invalid, like a ministering angel.

Lizzie kept out of the way until she'd gone, but even Sophie was rather short with her niece, Lizzie noticed. Stories of Rosamund's exploits with young men had spread through the village, as Lizzie had known they eventually would, until even Sophie came to hear of them. She had wondered if she should take her young niece to task, for her behaviour was becoming more and more embarrassing to them all, but she hesitated to approach the aloof and haughty young woman who now perched on the arm of David's chair and fed him grapes.

Rosamund couldn't stay long – she had a date, she explained – and left after a bare half an hour, and when Lizzie heard the horse's hoofs on the gravel, she emerged from the shed where she'd hidden herself. 'She's gone, the brazen hussy,' Millie said as she entered the kitchen. 'And good riddance, I say.'

Lizzie laughed. 'That's what I say too,' she said, and went across the kitchen on her way to the small sitting room and David.

Kathy didn't know what to do. It was now August, and soon her pregnancy would be showing. She thanked God she'd not had morning sickness, for she'd never have kept her condition a secret this long if she had. She'd seen Molly looking at her a bit quizzically a few times, and if she was to ask her directly she didn't know what she would say.

And then one night, as she tossed and turned, a solution of sorts came to her. She couldn't get rid of the baby, and yet she couldn't just carry on with the pregnancy as if nothing had happened. She would ring Sophie Barraclough from a public phone box. Maybe she knew somewhere Kathy could stay and hide away till the baby was born, and maybe Kathy could do housework for her keep. And later, when it was over, she'd give the child up for adoption; it was the only way. She couldn't expect Barry, or any of the family, to accept and provide for another man's child.

She must contact Sophie soon, she knew that, before someone tumbled to the reason she was behaving so oddly. She knew the family were worried about her. Maggie had gone as far as phoning the doctor from a phone box in Bristol Street. 'She's more than preoccupied, Doctor,' she'd said earnestly. 'She's withdrawn. She never speaks and doesn't answer if anyone speaks to her. All day she stays silent at her bench, and around the others are laughing, joking and singing, and you know, Doctor, she doesn't seem to hear any of it. I go to work with her in the morning and back in the evening and we have dinner together, and honest to God, she might as well be a corpse for all the conversation she has.'

'It sounds like depression to me,' the doctor said. 'If you could get her to see me . . .'

'Oh God, Doctor, she won't,' Maggie cried. 'We've all tried and she goes mad. It's the only thing that seems to rouse her. She'd kill me if she knew I'd phoned.'

'Then I can do little,' the doctor said. 'I don't know what to suggest. Maybe a priest could help.'

The doctor wasn't surprised that Kathy O'Malley's nerves had snapped. The family had suffered more than some and less than others, but the human mind was a funny thing, and some could take more pressure and pain than others. He hoped the priest would be able to help Kathy O'Malley, help them all, for whatever was ailing her was affecting the rest of the family.

Father Cunningham already knew something was troubling Kathy. From mid-July she started to attend evening

278

mass a couple of times a week, and for weeks she never missed benediction. As well as this, he'd often spotted her with her head bowed in prayer, or lighting candles in the evenings, but she always scurried away if she saw him approaching and never lingered after mass. He'd wanted to speak to her for some time, but there were so many pressures he hadn't got around to it before Maggie called to see him and asked him to speak to her sister.

By that time Kathy knew there was going to be no divine intervention to deliver her from the heavy weight of guilt and shame she carried around with her. She'd prayed, begged and implored God to help her, offered up masses, lit candles and pleaded with the Virgin Mary, but all to no avail. She didn't want to talk to any priest, for what could she say? She was in a state of mortal sin anyway, because, although she'd gone to confession, she could not bring herself to tell a priest she'd known most of her life of her evening of lust with Doug Howister. She knew priests could not repeat what they'd heard in confession, but both of them knew Kathy well enough to recognise her voice, and they were only human. She wouldn't be able to bear the look of disgust she'd see later in their eyes; really, she felt she had enough to cope with at that moment.

If she'd been able to go to confession at another church, where no one would know her, she would have done so, but what reason could she give to the family for going anywhere but St Catherine's? Every time she went to the rails for communion, she was making it worse, as it was another sin to receive the host unless you were in a state of grace, but if she hadn't gone to communion every Sunday morning the family would have remarked on it.

The last person she wanted to see, therefore, was a priest, and when Father Cunningham called, he found her in a strange mood. She was obviously troubled about something

– he could almost feel the tension running through her – and yet she was short with him. She said there was nothing bothering her, she didn't want to talk about anything and there was absolutely nothing he could do for her. Father Cunningham left, shaking his head and more worried than ever. Unless he was very much mistaken, he thought, Kathy O'Malley was heading for a breakdown.

Still Kathy hesitated to make the phone call to Sophie. Afterwards, when she analysed it, it was as if she was waiting for something. That something came one morning towards the end of August, and somehow Kathy knew. She knew when she saw Molly rushing across the factory floor towards her, her grey hair unpinned and straggling down her back as she tried to hurry, her apron still tied about her waist and her old threadbare slippers on her feet, and as she watched her mother-in-law approach, the blood froze in Kathy's veins.

Molly was panting heavily. Sweat ran down her face and mixed with the tears from eyes wild with grief as she waved the telegram at Kathy. 'Missing, believed dead!' she cried. 'That's what it says. And that's only because they haven't found his bleeding body yet.'

Kathy saw the woman before her as if she were a long way away. She knew God had taken Barry from her because she had sinned. It wasn't fair. Barry had done no wrong, but she had, and now she had no husband and the children no father. 'Oh God, no,' she cried as she crumpled to the floor in a dead faint, cracking her head on the bench post as she fell.

It was Maggie who accompanied her sister to the hospital. Molly, after delivering her message, was overcome with a paroxysm of grief and someone took charge of her and took her to the canteen for a cup of hot sweet tea. Maggie gave the hospital all her sister's details and then waited for what seemed like hours in a grim hospital corridor, hoping that someone had told her mother, and the children had been given their tea and put to bed.

But really most of her sympathy and thoughts were for Kathy. How in God's name would she cope without Barry? He'd been the only man in her life ever since she could remember. She never even joked about infidelity like the others, and Maggie knew that some of the women's jokes and crudity and lax morals had shocked her sister to the core.

Maggie sat on the hard bench seat, shut her eyes and tried to pray, although she found it harder daily to believe in a God who allowed such killing and horror in people's lives. And it was there that the young doctor found her.

He coughed to attract her attention, not sure if she were dozing or not, and she opened her eyes to see a young man in a short white coat with a stethoscope around his neck and a clipboard of notes in his hand. He smiled at Maggie and said, 'Did you come in with the other young woman?' He glanced at the notes. 'Katherine O'Malley?'

'Aye, she's my sister,' Maggie said.

'And she fainted as a result of some shock, I believe you said?'

'Aye,' Maggie said sadly. 'She'd just heard her husband was missing, believed dead.'

The doctor nodded his head. It wasn't that uncommon an occurrence these days.

'How is she, Doctor?' Maggie asked urgently.

'Well, she gave her head quite a crack,' the doctor said. 'We've had to stitch it, so we had to shave part of her hair away, and she's confused due to the concussion, so we'd like her to stay in for a day or two so we can keep an eye on her. But I'm very sorry to tell you, especially as her husband has been reported missing, that we were unable to save the baby. Your sister miscarried a little while ago.'

Maggie's mouth dropped open. 'A baby?'

'You didn't know she was pregnant?' the doctor asked in surprise.

'No,' Maggie cried. 'She couldn't have been pregnant, there must be some mistake, you must have her mixed up with someone else.'

'I assure you, your sister was over three months' pregnant when she was admitted,' the doctor said.

'But . . . but her husband has been away since nineteen forty,' Maggie said.

The doctor shrugged. 'These things happen,' he said.

Maybe, Maggie thought, but not to Kathy, she's not that type at all. She must see her, speak to her, find out what had happened, but the doctor said she was sedated and couldn't have visitors until the next day. 'I'll come tomorrow,' she promised. 'And I'd be very obliged if you'd not mention the miscarriage to any of the family.'

Again the doctor shrugged. 'I'll inform the nurses on the ward.'

'Thank you,' Maggie said. 'I need time to talk with my sister.'

All the way home, Maggie thought about it. Over three months, the doctor said, and now it was August. That meant something must have happened some time in May. And then she remembered the night Kathy had gone to the pictures alone to see *Mrs Miniver*. Sid and Enid had told Maggie later that they'd waited up till nearly eleven o'clock, but Kathy hadn't returned home, and the next morning Molly had found her asleep in the cellar with her head on the table.

'Her clothes were all rumpled up, and her eyes so red and swollen, I knew she'd been crying for hours,' Molly had said to Maggie. 'She said she'd had a headache, but it was more than any headache, I'd say.'

And when Maggie had asked her the next day about the film, she'd said it had been all right and made it plain she didn't really want to talk about it. 'Enid and Sid said you were in rather late,' Maggie had said.

'What is this?' Kathy had retorted sharply. 'Am I a child to be told when to come in? I met an old friend and we got talking.'

For two hours? Maggie might have said, for since the start of the war most of the picture houses closed at nine o'clock. She could have asked who the friend was, but she didn't, for she knew Kathy was lying, there was no friend. And it was shortly after that that her behaviour had become odd.

And suddenly Maggie knew what had happened that night. Kathy had been raped on her way home! Obviously she'd been upset and ashamed about it and not wanted to tell anyone. And then to find herself pregnant – she must have been out of her mind with worry. Still, at least she'd miscarried, and maybe that was a blessing. Tomorrow Maggie would see her and tell her there was nothing to be ashamed of; she was not to blame at all and there was no need for the family to know if Kathy didn't want to tell them. In all honesty, she'd have enough to do coping with the fact that Barry was unlikely to come home again, Maggie thought, and she made her way home to tell the family how Kathy was.

'All I'm saying is she's not the only one to lose her man,' Bridie said.

'For God's sake, Bridie, show some compassion,' Mary cried. 'You of all people must know what she's going through.'

'I didn't faint all over the damned place and languish in hospital,' Bridie snapped.

'She's split her head open, you stupid woman,' Maggie spat, furious at Bridie's complete lack of sympathy.

When Maggie had returned from the hospital, she'd popped in first to Kathy's house to find Molly beside herself with grief. Maggie felt helpless. It was Molly's third son to die, she told herself, looking at the woman's heavy shoulders and face awash with tears, and Barry had been her favourite, according to Kathy. Eventually Maggie left her in the capable hands of Sid and Enid. The old woman's sadness had reduced her to tears too; all these young men dying and still the war wasn't won, she thought, making her way to her mother's. She loved Kathy dearly, and she'd been very fond of Barry and would miss him sorely. Then at Mary's house, Bridie had been holding court, giving out about Kathy making a fuss about something that had happened to many women.

'Don't you get on your high horse with me,' Bridie yelled at Maggie. 'She cracked her head because she fainted. Why did she faint, that's what I want to know.'

For a second Maggie paused. Had her sister's faint been caused by shock alone, or was her pregnancy something to do with it? she wondered. But Bridie couldn't know about the pregnancy. Nobody knew but her. She thought her slight hesitation went unnoticed, for Mary cried, 'For the love of God, Bridie, are you mad or what? It's enough to make any woman faint when she'd told her man's missing, presumed dead. You know what Kathy and Barry thought of one another, they've been made for each other since they were weans together.'

Bridie, however, had seen the panicky look in Maggie's eyes and said now, with almost a sneer in her voice, 'I know as well as anyone how it used to be with Kathy and Barry, but I wonder if she feels the same now. Sadie who lives next to me said she saw her being very friendly with a soldier outside the Broadway some months back, and him a Yank and all.'

A Yank! Maggie thought. It was a Yank that raped our Kathy. Unless it was Doug Kathy had been seen with, but she dismissed that, for they'd been so sure that Doug and Phil had been transferred somewhere. Anyway, if she'd met Doug, she'd have mentioned it, surely?

'And what exactly do you mean by that remark?' Mary snapped.

'They were just being very friendly,' Bridie said. She smiled to herself; she was enjoying this. She'd waited with the information and watched Kathy carefully. Everyone knew what Yanks were. Bridie didn't know whether it had gone further than cuddles and the silly bitch had fallen for a baby or not. Oh, she'd like that, it would take the smile off Kathy's silly face and stop the family thinking she was some sort of saint; in fact, it would bring the whole family name down in the mud. The Sullivan clan made her sick, going about as if they were something special all the time.

'Don't be so stupid, you malicious old bugger,' Maggie burst out.

'Don't you call my mother stupid,' Sheelagh cried from the corner. 'And we're not lying, Auntie Sadie did say they were being friendly. She said they were kissing and cuddling.'

Oh, God! Maggie cried silently. If Kathy had done anything wrong and she had to be seen, why did it have to be by Bridie's neighbour? She looked at Sheelagh with distaste. Kathy had been right in her reservations about a convent education for the girl. She was fourteen now, and very tall and slim, and her face would be pretty if it wasn't always so petulant. There was no trace of a Birmingham accent in her voice, nor of the Irish lilt of her parents and grandparents. She called Bridie Mother instead of Mammy and hardly deigned to speak to the other people in the neighbourhood at all, except Sadie Griffiths, who lived next door and was as nasty, vindictive and gossipy as Bridie was.

285

And when she did speak, it was with a haughty lift of the chin and often a sneer in the voice.

Mary said she was sure there was some explanation for what Sadie had seen; maybe she was mistaken. Eamonn was thundering around that he wouldn't believe a word the bloody woman said anyway, but what was the world coming to when a slip of a girl could speak as Sheelagh did to her elders? Mary turned in appeal to Maggie and said, 'What do you think?'

What do I think? Maggie thought. I think my sister lies now recovering from a miscarriage that might be the result of a brutal rape and I'll know nothing more until I can speak to her. 'I think,' she said, 'we should stop tearing Kathy's character to pieces when she's not here to defend herself – if she has anything to defend. I wasn't able to see her tonight, as I said, and when she is fit for visitors, I'm sure she'll be able to clear up any misunderstandings.'

'Aye. Aye, you're right,' Eamonn said. 'We should be ashamed talking of Kathy this way. Hasn't she always been a grand girl altogether and not a whit of trouble?'

'Aye, that's right, Saint Kathy,' Bridie sneered. 'Well, I know what I know, and so does Sadie. Kathy isn't as goody-goody as you seem to think. She hasn't even time for her own weans. She was quick enough to send the two eldest away, and everyone knows Molly rears Padraic.'

'You look to your own bloody house,' Maggie said. 'Oh, you have Sheelagh strutting beside you every minute and dressed to the nines as well, but where's young Matt? You never seem to have a minute for him.'

'He's a numbskull, that's why,' Bridie snapped. 'And he'll be a bloody nowt and a nothing all the days of his life, like his father before him.'

There was a small shocked silence, and then Eamonn, though furiously angry, spoke quietly. Somehow it gave greater emphasis to his words. 'Go back to your home, Bridie, while you're still able, and take your daughter with you. I've never hit a woman in my life, but if I have to look on your face much more and listen to the venom from your mouth, I might start with you.'

Bridie stared at her father-in-law for a minute, aware she'd gone too far in putting Pat down in front of his parents, but she wasn't going to apologise; it wasn't in her nature to do that. 'Come on, Sheelagh,' she said. 'We know when we're not wanted,' and she swept out of the front door and closed it with a resounding bang.

SEVENTEEN

'Kathy, honestly, you don't have to tell me anything,' Maggie said. 'Oh God, don't cry, the nurses will throw me out.'

Kathy rubbed at her eyes and said, 'But I must, don't you see? I must tell someone the truth. Barry is dead because of me.'

'Don't be stupid,' Maggie said firmly.

'I'm not,' Kathy said. 'Wait till you hear what happened.' She stopped, almost afraid to continue, and then said, 'I'm sorry you had to find out about the baby in the way you did. I felt I couldn't tell anyone. In one way I'd like to be able to say yes, I was raped, as you thought when you first heard about the miscarriage. I'd like for you to think I was taken advantage of and was not a willing partner to what happened, but it's not true.'

The tears began to run again as Kathy continued, but she seemed unaware of them. 'If the baby had lived – and I'm really glad it didn't – the father would have been Doug Howister. We met by accident, at the cinema that night you weren't well enough to go. I knew he was attracted to me, you were right about that, and he'd told me himself before, and you were also right when you said I was drawn to him too. That's why I never wanted to be alone with him. I was afraid of our feelings overwhelming us, as they eventually did that night.'

'Oh, Kath, don't,' Maggie cried. 'It doesn't matter, nothing matters. Please, please don't upset yourself like this.'

Kathy struggled to control herself and said, 'We might not have this time alone again, and I want you to know everything. I . . . I did kiss Doug outside the cinema like Sadie Griffiths said. I know it was stupid, but I couldn't seem to help myself, and when we kissed I realised how much I wanted him. Oh, Maggie, how I ached to be loved. He didn't press me, in fact he told me to think carefully about what I was doing, but I was beyond reason. You have no idea.'

'Oh, I have,' Maggie said. 'It was like that for me and Con, and we didn't wait for marriage, Kath.'

'But you've not been unfaithful to him since.'

'No, but I can see how it happens. Four years is a long time, and sometimes I get so frustrated I could scream. You're only human, Kathy.'

'But I enjoyed it,' Kathy said.

'Did you think you wouldn't?'

'I mean more, much more, than sex with Barry,' Kathy said, and struggled to explain without embarrassment. 'It was . . . Doug is . . . we . . .'

'It wasn't just wham, bang, thank you, ma'am?' Maggie suggested helpfully.

'Well, yes, I suppose that's about right,' Kathy agreed. 'Even now, I can't fully regret it, though I'd have hated Barry to know; it would have hurt him too much. Doug moved out the following day. He said he thought they were heading south, and his unit must have been part of the invasion on the sixth of June, about the same time I realised my period was late.' She looked at Maggie with large frightened eyes. 'I can't tell you how scared I was. I nearly went mad. I couldn't eat, or sleep, or even think straight. I prayed, dedicated masses, lit candles, said novenas, but it did no good. I know everyone was worried about me, but I couldn't tell anyone anything.'

'What were you going to do?' Maggie asked gently.

'Ask Sophie Barraclough's advice,' Kathy said. 'Go and see her and throw myself on her mercy and ask if she knew of anyone I could hide out with for a while until the baby was born.'

'You'd never have got away with it. Mammy would have gone mad if you'd just disappeared for months, and what about Padraic? You couldn't have left him totally with Molly.'

'I know,' Kathy said. 'I'd have had to write to the weans too, and I'd soon have been traced. I didn't think it out well at all, but you must remember I was beside myself.'

'I can imagine,' Maggie said, and added, 'And you think God punished you for having sex with Doug Howister by taking Barry from you?'

'Aye,' Kathy said. 'Because I never told the priest about it, you know, in confession.'

'Why not?'

'I was afraid.'

'Kathy, they hear worse than that,' Maggie said. 'You must tell them and get it off your conscience, then you'll feel better about it.'

'I will, I suppose,' Kathy said. 'It's worried me going to the rails with my soul as black as pitch with mortal sin, but it hardly matters now. More important is how I'm going to get through life without Barry. I . . . I didn't want to wake up today. Yesterday I was sedated and knew nothing, but this morning, when I woke, it all came flooding back and I wanted someone to come in with a needle so I could float away again and not feel this pain. It hurts so much.' Kathy looked sadly at Maggie and said, 'Sometimes I wonder if it's worth going on, you know?'

'Now this is stupid. You've got your three weans that still have to be seen to, and Mammy and Daddy who'll miss Barry too, like another son, and Molly who will need you more than ever.'

'And what would they think of me if they knew I'd killed him?'

'You didn't kill him. Stop that talk.'

'God was punishing me.'

'He wasn't, he doesn't work that way,' Maggie said decisively. 'When you're well, we'll go to Father Cunningham and ask him.'

But before she could ask the priest's advice, the day after Maggie's visit she had to face her parents. She'd worked out a tale to tell them that she hoped would satisfy them, because though they'd dismissed Sadie's claims as untrue, fanciful or exaggerated, Maggie said they were bound to be curious and a semblance of the truth had to be told.

So she told them she'd met Doug and Phil the night she went to the pictures to see *Mrs Miniver* and had hugged them both outside the cinema because they'd told her they were moving off at dawn the following morning. Sadie had got totally the wrong end of the stick, she said. She'd gone to the pub with them for a last farewell drink, just as she'd done that time with Maggie, and that was why she was late home.

Mary patted her hand and said she was not to worry, that Sadie Griffiths had always been one for bad-mouthing people. 'She's that bad herself, she thinks everyone's the same. I knew you wouldn't be up to doing anything like that.'

Kathy knew she was blushing, and she felt rather sorry for Sadie, who had, for once, been telling the truth. She also knew she'd told yet another lie, and thought that if she didn't go soon to the priest she'd have a list of sins as long as her arm.

Eamonn said he'd not give house room to the woman and he was surprised Mary had even mentioned it to Kathy. Couldn't she see the state she was in already and hadn't she enough to cope with? And then Kathy began to cry, and Mary gave out to Eamonn for upsetting her with his clumsiness. Eamonn, angered, said someone had to say they missed Barry, and wasn't the loss of him more important than repeating some rigmarole an old trollop bent on making mischief had told them?

The nurse told them they'd have to leave, they were upsetting the patient. They went complaining and blaming each other, and Kathy continued to cry. In the end she got her wish, for the doctor was concerned about her and said she should be given another sedative, and she slipped thankfully into blessed oblivion again.

It was the next day before Kathy was able to think of the children and who was to tell them about Barry. She wanted to go to Hereford herself, but she was too weak. It wasn't the sort of thing she felt you should write to two children, and when Maggie offered to go for her and tell them about their father, Kathy accepted gratefully.

She was eventually allowed home, the very day Maggie set off for Hereford, but she was told to take things easy, at least until the stitches had been removed from the head wound. However, Molly seemed to have had the life sucked out of her and spent the day either staring into space or crying into a hanky. Kathy was finding Padraic a handful, for it was the summer holidays and the nursery school was shut. He was very interested in the hair that had been shaved from her head and the dressing and bandage that surrounded it, but not so bothered about the death of a father he'd not seen. 'He doesn't understand,' Kathy said, for Padraic's reaction upset Molly afresh. 'No four-year-old understands death, and he never even met Barry.'

'Oh God, fancy that, to die and not to have even seen your son,' Molly said, and burst again into shaking sobs.

Kathy could do nothing with her, and everyone else was at work, so she took the helm again. She was glad to do it, because she'd never been one to sit idle, and doing housework, shopping and cooking left her little time for thinking. She decided to take one day at a time and not to look too far into the future, and she prayed for the journey Maggie was making to tell her children their father would not be coming home again.

Lizzie was excited that her Auntie Maggie was coming and not at all worried about the purpose of her visit. Her mammy had been to stay when she wanted a wee break, so she presumed that now it was Maggie's turn. Sophie, however, knew why Maggie was coming, for Maggie had phoned her from Pickering's to tell her the news.

Sophie was greatly saddened by the phone call and told Millie and David in order to prepare them to comfort two very distressed children. Although David was still at home, the plaster cast had been removed from his arm, and Sophie hated to think that he'd soon be back in the battle ground. David, though, seemed anxious to be back. He went to physiotherapy once a week and carried on with the exercises at home. 'Quick reactions can make the difference between life and death, Mother,' he'd said one day as she watched him going through the routine. Sophie had turned quite grey, and Lizzie was cross with him for being so insensitive.

Maggie was surprised at how the children had grown and changed, and how well they both looked. They were very excited to see her, and as she hugged them both, her heart was heavy with the news she had to share with them

After answering all their questions about the family, she took them into the small sitting room, saying she had something to tell them, and they followed, puzzled but still unsuspecting.

Once in the room, she sat on the settee with a child either side of her and began, 'I want you both to be very brave. I have some sad and upsetting news for you.' Beside her she felt each child stiffen, but neither said a word, and there wasn't a sound. It was as if everyone was holding their breath. 'Your mother had a telegram the other day from the War Office,' she went on. 'It said your daddy is missing.'

For a moment there was a stunned silence, and then Danny gave a sob and, leaping to his feet, cried, 'That's what they said about Uncle Pat, and he was dead!' He looked at his aunt, tears trickling down his cheeks, and said, 'Our daddy's dead too, isn't he?'

Maggie nodded her head slowly. 'They think so, Dan,' she said, and gathered the weeping child in her arms. Lizzie got to her feet slowly, her eyes dry but glazed, and Maggie saw the hurt deep inside her, too deep for tears. She faced her aunt with a glare.

'He isn't dead,' she screamed. 'He isn't! He isn't! You're stupid and wicked to say things like that. I hate you!'

'Lizzie . . .' Maggie began, but Lizzie was across the room and out of the door before Maggie could move, and she felt she couldn't just abandon poor Dan to run after her.

David, Sophie and Millie had stayed in the kitchen where they might be on hand if needed, and so they heard Lizzie wrench the door of the sitting room open. David spotted her headlong flight down the corridor, and went out quickly through the back way, knowing that she would make for the little copse the other side of the lane. He'd seen her slip in there a few times when she wished to be alone. He wondered if she would want to be alone this time and if she would resent his presence, but he doubted it. Just in case, though, once in the shelter of the trees, he was careful to avoid stepping on crackling twigs, stumbling over tree stumps or getting entangled with trailing branches that might betray his presence.

Lizzie lay face down on a flat grassy area framed by trees and cried as if her heart was broken. She remembered all the things she'd done with her daddy when she was a little girl, how he would read to her for hours, and the way she always felt safe and protected when she was with him. She could remember the feel of his trousers against her bare legs and his scratchy cheek against hers, and the smell of his jumper, slightly sweaty and mixed with the cigarettes he'd gone back to smoking once he'd eventually got a job.

David was moved by the sight of Lizzie's distress and he slipped silently over the grass and lowered himself down gently beside her. Lizzie opened her eyes and the image of her father vanished, and she knew he was gone forever. For a moment she felt she couldn't cope with it. Surely you couldn't feel such pain and live, she thought, and she groped blindly for David's hand, needing the contact of another human being. David grasped her hand tightly and bent over her slightly, trying to comfort her with his presence.

He didn't urge her not to upset herself, as she might have expected, but said instead, 'It's good to cry, Elizabeth. It must be awful to lose your father like that. I was just a baby when my father died, and anyway he'd been an invalid for years. But I know how much you loved yours. I just can't imagine how much you'll miss him.'

'Oh, David,' Lizzie cried. She withdrew her hand from his as she spoke and put her arms around his neck, and together they fell back on to the grass. Lizzie lay with her head on David's shoulder, and his arms went around her waist to comfort her, and to his horror he found he was becoming aroused by the young body he held so tenderly. He was ashamed of his feelings. Lizzie was just a young, innocent girl seeking some comfort to help her cope with the devastating news she'd just heard, and here he was thinking of her in this way. He eased his body slightly away from hers and hoped she was too innocent to know what she'd done to him.

David had had no sexual experience at all. Some of his contemporaries at school had run forays into town, or even had little skirmishes with the laundry maids, and one chap, Gilmour, had boasted he'd done it with the French student who came to teach the boys conversational French. 'Taught her a thing or two I'd say,' Gilmour said. 'French girls definitely aren't as hung-up as the English, and she was as keen for it as I was.'

David was terribly envious of Gilmour and his confident manner. When he'd joined the RAF, he'd been ribbed unmercilessly when they found out, through a slip of the tongue, that he was still a virgin. Determined to make a man of him, they took him into town, plied him with drinks and delivered him to a prostitute called Carla, used at one time or another by most of the RAF lads stationed there. 'In fact we think she should be given an honorary title after the war,' one young cadet confided to David. 'For raising morale, you know? Anyway, if you get the sexual frustration bit out of the way, you can concentrate more on the job in hand.'

David was repelled by Carla. Her voluptuousness and crude sexuality offended him and he felt his libido, egged on all night by alcohol and blue jokes, slide away from him. He was suddenly more sober than he'd been all night. Carla, scantily dressed, surveyed him from across the room and said, 'You're scared shitless, aren't you?'

Miserably David nodded, and she said, 'It don't mean much, you know, if you are. One of these days you'll meet a girl who will bring an ache to your loins and you'll know what to do all right. I could teach you a few tricks to have them queuing up, but you aren't ready yet.'

David still didn't speak, and she said, 'How old are you, son?'

'Seventeen,' David said. 'I . . . I lied about my age.'

'To join the show before it's over, I suppose,' Carla said, and added, but kindly, 'Bloody young fool.' Then she gave a laugh and said, 'If you'd been a couple of years younger, I could be your mother,' and David realised with a sense of shock that Carla wasn't the young girl he'd first imagined, but someone much older, early thirties he'd have said. The other thing he realised was that she was easy to talk to, and that he liked her.

'You're a nice youngster,' Carla said. 'You've no need to tell those numbskulls about our little conversation. You just say it was great.' She patted David's knee and went on, 'One day some young girl will set you on fire, my lad, and what to do will be as natural as day following night.'

And now that David had met the girl who'd set him on fire, he could do nothing about it. She was only thirteen years old, for all her shapeliness, and she was also in his mother's care. It was almost incestuous to feel the way he did about Elizabeth O'Malley, who'd shared his home for four years.

Lizzie's heart-wrenching shuddering sobs had stopped, and yet still David lay beside her, with his arms around her. In truth he didn't want to relinquish his hold. After a moment or two she said, 'You're very special to me, David,' and then she uttered the words she thought she'd never say. 'I . . . I think I love you, David.'

David's heart began thudding against his ribs, and he realised he loved her too, and with a passion he was fighting at the moment.

'I feel so miserable,' Lizzie said. 'I can't really take it in about Daddy. I loved him so much, I sort of felt my love would protect him in some way. I know that's silly.'

'No it isn't,' David said. 'A lot of people feel that.'

'Do they?' Lizzie said. 'Well, it doesn't work, and the awful thing is, the last time he was home I didn't like him much and was glad when he went back. Oh God, David, I feel so miserable.' She wriggled in his arms and said, 'I'm glad you're holding me, I feel better to know you care.'

David's heart seemed to do a somersault. Lizzie lay still and quiet for a moment, and then suddenly she said, 'David, will you kiss me?'

David, struggling to keep his arousal in check, said huskily, 'I don't think that would be a good idea, Elizabeth.' He leant up on one elbow as he spoke, releasing Lizzie so abruptly that she rolled almost underneath him.

'Elizabeth,' she said dreamily. 'You always call me Elizabeth.'

David didn't need a Carla to show him what to do, or mates urging him on with vulgarity and pints of beer. He knew what he wanted to do with the young girl beneath him, but he held himself in check. A chaste brotherly kiss wouldn't hurt, though, he thought, it might even help, and so he bent his head and kissed her cheek gently and tenderly, with his heart racing. Then, unable to help himself, he kissed the tears away from her eyes and cheeks, then more urgently put his lips to hers.

Lizzie was astounded. Her love for David had been based on the romantic, but David's kiss released emotions she didn't know she had. And then his hands were cupping her small rounded breasts, and though she knew she should stop him, she wasn't able to. She felt as if she were drowning in his kisses, and she was giving little moaning sounds that were driving David crazy.

Panting slightly, he moved to unfasten her top, but her body immediately went rigid and she pulled away a little from his embrace. 'No, David, we mustn't.'

David could have groaned in frustration. 'Shh,' he said desperately, and began fumbling again with the buttons. 'I won't hurt you.'

Lizzie pushed his hands away. 'It would be a sin,' she said. 'I can't.'

She was sure it must be a sin; even to let David feel her breasts outside her clothes must be wrong. She didn't know if the feelings she had in her body when David kissed her were sinful too. She knew only she'd never had them before, and it took all her willpower to stop David unbuttoning her blouse. She'd wanted to help him and was shocked at herself.

David sat up, head in his hands, trying to still the frustration tearing at his insides. He was ashamed of himself for what he'd tried to do, and knew he would have gone on to do more if Lizzie had let him. She was only a child, he told himself firmly, and he had to forget the incident had ever happened.

Lizzie had lain watching David anxiously, and now she sat up and touched his arm lightly, and it was as if an electric current had run through him. 'I'm sorry,' she said, and David despised himself still further.

'It doesn't matter,' he said brusquely.

'If I could let anyone, it would be you,' Lizzie said.

'Oh God, Elizabeth, don't go round saying that sort of thing.'

'I don't,' Lizzie protested. 'I'm just telling you,' and then she said again, 'I really think I love you, David.'

Oh God, David thought. He had to get Lizzie back to the house before his good intentions went out of the window. He glanced at her. She was still looking at him with a worried expression on her lovely face and a slight frown puckering her brow. She was so beautiful that David suddenly felt short of breath.

He got to his feet and held out a hand. 'Do you feel all right to go in now?'

Lizzie nodded, her eyes sad and sombre-looking.

'I know it's hard for you,' David said. 'But the pain will go after a time.'

Lizzie doubted it. She couldn't remember a time when she hadn't loved her father. But David was so nice, and so kind, and then a spasm of horror went through her and she realised he could be killed too. 'I'm afraid,' she said, and shivered.

David put his arms around her again, and immediately his pulses began racing. He'd have to keep right away from Lizzie if he wanted nothing to develop between them, he thought. But he didn't want that, and it would destroy her, especially as vulnerable as she was at that moment. He'd just have to go very slowly and do nothing to hurt or worry her.

And with this decision made, they returned hand in hand until the house was in sight. Both knew that they mustn't speak to anyone of what had happened in the wood.

But though they said nothing, Maggie saw the shining light in her niece's eyes and knew something had happened to her. She'd run out on the news of her father's death, unable to bear it, and come back with her eyes shining, though the redness and puffiness around them showed the tears she'd shed. Maggie glanced at David and saw the same glow. So, she thought, that was the way of it. Kathy said Lizzie had been in love with David for years, but that was a form of hero-worship; this, unless she was much mistaken, was something more serious.

But then, she told herself, how could it be, with Lizzie a mere child? Anyway, Lizzie would be back at school in a few days and then David would be away to his planes and that would be that. It was young love, a new experience for both of them probably, and brought to a head perhaps because David had been comforting Lizzie. And if it helped her cope, where was the harm? It wouldn't last, but there was no need to worry Kathy about any of it; she had enough on her plate and she'd be down to see both children before too long.

Neither Millie nor Sophie had noticed anything amiss when David and Lizzie returned to the house together, nor did they during the next few days, the last of the summer holidays. Maggie left the following day, and Millie and Sophie's attention was taken up with Danny, who'd become silent and withdrawn since hearing of his father's death. Lizzie was ashamed that she couldn't feel that measure of grief, and that in the middle of thinking about her daddy and how she would miss him, she'd remember David and a bubble of happiness would rise inside her that she wasn't able to suppress.

David and Lizzie were able to spend their last days together uninterrupted. Sophie thought David was doing it as a kindness, and even remarked on it. 'It is good of you, David, especially when little Dan is still so upset.'

Lizzie felt slightly guilty, and yet she didn't want to stop seeing David. Twice they took a picnic, and once they stopped at a village pub and David had a foaming pint of beer, and later Lizzie thought his lips tasted funny. They walked miles along the River Wye, up hill and down dale they went, and hand in hand through the woodland, and they talked as they had never talked before. In fact David talked and Lizzie listened as he went on about his hopes, dreams and beliefs. She loved to hear him and watch him; she loved everything about him, so much so that at times, he ached with it.

She loved him to hold her tight and kiss her until she felt dizzy, despite being scared of the emotions pounding

301

through her body. She even felt the excitement in David and was frightened of that too. Although David never did any more than kiss her, the kisses were enough to set them both on fire, though Lizzie didn't quite understand what was happening to her.

Then it was Saturday, and confession. Lizzie had been dreading it. Sophie said that Danny was not to go as he was still not very well, and on the Buxton farm every hand was needed to get the hay in, so Alice wasn't able to go into Hereford either, and Lizzie felt ashamed that she was glad Alice was so busy. She had David to herself because he'd told his mother he'd enjoy the outing, and they took the bus together.

David tried to convince Lizzie not to go to confession just this once and spend the time with him instead, but she was horrified, knowing she needed the absolution of the priest more than ever before. But she told herself that David wasn't a Catholic and couldn't be expected to truly understand.

She left him in the porch, made the sign of the cross with holy water in the font by the door, bobbed her knee before the altar and stepped into the pew beside the others waiting by the confessional.

She knelt quietly, hands clasped, as she rehearsed over and over what she'd say to the priest. And then, before she was truly ready – though in her heart of hearts she knew she'd never be ready – the confessional door opened and with trembling legs she got to her feet and crept inside.

'Bless me, Father, for I have sinned. It's a week since my last confession,' Lizzie began.

She wasn't worried about the first part of the confession and rattled off her usual litany. Then she told the priest about her father's death and how sad her brother was and how she'd been impatient with him, and the priest said it was understandable. After that there was a silence while the priest waited and she racked her brain to think of further sins, until eventually he said, 'Anything else, my child?'

'Yes, Father.' Lizzie's voice was just above a whisper.

Again there was a silence and the priest prompted, 'Go on.'

'I've . . . I've . . . I've been having impure thoughts, Father.'

Behind the screen the priest smiled. You're not the only one, he might have said, but instead he enquired, 'What form do these thoughts take?'

'What form, Father?'

'I mean, are they about yourself?'

'Oh yes, Father, me and another person.'

'And who is this other person?'

'My . . . my boyfriend, Father.'

The priest sat up straighter. If he was not mistaken, the girl on the other side of the confessional was the little one evacuated to Hereford with her brother; he'd have recognised the accent anywhere. They were living with a non-Catholic lady who'd introduced herself to him as Mrs Sophie Barraclough. He wondered if she was aware her ward had a boyfriend.

'How old is your boyfriend, child?'

'Seventeen, Father.'

'And how old are you?' he asked.

'Thirteen, Father.'

'Hmm,' said the priest. 'You're rather young to have a boyfriend.'

Lizzie had known in her heart of hearts that that was what the priest would say. 'Yes, Father,' she said miserably.

'And even younger to have impure thoughts about him,' the priest went on.

'Yes, Father.'

'Do you go out with him, this boyfriend?'

'Yes, Father.'

The priest cleared his throat. He wanted to leave it there, but he couldn't. He had the girl's spiritual welfare to look after. 'Has he, your boyfriend, has he ever touched you?' he asked.

'Yes, Father,' Lizzie said. 'He's kissed me.'

'Is that all, just kissed you?'

Is that all? Lizzie thought. You wouldn't say that if you knew how it made me feel. But the priest hadn't asked how David's kisses had affected her; he'd asked if he'd touched her anywhere else. She went hot as she remembered his hands cupping her breasts the day he'd found her crying in the wood.

'No, Father,' she said.

'Go on.'

How could she go on? How could she say the word 'breast' to a priest?

'I can't, Father.'

'He touched your body?'

'Yes, Father.'

'What part of your body?'

'My . . . my . . . chest, Father.'

Oh, dear God, the priest thought, a young man was violating this young girl. 'Did you protest, my child?'

'Yes, Father. When . . . when Da . . . my boyfriend tried to unbutton my blouse. I did then.'

The priest let out a sigh of relief. 'So he touched you outside your clothes?' he said, glad that the situation had not got as out of hand as he'd feared. But he'd better be certain. 'And he didn't touch you anywhere else?'

'No, Father,' said Lizzie, and the priest smiled as he heard the indignation in the child's voice.

But this was no time for levity. 'Now listen,' he said sternly. 'Allowing a young man to touch you anywhere, even outside of your clothes, is a sin. Do you understand?'

'Yes, Father.'

'And that is what has led to these impure thoughts?'

'Yes, Father.'

'Even kisses you have to be careful of. A friendly kiss is no harm at all, but you shouldn't kiss anyone in any other way at your age. You do understand?'

Oh, Lizzie understood all right. Even as she chanted, 'Yes, Father,' she was thinking that she couldn't in all honesty describe David's kisses as friendly, not of course that you'd kiss your enemies that way either. But what the priest was actually saying was that she couldn't kiss David or touch him at all, or allow him to kiss or touch her. It didn't sound very hopeful to Lizzie. In fact the future of their relationship looked very bleak indeed. She tried again. 'I love my boyfriend, Father, and he loves me, and soon he will be rejoining his squadron. He's in the RAF but he was injured.'

And the uniform had attracted an impressionable young girl, the priest thought, and his injury had evoked sympathy, and then with her father dying, perhaps she turned to this young man for help and comfort and he took advantage of her. Thank God he'd soon be out of reach. 'You must pray to Our Lady for strength, my child,' he said. 'And pray to her for guidance. If you and your boyfriend love each other as you say, he will wait for you and not ask you to do things you feel are wrong.'

'No, Father,' Lizzie said dully.

She knew she had lost, and that whatever she did now with David was sinful and would have to be confessed. She mumbled through an act of contrition without thinking about the words, accepted her penance of a decade of the rosary and escaped from the box thankfully. As she knelt at the rails, she thought about her first confession and how Mairead Cleary had been given a decade of the rosary for her penance. I wonder if that was for impure thoughts, thought Lizzie. I wouldn't have known what an impure thought was in those days, even if one had leapt up and hit me on the nose.

But, she told herself, it was no good worrying about all that now. She'd confessed her sins and received absolution, and as long as she said her penance she would be clear of sin till the next time. David was waiting outside and they had the day to themselves, but she lit a candle before the altar of the Virgin Mary for good measure.

Outside, David went to pull Lizzie into his arms, but she drew back. 'What is it?' he asked, concerned.

'It's . . . Oh, David, the priest said we mustn't.'

David was mystified. 'Mustn't what?'

'Do this.'

'Do what, for heaven's sake?'

'Anything,' Lizzie cried miserably. 'Kiss and all that.'

'You're joking?'

'No, I'm not. I only wish I was,' said Lizzie. 'I told him . . . you know, about us, and he said we hadn't to do those things.'

David stood stock still and held Lizzie away from him. 'Why did you tell him?' he said, angry that she should talk about such private things to a virtual stranger.

'I had to. I told you, I must tell all my sins.'

'And he said it was wrong, did he?' David snapped.

Lizzie had seen David angry before, but then it had been directed at his mother, never at her. It scared her, and so did the blue eyes, cold as ice, that glared at her. She recalled again the words of the priest, and for the first time wondered if he might have been wrong. It was almost a blasphemous thought for her, because in the past she'd always thought priests infallible.

After all, she thought, what does he know? Priests don't marry, and he's probably never had anyone kiss him like David kisses me. He couldn't imagine what my feelings are, and how my impure thoughts are only really what I'd like David to do. Though I know that if he did those things I'd have to stop him, or it really would be a sin.

And while these thoughts were tumbling around in her head, David, the person she loved above everyone in the whole world, was waiting for an answer. 'I'm sorry, David,' she said. 'I must kiss the man I love. I see that now.'

'Ah, Elizabeth,' said David, and he opened his arms and she snuggled into them. The kiss between them was a form of release for Lizzie. She'd defied the priest and could feel almost sorry that he could never enjoy such pleasures himself, and when David's kiss became more ardent and he pressed her tighter to him, she responded so passionately that even David was surprised.

When they eventually broke apart, David said shakily, 'I think I'll take you to confession more often.'

'Well, what does a priest know anyway?' Lizzie said.

'Nothing at all,' David agreed, and placed a gentle kiss on Lizzie's lips. But when she would have continued the embrace, he withdrew slightly, having enough trouble controlling his feelings as it was. 'Come on,' he said. 'We'll never see anything of Hereford at this rate.'

Lizzie wouldn't have cared, but to please David she took his hand and they walked out of the churchyard and into the town.

EIGHTEEN

'Oh, Lizzie, how awful,' Alice said. It was the first day back at school and they were eating their dinner together. Lizzie had told her of Maggie's visit and the news she'd brought. Alice's eyes had filled with tears, and Lizzie knew she was remembering her second brother, who'd been killed two years before. 'You must miss your father very much.'

'Well yes, I do,' said Lizzie. 'Or at least I will, I suppose. The point is, it isn't like you missing your brother. I mean, he'd been at home until he joined up, but I haven't seen my daddy for four years. It's strange to think he's actually dead, and sad that I'll never see him again, but I don't think it will really hit me until the war's over and he doesn't come back, you know?'

Alice nodded. But she knew how important Lizzie's family were to her, despite the fact that she'd been separated from them for years, and she thought her very brave. 'Anyway,' Lizzie went on, 'something else happened on that day too, the day my aunt came.'

'What?'

'I'll tell you,' Lizzie said, 'but it's a secret. You've got to promise.'

'I promise. Cross my heart,' Alice said earnestly, then listened open-mouthed as Lizzie told her what had happened in the copse between her and David. She omitted to tell her friend about David's hands cupping and caressing her breasts, but what she said was enough. 'He kissed you?' Alice burst out. 'Really kissed you?'

Lizzie nodded. Before, she wouldn't have known what a real kiss was, but what David had done was real all right.

'What did it feel like?' Alice asked.

How could Lizzie describe David's kisses to Alice? She could hardly have said they drove her wild and set her whole body tingling with desire, and that when David eventually released her she found she was a little out of breath and wanting more.

She spread her hands helplessly and gave a shrug. Alice persisted. 'Were they terribly exciting, and did they transport you to paradise, like we read in one of the magazines the land girls left about?'

How they had laughed at the time at those phrases, and others like 'brooding eyes', and 'lips like wine', Lizzie thought, but now suddenly it didn't seem so funny. 'It was a bit like that,' she said to Alice.

'Don't they mind, Mrs Barraclough and Millie?'

'They don't know,' Lizzie said. 'I mean, I've been out with David, but they don't know how we feel about each other. Auntie Sophie thinks David is being kind to me because I'm upset over Daddy dying.' She glanced at Alice and said, 'I felt a bit sneaky about it, but I wasn't passing up a chance to be with him. He rejoins his squadron on Wednesday, so we just have today and part of tomorrow left. Auntie Sophie's having a little party for him tomorrow night, so we'll hardly have any time together then.'

'Will you write to him?'

'Of course.'

'Ooh,' said Alice with awe. 'It's so grown-up to have a boyfriend. Do you feel grown-up?'

'Not really,' Lizzie said. 'I just feel wonderful. I think I've loved David for years, and now I think he really cares for me too.'

Alice felt a little left out. She had no wish to get married for ages, but to fall in love was every girl's dream, and she wondered how long it would be before she'd feel that way about someone.

The war dragged on and Kathy was slowly coming to terms with the fact that when it ended she'd have no husband to welcome home. Yet every day she woke up thankful that she hadn't to admit to everyone that she was carrying a child. She truly believed the shame would have killed her. She knew Maggie would say nothing, and she was the only one in the family who knew the whole story.

She'd had a letter of condolence from Sophie Barraclough, expressing her sorrow at her loss and urging Kathy to come down to stay for a few days. She'd have to take Padraic with her, because Molly hadn't really recovered yet from Barry's death, and Kathy wondered if she ever would. She felt immensely sorry for the woman who'd brought four sons up to adulthood almost single-handed after losing her husband and two youngsters to TB, and then had her house bombed around her and her sons killed off till only one was left.

The doctor whom a worried Kathy eventually summoned to the house was also concerned about Molly. 'Depression,' he said. 'Can't wonder at it, really. I'll leave her some tablets and a tonic to buck her up a bit. She's lost a fair bit of weight, hasn't she?'

She had, Kathy knew. As long as she'd known Molly, she'd been a big woman – Barry used to say she was as long as she was wide. But now the apron that used to

310

strain across her ample stomach had plenty of slack on it, and the yellow-coloured flesh of her face seemed to sag, causing pouches to form under her eyes and folds around her neck.

Enid Sutcliffe, knowing that Kathy was worried about leaving Molly, promised to take time off to keep an eye on the older woman. Kathy was relieved and rang the Barracloughs from Pickering's to arrange train times.

On Tuesday afternoon, David was waiting for Lizzie outside the school as he'd been on Monday. Both knew that this was the last time they'd be together for some time, so Lizzie said to Danny, 'Run up home and tell Aunt Sophie I'm going for a walk with David.'

The old Danny would have refused or complained, said it was not fair or demanded to go too, but he had been badly affected by his father's death and was still very subdued. So he just looked from Lizzie to David and then turned for home without a word.

Normally Lizzie would have been worried about her young brother, but today she had eyes only for David. With one accord, they slipped into the shelter of the trees at the edge of the road, where he drew her to him with a sigh of relief. 'Oh, Elizabeth, my darling,' he said. 'This might have to last us months.'

'I know,' Lizzie said. The kiss was first gentle and then more demanding. Lizzie felt herself melting into David's arms, and she clutched him tighter still. She wished she could stop time for just an hour or so, for she knew that if they were too late home that day, questions would be asked.

Eventually David pulled away and said huskily, 'Let's walk down by the river.'

As they emerged from the shelter of the trees, a lone rider watched them from a hill opposite. Rosamund had missed David. She'd been invited to the party that night, but she'd thought he'd have made his way over to the Grange at least for one day before he went back. Her Aunt Sophie had told her mother he was spending a lot of time with Elizabeth, helping her recover from the tragic death of her father. Rosamund could see how David would feel obliged to do his bit, but he surely could have spared her one day!

Her eyes narrowed as she watched the pair emerge from the trees. They were running hand in hand, laughing together. It didn't look as though David was looking after Lizzie. It looked like they were . . . Surely to goodness David wasn't attracted to that common little guttersnipe? But then, she reminded herself, David was easy-going by nature and could be involved in something before he was really aware of it. She could well imagine that Lizzie O'Malley, who was slightly pretty, in a common sort of way, would have worked on David until he imagined an attraction that was all in her head.

David needs rescuing from the likes of her, Rosamund thought, and she slid from her pony, tethered it to a tree and crept down the hill, keeping the two in view all the time. They seemed deep in conversation and were totally unaware of Rosamund trailing them. In fact, they were so wrapped up in each other, she doubted if they'd notice if she ran right past them completely naked.

David suddenly pulled Lizzie towards him and kissed her hungrily. A spasm of jealousy overwhelmed Rosamund, so sharp and painful that she gasped out loud. David was hers, he'd always been hers, everyone knew it. Her mother and David's had talked about it since they were babies, and no grubby city brat was going to snatch him away. True, she'd had her fun with plenty of young men for a year or two, but she was only waiting for David to grow up. And now here he was, and grown very nicely indeed, and it was time for her to take an interest in him. After all, what age was the O'Malley child? She could only be about thirteen. She was far too young for David, while Rosamund was just one year younger than him; another year or so and they might think about engagement, especially if this damned war was over by then.

David spread out his tunic and they both sat down on the river bank, watching the September sun dance on the ripples of the river. 'We'll have to make our way back soon,' Lizzie said.

'Not yet.'

'We'll get into trouble.'

'I leave at first light,' David reminded her, as if she needed it. 'No one will tell me off tonight.'

'No, I'll get it instead,' Lizzie said, but she smiled at David, for she didn't want to go back either.

The smile made David's heart turn a somersault. 'I love you, Elizabeth,' he said.

Lizzie's heart skipped a beat, for it was the first time David had actually said he loved her. Suddenly his lips were on hers, and they fell back on the grass together. Both knew that this was probably it for months, and in Lizzie's heart was a fear that David might be killed like her father and uncle. She kissed him with a passion that for a moment took away his good resolutions. As his hand brushed her breast, Lizzie gave a gasp but didn't push it away. His senses were reeling and his body begging for a release that he knew he couldn't take from Elizabeth, even if she were to allow him to. He caressed her breasts and she moaned with pleasure, and when a button of her school blouse popped open, and he slipped his hand inside, she said nothing, but wriggled beneath him, driving him wild. Swiftly he undid the other buttons until her breasts lay naked in front of him, and the sight made him dizzy.

Behind her tree, Rosamund trembled in rage. The little tramp! she thought. Dirty little whore! She almost expected to see David strip off the rest of her clothing and kick off his own trousers, but he had already gone further than he meant to, although Elizabeth didn't seem to mind and just gazed at him with her large brown eyes. 'I love you, David,' she said in a whisper.

'Oh, God, Elizabeth,' David said, and gently caressed her breasts till the nipples stood in peaks while he kissed her neck, throat and lips and she tingled with desire. She was enjoying what David was doing to her and never wanted him to stop, and yet she knew what she was allowing him to do was wrong, and so when he stopped abruptly, because he wasn't sure he could trust himself, she was disappointed, but said nothing.

David forced himself to speak lightly. 'We can't stay here all day, sweetheart,' he said. 'We've got a party to attend.'

'Not yet.'

'I'm afraid so,' David said. He leant forward and kissed her gently on the lips, pulled her blouse around her and began fastening it up. 'I'm sorry I did that,' he said. 'I didn't mean to. I know we agreed just to kiss, but I went crazy for a minute and forgot myself.'

'I could have objected,' Lizzie said, 'but I didn't. It wasn't just your fault, you know.'

'Will you have to confess it?'

'Probably,' Lizzie said, knowing she most definitely did and that the priest would go mad, but she wouldn't think of it on this, David's last day.

He put out a hand to help Lizzie up, and behind the tree, Rosamund fumed. Prim little cat, she thought. Lies there naked to the waist like she's offering David the moon, and then retreats at the last minute. She's such a child, that was probably excitement enough for her, but I bet David's as

314

frustrated as hell. She smiled to herself. I'll see if I can offer him some consolation before he returns to his squadron. My contribution to the war effort. And so decided, Rosamund crept up the hill unseen to where her pony stood patiently waiting for her, then rode home deep in thought.

At the party that night, Rosamund monopolised David. She seldom left his side and plied him with drink, Lizzie noticed. But it was a party in his honour, she told herself, and it couldn't be wondered at if he got a bit merry. She told herself it was silly to feel uneasy, but she did.

David was feeling very mellow and everyone was being kind to him. He knew this was the party his mother should have given when he first enlisted, but she had been too angry and upset, and he himself too bolshie. He could remember his brother having a send-off party when war was declared and patriotic fervour was at its height. This was his mother's way of saying sorry, and declaring publicly how proud she was of her second son. David was dragged off to meet friends of his mother and of the father he couldn't remember, to be hugged and shaken by the hand and told how brave and heroic he was.

He thought often through the night that he would have swapped it all for a minute or two in his Elizabeth's company. But she wasn't even a proper guest, but pressed into service with Millie in the kitchen and then sent out with trays of drinks, or more savouries to put on a table already bulging with food.

He was glad that Rosamund had been invited, for she was the only other person anywhere near his age. She was the only one able to understand the tedium of being shaken by the hand by men almost old enough to be his grandfather, and told what a fine young man he was and how his father would have been proud of him, or hugged by powdery old women smelling of lavender, who exclaimed on how he'd grown and lamented the passing of the years.

Eventually Sophie decided that Lizzie and Danny must go to bed. Someone had put old-fashioned dance music on, and David almost envied Elizabeth and Dan being able to escape from it all. And yet he was sorry to see his sweetheart, his love, leave the party, for it really was the last time he'd see her for ages. When she stepped in front of him to say goodbye, her face flushed crimson, and his heart began to thud against his ribs.

'Goodnight, David,' she said, and she hoped the break in her voice was not apparent to anyone else. 'Look after yourself.'

'Good . . . goodnight, Elizabeth,' David said stiffly and awkwardly, hating himself for his manner. 'I'll be fine,' he added, 'don't you worry.'

Lizzie stood on tiptoe and kissed him hastily on the cheek, and then it was David's turn to flush. He wondered what would happen if he was to declare then and there that Lizzie was his girl and kiss her as he wanted to. Many would be scandalised; others would declare he was drunk, but he wasn't that drunk, not yet at least. Yet when Lizzie had eventually disappeared upstairs, he had the urge to get very drunk indeed, and damn the whole lot of them.

Suddenly Rosamund was at his side again. He smiled at her, for she'd been different that night. There had been none of her snide comments about people, and she'd been kindness itself to him; she'd even been gracious to Elizabeth. Maybe, he thought, she's growing up at last. She grasped his arm. 'Shall we slip away?' she said.

'Can we?' David asked.

'Look around,' said Rosamund, and David looked. His mother and his aunt were in the kitchen with Millie, and everyone else was gathered in cosy groups reminiscing deliciously, while music that had been popular before David's birth was pouring forth from the gramophone.

'Let's get out of this for a bit at least. I'm feeling stifled in here,' Rosamund said, and grabbing a couple of bottles of cider from the table she added, 'Bring your glass with you.'

To go through the kitchen meant meeting up with their mothers and Millie, so they sneaked down the passage and out of the front door, ran along the gravel path down the middle of the front lawn and across the road into the copse where David had found Lizzie that fateful day.

They slipped between the trees, and once safely hidden, Rosamund sat down on the grass with a sigh. 'Oh God, what a bore these things are.'

'Yes,' David agreed, but he knew that without Rosamund's urging he would never have left the party. He knew too what bad manners it was, but such things never seemed to bother Rosamund. He smiled at her, glad they were friends again, and said, 'We can't stay long, we'll be missed.'

Rosamund didn't reply. Instead she opened the first bottle of cider, filled up their glasses and said, 'Where do they find all the old relics? They should be in a museum, some of them.'

David laughed. While recognising the cruelty of Rosamund's words, he had to admit that though the old people had seemed ridiculously proud of him, their opinion, good or otherwise, mattered not a jot.

'Poor David,' Rosamund said. 'And there you were, I suppose, dying to spend some time alone with Elizabeth O'Malley.'

David's eyes opened wide with shock and he took a large gulp of the cider. 'You know?' he said.

'It's obvious to anyone who knows these things,' Rosamund said. 'Oh, don't look so frightened. It won't be to anyone else. After all, neither your mother nor mine would suspect

317

a thing. They've been expecting us two to get it together since we were in our cradles.'

David knew that Marjorie had always had hopes that way, though he wasn't sure if his own mother felt the same, but he said gallantly, 'Yes, I know. I'm sorry.'

'Hey, it's all right. These things happen,' Rosamund said. 'It's you I feel sorry for.'

'Me?' David said, finishing off his cider and looking at Rosamund in a puzzled way. 'Why's that?'

Rosamund refilled his glass and passed it to him. 'Well, she's so young, isn't she, your Elizabeth?' she said. 'What age is she?'

'Thirteen.'

'Four years younger than you,' Rosamund said, and she placed her hand on David's arm. 'She's just a child yet. She'd be afraid to love you as you want, and you'd be wrong to press her.'

'I know,' David said gloomily. 'We've talked about it. The point is, with Elizabeth everything enjoyable seems to be a sin.'

'Oh God, of course, she's a Catholic,' Rosamund said, her voice high as if she were surprised. 'We've had a few Catholics at school with us. They say that for them, sex must be for the procreation of children, and that's the only reason they're supposed do it. After the family is completed it's not allowed again, and that's that for the rest of their married lives.'

David looked at her, horrified. He knew little about Catholicism but Rosamund seemed to be very well informed.

'That's why most Catholics have large families,' she went on. 'I know for a fact that two girls at our school said their mother put a bolster down the bed after the birth of the child they decided was to be the last. Two others said their parents slept in separate rooms.'

David listened in disbelief, draining his glass of cider almost without being aware of it, as he was unaware of Rosamund filling it up again.

'I mean, I bet Elizabeth hasn't let you go very far,' Rosamund said.

Had David not had so much to drink, he'd have wondered at the insensitivity of Rosamund's question and told her to mind her own business, but the alcohol loosened his tongue and he found himself saying, 'No, she hasn't,' and remembered that what she had agreed to do, she'd confessed later to the priest.

'Poor you,' Rosamund said. 'You'll have to wait until the girl grows up and then overcomes the constraints of her religion before she'll let you do more than kiss her, I'd say.'

David was pretty sure Rosamund was right. She'd certainly been astute so far, and he saw a frustrated courtship ahead of him with a young girl just into her teens. Really, he thought, he had no right to feel anything for her other than a sort of brotherly love.

Rosamund watched him for a moment and smiled to herself. She touched his cheek gently with her lips while she stroked his other cheek with her hand. 'What you need to do,' she said, and her voice was low and husky, 'is find some release for your frustration, so that you can woo Elizabeth in the patient and fairly innocent way she wants. Find someone who isn't after a romance and wedding bells, but is willing to help you ease your sexual urge.' She paused. 'Someone like me, in fact.'

'You?'

David was one of the few people who hadn't heard of Rosamund's reputation. He had been somewhat protected from the village gossip, and neither his mother nor Millie would have dreamt of discussing Rosamund's affairs with him. She'd counted on that, and knew when she saw the amazement on his face that what she'd said had stunned him totally.

She lowered her lids and said, 'I went out with one or two of the officers at the Grange a couple of times, fancied myself in love and I'm afraid I got carried away.' She grasped David's arm again. 'Don't think badly of me, but I have gone all the way with some of the young men I dated.'

'I don't think badly of you,' David said. He knew just how easily it could happen, and he was shocked by the reaction of Rosamund's touch. His whole body was tingling and he took a large swig of cider to see if it would help the shaking that seemed to be affecting him.

As he drained the glass, Rosamund whispered in his ear, 'Elizabeth need never know, you see. For you and me, it will be just the sexual act between us, and then you will be able to wait for her to mature with no worries.'

It was the answer, David knew, but he shook his head. 'I couldn't do that,' he said. 'For one thing, I really love Elizabeth, even though she's so young, and for another, I couldn't use you like that. And,' he went on, 'I don't know how, really. I've never . . . never . . . never done it, you know.'

Rosamund was elated. David was a virgin, and she knew things to do and ways to excite him that would mean he'd never go back to Lizzie by the time she'd finished. She held his hand and said soothingly, 'Don't worry, you just lie back and let me do all the work. Trust me. I don't mind helping you out in the slightest, and what we do won't hurt Elizabeth.'

David protested no more, affected as he was by his cousin's nearness, and when she slipped her clothes off and stood before him, despite himself he was aroused by her beauty and perfection in the faint glow of the moonlight peeping through the trees.

She sank down beside him and said, 'Kiss me,' and he rolled on top of his cousin and had no hesitation in obeying, but where he'd been in control of the kissing and arousal of his darling Elizabeth, it was soon apparent that Rosamund was in charge of this. She stripped him, directed him and guided him, and led him to heights of passion he didn't know existed. Again and again he cried out as his senses exploded inside him and he could no longer contain himself, and any thoughts he had had of returning to the party went totally out of his head.

Much, much later, when they crept back to the house dishevelled and unrepentant, they found only Marjorie and Sophie waiting for them. The party had broken up long before. Sophie had had to make excuses for the two young people's absence, and had sent a weary Millie to bed while she and Marjorie waited. Sophie could barely contain her anger at David's lack of consideration for his guests, but when she saw them, she knew that any recriminations would fall on deaf ears and were, in any case, far too late.

Both of them were very drunk, for after their sexual appetites were somewhat satisfied, they'd finished the two bottles of cider before the passion rose in them again. By the time they returned they were both unsteady on their feet and inclined to find most things incredibly funny. Rosamund had not troubled to fasten her blouse properly, and David's shirt was unfastened at the collar and not tucked into his trousers, while his jacket and tie were missing altogether. Both had grass sticking to them, in their hair and clothes, and seemed to care not a jot.

'Look at the state of you,' Sophie said, but her heart wasn't in the rebuke.

'Yes, just look at us,' David said, and his voice was slurred. 'Disgusting, we are,' and he fell against Rosamund and she leant against him laughing.

'David!' Sophie rapped out.

He attempted to straighten up, still with the silly grin on his face. 'Ssh,' he said, and with an exaggerated movement put a finger to his lips. 'Mama is not amused.'

'Don't make such an issue of it, Sophie,' Marjorie said quietly. 'All right, they've both drunk too much and have been indiscreet, but after all, they are made for each other. We've known it since they were children.'

You may have, Sophie thought, but I know Rosamund will destroy my David. Ah, but then, she thought, maybe the Germans will destroy him first, and angry and disappointed though she was, she would not have her last words to David be those of censure. She pushed him into a chair and said, but gently, 'You'll have a sore head in the morning, my lad. Let's see if we can get some black coffee into you before you collapse totally.'

And David smiled idiotically and submitted to his mother's fussing, and waved amicably to Rosamund as she and her mother went out to get into the car to make for home.

Lizzie was glad her mother was coming down for a visit, because David had gone and life was very flat. She knew something had happened at David's party after she'd gone to bed, although she hadn't been able to find out what it was. It was hinted at, but not explained. It was just the hateful Marjorie who kept talking about how naughty David had been. Sophie had silenced her quickly, but it left Lizzie speculating, though she wouldn't write and ask David about it. He had more important things to worry about.

David himself had little recall of how he had got into the copse with Rosamund in the first place. He presumed he must have asked her, and felt that in some way he'd let Elizabeth down. He'd let her down further when he'd made love to his cousin – not just once either, but many times. Despite his slight shame, he could not regret or forget the exhilarating joy that had coursed through him again and again. Even the next morning, when he could barely lift his head from the pillow without agony, and his stomach churned and the thought of food made him want to vomit, the memory stayed with him.

He also remembered that Rosamund had said she'd be returning to school a day or so after he left, while he would be travelling to the south coast. 'If you need me,' she said, 'you know what I mean by need, I'll come.'

'But how?'

'I'll forge a note to say that my mother has requested me home, but instead I'll come to you,' Rosamund said. 'You'll have to work it out at the other end, where we'll stay and so forth.'

'Have you done this type of thing before?' David had asked, and Rosamund, gazing into his eyes, decided that in this case honesty was definitely not the best policy. 'Of course not, what do you take me for? But I'd do it for you, for after all we have always had a special relationship. Anyway,' she added, 'you've got some catching up to do. Most boys of nearly eighteen have done it a fair few times.'

David knew that was right, if only half the tales were true, and yet he felt bad about just using Rosamund in that way, although he had to admit she seemed to enjoy it as much as he did. There was also the difficulty of writing to her. She'd impressed on him that he mustn't write to the school. His letter would probably be intercepted and read and the fat would be really be in the fire.

'Last year one of the girls had a young aunt living near the school who used to receive letters from girls' boyfriends,' she said. 'If she's still there and willing to do it again, I'll write and let you know.' David was pleased, despite his misgivings, that there was probably a way of getting in touch with Rosamund if he really had to.

Lizzie, for her part, treasured the letters David sent her. *Darling Elizabeth*, they began, and often throughout the letters he told her how much he loved her and missed her and longed for them to be together. Sophie and Millie seemed glad that Lizzie was writing to David and said that it would cheer him up.

She'd received three letters from David by the time her mother arrived, with Padraic, now a sturdy four-year-old, holding her hand. Danny cried when he saw his mother, and seeing his distress brought a lump to Lizzie's throat too. Padraic watched the brother and sister he hardly knew and wasn't sure whether he liked them or not.

Remembering the tantrums of the spoiled three-year-old, both Lizzie and Dan were nervous of their little brother at first. But nursery had done Padraic good. He still pouted and sulked and wanted his own way, but he was learning not to snatch and grab. He still pinched and slapped when other children – including Lizzie and Dan – wouldn't give him what he wanted, but despite that the visit went off quite smoothly all in all.

It was Dan who was the problem, for he wanted to sit close to Kathy all the time she was there. He trailed around after her when he wasn't at school, and it fell to Lizzie to entertain her youngest brother. 'Dan's sloppy,' Padraic said to Lizzie one day as they walked up to Alice's farm, and Lizzie had to agree with him. Something was certainly up with Dan, and had been since he'd heard his father had died. She felt ashamed that she hadn't seen earlier that he had a problem and tried to do something about it. Maybe Sophie would have got the doctor if she'd spoken to her, but Lizzie had been too engrossed with David and the need to be near him. So engrossed she'd allowed him to touch and fondle her bare breasts. She must have been crazy, for even to think about it now filled her with shame.

The priest had gone mad when she'd told him in confession, and she'd not protested, for she felt she deserved the telling-off and the three decades of the rosary she had to say in penance. 'Get down on your knees and repent to the Lord for the way you allowed this young man to defile your body,' the priest had thundered, and Lizzie had trembled that anyone waiting outside would hear his remarks. She'd crept out, her face aflame, chastened and disgusted with herself, but even as she asked God's forgiveness, she also thanked him that David was miles away, for she knew that if he looked at her the way he had, and kissed her with the same passion and urgency, she'd probably let him do it all over again.

Both Danny and Lizzie cried when Kathy was ready to go. 'I want to come home,' Danny said, and Kathy, holding her own tears in check, told him it wouldn't be long now. 'Just a few more months,' she said. But months was a lifetime to Danny and he wouldn't be consoled. Millie had to hold him back forcibly as Kathy climbed into the car beside Sophie.

'Do you really want to go home, Danny?' Lizzie asked later.

'I want to be with Mammy,' Danny said. 'I . . . I miss her and if . . . if anything happens to her . . . we'll be all by ourselves.'

'Nothing will happen to her, not now,' Lizzie said. 'We're winning the war and there aren't any bombs or anything.'

'Then why can't we go home?' Danny said. 'Mammy said when the bombs stopped we could go home, she promised.'

'But you didn't want to go home before,' Lizzie pointed out.

'Well, I do now,' Danny insisted, and he was so distressed that Lizzie held him close and comforted him, though the thought of returning to Birmingham made her feel as if a lead weight had been fastened to her heart.

NINETEEN

Danny was so unhappy after his mother's visit that Sophie Barraclough decided that if he really wanted to go home then he must, much as they would miss him. They took it for granted that Lizzie would want to return too, but she didn't. It was bad enough, she thought, to have to go home eventually, when the war would be officially over, but to be yanked back now just because Danny was unsettled seemed grossly unfair.

Alice was sympathetic, because she would miss Lizzie a great deal. 'Ask if you can stay at least to the end of the school year,' she suggested. 'It is your last after all. You and I will both have officially left by July. Surely she won't mind you staying till then?'

All night Alice's words went around in Lizzie's head. She didn't want to leave now, for she knew that once she was home her mammy would say it wasn't worth going to a new school for just a few months, and she'd either be hanging about the house, minding weans for people and doing the housework, or pushed into any sort of job before her fourteenth birthday. Neither prospect was as appealing as staying on in Hereford for another nine months. She wasn't asking for much, she thought; after all, hadn't her mother already deprived her of the chance of a grammar school education? Surely she wouldn't force her to go home when her last school year was just one third of the way through?

Lizzie thought she needed an ally on her side to plead her case, and the next day, knowing that Sophie and Millie, despite claiming they would miss them sorely, would never go against her mother's wishes, she went to Mr Donnelly, her teacher, and told him everything. He said he'd certainly not want Lizzie to return home without completing her last year and promised to write to her mother saying so. Lizzie wrote too, and waited with trepidation to see what the outcome of the letters might be.

'Our Lizzie doesn't want to come back until she's finished school officially,' Kathy said to Maggie in the tea break a couple of days later. 'And though I'd like her back for Christmas, I can see her point, and that of her teacher. He was the one pressing for her to take that eleven-plus exam, and though I didn't like that idea much at the time, he sounds quite a decent bloke, on paper at least.'

'So you're letting her stay?'

'I think so,' Kathy said. 'This Mr Donnelly also said our Lizzie would get a better-paid job later if I could afford to send her to a commercial college somewhere, where she could learn secretarial skills, rather than make her start work straight away. He says she's a bright girl.'

She looked at Maggie and went on, 'I'm often troubled by the thought that I should have let her take that exam when it was suggested. I see Sheelagh swanning about and know our Lizzie is worth ten of her, but I never gave her the chance to prove it. In a way I think I've failed her.'

'Oh, now that's silly!'

'No it isn't. Listen, Maggie,' Kathy said earnestly. 'The war has turned the world on its head. I mean, the way I see it, women have been doing jobs usually done by men since nineteen thirty-nine. And so many have been killed in this war, there might not be the men to fill all the jobs when the war's over. The opportunities for women have never been so good. Our Lizzie doesn't have to go into a shop or factory like we did. You can lose a man for lots of reasons and have to provide for your family. I'll be hard pressed to earn enough to keep mine, I'll tell you. What the hell do I know? Damn all except how to make distress lamps. I don't think there'll be much call for that in peacetime, do you?'

Maggie couldn't argue with her sister, and Kathy went on, 'I'll enquire and see how much a commercial college costs. Barry would like Lizzie to have the chance of bettering herself.'

Maggie watched her sister's face and knew that when it was all over, she'd miss Barry all over again. She gave a sudden shiver of fear. What if it had been her Con? She didn't know how she'd cope either. Mentally she shook herself and told herself not to be so stupid, worrying like that over things that hadn't happened. But she was glad when the buzzer went, summoning her and Kathy back to work, and she knew that the chatter from the woman working with her would dispel her melancholy.

Mr Donnelly was glad to get Kathy O'Malley's letter giving permission for Lizzie to finish the year and saying she would look into the possibility of her taking a secretarial course. She sounded a nice, amiable woman who was not naturally averse, as some were, to the chance of her daughter bettering herself. He wished now he'd written himself to ask that Lizzie be allowed to take the eleven-plus, and not left it to Mrs Barraclough.

Lizzie was delighted when Mr Donnelly told her he'd had a letter from her mother allowing her to stay on until July. He said nothing about the secretarial course, in case Kathy eventually decided against Lizzie going, and in Kathy's letter to her daughter she said nothing either, but Lizzie wouldn't have cared; she was looking no further than July anyway.

In the Barracloughs' house, preparations were being made to send Danny home. Sophie and Millie were busy knitting jumpers and socks and balaclavas, and David's old boots were got out and polished and his winter coat was turned up. Danny was due to go in December, just as the term ended and a few days before Christmas, and though he seemed excited, Lizzie knew she would miss her little brother.

She told David all about it in her letters, glad she was able to write and confide in him. He wrote back fairly often, and she lived for his letters. He didn't say he loved her as much as he once had, but Lizzie wasn't worried; she supposed there were only so many ways you could say you loved someone. He also started his letters now with *Dear Elizabeth*, instead of *Darling Elizabeth*, but Lizzie wasn't worried about that either. His letters were warm and friendly and often so funny, as he described places and people and situations in such an amusing way that she often laughed out loud.

Lizzie wasn't to know how David sat and thought for hours over his letters to her. Away from her, he wondered if he really loved her as much as he said. He was fond of her, certainly, but love – he wasn't sure about love. She was very young, far too young for him really. Then of course there was the whole religious aspect of things, and yet he was almost a man, with a man's needs. Rosamund enjoyed sex as much as he did and made no demands on him for love or commitment, and she most certainly didn't see their lovemaking as a sin.

She'd had no problem getting out of school, as she'd prophesied, and to all intents and purposes the school thought she was returning home each weekend. David had installed her in a little guest house near to the camp.

'Easy as pie,' she said, their first evening together.

'What if they ever find out?' David said. 'Your mother, or mine, or the school?'

Rosamund pulled David down on the bed beside her and said, 'Why should they? Anyway, what could they do? The school would probably throw me out, but I wouldn't care about that. I've had enough of it anyway, and if I was to be sent home in disgrace I could handle Mummy. She's had quite an active war too in her own way, and hasn't exactly acted the dutiful wife, so she can't really say anything to me.'

David gaped at Rosamund. He could hardly believe what he was hearing about his aunt, who always seemed so correct and proper. 'Hasn't she?' he said.

'I suppose you can hardly blame her,' Rosamund went on. 'Remember, the Grange has been half full of men all through the war, and she's been alone for months while I've been away at school.' She tossed her head and said, 'I've caught her out on more occasions than I can remember.'

'Don't . . . don't you mind?'

'Why should I?' Rosamund said, surprised. 'I let her know that I'm aware of it and it keeps her off my back.'

David shook his head. This was all strange to him. They were a randy enough lot in the Air Force, and he was a normal hot-blooded teenager, but he hadn't thought parents behaved like this, and certainly not people he knew and was even related to. 'Don't look so shocked,' Rosamund said. 'My mother's not totally to blame. I mean, Daddy's a dear, but he's never been totally faithful to Mummy, almost since the day they married.'

David suddenly felt very sorry for Rosamund, but to tell her so would inflame her temper. He knew her well enough to realise that, so he just put his arm around her and held her close. It was some time before he realised she'd unbuttoned his tunic and shirt and had her hands inside, running her fingers over his bare flesh. 'Oh, Rosamund,' he groaned.

'Come on, David,' she said. 'Let's forget about parents and get on with what we want to do.'

David needed no second bidding. He could hardly wait to strip off his clothes. It was afterwards that the guilt came and he would lie torturing himself with images of Elizabeth. He really should tell her how he felt, but Rosamund wasn't ready yet for him to do that; she had to hook him properly first. He was helpless against her and she knew it, and revelled in the power she had over him.

Rosamund taught him methods and techniques of lovemaking he'd never have known, and had ways of stroking, kissing and caressing him that set him on fire and made him feel he'd explode if he didn't have release soon. Afterwards he was brought to such a pinnacle of joy that he'd call Rosamund's name again and again. Once he cried out that he loved her and was horrified. He didn't love Rosamund, nor she him, but then she'd know he didn't mean it; it was just something you said in the heat of the moment.

David swapped, wangled and bribed to get as much time off at weekends as possible. Often the other men at the camp chaffed him about it. They all knew that he had a girl secreted away somewhere and thought it was about bloody time. All of them were curious, but David was not willing to share Rosamund with anyone.

But sometimes David didn't get off at all over the weekend, or could only see Rosamund for a few stolen moments. Then he worried about her and wondered what she'd find to do with herself. But when he asked her, she refused to tell him.

'We're free agents, you and I,' she said. 'We're together for our mutual convenience. I ask nothing of you and you're wrong to question me.'

But David was jealous, and horrified that he should be jealous of Rosamund when it was Elizabeth he was supposed to care about. He often wondered if Rosamund was sharing her favours with other men, maybe fellow pilots on the camp. Then he'd admonish himself that she wouldn't do that and he was wrong to think she would. But the suspicious thought kept going around in his head. Rosamund refused to reassure him. 'Hush, David,' she'd say, her voice sexy and her manner suggestive. 'Let's go to bed,' and David was powerless against her and scared of her withdrawing her favours if he continued to ask awkward questions.

But the illicit weekends he was spending with Rosamund made letters to Elizabeth difficult. He could write a little bit about the camp and his fellow pilots and what he did in his free time during the week, but he never wrote about the weekends. He'd hoped he'd have a decent few hours off at Christmas so he could get to see Elizabeth, for he knew Dan was leaving and returning to Birmingham.

'And Elizabeth is staying?' Rosamund exclaimed. 'How odd!'

'Not really,' David said. 'It's her last year at school and her mother is letting her finish the year. I don't think she's as keen to go back as Danny anyway.'

No, she wouldn't be, Rosamund thought, but she said nothing. It wasn't in her plan to poke fun at the evacuees now. She'd decided that she was going to make David fall madly in love with her, then she could do what she liked. But for now she had to appear kind and concerned. Really, she thought, David was just so easy to fool.

Everyone back home in Birmingham was excited that Danny was returning, but the prospect of having him around at last galvanised Molly into action. She saw some purpose to her life again. True, she had but one son living, but her favourite had left behind two sons and a daughter. Soon they'd all be home again and Kathy would be needing a hand rearing them. It was no good carrying on crying for the loss of Barry; she had to get on with helping to raise his children.

A few Christmas cards had begun arriving towards the middle of December. One was from Rose, with a letter inside saying she couldn't wait until the war ended and she could come home again. But what home? Kathy stood with the letter in her hand, staring out of the window on to the sea of rubble where Rose's house had once stood. She must come home, certainly, but where she'd stay was anyone's guess.

Still, she told herself, it would pan out in the end, it usually did, and all the worrying in the world would not change things. She picked another letter from the pile on the table and turned it over. The writing was unfamiliar and the stamp was foreign. She slit the envelope and drew out the letter curiously.

Dear Kate. Her heart skipped a beat. No one but Doug Howister called her Kate. She read on eagerly.

I hope you won't mind me writing to you at this time. I've thought about you often since our last night together, and it has comforted me over the past weeks when I've been too weary and battle-worn to think straight . . .
I know D-Day has been heralded as a great success, and so it was, but when I saw the numbers killed, I began to realise the true cost of victory in lives lost.
One particular loss affected me personally, because Phil Martin died right beside me. He was very fond of your family and he was forever the clown, always good for a laugh, and he'd been my buddy since first grade. We'd

been together all through high school and college and joined up because we wanted to do something in this goddamn war.

We'd had a taste of jungle warfare fighting the Japs in '42 and '43, but nothing prepared us for D-Day. You'll know all about it in Britain now, I guess, but the landing in Normandy was a fantastic achievement and yet many were killed. Opposition was stiff, but we continued to advance and Phil and I began to think we were invincible. We couldn't seem to put a foot wrong and everywhere the Allies were claiming victories. By August, we were moving east to encircle the German army. And that's where Phil bought it, gunned down along with so many others. I could hardly believe it, we'd gone through so much together. I wanted to stay with him, but knew I couldn't. He was dead and I daren't waste time and risk other lives. Afterwards came the guilt. Should I have insisted I stayed with my best buddy? Perhaps he wasn't killed outright? Maybe I could have done something for him? Or maybe he would have just been glad of my presence? I don't know. I suppose whenever you lose someone close, you are riddled with doubts that you did the right thing and guilt that you're alive and they aren't, but I've wanted to die many times since, when I realise how I'm going to miss that crazy guy.

Kathy could read no more, for her face was awash with tears. Doug's hurt and pain came through the pages of the letter and her heart ached for him. She remembered how Barry had gone through something similar when Pat was killed, and how later, when he was home, recovering from his own injuries, he had vented the frustration and anger he felt on losing Pat on her and the children. And she remembered that she hadn't been very sympathetic or understanding of

335

what he was going through and instead had shouted back at him. Since the news of his death, she'd gone over and over the angry words she'd hurled at Barry, and oh, how she'd wished them unsaid. But it was too late, and now she'd never be able to make it right with him again.

She brushed the tears from her eyes and returned to the letter.

What has sustained me, Kate, and I think kept me from going completely mad, was the thought of you and your sweetness and simplicity. You are the epitome of all that is good and wholesome in the world and what men like your brother and my buddy are willing to fight and die for to protect.

When grief for Phil threatened to overwhelm me, I would conjure up your face, and the one night of passion we shared. Oh God, I wish it had been more, but you could have a whole lifetime and never experience what we had that night. I hope you didn't feel guilty or ashamed, for you had no need to. It was beautiful, and because of it I will get over my buddy's death. I will probably never see you again, Kate O'Malley, but I love you and will continue to love you with all my heart, till the day I die. Doug.

'Oh, Doug!' Kathy cried, and the tears rained down her face once more, even as she told herself to give over, for the others would be in on top of her in no time. Eventually she did manage to stop crying and sat and read the letter again. The question was, what was she to do with it? To keep it was folly, and yet she couldn't bear to part with it. She threw the envelope in the fire to stop any awkward questions, but the pages of the letter she folded and popped down the front of her dress just as the door opened and

Molly and Padraic burst in with bulging shopping bags.

Later that evening, before Padraic went to bed, Kathy examined the mattress in the bedroom. She had realised that she had nowhere in the whole house that she could call her own, where she might put a letter and be sure no one else had access to it.

She stripped the sheet from the double bed, then felt over it with her fingers. Molly's side had sagged slightly, and because of her extra weight the bed springs had made small holes in the underside of the flock mattress. Kathy worked on one of these tears, ripping at it slightly until a sizeable hole appeared, and then folded the letter up small and tucked it well inside. No one but her would ever know, and it would give her a measure of comfort, she thought, as she made up the bed again and went downstairs.

Lizzie thought it was a strange Christmas without Danny, though as always Sophie and Millie did their best to make it a good one. David was there on Christmas Eve and Christmas Day, but had to return on Boxing Day, and Lizzie was delighted to see him. She was sure he'd grown, for he seemed to tower above her, and she felt very protected and safe in the circle of his arms.

They went for a walk on Christmas Eve afternoon. It was the only time they had alone, and as usual they made for the woods. Ever since Lizzie had known that David was definitely coming home, she'd been telling herself she hadn't to be so silly about letting him touch her. He was going on for eighteen now and couldn't be expected to make do with a chaste kiss, and afterwards she could go to confession and repent of it all.

But David made no move to go further, even when she snuggled into him as their kiss became more ardent. She yearned for him to touch her, but didn't know how to tell him. He must have felt her heart thudding against her ribs, but he made no sign that he had. Lizzie had kissed him with all the throbbing emotion that was in her and felt his body harden against her, and it excited her.

And then David had broken away and said huskily, 'We'd better go back. You'll be frozen, Elizabeth.'

'I'm not cold, David.'

'Neither am I, my darling child. I'm burning hot for you,' David said. 'But it wouldn't be right, we both know that.'

'I . . . I don't mind.'

'But I do,' David said. 'I love you too much to cheapen you and do things your conscience and your Church tell you are wrong.' He took Lizzie's hand and kissed it. 'Come on, cheer up, darling,' he urged. 'I only have a few hours. Let's enjoy them.'

After that, what could Lizzie say? Once they'd got back to the house, they were thrust into the preparations for Christmas and everyone was talking of the VI bombs that had dropped in Manchester early that morning, killing and maiming people. It was the first such attack outside London and the south coast, and Lizzie was worried that they might reach Birmingham in the future. Sophie reassured her, though she'd been shaken herself by the attack on the northern town. 'Their range is not great enough to hit Birmingham, Elizabeth. You're two hundred miles from the coast, after all.'

'I thought the RAF were meant to take out the factories in September,' Millie said, looking at David. 'The threat was supposed to be over.'

'Don't look at me,' David said. 'I'm a fighter pilot. I don't bomb anyone, I just shoot down the buggers.'

Sophie raised her eyebrows, but said nothing. Once Lizzie knew she would have done, and David knew it too and grinned at Lizzie and gave her a huge wink. Millie had missed the exchange as she'd had her back to them all, and she said, 'Still, I thought you might know something. I mean, it's all RAF, isn't it?'

'Bomber Command is different, Millie,' David said. 'But even if I knew anything, I could hardly tell you. Careless talk and all that . . .'

'Pity someone couldn't have told them poor buggers in Manchester and given them a chance to take cover, or those in London and the south,' Millie said. 'Imagine hearing the scream of the bomb above you, then the engine cutting out and you just have to wait to see if you're going to be meeting your maker that day or not.'

'The V2s give no warning at all,' David said. 'And each one carries a ton of explosives in its war head.'

Lizzie gave an involuntary shiver, and Sophie said briskly, 'Come on now. I'm sorry for all those killed, but it's Christmas, and Elizabeth's last with us, and David only has two days, so let's not spoil it.'

After that, it had been almost as good as other years, except quieter without Danny. War talk was banned from then on, and even the following day, when Marjorie and Rosamund came for dinner as usual, Marjorie was not allowed to dominate the conversation with her gentlemanly officers and their goings-on.

David looked at his aunt in a different light after Rosamund's revelations. He couldn't help it, but he felt quite repelled by the idea of Marjorie carrying on with many of those men billeted at the Grange through the war. Rosamund had said her father wasn't faithful either, and maybe he wasn't, but . . . well, damn it all, it was different for a man, everyone knew that. But then how was it he wasn't repelled by Rosamund? He didn't really know. Perhaps he was slightly, because sometimes Rosamund appeared almost too eager for sex, and he was a little disgusted by himself that he seemed incapable of refusing what she was offering him. But at least it meant he didn't feel the need to press Elizabeth to go any further in her lovemaking than she wanted to.

He wasn't to know that Lizzie had come to her own decision as they strode through the wood that Christmas afternoon. She'd thought they might have to suffer Rosamund's company, as David had said he'd have to ask her. Lizzie had her toes screwed up as she waited for her answer, but Rosamund said she was tired and cold and would stay by the fire, and Lizzie hoped the relief that flowed through her wasn't evident to anyone.

She'd decided she would have to show David what she wanted and so she'd slipped upstairs and removed her brassière. As she walked, her nipples rubbed gently against the soft peach-coloured sweater Millie had knitted her for Christmas from a mohair shawl of Sophie's that they had unravelled together.

Lizzie's whole body was tingling in anticipation of David's touch. They were barely inside the shelter of the trees when she kissed David with an intensity that surprised him. 'Oh God, Elizabeth,' he was able to say at last. 'You're beautiful.'

'Do you love me, David?'

David evaded the question and instead said, 'Do you need to ask?'

'Do you want to love me?'

David ran a finger down her cheek, realising that it would be like rape to make love to Elizabeth. It was different with Rosamund, pleasurable for both of them. She knew the score, and she wouldn't be off to tell the bloody priest all about it.

So he smiled at Elizabeth and said, 'More than anything in the world. But I won't. Not yet, you're not ready.'

Lizzie shivered. She was frightened, there was no denying it. 'Maybe not,' she said. 'But I'm ready for more than a kiss,' and as she spoke she unbuttoned her coat, took David's hands in her own and placed them inside her jumper as she snuggled against him.

'Ah, Elizabeth,' David moaned. His lips sought hers, but as his passion mounted, he told himself to go steady and pulled away. He was never more glad of Rosamund than at that moment. In two days' time she would be installed once more in their little love nest and would help to still the ache of desire that was growing in him by the minute.

'What is it?' Lizzie asked.

'What is it?' David cried. 'I'll tell you. At this minute I want to lay you on the ground and make love to you, and the fact that I can't is like someone tearing my insides to pieces.'

Lizzie licked her lips and said, 'You can, if you want to.'

'Oh God, Elizabeth, shut up. Of course I bloody want to, but it wouldn't be right.'

Lizzie bit her lip, not knowing what she'd done to make David so angry. Instantly he was sorry. 'Oh, Elizabeth, you don't know what you do to me,' he said, holding her close. 'You drive me mad. Eventually, one day, it will be right for you, but not yet.' He kissed her on her forehead, her eyes, the tip of her nose, her lips, and said, 'Until then, my darling, we must wait.'

Lizzie, both disappointed and relieved, made no further comment, and hand in hand they returned to the house.

Christmas seemed a bit flat after David had gone. Lizzie told Alice a few days later. 'I mean, even Miss High-and-Mighty Rosamund has gone visiting some friend of hers for the rest of the holiday.'

'Thought she hadn't got any friends?'

'Well, she can't have many, none come down here,' Lizzie said. 'They're probably all as stuck-up as her.'

'Maybe,' Alice agreed. 'But you said she'd been nice to you this holiday.'

'She has,' Lizzie agreed. 'It was unnerving. David said she can be nice when she puts her mind to it, but I've never seen it before. I thought she might have some idea about us, you know, but David thought not. I'm not so sure. I caught her looking at me funny a time or two. And then there was Christmas Day, when we went for a walk and she chose not to come. She said she was tired.'

'Maybe she was.'

'And maybe she wasn't,' Lizzie said. 'I'm glad she stayed behind. Don't get me wrong, but I started wondering why she had, and as we went out of the door I was almost certain she gave David a wink.'

'Almost certain?'

'Well, I didn't bloody ask her,' Lizzie snapped. 'I tell you, Alice, I don't trust Rosamund Harrington as far as I could throw her. And despite her record with seemingly most of the armed forces, she's always had a soft spot for David.'

'He's yours, stupid,' Alice said. 'And now he's away in the RAF, Rosamund can't get her grubby hands on him even if she'd like to. He's safe from her. Maybe this friend she's gone to visit is male.'

'It wouldn't surprise me,' Lizzie said. 'She is shameless. But I don't care anymore. She can sleep with the entire male population for all I care, as long as she leaves David alone.'

'Don't give her another thought,' Alice said. 'She's not worth it. Concentrate on what you and David have between you, because it's worth hanging on to.'

And Lizzie knew Alice was right, and gave her friend a hug.

TWENTY

Everyone knew as 1945 dawned that the Allies were winning the war. They listened avidly to the news on their wirelesses of the towns liberated from Nazi rule, and they knew the German army were on the run. There was an air of expectancy, but as winter finally gave way to the unsettled weather of early spring, there was nothing definite in the news, and yet daily victory seemed to draw closer, and many people were becoming impatient.

David had managed to wangle a few days' leave while Lizzie was home from school for the Easter holidays, and she was delighted to see him. But she found him moody and unpredictable. He knew as well as anyone that soon the war would be over and he would be demobbed, and really he didn't want that. He'd enjoyed the life and the camaraderie of the RAF.

Then there was Rosamund, who'd got under his skin in a way David had never intended. His heart still turned over when he saw Lizzie, and when he took her in his arms his pulses raced, but when he felt her body stiffen slightly, it annoyed him. She wouldn't be fourteen until June and would be leaving Hereford in July, his mother had told him. Really it was madness for them to have embarked on any kind of relationship. It might never have happened, he knew, if she hadn't got so upset over the news of her father's death, and she was such a child still. He didn't want to tie himself down to any one girl yet, not even Rosamund. Things were very pleasant for both of them at the moment, but he wasn't ready for commitment.

He knew he should be honest with Elizabeth and tell her that though she'd always hold a special place in his heart, he thought it was better that both of them were free to see other people, as they were so young. He realised it had been a kind of half-love he'd felt for Elizabeth, intense at the time but not real love at all. But he couldn't bear to see the hurt he'd inflict on her. Anyway, he told himself, why spoil her last few months in Hereford? Let her have her dreams, and when she was settled back at home, he'd write and tell her.

But with such thoughts whirling in his head, he was often brusque and short-tempered with her. He didn't seem to want to be alone with her either, because to continue to kiss and cuddle her feeling as he did would only make things harder later. Lizzie, however, ached to feel his arms around her. He had also taken to going for long, solitary walks and refused Lizzie's company when she asked to go with him. 'I'm surrounded by people in the camp all the time,' he attempted to explain. 'I need my own space.'

Lizzie didn't argue further, but let him go, and David would tramp the hills trying to make sense of his emotions. He knew he was fairly besotted by Rosamund, and he'd become more jealous of her as his feelings for her increased.

Rosamund had to be very careful near the camp that David never saw or heard anything to make him suspicious of her. In actual fact, on the weekends when he couldn't see her, she was never lonely, and had entertained many a young airman in the rooms David paid for. She didn't feel guilty about it at all. David could hardly expect her to kick her heels alone in the place, and men were always more than willing to keep her company.

Only David would keep on about what she did when she wasn't with him. She put him straight that she wasn't going to be quizzed; after all, she didn't belong to him, so he had no right to ask. If she had her way, and she usually did, one day she'd have David's ring on her finger, but not yet awhile, for now she just wanted to have fun.

Lizzie was sad when David returned to camp, and yet she'd sensed a distance between them that hadn't been there before. 'Cheer up, lovey,' Millie said, seeing her doleful face the day after he'd gone. She knew what had made the young girl miserable. David had been proper cool with her at times, even though he'd always known how fond of him she was. 'Men are funny creatures,' she said. 'They get odd moods and don't talk about what's worrying them like women do, and then they just bite the head off you for nothing.'

'Do you think David is worrying about anything?'

'Why, of course he is. If the truth be known, he don't want this war to end,' Millie said. 'He doesn't want to go back to school, that I do know, and he doesn't know what else to do with himself.'

'Do you think that's all it is really?' Lizzie asked.

'Well, course it is,' Millie said. 'What else could it be?'

Lizzie let out a sigh of relief. Millie must be right. She'd known David since the day he was born, and after all, Lizzie had little experience with young men. She went up to her room and got out pen and paper, intending to write David a long and very loving letter to cheer him up at the camp.

Hider died on 1 May, and people danced in the streets. It was the beginning of the end. On 7 May, Germany surrendered, and the VE celebrations on the 8th were a sight to behold, with every city, town and village joining in. Lizzie wrote to her mother about the party held in Millover village.

There was a big tent, Aunt Sophie said it was a marquee, and big flags in red, white and blue and more food than I've ever seen. There was a bonfire on the village green and everyone said the grass will never be the same. Mr Carr brought out a few boxes of fireworks he said he'd kept back from 1939 for such an occasion. There was dancing after and everyone came, even the men from the air force stationed at Madeley, and no one went to bed for ages and ages and it was a good job because at midnight all the bells started ringing in St Peter's church.

Kathy smiled as she read Lizzie's account of the party. Oh, she missed her daughter and was counting the days till she came home. There had been two letters that morning and she'd opened Lizzie's first, as she always did. The other one was in a hand she didn't recognise, but the stamp was foreign, and she hoped it wasn't from Doug. She could do without hearing from him on anything like a regular basis.

She was glad she was on her own, unless you counted Danny and Padraic, who were eating bread and dripping at the table. She hadn't been able to lie in bed, she was too used to getting up at some ungodly hour, so when the two boys had woken up and gone downstairs, she'd crept down to join them, and had been making them something to eat when she heard the postman rattle the letter box and saw the two envelopes on the mat.

Now she opened the second letter cautiously, and when she let out a cry, Danny and Padraic were alarmed, for though she appeared to be smiling, tears were raining down her face. Danny leapt to his feet, the chair scraping the linoleum, and said, 'What's up?'

Kathy, however, took no notice of her son's question, but went bounding up the stairs. 'He's alive!' she screeched, in a voice guaranteed to rouse the house. 'He's alive! Barry's alive!'

It took some minutes for the news to percolate through to the rest of the occupants. Then Sid came tumbling out of the attic half dressed, doing up his trousers, with Enid behind him still in her nightie with her head swathed in a scarf to hide her curlers. Molly, half asleep still, and without her teeth, emerged crying, 'What is it? What is it?'

But downstairs Danny knew. 'Is it our daddy?' he said. 'Is he alive after all?'

'Yes, Danny, yes he is,' Kathy said, hugging both her sons tight, and though her eyes still glinted with tears, her face had a smile so wide it near cut it in two.

The news flew around the family rapidly, and all of them crowded in to celebrate with her. Only Bridie said it was all right for some, and women who were true widows got no consideration at all. But Kathy couldn't care about Bridie, nor could she feel sympathy for her; she was too overjoyed.

She was glad there was no work that day, for she couldn't have concentrated. In fact the whole factory was being closed down, and just before she'd opened the letter she'd been telling herself she had to find another job, and quickly. Now she had a husband coming home, though, there was no rush. Sid had to go in, being a supervisor, but Enid, Maggie and Kathy weren't needed that day. Instead, once the children had been packed off to school and nursery, they sat in Kathy's house with Eamonn and Mary, Bridie having departed in a huff, and talked it over for hours.

Molly hadn't seemed to take in the news at all, and sat slumped in a chair, every so often saying, 'I can't believe it, oh, praise be to God.' Eamonn wanted to know how Kathy had learnt about it, and she passed him the letter. But why, he wanted to know was Barry not in a POW camp?

Kathy didn't know. It appeared he'd been put in a labour camp, which was one of the reasons she hadn't been informed earlier that he was a prisoner. The man who'd written to her was a Corporal Wallis. He'd been with a company of men who'd liberated the camp, and said that most of the inmates, Barry included, had been in pretty poor shape

'I'm sure he'll be able to tell us, Daddy,' Kathy said. 'Corporal Wallis says he's recovering in a military hospital and we'll be able to write soon.'

But Kathy didn't care about the whys and wherefores. She knew only that the man she had thought dead was not. He was sick, but he'd recover, and he'd come home to her, and with their children around them they'd be a family again.

'Who will tell Lizzie?' Mary said.

'I'll go down,' Kathy said.

'Aye, but she should know today,' Mary said. 'For you know what she thought of her daddy.'

Everyone knew. 'But she'll be at school now,' Kathy said. 'I'll ask Mrs Pickering if I can phone at half past four and I'll see about trains down to Hereford for tomorrow.'

All day Kathy was in a dream. She couldn't believe it was happening. After a dinner Enid had prepared – for neither Kathy nor Molly was in a fit state to do it – Kathy wrote immediately to Barry. Then she went down to the station to book her ticket to Hereford, before making her way to Pickering's to phone Lizzie. She was cheered and congratulated by people standing on the streets and in their doorways, as if she'd done something wonderful. Kathy didn't wonder how they all knew, for word spread like wildfire in the street, and she was especially touched by the women who'd lost their own men but rejoiced with Kathy that hers was safe.

Kathy had never got used to the phone and tended to bellow down it, so Millie, who answered at the other end, knew who it was straight away. 'You want Elizabeth?' she asked. 'Is something wrong?'

'No, nothing,' Kathy said, and longed to call out her news, but that wasn't right, for Lizzie must be the first to hear.

Lizzie also thought there was something wrong. 'What is it, Mammy? What's up?' she said, and prayed that nothing had happened to her grandad, who'd been ill almost from the day the war started.

'Lizzie, I've some wonderful news,' Kathy said. 'I had a letter this morning, and, well, you'll never believe it, your daddy is alive.'

Lizzie couldn't take it in. First she felt numb all over, and then pure joy filled her body with heat and her voice came out all squeaky. 'You . . . you mean it?'

'Would I joke about a thing like this?' Kathy said.

'Well, no, but how . . . why . . . I mean, they said he was missing, presumed dead.'

'He'd been sent to a labour camp, not a proper prisoner-of-war place, but he's all right. I mean, he's a little sick and weak and in hospital. I've written to him today.'

'Oh, Mammy, you're right, I can hardly believe it.'

'Nor me. I needed you here today, my darling girl,' Kathy said, her voice breaking with emotion. 'I'm coming down to see you tomorrow. I can't wait to give you a hug.'

'Oh, Mammy.'

'Now, don't be crying,' Kathy said. 'Go in and tell Sophie and Millie, for they'll be wanting to know, and tell Sophie I'll be arriving in Hereford at two thirty-five p.m. or there-abouts, depending on how many stoppages we have.'

Lizzie put the phone down and went along the corridor to the kitchen. She felt as if she was walking on air, floating, and as she opened the door, Millie and Sophie, sitting at the table drinking tea, turned anxious faces towards her. Sophie noticed how pale Lizzie was, and said anxiously, 'What is it, dear?'

349

'Nothing,' Lizzie said. 'I mean, nothing bad. My daddy's been found, he's not dead at all.' And she burst into tears.

Kathy's visit that time turned into a celebration. Lizzie had the afternoon off from school so that she could go with Sophie to fetch her, and at the station they clung to each other and cried. 'Shall I come home, Mammy?' Lizzie asked. Kathy wanted to say, 'Yes, come back with me, we'll go and pack this minute,' but instead she said, 'There's no need for that, pet. You didn't come back when we thought your daddy had died, and there's no need now. Sure, you'll be home in no time anyway.'

Lizzie was pleased she'd have a few more weeks, and she kept hold of her mother's arm as they made their way to the car. Back home, Millie had prepared a banquet, and after they'd eaten, Marjorie arrived with two officers in tow and two bottles of champagne. 'Left over from the VE celebrations,' she said vaguely when Sophie raised her eyebrows quizzically. Sophie thought it wasn't the moment to ask where she'd got them in the first place. 'After all,' Marjorie went on, 'what better occasion than this to celebrate?'

Everyone in the village was pleased Lizzie's daddy had been found alive, and to hear about it after all this time seemed like a miracle. Lizzie thought so too, and so did the children at school, especially Alice. Lizzie felt sorry for Alice, who she knew would have liked to have a letter like the one which had come to Kathy, saying her brother was safe too. But Alice was too good a friend to brood for long, and she hugged Lizzie and said it was 'Great news, absolutely great.'

And Kathy returned to Birmingham the next day with her heart lighter than it had been for months.

David had promised to see Lizzie before she left Hereford, but now he wrote to say his leave had been cancelled.

He knew he would find it more difficult to appear natural with Lizzie when his time with Rosamund was filling his mind all his waking hours, and he confided his doubts to Rosamund after his leave at Easter. 'If you don't love her anymore,' she said, 'you should tell her how you feel, before someone else does. I think Mummy has a good idea of how things stand.'

But Marjorie had more than an idea, and couldn't help boasting of it to Sophie one night, just a few weeks before Lizzie was due to leave. 'I think Rosamund and David are becoming very pally. They write to one another, you know,' she said. 'Mind you, it's only what we expected, isn't it?'

The news didn't please Sophie, but only Millie saw the blood drain from Lizzie's face. 'I don't know about that,' Sophie said. 'Rosamund hasn't bothered with David much of late, but everyone has noticed she seems to have a long string of admirers.'

Marjorie laughed to show she wasn't annoyed, a tinkling, false laugh, and said, 'Oh, it's true Rosamund was a little wild, a year or so ago. All those gorgeous young men about the Grange would turn any girl's head for a time. But it's definitely David she's gone on now, she almost said so. She's met him a few times too, when she visits that friend in the south of England.'

Marjorie in fact suspected there wasn't any friend in the south of England but David Barraclough. She had asked once, and her daughter had looked at her in the haughty way she had and said, 'Don't pry too closely, Mummy, you wouldn't like what you'd find out, and I might find myself obliged to write and tell Daddy what you've been up to.'

After that Marjorie said no more to her wayward daughter, especially as nothing would please her more than for Rosamund to settle down with David Barraclough. She would be seventeen in July, and was a sensual girl with strong sexual needs. Marjorie knew, for she was the same herself, and she'd like to get Rosamund married respectably before she made a name for herself. In wartime, the moral code was allowed to slip a little, but the same laxity was frowned upon in peacetime. Also, Rosamund would be leaving school in a year. With Europe in such disarray, a finishing school in France or Switzerland would be out of the question, and what would Rosamund do all day? No, Marjorie thought, the sooner she's married, the better.

She didn't see the effect her words had had on Lizzie, who'd risen to her feet and stood trembling from head to foot. She wanted to scream at this woman she'd always disliked that what she said was lies, all lies. Rosamund meant nothing to David, nothing at all. She was a whore, that Rosamund, and everyone knew it, and David had little time for her. If he'd seen her, he'd have told Lizzie. It wasn't true.

But though Lizzie opened her mouth and licked her dry lips, no sound came out. Millie was alarmed by the look on her stricken face. Her eyes standing out huge in her head were so filled with hurt that Millie's heart ached for her. She realised that Lizzie too had loved David, but suspected that whatever had been between them had been destroyed by that Marjorie, who'd never had a decent thought in her head.

Lizzie's love for David, though, wasn't destroyed; just dented slightly by doubts that she was sure he could soon clear up. She wrote to him telling him what Marjorie had said, and waited anxiously for his reply.

When it came, she was amazed that he'd made no reference to Marjorie or Rosamund and offered no explanation for the things Marjorie had said. Lizzie sat on her bed with the letter in her hand, and faced facts. She knew Marjorie was a malicious old gossip and a troublemaker like her daughter, but neither of them had any reason to lie – it didn't make sense.

352

She saw then that her relationship with David had been based on deceit, for she knew now that he had met Rosamund and written to her, and she also guessed that his odd behaviour at Easter had probably been due to guilt. In her heart of hearts, she knew David was tired of her and it was over between them.

So she decided she would turn her back on him as if he'd never existed, like she was going to turn her back on everything about the Barracloughs' home and the village of Millover. She would prepare herself to go back to the back-to-back house in Bell Bam Road and the attic bedroom she'd share with God alone knew how many people. David would be just one more thing to forget. She had a week left before she was due to go home, and she resolved not to think of David at all.

It wasn't easy, because Sophie was cross with David for not turning up to say goodbye to Lizzie. 'I did think he might come,' she said, the evening before Lizzie was to leave. 'After all, things must be winding down now, and a twenty-four-hour pass would be better than nothing. I mean, Elizabeth, you have been here five years.'

Lizzie said nothing. She couldn't trust herself to speak. Instead she pleaded tiredness so that she could escape to the bedroom and nurse her disappointment and hurt in private.

It was as she was about to leave the room for the last time the next morning that she found her doll, Daisy, covered with fluff, under the bed. Her painted eyes were as blue as ever, but her lips were faded and the crimson spots on her cheeks were gone altogether. Poor Daisy looked very bedraggled, with her plaits unravelling and shiny patches on her velvet dress, the lace turned grey and torn in places. Once she had been important to Lizzie, a link with her daddy, someone to tell secrets and fears to and to combat homesickness. But as Lizzie had settled down, and in particular made friends with Alice, she hadn't needed the rag doll so much and hadn't thought of her for years. And yet she still didn't want to abandon her to be thrown away, or given to a village child who wouldn't love her as Lizzie once had, and so she opened her packed case, shoved her inside and left the room without a backward glance.

Millie and Alice went with Sophie to take Lizzie to the station. She was settled into a carriage with books to read and enough food to feed an army. Everyone was urging her to write, and Lizzie was nodding and saying she would, but her eyes were misted with tears, and now the time had come to leave, she just wanted to be away before she broke down completely and upset everyone.

When at least she heard the slamming doors and the guard's whistle, she gave an inward sigh of relief, and as she waved to the three disconsolate figures on the platform, she told herself sternly not to cry. 'You're going home,' she said to herself. 'Your life in Hereford is over and your new life is about to start,' and she made a promise to herself that however hard she found it, she'd try not to complain.

But for all Lizzie's brave intentions, she was unprepared for life in Birmingham. New Street station itself unnerved her. The squeal of the engines, the screech of brakes and the loud hiss of steam as the great monsters pulled into the station took her by surprise, as did all the clamorous noise of the teeming mass of people. When they emerged from the station it was little better. Lizzie had lived in a sleepy Herefordshire village where cars were virtually nonexistent, as even those, like Sophie, wealthy enough to afford one could use it only sparingly, with petrol so scarce. Even in Hereford itself there had been nothing like the volume of traffic of Birmingham city centre. Rattling trams, buses, lorries and vans vied with the ordinary cars, and Lizzie stood in speechless amazement as they emerged from the station.

She was also aware of a smell in her nose and the back of her throat, acrid and unpleasant, and the dust that danced in the summer sunshine and made her sneeze. They had to take a taxi home, for they'd never have managed on the bus with her case and the hamper Sophie had packed, and she was glad. She had no wish to mix with the noisy people thronging the pavements. She remembered how she had once loved to look around the town, and the Bull Ring in particular, and wondered if she'd ever want to do it again.

She was horrified at the drab greyness of her street and the dirt everywhere. Everything seemed smaller, but she remembered the fireside chairs and the small settee drawn up before the fireplace, and above the mantelpiece the picture of the Sacred Heart of Jesus.

'Welcome home, Lizzie.'

There was a party tea laid out for her, and people were crowding in to welcome her home, but after five years they seemed like strangers. She was jealous of the obvious closeness between her mother and the Sutcliffes. She could hardly recognise Barbara and Kenny and was resentful that they lived in her house and had her mother as well as their own all the time.

And then there were Gran and Grandad Sullivan, both grown older and Grandad certainly frailer, and Maggie, whom Lizzie had last seen when she'd come to tell her her father was missing. Carmel was unrecognisable as the carefree young girl Lizzie had left behind, and even Gran O'Malley had changed. As for Bridie, she was even worse than Lizzie remembered, and Sheelagh had grown more vitriolic and stuck-up than ever.

She felt cut off from her family, on the outside of it, and she didn't like it. She'd been close to Danny in Hereford, but he'd returned seven months before and didn't need Lizzie anymore. The bombed buildings across the road provided an exciting place for him and other boys like himself to plunder and play in, and as far as he was concerned, he was glad to be home. Lizzie envied him, and wondered if she'd ever feel like that again.

Three weeks later she was still unhappy and unsettled. She shared a double bed with Enid Sutcliffe and Barbara, with one inadequate cupboard for her clothes and a chamber pot under the bed for if she was taken short in the night. She longed every night for her old bedroom, with the toilet next door and a bath every night of the week if she wanted one. Here she was still counted as a wean, and bath night was Saturday, though now she had hers after Danny and Padraic had finished and had been packed off to bed. Kathy, Enid and Barbara bathed on Friday, and Sid and Kenny went to the public baths in Kent Street a couple of times a week, but Lizzie could only have one bath a week.

That day she was feeling thoroughly depressed and dispirited, missing Millover village and particularly Alice very much. She'd woken with a griping period pain and then couldn't find her hair ribbon. Later she found that Padraic had taken it, to play with a kitten he'd found in the street, and when it was eventually retrieved it had been torn to shreds. It wasn't the first time Padraic had rifled through her things and borrowed items without asking, and knowing it was useless complaining to Molly, Lizzie went to her mother.

Kathy, up to her eyes in the family wash and fed up to the back teeth with constantly chastising her young son to no avail, snapped that Lizzie must put her things where Padraic couldn't get hold of them.

'Oh, where do you suggest?' Lizzie said sarcastically. 'The roof?'

'Less of your lip, young lady.'

Tears at the unfairness of it all sprang into Lizzie's eyes, and at that very moment a letter addressed to her landed on the mat.

Lizzie knew what it was. She knew as she held it in her hands and crept up to the attic to read it in peace. Hope still stirred within her. Just maybe it was an apology; perhaps she'd been mistaken about the coldness between them, and David would explain why he had not been able to see her before she left Hereford. Gingerly she opened the envelope.

Dear Elizabeth,
This is the hardest letter I've ever had to write as I have
no wish to hurt you. You are very dear to me and will
always have a special place in my heart. But you are very
young yet, far too young to settle down for many years.
Your schooldays are over now and in the world of work,
many new opportunities will be offered to you. You will
meet new people including young men and I do not want
you to feel tied to me in any way. I hope we will always
be friends, and though you may be upset now, in the
future you will see that this will be for the best in the
long run.
Love, David.

Why, if Lizzie had had an inkling of how things stood between her and David, was she so stunned by the letter? She hadn't known she'd feel so bereft that she'd lost the young man she'd loved for five years. She felt let down. He'd used her, told her he loved her and tossed her aside like a worn glove.

The tears came then, like a torrent. She wanted to howl but knew she mustn't, and she lay face down on the bed, glad she was at the top of the house, and tried to muffle her sobs. She knew she must stop crying, for someone would hear her and then they'd never stop asking her what the matter was, and no one must ever know. Someone was sure to come up the stairs in a minute; in a house so small, with so many in it, it was always the same.

But when Kenny did come up, she didn't hear him. He was whistling as he opened the stair door, but he stopped as he heard the muffled sobs from above him. He stopped on the bottom step and listened; yes, there was definitely someone weeping in the attic. He knew who it would be – Lizzie. She'd looked proper miserable since she'd come back home, he thought, though her appearance had improved. She'd been a right skinny nipper when she went away, and she'd come back a stunner.

Before she'd gone to Hereford, he could have a laugh and joke with her, but it was funny, he'd been a bit nervous of her since she'd come back home, and Barbara said the same. It wasn't just the way she looked, it was the way she spoke and the clothes she had that Barbara said were grander than any you'd see in the shops. Barbara said Lizzie didn't even wear her very best things these days, but kept them in her suitcase, with the tattered rag doll on top that she'd had from when she was a little girl.

Still, there was nothing grand about her blarting her eyes out, Kenny thought, and he slipped off his boots and crept up the creaky stairs. When he saw her spread-eagled on the bed, her shoulders shaking, he felt real sorry for her. He sat down gingerly on the bed, and though he spoke softly, she shot around and glared at him.

'Don't cry, Lizzie,' he said. 'Nothing's worth upsetting yourself so much for.'

'Go away,' Lizzie snapped, wiping her face hurriedly with the sleeve of her cardigan. It was a childish action, the sort of thing she'd have done when she was nine years old, and Kenny almost smiled but stopped himself in time. Lizzie was too forlorn to laugh at. 'Come on,' he said. 'What is it?'

'Nothing. Go away,' Lizzie said, and she opened her eyes wider and looked at Kenny. 'Why would you care anyway?' she asked sharply.

''Cos I don't like you upset. I don't like to see anyone upset,' Kenny said. 'Come on now, tell Uncle Kenny, 'cos I'm a nosy bugger and won't give up till you do.'

And Lizzie remembered how he'd always stuck up for her before she went away, and how he and Barbara had once been her friends, and yet she'd hardly spoken to them since she came back. Kenny, she realised, was the same age as David, or very nearly. He wasn't as handsome as David – his hair was ordinary brown instead of blond, and went back from his head in a wave, and his face was thinner and pointed at the chin. In fact his whole body was thinner, and he wasn't really very tall, but she realised that his eyes were kind and his mouth seemed to have a permanent quirk pulling it upwards. She gave an impatient jerk of her head. David was gone, lost to her, and the sooner she realised that the better she'd be. And she might as well tell Kenny what she was so upset about, for she'd have to tell someone, and somehow she knew she could trust him to keep it to himself.

'I got this today,' she said, and for the first time he noticed the crumpled note in her hand.

He smoothed it out and read it, then said, 'Who is this David?'

'David Barraclough, Sophie's son – you know, the people I stayed with.'

'Oh yeah, Auntie Kath mentioned it,' Kenny said.

'I thought, I thought he loved me,' Lizzie said. 'He said he loved me and I certainly loved him.'

Oh God, Kenny thought. He knew why boys told girls they loved them. Surely Lizzie wasn't that stupid? And had he any right to ask? Well, someone had to damn well ask, in case there was . . . well, you never knew. And he could hardly tell anyone else he'd seen Lizzie blarting her eyes out in the bedroom over a lad that didn't want her anymore. She'd never trust him again. So tentatively he said, 'You didn't let him do anything to you, did you, Liz?'

Lizzie's face flushed crimson, for hadn't she let him touch and even fondle her breasts on the last day before he rejoined his squadron. Of course she'd thought he'd loved her then, and that was what you did. But Kenny saw the blush and misinterpreted it. 'You didn't, did you, Lizzie?'

'Didn't what?' Lizzie said, and then she knew by his anxious eyes what he was asking her, and sat up in the bed indignantly. 'No, no, I didn't, Kenny Sutcliffe,' she hissed so no one else should hear. 'I'm not that sort of girl.' But in her heart of hearts she knew she could easily have done more if David had been willing.

Kenny let out a sigh of relief. 'Sorry, Lizzie,' he said. 'But I thought I'd better ask. And another thing, I know you're upset and that, but it's probably for the best, like he says. You was too young, and not just for him either. You was too young for any real boyfriends. I'll take you to the pictures and that, but just as a friend, like. I won't expect anything for it, you know what I mean, don't you?'

'Oh yes, Kenny, I know,' Lizzie said.

'And another thing,' Kenny said. 'That David what's-his-name should never have took up with you in the first place, and he should have been man enough to tell you face to face, not write it in a flipping letter for you to open and cope with on your own.'

Lizzie realised Kenny was right. It was cowardly to write a letter. David wasn't worth the tears, she decided. Kenny was pleased to see the determination in her face and he said, 'Now, chin up, Lizzie O'Malley, and don't let this David bloke get to you, right?'

'Right,' Lizzie said, and she lifted her head higher. Later, when Kathy asked her if the letter was from Hereford, she said it was, without a break in her voice, and smiled at her mother.

TWENTY-ONE

Lizzie couldn't help being upset by David's letter, but she tried not to let her sorrow show. Kathy, however, knew that her daughter was miserable, although she didn't associate it with the letter she'd received; she knew Lizzie had been unhappy a long time before that.

Lizzie poured out her heart in a letter to Alice, although she never told her friend of Marjorie's revelations which had induced her to write to David for an explanation. Alice therefore did not view the relationship she'd seen developing between David and Rosamund over the summer as anything other than one of Rosamund's many flirtations. Not, of course, that she'd seen much of either David or Rosamund herself, trapped as she was on the farm every day, but rumour was rife.

She personally didn't think the relationship would last five minutes; most of Rosamund's didn't. She didn't see the point in upsetting Lizzie afresh, for she had enough to cope with dealing with David's defection, and by the time Alice wrote, she thought the affair would probably be over anyway. So instead she said how disgusted she was with David, and amazed at the cavalier way he'd treated Lizzie.

She told her she was better off without someone so cowardly and ill-principled as to declare their love in one breath, and a couple of months later to write a letter saying it had been a mistake but he'd like to remain friends. Alice said Lizzie should count herself lucky that the relationship had gone no further than it had.

Alice's reply was immensely satisfying to Lizzie, and she was glad that David had not taken up the total surrender of the body she'd been ready to offer him. She was glad too that she'd not told Alice any intimate details of their lovemaking. She couldn't have borne it if Alice had felt let down by her behaviour.

Alice suggested that Lizzie should not think any more about David, and should 'keep busy', sound advice but, Lizzie thought, not easy to take. She lived in a small house with three women, idle now because the parts they'd assembled during the war were no longer needed. They got under each other's feet and there was certainly not enough work for them to do.

Lizzie was lonely. She needed someone her own age, someone like Alice to talk to, but there was no one. She did look up Maura Mahon, but her old friend wasn't all that pleased to see her. She'd begun work at a brass foundry in Nechells, and Lizzie realised within a few minutes that they had little in common. She was shocked by Maura and thought her quite fast, with her high heels, tight skirts and plastered make-up, and she knew Maura thought she'd become uppity since she'd been away.

Carmel she'd always got on with, but her aunt was no longer a child, Lizzie realised, but a young woman. Her primary concern was her sweetheart, Ricky Westwood, who was in Europe awaiting transport back to America, where he'd be demobbed. Then, he said, as a civilian, in charge of his own life once more, he'd come and claim Carmel as his bride, and Lizzie could see she was both fascinated and a little frightened by the prospect.

Since the episode of David's letter, Lizzie had got over her resentment of the Sutcliffes and tried very hard to shake off her depression and be friendly to the people who shared her home through no fault of their own. Barbara was glad that Lizzie seemed more approachable, and Kenny, true to his word, had taken her to the pictures a couple of times. But still the days were long, with all the young people working, and Lizzie wished the summer would speed by, for she was beginning at Aston Commercial College in September and she could hardly wait.

'She'll learn other subjects too, just like a proper school,' Kathy said proudly when she received notification that Lizzie had a place. 'They even learn French, but they do typing, shorthand and book-keeping too.'

'Second-rate education though,' Bridie said with a sniff. 'I don't know why you're even bothering, because you'll never make a silk purse out of a bleeding sow's ear.'

'How do you keep your patience with her?' Maggie said as Bridie swept from the room.

'With difficulty,' Kathy said. 'I understand why our Lizzie used to slap Sheelagh too. I've often wanted to do the very same to the mother.'

'They're a couple of bitches, that's why.'

'Well, I'm pleased at least that Lizzie isn't jealous of Sheelagh going to a posh school.'

Lizzie wasn't. She thought it all a load of swank. She considered the commercial college the very place for her, and in fact it was an excellent school. Mr Donnelly had written to plead Lizzie's case when Kathy had told him where she'd like her daughter to go. He'd explained to the headmaster that though Lizzie was bright, she'd been denied the chance to take the eleven-plus as she'd been living as an evacuee at the time, although he had no doubt she would have passed. He would be pleased to know that she'd have a second chance at the college, and his words had carried weight.

A couple of days later, the Sutcliffe family heard about the new prefabricated houses that were going up all around the city, and Sid went and put his name down for one of them. 'The bombed-out families have first priority,' he said, and Mary wrote to Rose and told her to come home quickly if she wanted a chance of one of the new houses. 'And what about you?' she asked Maggie. 'What will you do when Con comes home?'

'Oh, I have a bit saved,' Maggie said. 'I think Con and I are after buying a place.'

'Oh, aren't you the grand one?' Mary snapped. 'Well, I hope it stays fine for you.'

'Now what have I said?' Maggie asked, perplexed.

Carmel grinned. 'Mammy's always wanted her own place,' she said. 'But sometimes you could be the Pope himself and Mammy would find fault. Don't be worrying about it, Maggie. Isn't it just her way?'

'Aye, maybe you're right, and the sooner Con's home and we're out of here, the happier I'll be.'

But before the men returned, Rose came home. Pete was now nine years old and Nuala seven. Josie, together with her cousins Tim and Padraic, had had her fifth birthday in July, and all three would start at St Catherine's Infant School in September. Mary said she'd be glad when the school opened and got the weans from under her feet, for they were all cramped up in the house. 'But it's only right that Rose should be in line for a place of her own,' she said. 'Since the one she had was blown to kingdom come, and her husband a fighting man.'

Lizzie could remember Rose a lot better than Danny could, but the children had grown out of all recognition. Pete had been a thin, almost scrawny child, but now he'd filled out and had the longest legs Lizzie had ever seen on a boy his age. Nuala, the plump, gurgling toddler, had developed into a pretty little girl with a smile on her face the whole time. But it was Josie whom everyone noticed first, with her black hair, heart-shaped face and green eyes flashing with mischief. Rose said she stopped wailing when she began to talk, and she'd never stopped since.

Padraic and Tim were enthralled by the children, introduced as their cousins, whom they had no recollection of meeting before. They thought they looked strange and spoke funny, for they'd never heard brogues so thick, and were bowled over by Josie, by both her beauty and her presence. Though much smaller than they, it was obvious from the outset that she would be the commander of the small trio, and she would order them here and there and everywhere to do things for her. Kathy and Maggie were amused by their small sons' devotion to their wee cousin.

'I'm dying for Con to see his son,' Maggie said one day, watching the three little ones at play. 'I bet you're the same.'

'Oh, aye,' Kathy said, but in actual fact she was rather nervous of meeting Barry again after so long. She knew she'd changed in five years and through necessity had become more independent, and she wasn't sure how Barry would react to that, or how the war had affected him. Padraic was almost as bad. He didn't care that Kathy told him Barry was his daddy. The only daddy he knew was Sid Sutcliffe, who had lived with him all his life. Now Mammy said the Sutcliffes were all moving out to make room for this stranger, and Padraic found it all very unsettling.

Lizzie, however, had become resigned to being at home. She eventually grew used to the noise and smell of the traffic, living as she did only yards from Bristol Street, and was not so nervous of crowds of people either, and she

366

recognised the hullaballoo in her own house and streets as part of life.

Therefore, when she went into town with her mother towards the end of August to buy her uniform for Aston Commercial College, she was quite excited, especially to have her mother to herself for once without Danny or Padraic tagging along. She knew that they'd have to go to Lewis's for it, but she hoped there would be time to have a gander down the Bull Ring later.

But first Lewis's third floor, reached by an escalator, which was much more fun than the stomach-churning lift with its clanking metal doors which always took her breath away.

There were wooden sets of drawers with glass insets in them behind every counter, stretching as far as Lizzie could see, and they were full of jumpers, shirts, ties and sports wear for various schools, while dotted around were models dressed in this uniform or that.

Lizzie looked with distaste at the striped blazer and flared pinafores of St Agnes's Convent. The model also wore a felt hat with the same stripes on the band, and a similarly striped tie. Kathy, seeing Lizzie's scrutiny, said, 'Good job you've not to wear that get-up, you'd look like a blinking deckchair, so you would.'

Lizzie grinned at her mother. 'I don't like it anyway, Mammy. I think it looks silly.'

'Aye. Aye, it does. Come on and let's get yours, a much classier rig-out altogether.'

And it was. The gympslip was brown, with three pleats down the front, worn with a buff high-necked blouse, a brown blazer with the college badge on and brown stockings and shoes. Lizzie watched her mother parting with her hard-earned pounds, anxious that it was costing too much, but Kathy, aware of what her daughter was thinking, reassured her. 'I had it put away,' she said. 'And there's more where that came from. I intend to make a day of it anyway and have our dinner at Lyons'. Molly will mind the weans for me.'

Dinner out was a treat, Lizzie thought, and she tried to stop worrying and enjoy the day. Every time she thought of the uniform they had in the bags, she felt a thrill of excitement and knew she was longing for the term to begin.

Lizzie enjoyed the commercial college as much as she'd thought she would, and quickly made friends, especially with Carol Mason and Lynn Shaw. They often went out at dinnertime, arms linked, around to Aston Cross shops, looking at the things they couldn't afford and giggling hysterically about nothing at all. They treated with disdain the whistles and calls from the boys at the commercial college and the upper end of Aston Grammar School. Neither of her new friends had much time for boys, and after Lizzie's painful experience with David, she decided that no boy was worth the worry and the subsequent heartache.

But Lizzie didn't forget Alice, her best friend for five long years, and she wrote to her often. She told Alice that her teachers were strict but fair, and that she enjoyed the lessons, especially French. She was glad she could write to Alice about it, for she told them little at home in case they thought she was swanking. Alice would never think that, and Lizzie could even put a few French words in her letters, together with a translation, knowing Alice wouldn't take it amiss.

She also told her of book-keeping, which she considered common sense and, as her maths was quite good, had mastered quickly, and went on to describe typing, which she adored. The keys were masked so that you learnt the keyboard by memory, and you had to keep your eyes fixed on the grid in front of you. Lizzie often thought the typewriters all working together sounded a little like the battery of ack-ack guns she'd listened to as she'd cowered in the cellar in the days before evacuation changed her life. The only difference was that the pounding at the commercial college was punctuated by the teacher shouting 'Carriage return!' at regular intervals.

Shorthand, Lizzie struggled with. The college specialised in Gregg's shorthand and not the more usual Pitman's, and it was explained to the girls that the slope to the right, hallway to the next outline, was an aid to speed. Lizzie didn't know whether that was true or not; she just knew that the marks on the paper looked like hieroglyphics and were just as impossible to understand. 'It will come,' the teachers assured the bemused girls, but most felt like Lizzie and her friends Carol and Lynn, who all wondered if they'd ever master the strange alphabet.

Alice, though she looked forward to Lizzie's letters eagerly, burnt with envy for her friend, for she herself worked extremely hard and yet had little free time and no regular wage. Lizzie, on the other hand, was learning a useful skill and having fun with her contemporaries. She described cinema trips and dances, first with Kenny and Barbara and later with Lynn and Carol too, and as she got over her nervousness of the city centre she began again to enjoy her jaunts to the Bull Ring.

Alice stopped writing to Lizzie. She couldn't tell her how bad it was, but she felt achingly lonely. She had no one now to giggle with, or whisper secrets to. She met no one on the farm and seldom left it. She never went to Hereford, to the cinema or to look around the shops. What was the point on her own, she asked herself, even if she'd been allowed and had the money? She became severely depressed about the future, which she could see would be a life of total drudgery.

In early October, Barry's youngest brother Dennis was demobbed, and although the O'Malleys had a celebration for him and Molly was ecstatic, there was no room for him in Kathy's crowded house with the return of Barry imminent. Nor could the Sullivans fit him in, for they were already bursting at the seams and their own men were expected any day. Dennis lodged with a shipmate's parents in nearby Sun Street, and Kathy could see that Molly was unhappy, feeling that she'd failed her son.

Padraic was confused by the man his granny clasped to her and called her babby. He towered above his squat mother – in fact, he towered above most people, being over six foot in his stockinged feet. But then Padraic found a lot of what adults said and did confusing. Kathy knew just how Molly felt; she'd feel the same if it was one of her sons returned as a hero from the war to a muted welcome and no home, and she felt great sympathy for her mother-in-law.

Then, near the end of October, Sean, Con and Michael came home too. The family were delighted they were back, and Kathy tried not to be depressed that Barry was not yet well enough to come home with them. At the customary party to welcome home the victorious heroes, Kathy did spare a thought for Bridie, who sat alone in the comer of the room, holding a drink and seemingly wrapped in misery. 'She's bound to feel Pat's loss at a time like this,' Kathy said to Maggie.

Maggie, half drunk and deliriously happy to have her Con beside her once more, had little time or sympathy for Bridie. 'Why?' she said. 'For God's sake, Kathy, she never spoke a decent word to the man all the years they were married, and she goes on since he died as if it were the love match of the century. Sure, doesn't she enjoy being miserable? Hasn't she enjoyed it since the day she came into the world? You sympathise with her if you want, but don't expect me to. If you ask me, she likes her widow's weeds.'

Kathy, despite her sister's words, did try. 'I'm heart-sore that Pat's not home with the others,' she said to Bridie.

'I understand how upsetting it must be for you and your children. You must feel Pat's loss greatly at a time like this.'

'Pat's loss!' Bridie spat out. 'Dead loss, more like. He was never much use to me alive, and less to me dead. No, it isn't your dear brother I'm mourning, but living in this squalor, this dead-and-alive hole. Your family seem happy enough to stay here like pigs in muck, but I've got plans for my life and they don't include living in a slum.'

Kathy was stunned by her reply. Too stunned to remind Bridie that her own family, including her married brothers and sisters, lived in the streets and courts in and around Bell Barn Road. Instead she retreated from Bridie's attack. Maggie was right, she thought, she enjoys misery. She decided to let Bridie be and celebrate her brothers' home-coming with style.

None of them looked much the worse for their wartime experience, she thought, though Michael the boy was gone for ever. The man Michael had a definite chin, and even the beginnings of a moustache above his upper lip. His face had lost the roundness of adolescence and become chiselled instead. He was a very handsome man, Kathy realised with slight amusement. His jet-black hair, grown longer since he'd left the army, made him more attractive than ever, and his eyes were dark-velvet-brown. Kathy guessed he'd break some hearts before he was ready to settle down.

Con and Sean just seemed happy to be home, delighted with the son and daughter they'd never seen. They seemed resigned to sleeping downstairs with Michael while the women and weans had the attic, although Kathy guessed they wouldn't put up with that indefinitely. She had been stupid to have doubts or feel nervous of her own husband; now she wanted her Barry home too, where he belonged. She'd known him so long and so well, she was sure they would soon settle down together as before, and she began to look forward eagerly to his return.

It was the first week of December before Barry came home, and his appearance shocked the family. He'd written to Kathy that he wanted her and the children to wait in the house, where he'd always imagined them, so Sean, Michael and Con went to meet him at the station. Back home, a 'Welcome Home' banner fluttered from the upstairs windows and a banquet awaited him inside, and as the minutes ticked by, Kathy became more and more nervous. Dusk came early that dismal winter's day, the purple-tinged clouds seemed low and oppressive and icy rain spears lashed the pavement. Kathy lit the gas and banked up the fire and gave a shiver of apprehension.

How often during the long separation had she longed for this moment? She'd imagined she would fly into Barry's arms and the last five years would be wiped out. Only Molly remained with them to welcome Barry; the Sutcliffes had taken themselves off for the day and said they'd be back later, and the rest of the family said they'd leave them in peace too.

But as Kathy eventually stared at her husband across the room, she wished they were there beside her to cover the awkward silence, for the man who stepped through the door bore little resemblance to the Barry who'd gone away. His hair was pure white, his face was scarred and pock-marked and his cheeks were sunken in, as if he had no teeth. He was so incredibly thin, and a little stooped. She wanted to weep for the fit young man who'd turned old in the space of five years.

'Hello, Kath,' Barry said. Kathy noted with relief that at least his voice hadn't changed. She had the urge to fly across the room and put her arms around her husband, not as a wife or lover, but as a mother might, to comfort him. And as she did go forward, a smile of welcome on her face, she noticed that his bleary eyes were filled with tears.

Then, as if his words had released everyone else too, Lizzie and Danny stepped forward and Molly cried, 'Mother of God, son, what have they done to you?' So saying, she pushed everyone else out of the way and enveloped her son in a hug. Over Molly's shoulder, Kathy caught Barry's anguished eyes and the tears trickling down his cheeks. She spoke as if he was the Barry they'd always known and not some emaciated stranger. 'Come on, Molly. Don't be strangling the man to death before the rest of us have a chance to welcome him home.'

Molly released her son, but still stood beside him, sobbing and wiping her tears on the hem of her apron. Barry drew his sleeve over his own eyes to wipe the tears away, and in a voice broken with emotion cried, 'Give over, Ma, for God's sake. OK, so I'm no bleeding oil painting, but I'm alive. You should see the state of the poor buggers who didn't make it.' He looked across to Kathy and said, 'How about it, Kath?'

Kathy was consumed with pity. 'Oh, Barry,' she said, and started forward again, but Padraic, frightened of the charged atmosphere, held her back by hanging on to her skirt, and Dan and Lizzie got there before her.

Barry was knocked out by the sight of his older children before him. When he'd left, Danny had been only six, and now here he was aged eleven, tall and healthy, and Barry's heart swelled with pride. 'You're catching up on me, son,' he said, putting a hand on his shoulder. Lizzie, though, was something else, he thought. Not much bigger than her brother, she had her mother's slight build, dark eyes and jet-black hair, and he was reminded of the time he'd first seen Kathy and recognised her as a desirable girl, rather than just Pat's kid sister. He'd known at that moment that he was determined to marry her, and had never regretted it, and now he hugged his daughter fiercely. Then he went across to the other wee boy, again the image of Kathy, hiding behind her skirts. It shook Barry that the child should be nervous of him, and he bent down to his level and said, 'Hello, Padraic.'

The child made no answer, but stood finger in mouth and looked at him out of large brown eyes. 'Say hello to your daddy, Padraic,' Kathy said. 'You mind I told you he was coming home today?'

Padraic stared at him. The only recent photograph Kathy had of Barry showed him at the beginning of the war in his uniform. Padraic had often looked at it, and the strange man before him wasn't anything like the photograph. He couldn't be his daddy, and yet Lizzie and Danny had called him Daddy and his granny had called him her son. 'Are you my daddy?' he said at last.

'Aye, I am.'

'Are you old?'

Barry chuckled and said, 'I suppose you'd think I was.'

Padraic considered it. 'Well,' he said at last, 'you've got white hair.'

'Aye, I have, and I'll tell you all about it when you're older,' Barry promised.

'Are you too old to play football with me like Grandad?'

'No, I'm not,' Barry said. 'Have you got a ball?'

'Yeah, but I have to share it with Tim. A man give it to us.'

Kathy held her breath, but Padraic said no more and Barry didn't seem disturbed about it at all. 'That was very kind of him,' he said. 'Later I'll give the pair of youse a game, OK?'

'OK,' Padraic said. A smile spread over his face and he went on, 'I'm glad you came back.'

'And me,' Barry said, getting to his feet, reaching out for Kathy's hands and drawing her close. 'Oh God, how I've dreamt of this,' he said, and Kathy submitted to her husband's embrace and tried not to think of the person who had last held her in the same way, eighteen months before.

She nearly succeeded. But as Barry's lips descended on hers, Padraic suddenly said, 'Doug said you'd play with me when you came back.'

Kathy, with her eyes closed, had a vision of Doug's arms around her and his lips on hers, heart-stopping and yet tender. In comparison, Barry's kiss was like a stamp of ownership, a hard kiss that bruised Kathy's mouth as she felt his teeth bite into her lips, and she pushed him away with a cry of alarm. 'What is it?' Barry cried.

'Nothing.' What could Kathy say? She wondered if he'd always kissed her like that and she'd never noticed. But the memory of Doug Howister's lovemaking was in her mind and she was suffused with guilt and didn't really know how to answer Barry standing in front of her. 'What could be the matter?' she said lightly. 'Except that Molly and I have been cooking for days and we have a banquet waiting for you.

Barry watched Kathy with narrowed eyes and wondered why she was nervous, for her hands were shaking and she seemed odd. He'd not really heard Padraic's comment – his mind had been elsewhere – so he didn't know what had caused Kathy to push him away. But he excused her. She hasn't had a man near her for five years, he thought, it's bound to take some getting used to, and then of course she may have been embarrassed in front of the weans. So Barry said pleasantly enough, 'I am a wee bit hungry, though I haven't been used to big meals for months now, so I won't be eating you out of house and home.'

'You can do that with pleasure, lad,' Molly said. 'I'd do without myself to give it to you. My bulk could keep me going for many a day, but my God, you've no flesh on your bones, you need feeding up, you do.'

'And you're the one who'll see to it,' Barry said with a smile. 'Lead me to it, Ma, and I'll eat everything I can.'

Kathy had been sure Barry would be angry with her, and blessed Molly, who had noticed nothing wrong and yet had lightened the atmosphere. She breathed a sigh of relief. It will take some adjusting having him back, that's all, she told herself, and she smiled at her husband and took hold of his hand.

Neighbours and friends crowded into the little house that evening to welcome Barry home, and the place resounded with noise. Everyone brought a bottle of something and many wives contributed to the food, and Lizzie saw Padraic, Tim and Josie retreat under the table with a plate of purloined goodies and smiled as she remembered doing the same thing at their age.

Eamonn was interested in why Barry had been sent to a labour camp, and he told them all of how he'd come round in a Belgian farmhouse after the farmer and his son had rescued him from a nearby field littered with his dead companions. Fitted out with false papers, and known as Gustave, a deaf mute, he'd been rounded up with all the other able-bodied men in the area and marched off to a labour camp before the farmer had been able to smuggle him out. Had he revealed who he was, his rescuers and their family would have been shot, so he'd kept quiet.

He didn't go into details of the rigourous march day after day, during which many died, or of the conditions at the camp, where food and water were barely adequate and beatings commonplace, and they toiled daily repairing supply routes bombed by the Allies as the invasion of Europe continued.

The guards just disappeared one day, and even the meagre supplies of food dried up completely, and eventually dysentery broke out amongst the weakened prisoners and many died. 'Including the farmer and his son who'd rescued me,' Barry said, and Kathy noticed the tears glistening in his eyes at the memory. 'Two days later the Allies liberated the camp and I was able to croak out my name, rank and serial number before I collapsed.'

It was a dreadful story, and Kathy knew Barry had played down his suffering. But something had turned his hair white and made the marks on his face. Later she was to see the sickening criss-cross stripes lining his back, though Barry made a joke of them.

But even before witnessing evidence of further physical cruelty, she knew that Barry hadn't emerged mentally unscathed either, and might carry those scars also to his grave. It was up to her, as his wife, to make it up to him, and she squeezed his hand and said, 'It's good to have you home, pet.'

Molly had taken Lizzie's place in the attic beside Enid and Barbara, and Lizzie lay along cushions covered with a blanket in her parents' bedroom with her brothers. Fortunately they would not be so squashed for long, for the Sutcliffes had been given one of the new prefabs, and the following day Lizzie and her parents were going off to see it. Molly had already been, and Maggie and Rose and their husbands, and all were mighty impressed with the Sutcliffes' place. It was on the edge of an estate to the north of the city called Pype Hayes, and they were just waiting to see if they would be issued with utility furniture before they could move in.

Part of Lizzie was pleased, and part of her knew she'd miss them all, but now that her daddy was home it was right that the Sutcliffes should move out. Kathy was sad to think of them leaving, for they'd been such a tower of strength to her and they'd been through a lot together. The children were grown now, fine and healthy and a credit to their parents, and she'd miss the life and energy that they'd injected into the house, but realised they should be on their own again.

These thoughts were whirring around Kathy's head that night as she watched Barry stumbling about the bedroom, getting ready for bed. He'd not drunk that much, but he was so thin and undernourished and unused to it that it hadn't needed much to get him rolling drunk. Kathy was pleased, and shocked at herself for being pleased, for she didn't want Barry to touch her that night, not after what had happened when he'd first arrived home. As he slid naked into bed beside her, she remembered how she and Doug had lain together. She hoped Barry had had enough to drink to make him too sleepy to be bothered, but he'd barely got into bed before his arm went around her, drawing her closer, fondling her breasts under her nightie. 'Take that bloody thing off,' he said, pulling at it. 'Don't know why you put it on in the first place.'

'Barry, don't,' Kathy protested. 'The weans.'

'What about the weans?' Barry demanded impatiently. 'They're asleep, and if they're not, they should be,' and he began unfastening the buttons at the neck of the nightie.

Kathy pushed his hands away. 'Don't,' she said again. 'They'll hear us above, your mother and the Sutcliffes.'

'So what if they do, we're married,' Barry snapped irritably. He sat up, leant over Kathy and said, 'What is it with you anyway? Five bloody years I've been away and you can think of every excuse under the sun why I shouldn't have sex with you this night.'

Barry couldn't understand it. He would never have described Kathy as a shrinking violet and would have said she'd be as keen to get back to a normal married life as he was, yet she obviously wasn't. Did she think all he wanted to do was hold hands?

'I don't . . . it isn't . . .' Kathy was flustered. How could she say she didn't want him to touch her until any memory of Doug Howister was erased from her mind?

378

Barry was growing angry that Kathy could give him no explanation for her reluctance. 'Look,' he said, 'I am home now and your bleeding husband, and whether you like it or not I intend to have sex with you tonight. I told you once before, I am not like your brother Pat. I'm wouldn't have put up with the shenanigans Bridie put him through for years. Now you can take that bloody nightie off yourself, or I'll take it off for you. You can have sex willingly, or unwillingly, it won't matter to me, but I'll have you either way.'

Never had Barry spoken in such a way to Kathy, she thought miserably as she tugged her nightdress over her head, but then he'd never had to. She'd always gone into his arms willingly enough.

'Ah, Kathy,' Barry said as he gazed at the naked body of his wife in the dim light coming through the curtains from the streetlamp outside. If then he'd spoken soft words of love and let his hands gently tease and tantalise her body as Doug had, and told her how beautiful she was, it might have been all right. But Barry was not used to such niceties with his wife, and he was in any case in too much of a hurry.

He lay across her, his weight pinning her to the bed and almost suffocating her, while his tongue sought her mouth. She smelt stale cigarettes and whisky, and as his tongue probed deeper and deeper, Kathy felt she might choke. She tried to turn her head away, but was unable to.

Despite herself, Barry's rough handling of Kathy's breasts had caused the sexual urges she'd dampened down to rise again in her, and she longed for Barry's hands to trail down her belly and between her legs so that she might want the eventual coupling as much as he did, but he could not wait for her to be ready, and as he spread her legs and prepared to enter her, she wanted to cry, 'Not yet, not yet!'

But her mouth was covered by Barry's and her moans went unheeded. Barry's caressing of her breasts had turned into a pummelling as his excitement mounted, and now he was hurting her. She hadn't been ready for him, but he didn't seem to care, and she lay passive beneath him and felt as if she'd been raped by her own husband. Tears trickled down her cheeks as she waited for him to be finished.

Lizzie pulled the blanket over her head, not wishing to witness what was going on, though she knew well enough what was happening. Eventually she heard her father's grunts turn into a cry, and then he was quiet.

Kathy realised after a minute or two that he'd gone to sleep, and she eased him from her and curled into a ball, her arms around her aching breasts and aware of the throbbing pain deep inside her. Then she cried for the gentle man she'd loved with all her heart who'd marched away to war, and the stranger who'd returned.

Lizzie listened to her mother crying and knew she could do nothing about it. Her mother would hate to know that she had seen or heard the confrontation with Barry, and Lizzie herself didn't fully understand what it was about. She stayed still where she was, the only sounds in the room the snores of her father and the sobs of her mother, and closed her eyes tight and eventually slept.

TWENTY-TWO

The next morning the atmosphere between Kathy and Barry was strained. Kathy was nervous of the man she thought she scarcely knew any more, and Barry was slightly ashamed of his behaviour of the previous night. He had a raging hangover so wasn't in the best of humour, and tried to excuse himself. After all, he thought, did Kath expect I wouldn't want her after all this time, when it was all I thought about all my weeks in hospital? And then for her to turn away with bloody excuses about the weans and the people in the attic. Did she expect me to say, 'OK then,' and turn on my side when my innards were screaming?

So he convinced himself that Kathy deserved all she'd got and was surly and bad-tempered with her. Only with the children, and particularly the wee fellow he'd just met, was he his normal, cheerful self, despite the throbbing headache.

He wished that Kathy, Lizzie and himself weren't going out on this jaunt to Pype Hayes, for he was dead tired. The previous day had been an emotional one and had drained him of the little energy he had. But Sid and Enid were anxious to show off their prefab, and all the family had been to see it but them.

It was an awfully long way out and none of them had ever been so far before. They passed Aston Cross, with the big green clock on the wall, and Lizzie was able to point out the road the college was on, but after that it was new to them all. Even Sid and Enid had only been a few times.

The canal appearing suddenly surprised Lizzie, under the bridge that spanned it which Sid said was called Salford. 'The canal has been there all the time,' Barry said. 'The canals run behind the factories and all the muck and waste is tipped into them. Something should be done, because they could be used. Birmingham has more canals than Venice, you know.'

Lizzie glanced at him, sure he was joking, but there was no smile on his face. She'd seen pictures of Venice in a book in the library in Hereford, and the canals there looked nothing like the mucky cut they'd just passed.

The bus turned right, and straight away the roads were wider and tree-lined, and the tramlines didn't run alongside them but down the middle of the street. Facing the road were lovely houses with bay windows and front gardens, and Lizzie saw her mother looking at them wistfully.

A little later Barry told them they'd be crossing Holly Lane in a minute or two. Lizzie knew that was where Fort Dunlop was, where her uncles, Sean and Con, worked. She didn't envy them the long journey they both had to make every day.

They were in Pype Hayes now, Enid told them as they crossed Holly Lane. 'But we're on the very edge of it, by the park.'

The roads were still tree-lined, even those leading off the main road. Enid told Lizzie there were no back-to-back houses with dingy courtyards, and that every house had a back and front garden.

After the neat, tidy houses with net curtains at the bay windows, the first sight of the prefabs was a bit of a shock, for they looked like tin shacks.

True, they were in a nice place, backing on to Pype Hayes Park, opposite a pub called the Bagot, close to shops and handy for buses and trams, but they looked awful, like garden sheds, and even the little fences around what would probably eventually be the front gardens did not make them look any better.

Enid guessed Kathy and Lizzie's thoughts, for she'd had them herself when she'd first set eyes on her new home. 'They look dreadful, don't they?' she said. 'I thought they looked like something you'd have standing on an allotment plot, rather than something you'd live in, but wait till you see inside.'

Enid wasn't exaggerating, for the prefabs were surprisingly roomy and comfortable. Even the hall was very spacious and not the poky corridor one might imagine. The living room had a coal fire, with a fitted cupboard on one side and on the other a glazed panel to the kitchen. 'The fire heats the water for the place,' Sid said. 'Then, in the summer, we have an immersion heater in the kitchen.'

'Yes, but that's not all,' Enid put in. 'There are air ducts to the bedrooms, so when the fire's on it heats them too.'

Kathy remembered the iciness of her bedrooms in winter, so cold that there was often frost on the inside of the windows, and wispy trails escaped from her mouth as she spoke. She envied Enid her warm and cosy home. 'There's only two bedrooms though,' Enid said. 'We don't know whether to let the kids have the big one and Sid will rig up some sort of partition between them, or give them one each and buy a studio couch that we can sleep on in here.'

'We'll have to see what we can get with our money,' Sid said. 'Every family can spend just a maximum of a hundred pounds on utility furniture. It's not a lot when you have to completely furnish a house.'

No, Kathy thought, it isn't, and nothing can replace the little things that make a home, like the ornaments or pictures you particularly liked, or the things the weans bought or made at school, or treasured photographs of your family. Yet many families had had those things destroyed, and it was right they should have these ready-made houses.

Lizzie liked the built-in wardrobes in the bedroom and wished her attic room had one so that she could lock her things out of Padraic's reach, and everyone was impressed with the bathroom, with its panelled bath and toilet and wash basin too. 'No more going out to the lavvy in the middle of the night,' Enid said happily.

'No indeed,' Kathy agreed. 'And does the water actually run hot?'

'Oh yes,' Enid said. 'We can have a bath any day of the week.'

Lizzie, peering over her mother's shoulder, remembered the bathroom she had shared with Danny at the Barracloughs' house and suppressed a sigh.

The kitchen, however, took everyone's breath away. There were cupboards built all round the room, and one was even fitted with open baskets for storing vegetables. There was a stainless-steel sink and drainer, and under the sink was a cupboard and under the drainer a boiler, and to complete the kitchen there was a gas fridge and a cooker. Kathy stared open-mouthed and looked about her. It was nothing like the Barracloughs', and not even one-tenth the size, but it had been planned to make use of every bit of space, and Kathy would have loved a kitchen like it. 'Oh, Enid,' she said.

Enid's smile nearly cut her face in two. 'I know,' she said. 'I'm that pleased to get one. Me and Sid will be as happy as Larry here.'

'I should think so,' Kathy said as they all trooped into the back garden after Sid.

'The gardens are all fenced,' he said. 'Ready for digging and planting. I can grow a fair few vegetables, and some flowers out the front for the wife, and of course we've got the shed for storing things in.'

'I'm pleased for you, Sid,' said Barry sincerely. 'And such a view out over the park.'

The view was beautiful even on a bleak winter day. The grass rolled gently and put Lizzie in mind of Hereford, but to her left she could see tennis courts and ahead a glint of water that Sid said was a lake, and she knew she'd like to live in one of these prefabs.

'Won't look so bad either when they're weathered a bit,' Sid said. 'And when all the front gardens have got a bit of a lawn and flowers growing around the edges, it will look better still.'

'Enid's right, it's a little palace,' Kathy said, and her voice was wistful.

'Never mind, Mammy,' Lizzie said. 'We'll have a new house one day.'

'And pigs might fly,' Kathy said. Lizzie knew exactly how she felt. It was hard to leave the comfort of the prefab and return to the inadequacies of their own place.

Harder still, though, was the finding out later that Maggie and Con and Sean and Rose had been so impressed by the Pype Hayes area on their own visit there a fortnight before that they had decided that they'd like to move out there too, especially as it would mean they'd be much closer to Fort Dunlop. Maggie and Con found a home actually in Holly Lane almost immediately, empty and ready to move into. It wasn't on the large council estate itself, but to the side of it, near Woodacre Road, some way from the Sutcliffes', whose prefab faced the park on the opposite side.

Kathy and Lizzie, taken on a visit to Maggie's house, were full of praise. It had a small, quite narrow hall with two rooms off, and a fairly tiny kitchen at the end. Upstairs were two big bedrooms, one smaller one and a bathroom. 'It's lovely, Maggie,' Kathy said warmly.

Maggie pulled a face. 'Not yet it isn't,' she said. 'It's been a bit neglected, which is why we've got it so cheaply, but we'll soon do it up bit by bit.'

'Och, Maggie,' Kathy said. 'Sure, the house itself is lovely. God, you could do what you liked with the houses we have and they'd be no better. But with a lick of paint, a nice bit of wallpaper and new curtains, you'll have a wee palace here, so you will.'

Kathy's opinion had always mattered to Maggie, and she was pleased with her sister's praise. 'Con said he'll plant flowers in the front garden,' she said, leading them outside. 'The bottom half of the back garden he said he'll set aside for vegetables. I mean, we have plenty of room, but at the moment it's like a jungle, as neglected as the house.'

Kathy nodded wistfully. What she'd give for a place like this for her own! She suppressed a sigh, but her eyes were sad and Maggie put her arms around her sister. 'Oh, Kathy, I'm going to miss you,' she cried. 'We've never been more than a few doors apart. It's a lovely house right enough, but God, I'm going to be lonely here by myself.'

'And me,' Kathy said as the two sisters cried together. Lizzie felt her own eyes smart, and she told herself sternly not to be so soft.

But it got worse. Kathy thought she'd have Rose and Sean and their weans a wee while yet, as they hadn't found a house that would suit, but one day, just before Maggie moved out, Rose called in on Kathy. She'd decided to go in with Maggie for the time being, she said, and would be leaving them a week to settle themselves in before she and

Sean joined them with the weans, so that both families would be in just before Christmas. 'It makes sense,' she said when Kathy queried her decision. 'We want a house in that area too, as it's a desperate trek out there for Sean every day. Anyway, there's so few houses on the market and so many needing them, they are snapped up straight away and you need to be on the spot.'

'You wouldn't think of putting in a for a prefab like Mammy suggested?' Kathy said. 'You know, with you being bombed out and all?'

'What good would a two-bedroomed prefab be to us?' Rose asked. 'Sean won't be happy until he has a football team around him, I'm sure.'

'You're not . . . '

'No, I'm not,' Rose said with a grim laugh. 'But that's only because we've not had the opportunity.'

Kathy knew she was right, but she hated the idea of Rose going too. It was as if her whole family was fragmenting. Michael was courting heavily, while young Carmel was still writing to Ricky Westwood, and Kathy knew he was pressing her to go over and meet his family. She'd hesitated so far, and Kathy could hardly wonder at it, and yet she felt her youngest sister truly loved Ricky. God, what a decision to have to make. It would break her mammy's heart to have her daughter on another continent. But then Mary had left her own family and gone to England with Eamonn and her weans, and none of the family should try to stop Carmel seeking happiness in her life, Kathy reasoned.

It was as Kathy lay in bed that night, after Barry had fallen into a stupor beside her, that she realised she hadn't had her period that month. It had been due just a few days after Barry's demob, but nothing had happened. She might easily have become pregnant from that first disastrous night, or from any of the far from successful nights since, for however she felt, Kathy knew it wasn't necessary for the woman to enjoy sex in order to conceive. Many women around the doors would testify to that themselves. Anyway, if she was having a baby she was and there was nothing to be done about it. She was grateful she hadn't started being sick yet, though she'd felt nauseous the last few mornings. She wasn't upset, but neither was she jumping with joy, though she might have been if things had been right between her and Barry. Maybe he would leave her alone a bit after this, she reasoned, but she wouldn't tell him, she wouldn't tell anyone yet; she'd wait until she was sure.

Barry's sexual demands were far more regular now than they had been before he'd left. There was no longer any attempt at tenderness; he would get into bed, roll on top of Kathy and take what he considered his due. Any attempts she made to refuse him, or even delay the lovemaking, led to further roughness from her husband. She'd learnt to lie and accept the assault – for that was how she thought of it – without a sound, and when the grunting finally stopped and Barry was satisfied and rolled away from her, she breathed a sigh of relief.

But it often took a long time for her to sleep afterwards. Her thoughts would go round and round in her head as she listened to her husband's snores, while her body would often be throbbing with pain from Barry's rough handling. The tears would come then, but even smothered in the pillow, Lizzie often heard. Now that the Sutcliffes had gone, she shared one of the double beds in the attic with her gran, while the boys had the other, and she'd lie stiffly beside Molly, listening to the sounds from the bedroom below. She knew that Molly was awake, and Molly knew that Lizzie was, but neither spoke, nor did they ever refer to it afterwards. Lizzie knew she must never speak of her mother's tears, but she lay in helpless misery and wished she could help her parents in some way.

They were polite enough to one another, most of the time almost too polite, but the spark between them was missing. And Barry was further annoyed that the weans went to their mother if they wanted anything, not used to their father being around yet. But he never showed his anger to the weans; it was Kathy who got a tongue-lashing.

He also made it obvious that Padraic was the one he doted on. Though Molly loved her youngest grandson as if he were her own, she didn't believe in showing such blatant favouritism. You could have favourites – after all, a person was only human – but to show it so openly was wrong. Padraic was no fool and was quick to take advantage of the new situation. He missed his cousins terribly when they left, especially Tim, and was glad to have a father to take him up the park and play football with him, and a bored and unemployed Barry was always glad to go.

Barry felt cheated of his other two weans. He'd seen none of their growing up, and they were closer to Kathy than they were to him. Christ, if Kathy wasn't there, they'd go to Molly before him, but Padraic was different. He was only five, young enough for Barry to enjoy his company for many years yet. Barry didn't understand why Kathy was sometimes hard on him, but presumed it was because the child loved him and that annoyed her in some way. She didn't care for him any more – she made that quite clear, the way she lay like a bloody doormat every night – but love him, or hate him, he'd make sure she did her duty by him. The fact that Padraic thought he was wonderful, though, salvaged some of his pride and self-esteem, and sometimes seemed to be the only good thing to have come from this God-awful war.

Kathy was frustrated and unhappy because of Barry's attitude with the children. He seemed to have eyes and attention only for his younger son Padraic was still a difficult child, for despite nursery and school, he still wanted his

389

own way, and as Molly had given into him all the time, he was used to getting it.

Now his father endorsed that. Barry often countermanded Kathy's instructions, gave him things Kathy had previously forbidden him to have and almost encouraged him to answer back. When Kathy, driven to distraction, shouted at Padraic, Barry would stick up for him, and Padraic's constant cry if she corrected him was that he would tell his daddy. When he did, Kathy was the one Barry went for. Once Kathy smacked Padraic's legs over some naughtiness, and she'd seldom seen Barry in such a rage about anything. Padraic told his father about the punishment as soon as he came in, and Barry went rushing down to the cellar, pinned Kathy to the wall by her arms and said that if she laid a hand on the child again, he'd do the same to her.

Kathy, though frightened of him, was outraged, and so was Molly. The other children were speechless, but Padraic was jubilant. When he calmed down, Barry was quite ashamed of what he'd done, but he was damned if he was going to say so, and after all, Kathy had no right to lay into the lad. He looked at the accusing faces of all those around him and said to Padraic, 'Get your coat, son, and you and me will go down the park.' Padraic, with a smug glance at his mother, ran to obey, and Kathy gave a heavy sigh.

'What's the bloody use?' Lizzie heard her say as she turned back to the stove.

On Christmas night they were all at a party at Mary Sullivan's, and Lizzie thought they seemed a very small family indeed. Molly was there, and Barry's brother Dennis, who had spent Christmas with them, and Bridie with her two children, and Michael's girlfriend, Pauline Maguire, and her parents. Lizzie tried to make a show of enjoying it for her mother's sake, but Kathy wasn't fooled. She knew that this Christmas was probably not a patch on those in the Barracloughs' home. However, in her heart of hearts she knew it wasn't only that. Lizzie was aware of the atmosphere at home. She couldn't blame her, for God, it was dreadful, and she was just glad Lizzie liked the commercial college so much.

She glanced across at her husband, laughing with Eamonn and Michael as if he hadn't a care in the world, and hoped the doctor would sign him off so that he could begin work after Christmas. Then maybe he wouldn't have so much pent-up energy to attack her in bed every night. God, she felt exhausted. Padraic had been at his worst that day, screaming each time he was slightly thwarted, and Barry had made Dan and Lizzie give him whatever it was he wanted. Any argument they tried, or indeed those of Molly and Kathy, had been shouted down, and the whole thing had wearied Kathy. She hoped Barry would leave her alone that night, especially as she was fairly certain now that she was pregnant.

Barry, however, didn't see it that way. He'd eaten and drunk better that day than he'd done since he'd come home, and a spot of sex was just the thing for rounding the day off well, he thought. Kathy was almost asleep when Barry eventually made it to the bedroom, and he stripped off quickly and, slipping into bed beside Kathy, reached for her immediately.

She was jerked awake by a hand kneading her breast and said irritably and still drowsily, 'Not tonight, Barry. Leave me be.'

Barry laughed, but it was a humourless sound. 'Leave you be? What you talking about, girl, it's Christmas.'

Kathy, angry, said sarcastically, 'God, is it? How could I have forgotten? Is there anything else you wanted for your Christmas box?'

She felt Barry stiffen in anger beside her, and he said sharply, 'Come on, Kathy, don't be stupid.'

'Stupid, am I? Aye, I must be, putting up with you so long,' Kathy cried. 'Bloody hell, can you never go to bed without reaching out your hands to me? Do you ever ask if I want to? No, you bloody don't, because you'd know that sometimes I might say no. Tonight I don't feel like it.'

She pushed Barry's groping hands from her body and said, 'You say it's Christmas, and so it is, and the season of goodwill to all men, and women too, don't forget. I'll tell you what I'd like for Christmas, and I've got very little from you so far. I'd like to be left alone. I'd like to go into my side of the bed and know I'll be able to sleep unmolested. Is that too much to ask for one night of the year?'

Upstairs in the attic, Lizzie and Molly listened to Kathy in horrified fascination. For the first time, Lizzie was so scared she let her hand slide across the bed until it connected with Molly's body. Molly's big, soft hand cradled Lizzie's, and she felt safer as she heard her father say coldly, 'You're my wife, Kathy, and it's about time you realised that. You promised to love, honour and obey, or have you forgotten all that?'

'I've forgotten nothing.'

'Then what's it to be?'

'God, Barry, will you leave me be just this one night? I'm bone weary, so I am.'

He ignored her plea and began to straddle across her, pushing her nightie up as he did so. She cried desperately, 'For Christ's sake, Barry, leave me alone! You've done your work well. I'm pregnant, for God's sake, and not feeling so good.'

Barry stopped and stared at Kathy in amazement, while up in the attic the hands of the young girl and the old woman clasped together tighter. 'God, Kathy, d'you mean it, you're pregnant?' Barry said delightedly. 'You're sure?'

'I'm as sure as I can be,' Kathy said. 'But I've seen no doctor yet.'

'And you don't feel well?'

'I'm just tired.'

Barry felt exhilaration tingle all through his body. This child Kathy was carrying he would see grow up. God forbid there'd ever be another war to separate him from his family so that his wife viewed him as an unwelcome visitor in his own bed and his weans as a stranger in their midst. He'd proved to himself and anyone else who was interested that he was as virile as the next man, and in a few months his wife would be showing evidence of that. For now, though, he thought, she needed a bit of consideration. To Kathy's grateful relief, he gave her a chaste kiss on the cheek and said, 'You should have told me about the baby before and I'd have eased off a bit. I'm not a bleeding monster.'

'I . . . I wasn't sure till now,' Kathy said nervously. 'I'm sorry I blurted it out like that.'

'Well, never mind,' Barry said. 'I'm pleased however I was told, and it's small wonder you're tired. You need to get your head down and rest, if you ask me.'

Kathy couldn't believe it. As she settled herself she thought that if Barry had been like that in the beginning they might have had a chance, and she wondered as she drifted off whether the baby might signal a new start for them all.

Up in the attic, Molly and Lizzie looked at each other and smiled in the near-darkness of the room. 'A baby,' Lizzie breathed.

'Aye, praise God, another wee O'Malley,' Molly said. She had no doubt the child would be the making of Barry and Kathy. The first child of the family to be born since the end of the war, and that would mean something. This was what was needed to put all that happened over the last six years to the backs of their minds and look to the future. And for the first time in days, Molly slept well and deeply.

TWENTY-THREE

By the new year of 1946, Molly had become restless about her son Dennis, who still lived with his shipmate's parents and had to sleep on a sofa. She'd been on about it at Christmas, when she'd said he looked proper peaky in her opinion, and since then had been down to the council two or three times a week complaining about it. In the end her persistence paid off and she was given one of the flats in the St Martin's complex in Vaughn Street in Deritend. They had only been built in 1939 and so were very modern and comfortable, and she told Kathy she'd be moving in in March.

Kathy respected Molly's decision, but she knew she would be sad to see her go. They'd been through a lot together and she was glad Molly was staying so close at hand. For her part Molly would miss Kathy and the weans, especially Padraic, but with Barry home and a new wee O'Malley expected, she thought they needed a bit of privacy. She knew Barry and Kathy had had a few problems living together again after so long and was glad things seemed to have improved just lately.

Kathy thought so too. Barry hadn't insisted on his rights every night since she'd told him she was pregnant, and she was glad of the respite. She'd become detached about it all anyway, something to be done before sleep, like visiting the lav, or cleaning her teeth down the cellar, and just about as enjoyable. But she didn't complain, knowing many woman had worse to put up with.

Barry had been signed off as fit for work in January too, and he now worked at the Claredon Stamping Co., which made brass fittings. 'The biggest money-spinner is the brass bedsteads,' Barry told the family when he'd been there a week or two. 'And,' he went on, 'we sell most of them to Africa.'

'Africa?' Danny exclaimed. 'Darkest Africa?'

The Church was always going on about Africa, and missionaries often came from there to preach about the heathens. It was such an alien place, but they knew all about it. It was always hot, much of it desert or steamy jungle, and lots of people with black skin who wore little or no clothing lived there. Brass bedsteads made in Aston, Birmingham, didn't fit into their preconceived ideas of Africa.

Barry was pleased he'd got everyone's attention. He'd not believed it himself when he'd first heard. 'Aye,' he said. 'Apparently white ants eat away at wooden ones, or else they rot in the extreme climate they have.'

'Well, well,' said Kathy. 'It's almost unbelievable. I wouldn't have thought there would be much call for any sort of bedstead in Africa.'

'Nor I before I went there,' Barry said. 'But a bloke told me, straight up. There's this African agency that deals with all the orders from there and it kept the whole factory going through the slump when millions were out of work.' He looked across at Kathy and said, 'I should have been working there a few years ago, and we'd not have had the means test people in then.'

Kathy gave a shiver, for even the thought of returning to the poverty and hopelessness of those days chilled her to the bone. 'Well, never mind, you're there now. That's all that matters.'

Lizzie had also got a job, on Saturdays and the odd evening after school, at Woolworth's at Aston Cross, after her father heard they were on the look-out. She was glad, for she hated taking money from her mother, only too aware that she could have been working full time in a factory or shop since she'd returned home, and contributing to the family instead of them subsidising her further. Now she was able to stand her corner with her friends when they went together to a dance or the pictures. And if clothes ever came off dreaded points, it would be nice to have a bit of spare cash to treat herself.

Now that Barry was at work all day, he had less time and energy to spend with Padraic. He'd arrive home at half six, starving hungry, and the children knew it would be no good talking to him till he'd had his dinner. Kathy would always have it ready, and he wasn't human at all until he'd eaten his fill.

By then, usually Padraic was drooping with tiredness. Barry would put him to bed, as he'd done since he returned home, but after a day at work he was in no humour to listen to a list of complaints from the little boy. Padraic was bright enough to know this, and had no wish anyway to alienate his father, who would read him one or two stories most nights if he thought he'd been a good boy.

However, Padraic was totally unprepared for Molly moving out. Kathy thought he'd realised and become resigned to it, but to Padraic it was the final betrayal, and though he stormed and shrieked and threw himself to the floor, he knew there was nothing he could do. Everything had changed. All the people he loved, who had been a constant in his short life, had disappeared, and he was helpless against it all. Lizzie, who tried to calm her young brother, had a measure of sympathy for him, and Kathy felt almost desolate at times with the way her family, who'd once lived on top of one another, had scattered themselves.

Even Bridie was on the move by the first week in April, to a flat found for her by the Catholic Housing Association with whom the nuns from the convent Sheelagh attended had put her in touch. Using Mart's lameness as the reason her back-to-back house was unsuitable for the family, she made an application and was allocated a ground-floor flat in a converted house in Church Road, Erdington. It was much nearer to Sheelagh's convent and not that far for Matt, who would attend St Thomas's Secondary School at the back of the Abbey School.

Bridie, as expected, was inclined to be boastful about her new place and the way she'd got it, and disparaging about Kathy left in a 'depressing bleeding slum'. Kathy in one way was pleased Bridie was moving out, because she'd been a thorn in her side for many years, but it was another branch of the family to leave the area and she was fond of Matt, who grew more like his father in both looks and temperament every day.

'God above, the family will be taking over the whole of Erdington and Pype Hayes at this rate,' Mary said when she heard.

'Well, here's one who won't,' Kathy said. 'I'm afraid you're stuck with me.'

'It's glad I am to have one beside me,' Mary said. 'For you know Carmel won't bide long, and she won't be living up the road either, but on another continent altogether.'

Kathy knew only too well, for Carmel was not long back from an all-expenses-paid holiday visiting Ricky Westwood's family in Pittsburgh. She'd been as excited as a child, and no wonder. She'd never even travelled on a train before, and to have the opportunity to fly miles above the earth and over the ocean to see a new country made all the family a bit envious.

But the Carmel who returned was more restless than ever and confided in Kathy that the only thing she was sure of was that she loved Ricky as much as ever and wished she didn't. However, she also knew, as all the family did, that her father was dying. Not even Dr Casey, who'd attended the family for years, thought he'd recover this time. 'I think you must prepare yourself, Mary,' he said.

Mary's eyes glistened with tears as the doctor went on, 'Now, now. He's done well. Few men with lungs as bad as his last so long. You have nothing whatever to reproach yourself for, you've looked after him well.'

It was just a matter of time for Eamonn Sullivan, and Carmel knew she'd have to stay until her father breathed his last and that Ricky would have to understand that. Mary knew how her youngest daughter felt, and she also knew that when the time came for her to leave, she'd wave her off and hide her tears and heartache, as her own mother had done when she and Eamonn had left Ireland. She had come to England for a better life, and she couldn't deny the same to one of her own, though it would be heartbreaking to see her go. She had a special feeling for Carmel, her baby, and for Kathy, the eldest of the family, and though she'd never admit to having favourites, she was glad Kathy had no plans to move away from Edgbaston.

Everyone seems to be moving out, Lizzie wrote to Alice.

Uncle Sean and Auntie Rose moved into their own house last week, so Auntie Rose was probably right about being in the spot where you actually want to live, because it's in Holly Lane too, but just a bit further down the hill, even nearer to Dunlop's factory. Mammy said it was time they

had a house of their own and they were very squashed,
but we all miss them. Mammy's getting very big now and
yet the baby's not due until the beginning of September.
Granny Sullivan says she wouldn't be surprised if it's
twins.

Write and tell me how things are with you, it's ages since
you wrote. I hope things are easier for you now the
winter's over. I think it's hard getting up in the dark and
cold. I'm going on all right myself and I'm beginning to
understand shorthand and I never thought I'd be able to
say that. My typing speed has increased too. We type to
music now to keep the rhythm steady and they play 'Red
Red Robin' and 'The Star-Spangled Banner' on the gramo-
phone. The older girls say we'll know we've really made it
when we can keep up with 'The William Tell Overture'.
I've finished my domestic science apron and headband at
long last and you should see what a mess I've made of it. I
often wished I had you beside me, remember how you used
to help me with sewing in the village school? Carol and
Lynn are all right as friends, but as bad at sewing as I am.
The cookery classes are not too hard at all, except that
with the rations as they are, there is so little to cook . . .

Alice read the letter and felt despondency settle on her. She
hadn't written to Lizzie for such a long time, because she
was too depressed to do so. Lizzie was right, Alice would
have loved the sewing classes and her apron would have
been finished quickly and beautifully, not at all like the
cobbled effort she could imagine Lizzie had turned out.
She'd never had anything interesting to sew, just reversing the
frayed collars and cuffs of her father's and brothers' shirts,
or cutting the sheets and seaming the edges together to get
more wear out of them, which made them uncomfortable
to sleep on, or darning interminable holes in the socks of

the men of the family. But still her stitches were even and her darning neat.

Alice sighed and scanned Lizzie's letter again. Why, she wondered, did Lizzie imagine it might be easier now the spring was here? If anything, the work load had increased, for it was the time for crop sowing, and often she was drafted in to help there too, when her mother let her out of the house and away from the spring cleaning. She clenched her fists suddenly. She'd go mad if she was cooped up on the farm for much longer. It wasn't fair. She saw and spoke with other girls she'd been at school with on Sunday if they went to church, or occasionally on market day, and none of them had a life like hers. She was fed up with it and tired of pretending everything was all right. In the past she'd always told Lizzie everything, and she decided there and then that she would write to tell her exactly how bad it was. She felt guilty that she hadn't written before anyway, and told her how things were between Rosamund and David. Lizzie deserved to know.

Alice's reply to Lizzie's letter came almost by return of post, and for the first time she poured out how boring and soul-destroying her life on the farm really was. Lizzie was filled with sympathy for her and knew her friend was desperately unhappy.

She wasn't totally surprised by the news about the deepening relationship between Rosamund and David. Alice wrote that David hadn't wanted to go back to school at the end of the war and instead had started private lessons with a professor in Hereford to cram him for his Higher School Certificate, and with Rosamund expelled from school – or that was what people said, anyway – they both had a lot of free time. Alice supposed that that was why it had started.

But Lizzie knew it had started some time before that, and she felt furiously, blisteringly angry that she'd been taken for such a fool. Rosamund regarded David as her property; she would never let him go now, she knew. She also knew she'd swallow him whole and spit out the pieces, but that was his look-out.

She wondered what Sophie thought, and guessed she wouldn't be happy about developments. She wondered if she was aware of the relationship at all, for she'd never mentioned it in her letters. In fact, Sophie had been ignorant of it for some time, for despite David's drunken behaviour the night of his party, she'd seen nothing untoward between the young couple till the autumn, and even then thought it natural that they should go around together for, after all, they always had done. If David got the passes needed, he wanted to train to be a pilot in civil aviation, and though she would miss him – for he wouldn't live at home – she was glad that he would be out of Rosamund's reach too. She also knew, because he'd told her, that he had no intention of settling down for some years yet, a fact which Sophie was very relieved about. So even when Millie expressed disquiet, Sophie was unwilling to see a problem. 'Rosamund's only amusing herself,' she said. 'You know how she is. It's just harmless flirtation and she'll soon tire of David. My niece is hardly what you'd call the faithful type.'

Millie wasn't convinced, but she kept her doubts to herself.

Lizzie didn't really care any more what happened to Rosamund and David, or Sophie's reaction to it, but she was concerned for her unhappy friend. Alice needed a prod, a spur, to encourage her to stand up to her domineering mother. In the end, in Lizzie's reply she told Alice the news David had unwittingly disclosed about the eleven-plus exam Mr Donnelly had wanted her to sit but that her mother had vetoed. She didn't know how Alice would use the information, or whether it would cause her to be angry enough to make a stand, but it was all she could do.

Just after Alice's letter that so disturbed Lizzie, Kathy received one that upset her totally. The Easter holidays had begun, but the children were all out and the house was mercifully empty when Kathy picked up the airmail letter with the American stamp.

One part of her hoped it wasn't from Doug, for it would cause immeasurable problems if he began writing to her again. Another part of her wanted to know how he was, to hear about his life, and she ripped the envelope open eagerly and withdrew the thin airmail sheets. What she read made her legs so shaky she felt they wouldn't hold her up, and she felt for a chair and sat down, trembling slightly.

The letter was from a Mrs Laura Howister, Doug's mother, and she wrote to tell Kathy of Doug's death on the last day of 1944. As Kathy's eyes blurred with tears, Laura Howister went on:

When his effects were sent over to me in the States, for some time I couldn't look at them. But when I was able to steel myself to do so, for life I knew must go on, I came upon a letter amongst them asking me to contact you if anything happened to him. He told me your name was Kate O'Malley and he said you'd brightened his life when he was in England prior to the invasion. He said you were very special to one another.
For that reason, Kate O'Malley, I thank you from the bottom of my heart because you made my boy happy. Doug was a warm, loving son and will be sorely missed in the family, but if you had a special place in his heart and he in yours, you too will feel his loss keenly. I'm sorry I was not able to tell you of his death sooner. Possibly you have been wondering why he didn't write to you.

Kathy looked up from the letter and tears ran unchecked down her face. Had she wondered why he'd written but once? Yes, she realised she had, even though she'd known that to enter into any sort of communication between them was dangerous. Yet she'd longed for his reassurance that he'd not forgotten her and what they'd shared together.

Funny that she'd never, ever thought Doug wouldn't make it. She'd always thought of him as a survivor. But now the fantasy was over, and Doug was no more. Laura Howister spoke of the effects sent to her, but nothing of the body or the funeral. Kathy guessed he was buried in foreign soil like countless others, and that Laura Howister, like her own mother, would not even have a grave to tend to help her grieve for the son she'd loved and lost.

And then she cried for Doug Howister, taken from her for ever, and was mightily glad Bridie had left. It wouldn't have done for her to come bursting in the door, without as much as a by your leave, and see Kathy mourning the loss of her American lover.

She read Laura Howister's letter again, and then burnt it and the envelope, but Doug's letter she couldn't bring herself to destroy, and she decided she'd try and get Maggie on her own on Saturday and tell her about it.

The weekends now had begun to form a sort of pattern. After Barry's Saturday shift, he'd come home for a bite of dinner, and then the whole family would set off for Maggie's, Mary too sometimes, if Carmel could give an eye to Eamonn. The men would go to the match at the Villa, taking Pete, Danny and sometimes Padraic and Tim with them. Rose would join the women, and they would prepare a big spread for the men's return.

In the beginning, Kathy and Lizzie would often go off to visit the Sutcliffes for an hour or two. It was a fair step, but if you cut across the estate there was a walkway through

St Mary's churchyard that brought you out on Tyburn Road, and then it was no distance at all, especially as Kenny would come over to meet them both. Kathy guessed that Kenny really came for Lizzie, and they'd often go for a tramp around together through the park, while Kathy went for a natter with Enid.

When Kathy became too heavy and weary for the walk over, especially when her legs began to swell, Lizzie continued to go on her own. Kathy viewed the growing affection between Kenny and her daughter with a little anxiety. 'I'm sure they're walking out together,' she confessed one day to Maggie.

'What if they are?' Maggie said. 'Kenny's a decent lad, despite being a Protestant.'

'Aye, but I'll have the priest at the door.'

'God, Kathy, the child's not fifteen years old,' Maggie said. 'Don't marry her off yet a wee while.'

Kathy said nothing to that, but she remembered the revelations Carmel had made in the hospital about her and Andy, and she'd been younger than Lizzie. She shook her head. 'Children grow up so quickly these days,' she said eventually. 'I suppose it's the bloody war to blame.'

'It may be,' Maggie said. 'It changed a lot of things, but with Lizzie and Kenny I think maybe you're getting in a stew about nothing.'

Lizzie could have reassured her mother, for though she liked Kenny, they'd only got as far as holding hands. He came down to see her sometimes on Sunday evenings too, and he'd taken her to the pictures at the ABC on Bristol Road and given her a bar of chocolate once inside. On another two occasions they'd gone for a walk, but that was as far as it went. Sometimes Lizzie was disappointed about it all, even though she was somewhat relieved he didn't push her. She often wondered what it would be like to kiss Kenny, for she'd never kissed anyone but David – and look where that had nearly led to. She supposed Kenny was right to take it so slowly, and no way was she going to indicate that she wanted to go further and have him think she was fast. She supposed she'd have to wait until he was ready. Lizzie knew Alice would be very disappointed and think it was not much of a romance at all, really. She often thought that Alice herself was waiting for a prince on a white charger to come and rescue her, marry her and live with her happily every after. Lizzie, more down to earth, knew princes and white chargers were in short supply, and that most people had to be satisfied with ordinary mortals like Kenny Sutcliffe.

But thinking of Alice brought to Lizzie's mind the letter she'd sent her friend. She'd worried about it often, wondering if she'd done the right thing in telling Alice about the eleven-plus, or if she'd made things even worse, and she wished Alice would write to her and tell her how things were.

However, it was almost May before Alice wrote to Lizzie, who was astonished to read that she'd at last stood up to her mother, taken herself off to Hereford and got herself a job at an exclusive dress shop.

The owner, Lena Carstairs, has been running it herself with just one assistant during the war, as once the rationing of clothes began it certainly suffered. Now she says she wants to engage more staff and took me on a trial basis. I can't tell you how happy I am.

Lizzie was pleased that her friend had her life sorted out and told Kathy, but Kathy hardly seemed to hear and certainly didn't make any sort of response. She seemed to have her mind on other things and a kind of lethargy had settled on her. She'd become depressed as the reality of Doug's death hit her, and because she couldn't tell anyone or mourn him openly, it was eating away inside her. She wished she'd been able to get Maggie to herself and explain it to her, but she'd never had the opportunity.

She tried counting her blessings, and knew in her heart of hearts that she probably would never have seen Doug again anyway. It was hard to think of him wiped off the earth altogether, but she tried to lift the despondency that often settled on her, and told herself she'd be better when the baby was born.

One Sunday afternoon in late June, Lizzie and Kenny were walking in Calthorpe Park. Kenny had been quite thoughtful all day, and eventually Lizzie said, 'Is anything wrong, Kenny?'

'No,' Kenny said. 'Course not. Why do you ask?'

Lizzie shrugged. 'Just wondered,' she said. 'You've been funny since you came. Sort of quiet.'

Actually she was very worried. She'd thought he was going off her. She'd read all about romance and relationships in the women's magazines her Aunt Maggie had delivered and it said in there that men often got moody and quiet when a relationship was going stale. She hoped it wasn't that because her feelings for Kenny had changed over the weeks and she realised she did care for him a great deal and had hoped he felt the same.

Kenny sighed and said, 'Well, I have got something on my mind.' Lizzie's heart seemed to stop beating. He turned to face her and went on, 'Right at the beginning, when you first came back home, I said I'd never expect you to do anything just because I took you out a few times. I meant it too. I never want you to do anything you don't feel right about, but I'm real fond of you, Lizzie. What do you think of me?'

Lizzie's breath, which she hadn't been aware she was holding, came out in a sigh of relief. She felt a bubble of happiness rise up inside her. 'I like you, Kenny, really like you,' she said, almost shyly.

'Enough to go out with me? I mean, properly go out with me?' Kenny asked, and Lizzie saw how nervous he was and felt sorry for him.

'Oh, Kenny, I'd love that,' she said.

Kenny smiled and blushed a little as he said, 'Can I kiss you then?'

In answer, Lizzie put her arms around Kenny's neck and closed her eyes. They bumped noses a little, and Lizzie had the urge to giggle, which she managed to suppress. She found Kenny's kiss was surprisingly sweet.

Kenny knew that for all her romance with David Barraclough, Lizzie was a naive young girl, and he didn't intend to rush her. His kiss was tender and something both were anxious to repeat, but he didn't push her to go any further than that. 'You'd better tell your mother,' Kenny said. 'I'd not want to go behind anyone's back.'

'Yes, I will.' Lizzie realised that their relationship had moved to a different plane, and that now they really were boyfriend and girlfriend, she was very happy about it and anxious to talk to her mother and tell her how she felt about Kenny. But when she mentioned it, Kathy seemed preoccupied and Lizzie was not even sure she'd heard what she'd said.

Hurt and disappointed by her mother's reaction, she decided to write to Alice. I know she'll want to know, she thought. She wished she could see Alice – she'd been a good friend to her – but she knew that with her grandad so ill and her mother heavily pregnant, she could not go running down to Hereford.

By mid-July, Eamonn, now totally bedridden, was only semi-conscious most of the time, and was gasping out his last days on earth. It was Saturday, and Kathy was sitting with her father while her mother tackled a large wash in the cellar. Carmel had been dispatched to the Bull Ring with a long shopping list.

The little room was stifling hot, despite the open window. Beads of perspiration stood out on Kathy's forehead and she could feel sweat gathering under her armpits and trickling down her back. She leant forward, dipped the flannel in the bowl of cold water beside the bed and wiped her father's glistening face. God, she hoped he wouldn't last long, for every tortured breath shook his feeble frame. She prayed that soon he'd find peace.

The sun slanting into the room set dust motes dancing, and Kathy transferred her gaze to the street outside and saw the children playing on the grubby pavements, leaping over the bricks and debris of the bombed buildings. In a week the schools would be closed, and then it would not be so easy to give a hand to her father. Still, in a week Eamonn might not still be with them, and it did no good worrying.

The door opening jolted her from her reverie, and she turned to find Carmel in the door with two cups of tea. 'I thought you could do with a drink,' she said.

'I could that,' Kathy said, taking the cup gratefully. 'I'm gasping, but I didn't know you were back.'

'I haven't been long,' Carmel said. 'Mammy's still hard at it. She told me to come and sit with Daddy in case you needed to slip home.'

'I'll need to soon,' Kathy said. 'The two lads will likely be in, plaguing the life out of Barry for something to eat. I'll go over and make them something and come back later if I can.' She took a mouthful of tea and said, 'I'll have this first, though. I was dying for a drink, to tell you the truth.' She waved her hand in front of her face and complained, 'I'm that hot.'

When she had drained the cup and got to her feet, Carmel put a hand on her arm. 'Kath.'

'What is it?'

'You know what it is,' the young girl cried.

'Ricky Westwood?' Kathy asked gently.

'Ricky Westwood,' agreed Carmel miserably. 'Yes, I do love him, Kath, so much it's eating me up inside.' She gave a wan smile and said, 'I know you've heard it all before. I did think I loved Andy, but I was just a kid. This is the real thing, but . . . but I don't want to live in America, miles from you all.'

Kathy sympathised with her sister, because although she knew that when you married a man you virtually belonged to him and had to be willing to follow him everywhere, in practice it was very hard. She was even sad that part of the family had moved out of Edgbaston and were no longer around the doors – and they at least were still in Birmingham, for goodness' sake. She was a fine one to talk.

'Oh, Kathy,' Carmel cried. 'How will I bear being apart from you all?'

Kathy put her arms around her sister. 'You'll bear it, Carmel. If the man loves you and you love him, that's all any of us can ask for, and it's a damn sight more than some of us get,' she said firmly, thinking of her own situation. Then she saw her sister's eyes on her, slightly puzzled, and went on soothingly, 'Pretty soon you'll probably have your own wee ones and no time at all to think of us all back here. You'll be living the life of Riley.'

Carmel gave her a watery smile, and Kathy went on, 'But I'm glad you've told me how you feel.' She bent and gave her sister a kiss and said, 'I must be off now, but if ever you want to talk, you know where I am.'

As she made her way home, Kathy realised she'd miss her younger sister, though she'd liked Ricky, as the whole family did, and the pair obviously loved one another.

Both Maggie and Rose seemed happy and were delighted to have their husbands back with them too. They assumed it was the same with Kathy, and it seemed disloyal to say anything else, but sometimes she got so depressed.

She gave herself a mental shake. This wouldn't do. Barry would know there was something up if she went home like this. She fixed a smile on her face and opened the front door.

TWENTY-FOUR

Barry hated it when the football season was over and there was nothing to look forward to after five and half days' hard graft. Not that they would have gone to the match anyway today, with Eamonn so ill; he knew that. Maggie and Sean were coming over to see their father as it was doubtful he'd last the weekend out. Barry was sorry, for he was fond of the old boy. He'd never said a word of condemnation when Barry was out of work all those years; both he and Mary had kept his elder children well nourished and decently clothed during those desperate times.

Barry was on his own in the house because Molly had taken Padraic and Dan to the Bull Ring with her, and he realised, as he made a cup of tea in the cellar, that it was the first time he'd been alone since he'd returned home. He wasn't sure he liked it much.

It was as he replaced the kettle on the stove that he felt the twinge in his back again. He knew what had caused it – that bloody mattress on his bed which had been flattened so much by his mother's bulk, he might as well have been lying on the bloody springs.

A new bed, or even a new mattress, was out of the question, he knew, and yet as he sat and thought, he remembered the two fairly new double mattresses brought in for the Sutcliffes when they'd been bombed out. They were both still in the attic; Padraic and Danny slept on one, and Lizzie had one all to herself since her grandmother had left. He drank his cup of tea and ran up the stairs. Lizzie's mattress had to be better than his, and he decided he'd change them over. She'd hardly notice the springs rising through the cover, but if she did, she could always sleep on the other side.

He pulled the bedclothes off the bed he shared with Kathy, and it was as he was attempting to fold the mattress in two to try and get it through the bedroom door that he spotted the folded paper sticking out of a tear underneath. At first he thought it had been used to pack the hole, but as he pulled it out, the pages fluttered to the floor and he realised it was a letter.

Intrigued, he picked it up and smoothed it out. Beside him the mattress unfurled as he read, but he was unaware of it. In fact he was unaware of most things as he tried to make sense of some American – and he knew he was a Yank, because of his reference to fighting the Japs – writing to his wife, whom he called Kate.

At first he was puzzled that Kathy not only hadn't told him about the letter, but had seen fit to hide it, but when he got to the end and the man described their night of passion, he was filled with fury. Hate for his cheating wife began to smoulder inside him, so intense that bright sparks jumped before his eyes. He'd been married to Kathy for sixteen years and bedded her often. She'd enjoyed it in the main, and he knew she'd often felt guilty that she'd enjoyed it. She'd never repulsed him, except that once after his return home, but he had to admit that though she'd

413

never tried to refuse him again, she only submitted to him now. And that was the right word – submission. She lay so passionless and unmoving beneath him, she might have been a lump of wood, and after it was over, he'd often felt a sense of loss.

Obviously, her Yank hadn't felt the same and she must have felt something for him, or she wouldn't have kept the letter. He wondered how often she'd crept upstairs to read it. God, it made him sick!

To think he'd felt guilty about his dalliance with the Belgian farmer's sister, Madelaine. As soon as he was well enough to work on the farm, she would sneak to find him, either in the orchard where he was collecting fruit, or in the far field scything hay, and eventually in his bed.

He'd felt bad about sleeping with the young girl, though he knew she enjoyed it as much as he did. He'd thought of Kathy and his family waiting for him back home – Madelaine had told him not to worry, that what they'd shared would never hurt his wife. 'She will never know about me, English man, but when you return, you will please her more from what I teach you.'

Barry knew he could never do the things they'd enjoyed together with Kathy. Sometimes, remembering them in the passionless light of day, he'd be embarrassed and he knew it wasn't the sort of thing to suggest to a wife. Wives needed more respect. Probably the pleasure he'd enjoyed with Madelaine had been heightened by the fear induced by the Nazi oppression that they all lived under. Madelaine would toss back her beautiful mane of dark hair and snap her fingers when anyone mentioned the Nazis. 'That is what I think of them,' she'd say, and Barry would be alarmed at her outspokenness.

She, herself, seemed not to feel the terror that affected almost everyone else. She was vibrant and full of fun and

414

had thrown back her head and roared with laughter when Barry asked her during their first time together, if she was a virgin. Her deep-brown eyes had sparkled with amusement and she told him she'd lost her virginity to a cousin enamoured with her when she was just fourteen. Barry hadn't been shocked or even surprised. It was an unreal time, where normal rules didn't apply.

Few would have condemned him for taking his pleasure where he could – and that's all it was. They both knew it would hurt no one. At least he'd never visited a prostitute, like many of his friends, though by God sometimes he wished he had. Some of his mates had got more than they had bargained for from the street women they lay with as well and had to go off and see the medical officer pronto.

He'd thought Kathy loved him. Right up until the day he was found unconscious in a Belgian field, she'd written him loving letters, for Christ's sake, full of funny things to make him smile, and she often said how much she missed him. It was all so much bullshit, for if that was the case, how had she lay down with a Yank – while he was risking his life daily in order that they all could live in peace again.

He sat down on the edge of the bed and tried to still the heart thudding against his ribs and rationalise the murderous thoughts in his head. He knew she'd had it hard, though she seldom spoke of it. God, they'd all had it hard. He'd been shocked at the devastation in Birmingham. The day he'd come home he could hardly take in what they'd been through, though Con, Sean and Michael had tried to warn him at the railway station.

He acknowledged the raids must have been terrifying. He knew about Rose's house being destroyed, of course, but he wasn't prepared for the sea of rubble opposite their own home. The house had been full of people, too, and that was bound to have been a strain, but Christ alive, she'd coped with that by going and getting herself a job. That had given him a bit of a jolt when he read about it and he'd been surprised that she hadn't written to ask him first. But he considered himself a reasonable man and he hadn't objected, like he hadn't objected later when she told him of the weekly visit to the cinema with Maggie, and all the time she was hoodwinking him. God Almighty, it hurt.

He could barely see the words of the letter for the tears that misted his eyes, but he didn't need to see them, they were burnt into his soul.

At the end of it all, the man said he would love Kathy till the day he died. By God, if he had been standing before Barry at that moment, he thought, he wouldn't have long to wait.

Barry had never raised a hand to Kathy yet, but he had the urge now to drag her back from her mother's and beat the living daylights out of her. He smashed his hand into the door, glad of the pain and the blood globules standing out on his knuckles. He tried to control himself but anger kept bubbling inside him.

All through the mud and blood and terror of war, Barry had clung to the thought of Kathy, his beautiful Kathy, and his two fine weans and the wee boy he'd never seen. When he was captured, he was marched to the labour camp in freezing conditions with thin, inadequate clothing and his shoes in tatters on his bleeding, blistered feet. They'd had little food and no water, and when people dropped around them like flies, they lay where they fell, usually with a kick from a guard to ensure they never got up again and the line went on. But all through the misery, cold and hunger more acute than any he'd ever experienced, he knew he would survive and come home to his Kathy.

Okay, he'd had the one affair himself. He *had* been slightly ashamed of it and knew at the time it was wrong, but it had meant nothing. Nothing at all. After all, he was a man, with a man's needs, and he'd been without a woman for a bloody long time.

But Kathy now, it was different for Kathy. She was totally his, for God's sake, and to think she'd been with someone else made him feel sick. He wrapped his arms around his middle and moaned. It hurt him so much, it was as if he had an actual physical pain. He would have staked his life on Kathy's loyalty and fidelity, and what a bloody fool he felt now. Perhaps she hadn't been that upset after all when he was posted missing, nor particularly relieved when he was found alive.

He remembered her post-office book she'd showed him so proudly, and the little nest egg she said she'd saved by doing war work. Bloody hell, now he knew the type of war work she'd been engaged in, and tears spurted from his eyes as he imagined Kathy selling her body to any who could pay.

He stood up suddenly, unable to just sit and act as if nothing had happened. The weans and Molly might be back any minute, or Kathy herself. He had to keep away from her or he'd do something he might later regret. But even as he got to his feet, he heard Kathy call out to him. He started down the stairs with a measured tread, his heart thudding painfully against his ribs.

Kathy didn't look up as he entered; her mind was full of the father she'd left lying unconscious on his bed. She took off her coat and hung it on the rail on the back of the entry door. She should go down to the cellar and make something to eat for them all, but she felt so tired. The baby was too active to give her much rest now at night, and her body was heavy and ponderous, and her legs and feet so swollen that to walk any distance was an effort.

But Barry didn't see his heavily pregnant wife with her bloated, misshapen body; he saw her still young, slim and desirable, and he felt sick with the force of anger inside him.

His breath was coming in little gasps. Kathy still didn't look at him, so he said, 'Hello, Kate O'Malley.'

The effect was electric. Kathy jumped and then turned to face her husband. She saw the letter in his hand and knew immediately what it was, and she felt faint with fright.

'You dirty, stinking whore!' Barry rapped out. 'I've a good mind to give you a bleeding good hiding.'

'Barry, I . . .' Kathy began, but stopped, for what could she say? The room swayed and tilted around her. She put her hand on the mantelpiece to steady herself and hoped she wouldn't pass out. 'Let me . . . let me try to explain.'

'I don't want you to bleeding well explain. I want you to tell me if you slept with this American, this . . . this Doug whatever-his-name-is,' and he waved the letter in Kathy's face.

Dumbly she nodded. Barry's fist caught her full in the face and her nose and lip spurted blood, which tasted sour in her mouth. She staggered back against the mantelpiece, but Barry's next punch caught her between the eyes and felled her completely.

Barry watched in amazement as Kathy crumpled to the floor. He rubbed at his bruised knuckles, which were bleeding again. Appalled at what he'd done, he dropped to his knees and, stuffing the letter in his pocket, began to rub Kathy's hands between his own, calling her name in desperation. 'Kathy, Kathy, come on. I'm sorry, I just couldn't stand it. Oh, Kathy, don't die, please don't. Don't leave me, Kathy.'

The front door opened and Mary stood there, and suddenly the news she'd come with didn't seem as important as the sight of her daughter lying before the fireplace, her face bruised and battered, and her son-in-law crouching beside her with raw, bleeding knuckles. 'What in God's name has happened here?' she cried.

Barry was filled with shame and could not bring himself to confess to his mother-in-law. 'She came over faint, Mary,' he said. 'I think she fell.'

Mary looked at him sharply. Marks like Kathy had didn't come from falling, even if she'd caught her face on the guard or the hearth, and something had made Barry's knuckles bleed all right. If he'd hit her – and it seemed certain he had – it would be the first time, to her knowledge. She might have taken the matter further if just then a shuddering groan hadn't come from the unconscious form as Kathy's stomach contracted.

'Oh, God in heaven, that's all we need,' Mary said, realising that her daughter had gone into labour. Barry would have to be dealt with another time; Kathy was Mary's main concern. Another contraction caused Kathy to groan again, and then another. God, Mary thought, things are moving fast.

'What the hell's the matter with her?' Barry cried in panic.

Mary looked at him coldly. 'She's in labour,' she snapped. 'It was probably being beaten half to death that's brought it on.'

'It's not due yet,' Barry said, and remembered their wee boy born prematurely who'd lived only a few days. He groaned and said, 'Shall I phone for an ambulance?'

Mary thought about it. There had been trouble in the house that afternoon and to call an ambulance would shout their business to the whole street. Once it pulled up outside the door, neighbours would throng around and more than one or two would notice Kathy's swollen, bruised face and bloodied nose. Then there'd be awkward questions asked at the hospital. If Barry had mistreated her daughter, he would be dealt with, but it would be kept within the family. For now Kathy's needs took priority. 'I don't think so. Go and get the bedroom ready,' she said coldly. 'Then you'll have to carry her up the stairs, but before you do that, get me a bowl of warm water and I'll try and clean her up.'

419

When Barry came down again, Kathy had her eyes open, though they looked like slits because they were so swollen. She didn't look at her husband or speak to him as he carried her, and Mary saw how she almost flinched from his touch. My God, when this wean's born I'll have Sean and Con give Barry a beating he'll never forget, she promised herself.

Barry himself seemed anxious to be away from them both, and Mary dispatched him to her house to tell them all of developments. He went gladly, and Maggie, who'd arrived at her mother's by the time Barry reached there, went round straight away to give her mother a hand.

Mary had tied a towel to the bed head and was urging Kathy to pull on it as she wiped her glistening brow with a flannel. 'Carmel's gone for the midwife,' Maggie said, and Mary nodded but didn't speak.

Kathy's face was contorted with pain as she writhed on the bed. Maggie thought she'd never seen her looking so ill nor her face so swollen. 'God, Mammy, she's in a bad way,' she said.

Kathy seemed to lack the energy to pull on the towel as she struggled to get away from the wild beast that was clawing her insides to ribbons. She was unaware of Bella Amis, the midwife, entering the room. As the hours passed and the long summer day eventually gave way to night, Mary became distracted, and even Bella was worried. 'I think,' she said at last, 'we'd better get the doctor.'

'I'll go,' Maggie said, glad to be given an excuse to leave the room, for she couldn't stand the sight of Kathy suffering.

At the sound of her sister's voice, Kathy opened her eyes and smiled, and then another pain assailed her. When she was through it, Maggie was gone and her mother was holding her hand. 'Daddy?' she asked weakly.

Mary paused for just a moment before she spoke. 'He's resting, cutie dear,' she said gently. 'Don't you worry about anything but this wean that doesn't seem to want to be born.'

420

Kathy didn't notice that Mary's eyes were misted over, for the man who had shared her life had slipped away just minutes after Kathy had left the room earlier, but she couldn't share this with the tortured woman on the bed. Nor could she share the fact that the priest had been sent for and would perform the Last Rites for her husband and she'd not be there beside him. She sighed.

Suddenly, a long shudder ran down Kathy's body and she screamed out, her eyes wild with panic and pain, 'Oh, Mammy, help me!'

'I will, I'm here, pet,' Mary said, and Kathy's hands held her mother's so hard her nails dug in. Mary hardly felt it. God help her, she said to herself, as she knelt beside the bed and prayed to the Virgin Mary, who knew the pain and trauma of giving birth herself. *Hail Mary full of Grace . . .* And as she prayed, on and on, she willed the doctor to hurry up, and listened out to hear his welcome step on the stairs.

Kathy had a long, arduous labour that went on all through the night and into the next morning. Often she thought she would die with the pain, and really she wouldn't have cared if she had. Time seemed to have no meaning, and as one pain superseded another, she felt she was trapped in a nightmare of agony that would go on and on.

Dr Casey had wanted to send her to hospital on Saturday night when he'd first seen her, but she'd become distressed. By Sunday morning she was half delirious and weakened considerably and he had serious doubts about her. He didn't think the baby stood much chance at all, coming six weeks early, but he kept these thoughts to himself. 'I think I'll phone for an ambulance,' he said. 'Mrs O'Malley can't take much more of this. She may need to have a Caesarean section.'

Even Bella Amis, who often felt affronted if a doctor was brought in to attend to a woman in labour and always maintained the home was the place to give birth, looked relieved. She was dead on her feet anyway, and the poor wee creature on the bed looked worn out too. She'd never have thought Kathy's baby would take this long to come, and she was glad that Maggie had made her mother go home. She knew for a fact that Mary had sat up night after night with Eamonn, God rest his soul, and Maggie told her that if she wouldn't go home and rest, she'd be the next one the doctor would have to attend to.

Maggie had sat through the night with her sister, holding her hand and suffering with her. She'd been an invaluable help, especially when the doctor had had to leave to see to other patients. She was a good girl, Maggie, and Bella knew that Kathy had missed her sorely when she'd left the area.

Funny about the husband, though, she thought. There'd been no sign of him, even when she'd arrived at the house, and she'd not seen hide or hair of him through the long night either.

Dr Casey, examining Kathy, thought it strange too. He'd been the Sullivans' and O'Malleys' family doctor for years and knew them all. He would have expected Barry to be anxiously pacing downstairs, ready to pounce on the doctor for news if he appeared, but he hadn't seen him, and Kathy had not asked for him once. She'd asked about the children, and Maggie had told her that Padraic and Danny were with Molly and Lizzie with Mary, but Maggie had not mentioned Barry either. It was strange, very odd, but then he had enough to do caring for the sick without delving into psychology.

Kathy's eyes were rolling in her head and Dr Casey said, 'I think you'd be better in hospital, my dear. I'll just pop to Pickering's to phone.'

Kathy made no comment, for her body was in the throes of a massive contraction and the breath seemed knocked from her body. At the foot of the bed Bella said, 'It's too late, Doctor. I can see the head.'

'Come on, good girl,' the doctor said to Kathy. The contraction waned slightly and he said, 'Rest now while you can and get ready to push when I tell you.'

Kathy barely noticed him, but seconds later she heard Maggie urging her to push. She felt the pressure of her sister's hand on hers, as if she was giving her renewed strength, and she pushed with all her might.

The puny baby slithered into Dr Casey's waiting hands. The child was small, its slightly wrinkled skin almost translucent-looking, with a slightly bluish tinge, and its damp head covered with black down. It gave a cry, a lusty cry for one who looked so small and helpless, and Kathy smiled a tired smile and gave a sigh of satisfaction.

Dr Casey was not at all sure the baby would thrive, despite the cry, but it wasn't what Kathy wanted to hear at that moment. 'You have a fine daughter,' he said. 'Have you a name for her?'

Kathy was glad she had a daughter, and she knew too that her children would have to be her consolation now, for her marriage was in tatters, and all because of one letter from a man dead and gone. Now she remembered the other letter, from Doug's mother, telling her what had happened to her son, and she suddenly knew what she'd call her baby. 'Laura,' she said.

'Laura!' Bella Amis exclaimed. No one would call their child Laura. She should be called after her grandmother or aunt. Molly, perhaps, or Margaret, both were nice sensible names, but Laura!

But then Kathy was exhausted, and people had funny notions when they were that tired. No doubt she'd come up with a more suitable name in time. Indeed, the father, wherever the hell he was, might have some say in it.

'Well now, isn't that the grand name?' Dr Casey said, coming up to the head of the bed with the baby in his arms in a shawl. Now that he'd had a good chance to look at Kathy's face, when it wasn't etched with the pain of labour, it looked very strange indeed. Her nose seemed twice its normal size and there were bruises on her cheeks, and the black rings around her eyes were not entirely due to tiredness, he noticed. 'You look as if you've been in the wars,' he said.

Bella Amis looked up from the bottom of the bed and stared open-mouthed. Maggie, from her position close to her sister's face, had seen the puffy bruises and discoloration around her eyes, but was going to make no comment about it till they were alone.

'I fell,' Kathy said. 'I came over a little faint and I must have hit my head as I went down.'

Dr Casey and Bella both nodded, and Kathy knew neither of them believed her. Dr Casey knew she'd been knocked about, but he'd seen many women the same, and they nearly all denied it and put it down to clumsiness of their own. He'd never have said Barry was the type to beat his wife, but then who really knew what went on behind closed doors?

Bella shot Kathy a look of pity. So that was the way of it, she thought. No wonder that bugger Barry hadn't shown his face. Should be ashamed, laying into his wife like that and her so heavily pregnant, no wonder the bloody child came early.

Maggie said nothing. She wished they'd all go and leave Kathy alone. She didn't understand any more than they did, but she knew her sister was upset. Her mother had whispered that she'd thought they'd had a few words. Bloody hell, everyone had a few words, but God, Barry had made a mess of Kathy's face. He wasn't in the habit of it, she knew that. You couldn't live around the doors as they had and not know how things were, especially when they were as close as she and Kathy. Since Barry had come back, there'd been something not quite right between them, she knew. Con said Barry had been to hell and back and it would take time for him to adjust to civilian life, getting a job and living with his family again. Well, he'd had time enough to bash Kathy's face up, and if she was Kathy she'd arm herself with a poker and let him have it if he came at her again.

She wasn't able to have a quiet word with her sister, for before the doctor was even out of the door, they were all in on top of her to congratulate her and exclaim over the baby. Lizzie was the only one who asked where her daddy was, but no one answered her. Kathy didn't know anyway, or much care either in all honesty. She was too sore all over and too exhausted to worry much over Barry's absence. Mary, though, guessed where he'd spent the night. Pressed by Maggie to go home and rest, she'd scarcely been in the house before Sadie Griffiths was nearly knocking the door down. She'd been in The Sun public house, she said, drinking with a friend, and had seen Barry. He'd seemed upset, not himself at all, and at closing time he'd been very drunk and was helped out of the place by Connie McIntyre, the local prostitute, who was promising him a good time that night as she supported his staggering frame out of the door. Sadie said she was concerned about him and wanted to know if everything was all right, and was there anything she could do?

Mary felt her heart sink to her boots. If Sadie knew, so soon would the rest of the street, and she'd make it her business to contact Bridie and tell her. She stared at the woman and had a great desire to smack the smirk from her face. But that, she knew, would make matters even worse, so she thanked Sadie for her concern and said everything was fine. Barry had gone out for a few jars because Kathy was in labour, and having taken too much, Connie was kind enough to help him home.

425

Sadie's eyes narrowed. Mary Sullivan was taking her for a fool. Connie McIntyre helped no one home; she helped them to her house and charged them for the privilege. Sadie had watched their shambling progress at kicking-out tune, in the opposite direction from the O'Malley house. And here was something else, Kathy in labour and early too, by Sadie's reckoning. Usually a man didn't go out drinking while his wife was in labour. Afterwards, certainly, most would wet the baby's head too well and stagger home after it, but before a baby was born . . . Strange that. Still, it was a good bit of gossip to share around, and tomorrow she might take a dander over to see Bridie in Erdington.

Mary closed the door on Sadie with a sigh of relief, although she knew she'd not fooled the old gossip-monger, nor stilled her tongue. Sean and Carmel had waited up for their mother's return, and now Carmel said, 'What's up with Barry, Mammy?'

'Child, I don't know,' Mary said wearily. 'All I know is I found Kathy unconscious and in premature labour when I left here.'

'Unconscious?' Sean queried. 'How did that happen?'

'You know as much as I do myself,' Mary said.

'Well, when Barry called here to tell us what was happening, he looked strange,' Sean said. 'He said he was going for a walk and I said I'd go along with him, but he said he'd be company for no one the way he was feeling. Something's not right, Ma. Surely to God he's not got caught up with the likes of Connie McIntyre, however drunk he was.'

'God alone knows,' Mary said. 'But there was no sign of him returning when I came away from Kathy's. Thank God Lizzie is in bed and didn't hear what Sadie had to say.

'We'll say nothing in front of any of the weans, nor Kathy either,' Mary went on. 'It will hardly help, and Kathy's been through enough. Whatever is wrong between them is their business.'

'Aye,' agreed Sean. 'For now I'll say nothing. I'll wait till I can talk to Kathy herself.'

Early on Sunday morning, Bella Amis went to help Mary lay Eamonn out; it was the custom that the one who brought babies into the world, helped to prepare those leaving it. She was also able to tell the family that Kathy had had a baby girl, and they all went over to see them. Mary told Maggie quietly what had transpired the night before, and Maggie felt rage burn inside her. The doctor had done what he could with Kathy's face before the family saw her, but he could disguise little. Sean drew his breath in sharply as he caught sight of his sister, promising himself that if that was Barry's work he'd pay for it, and dearly.

Lizzie was pleased to see that her mother was all right, though her face looked odd; her nose funny and puffed up, and her eyes black. But she put it all down to having a baby. She couldn't remember how Kathy had looked when she had had Padraic, and no one else seemed to notice anything strange.

But still she wondered where her daddy was. She'd thought he would be downstairs, perhaps, or upstairs holding Kathy's hand or cuddling the baby. But he was in neither place, and when she asked about him she saw the glances between the adults and no one answered her question. There was silence for a minute, and then they all started to talk at once about who the baby looked most like, and Lizzie knew there was something she was not being told.

Lizzie was the only one there that afternoon, and was in the bedroom with her mother when her father eventually came home. She heard him come up the stairs, and stop outside the bedroom door. He'd been told he had a baby daughter by the neighbours – by all accounts a frail and puny child that no one really thought would thrive – and he'd been consumed with shame. How could he look on

427

her, and know his actions probably hastened her birth, or on Kathy, who he'd punched senseless?

He put his hand on the door knob and had almost decided to go in and say he was sorry and lift up the wean, whose birth he'd looked forward to so eagerly. But then he remembered why the whole episode had happened and he burnt with anger again at Kathy's duplicity with her American lover. She'd made a right bloody fool of him. Well, she could stew in it now, her and her bloody child, because he'd have no part in any of it and he turned from the door.

Lizzie heard her father's footsteps go up to the attic and she was glad her mother had been asleep with baby Laura tucked into Padraic's old cradle beside her. She was puzzled and she chewed on her thumb nail and wondered what was wrong between her parents.

Bridie had been told of the goings-on of her in-laws by a jubilant Sadie, who'd travelled up to see her on Sunday afternoon, when she was also able to tell her about her father-in-law's death and Kathy's baby daughter. A very smug Bridie then put in an appearance on Monday morning, to pay her respects to Eamonn, she said, but really to get to the bottom of what was happening in the O'Malley home. She sat beside Kathy's bed, cuddling little Laura, and said with a smirk, 'What does Barry think of his new daughter then?'

Barry had not even come in to see the child, but Kathy was hardly telling Bridie that. 'He likes her fine,' she said shortly.

'Well, he was celebrating before she was born, by all accounts,' Bridie said. 'At The Sun, and drunk as a lord. Sadie saw him herself.'

Kathy hadn't known that, but she wasn't surprised that he'd dealt with a situation he found intolerable by getting drunk. However, Bridie's next words shocked her to the core. 'Connie McIntyre was with him, Sadie said. She saw them go home together.' At this Bridie gave a little laugh and said, 'She said she'd see him right and give him a good time. You know what that means?'

She could see from the look on Kathy's face that she'd hit the mark. The silly bitch hadn't known a thing about it and was unable to say anything. 'Still, that's men for you,' Bridie went on. 'A bellyful of beer and any brains they have fly out of the window. Mind, I wouldn't have liked my Pat to get mixed up with that McIntyre one.'

Kathy continued to stare at Bridie. She knew why Barry had gone home with Connie. It was to pay her back, to go with a common trollop and to do it in such a public way. God, it was a desperate thing to do altogether.

Bridie surveyed her sister-in-law's stricken face and bent her head to the baby to hide her smile of satisfaction. 'Ah, but isn't she the wee dote?' she said. 'Sadie tells me it's Laura you're calling her?'

'Aye, aye, that's right.' At last Kathy found her voice.

'Odd name that, a wee bit fancy. What brought it into your mind?'

'I like it, that's all.'

'And Barry, does he like it too?'

'Aye, aye. It's up to me, he said.'

Bridie looked up from the baby and studied Kathy's face again. Surely there were bruises there? It looked like someone had given her nose a punch, spurring her lip at the same time, and both her eyes had been blacked. This was something Sadie hadn't known about, because she hadn't been in to see Kathy before she set off for Bridie's. 'Someone been beating you up?' Bridie said.

'No, I fell and hit my face on the fender,' Kathy said.

Bridie had felt the weight of her father's fist many a time and she knew what a bashed-up face looked like. She gave Kathy a pitying look and said, 'I wasn't bleeding well born yesterday, you know. I know a beating when I see one. You might fool others, but you won't fool me. What did Barry hit you for?'

'He . . . he . . . It wasn't. . .'

'Come on, Kathy, I'm not bleeding stupid. That's why he went out and got plastered, isn't it?'

Kathy didn't answer, but Bridie went on anyway. 'And then McIntyre got her clutches into him. Mind, he wasn't struggling to get out of them, more snuggling in, Sadie told me. I still wouldn't have said he was the type to hit you. Pat never laid a hand on me, you know.'

'I know,' Kathy agreed miserably.

'Mind . . .' Bridie began, but whatever she was going to say was cut off by Lizzie coming into the bedroom with three cups of tea on a tray. Kathy could have kissed her daughter.

Later, when Bridie had gone to regale Sadie with all she'd found out, Kathy said to Lizzie, 'Never, ever leave me alone with Auntie Bridie, d'you hear? I don't care what you have to do. If she comes again, leave whatever it is and sit with us until she goes home.'

Lizzie knew what her mother meant. Bridie had often upset Kathy, and the doctor had said she mustn't be troubled by things. She also had to have plenty of rest to get better herself and to ensure she had enough milk for her frail premature baby.

Lizzie had already phoned the college and arranged to take that week off, the last before the summer holidays, to help at home. Now she held her mother's hand and said, 'Don't worry, Mammy, I'll stick to you like glue if Auntie Bridie comes here again.'

And Kathy smiled at her daughter and gave a sigh of relief.

TWENTY-FIVE

Lizzie was due to work most of the summer holidays at Woolworth's. She was reluctant at first, not sure where her duty lay, for her mother was not fully fit by any means. But Mary said she'd see to Kathy and Lizzie knew she'd probably get over her grandfather's death the quicker if she had something to do, and Molly had offered to fetch the family's rations and look after the boys, so Lizzie was able to rest easy.

She was pleased in the end, because she liked her job and was grateful for the extra money. Mary was particularly glad to have her out of the way every day, for Sadie and her ilk had done their work well, and rumours flew around the streets about the doings at the O'Malley household and the child born only seven months after the father had returned from the army. Meant to be premature, they said, but everyone knew what that meant.

Laura was five days old when Eamonn was laid to rest. Lizzie stayed with her mother, as she wasn't well enough to attend the funeral. Kathy wasn't surprised at the stream of visitors who called in later, using the pretext of coming to see her baby to study her face intently. Though many made oblique references to Barry and his carry-on, none were as blunt as Bridie had been.

Only Maggie knew the full story, for she had visited Kathy in a lull in the stream of visitors at the O'Malley house the day of the funeral. 'They're back at Mammy's stuffing food in their face as if they hadn't eaten for a week and don't know where their next meal's coming from,' she complained. 'Honest to God, Kath, some of those so-called mourners only came for the feed.'

Maggie was glad to see her sister smile at her outraged voice, for in all honesty she'd had little to laugh at since the day of Laura's birth, and Maggie knew that full well because she'd been every day to help Mary see to her. She didn't tell Kathy the funeral had been strained, with no one knowing what to say to Barry at all. Con said he wouldn't waste words on him, it was a good hiding he needed, but Kathy still maintained that she'd fallen and caught her face on the mantel shelf and so they could do nothing, but they were damned if they were going to be civil to the man.

She surveyed Kathy in the bed and went on, 'You can laugh. I tell you, it took Carmel, Mammy and me two days to cook the food that that lot of vultures will clear in less than half an hour, I bet. But I saved you something,' she said, drawing a bag from the inside of her coat. 'I didn't see why you and young Lizzie here should miss out.'

The bag contained delicacies not seen since before the war, pork pie and sausage rolls and fruit cake, and Kathy's eyes opened wide in surprise. 'The butcher said he keeps things like this for special occasions and special customers. Daddy was very respected, you know,' Maggie said. 'I don't know how much sausage is in the sausage rolls and I think there's more carrot than currants in the cake, but it's not bad.'

'More than we've had for many a year,' Kathy said. 'Run down and put the kettle on, Lizzie pet, and we'll have ourselves a rare old treat.'

Lizzie went willingly, and the door had barely closed on her before Kathy grasped Maggie's hand and told her quickly of the letter Doug had written to her and Barry's reaction when he'd found it. She also told her about Laura Howister's letter telling her of Doug's death that she'd later burnt. Maggie didn't interrupt once, aware as Kathy was that they might not have another chance to be alone.

When Kathy eventually stopped speaking, Maggie said, 'Is that why the baby's called Laura?'

'Yes, partly,' Kathy said. She remembered how Barry had gone mad about the name. 'What the bloody hell did she mean by naming the child without consulting me?' he demanded. 'And what a bloody name to choose.'

Kathy was afraid of his anger but refused to show it. 'You weren't here,' she said quietly.

'What bloody stupid talk is this?'

'I named her just seconds after she was born,' Kathy said and she looked at him coldly. 'No one could find you then, nor for hours after,' she went on.

Barry flushed and snapped, 'What nonsense are you on? The child is not being baptised yet . . . We had plenty of time to discuss it.'

'Discuss it? God, wouldn't that be a wonderful thing?' Kathy cried. 'You find it hard to look at me, let alone talk to me, and you barely know whether the child is alive or dead.'

'I'm still her father.'

'Then bloody act as though you are,' Kathy said, too furiously angry to be afraid any more. 'Till then you have no rights. I gave birth to our daughter while you were tipping beer down your neck and seeking comfort with another. I think that gives me the right to say what she's called.'

The force of Kathy's attack took Barry's breath away and, though he didn't understand what she was on about – 'seeking comfort with another' – he knew he'd acted badly.

Anyway, he thought, what do I care what she calls the child? She can do what the hell she likes as far as I'm concerned. Aloud he said, 'All right. Call the child what you will and remember I've had no hand in it.'

The christening had been put back until Kathy was on her feet again, but Father Flaherty had already told her that Laura was an outlandish name for a Christian child and she had to have a saint's name, too, and so now Laura Anne, with Maggie as godmother, was due to be christened in just over a week's time.

'You were a bloody fool to keep the letter,' Maggie said. 'Though I can understand why you did. Pity you didn't burn it like you did his mother's.' She hesitated a moment and said, 'How is Barry with you now?'

Kathy shrugged. 'How d'you think?' she said. Since the baby's birth he'd not been near either of them, and passed her door when he came home from the pub every night without pausing. Since the baby had been born, he'd shared the double mattress with Padraic and Dan, and used the excuse that he didn't want to disturb their mother. The boys accepted it. Dan knew his mammy had had a hard time, and Padraic liked having his daddy sleep in his bed anyway. Only Lizzie wasn't taken in by the reasons Barry used, but she didn't quiz her mother, sure it would upset her.

But Kathy could say none of this to her sister. Maggie wondered if she knew what was being rumoured about her, and decided she probably didn't. She never knew afterwards if she'd have told her or not, but at that moment Lizzie opened the door and came in with the tea.

There was eventually just the family left in the house after the funeral tea. Rose and Maggie had washed up everything and were talking about making for home soon, and collecting their children from the obliging neighbour who'd offered to mind them. Barry was sitting morosely staring at the fire, where he'd been since he'd come in. No one had spoken much more than a few words to him all day, and he hadn't seemed to care, but he'd helped himself liberally to the whisky.

He was suddenly sick of them all, and he got to his feet unsteadily. 'I'm away then,' he said.

'Off *home*?' Maggie said, stressing the last word.

'Aye, eventually,' Barry said. 'I'll go to The Bell for a quick one first.'

'You've had enough already,' Mary said sharply. 'Get yourself home, and don't be a bloody fool all the days of your life.'

Barry longed to tell the old woman to shut her mouth, but he didn't dare with the three lads standing threateningly beside her, so he shot her a look of hatred, inclined his head mockingly, and left without another word. Con, Sean and Michael looked at each other and, of one accord, slipped out behind him.

'Jesus, they'll kill him,' Mary said.

'No they won't, Mammy. You know it has to be done,' Maggie said. 'He can't get away with punching our Kathy into the back of next week, especially with her being pregnant and all.'

'It's hardly decent, with your daddy barely cold.'

'It's never decent,' Rose said. 'But Sean won't rest till he teaches Barry a lesson he won't forget in a hurry.'

'Kathy will go mad, she wasn't for it,' Maggie said.

'He has to be stopped,' Rose argued. 'What if he goes for her again?'

Maggie didn't answer. She knew Rose had a point and what could a woman do? What could she do if Con took to beating her, or spending all his time and money in the pub

– damn all, that's what! But for all their talk, the women were worried and waited anxiously for their men to return.

Eventually they burst in, rubbing at their grazed knuckles and the three women all looked towards them. 'Don't ask,' Sean said.

'Don't be stupid, Sean,' Maggie cried. 'We have to know what you've done?'

'Enough,' Con said. 'Don't worry. We made a mess of his face, like he did our Kathy's, and he'll have a few bruises on his body, but we only used our fists.'

'I wanted to kick the shit out of him, if you want the truth,' Sean said.

'Sean!' Mary admonished. 'Today of all days.'

'Aye, well. Look what he did to our Kathy,' Sean cried. 'And that was the day daddy died. He could have killed her, or the child inside of her, but he'll not do it again. I told him if he lays another hand on her, I'll do for him.'

Mary sighed and looked to her youngest son, 'And you, Michael? What have you to say?'

'Michael didn't touch him, Mammy,' Sean said. 'He kept watch. It didn't need the three of us, it didn't need two really. The man was half cut and didn't even try to defend himself.'

'I don't know what's happened to him anyway,' Michael exclaimed. 'We were mates once. He's the last one I would have expected to lash out at a woman like he did.' He shook his head in confusion. 'And he's always liked a drink, but now he's been legless every night – since the child was born.'

'Aye, well that's life, lad,' Mary said sadly, and hoped that whatever her sons and son-in-laws had done, it might have brought Barry to his senses.

Barry staggered to his feet in the entry. He knew he must look a sight. He felt his face gingerly, his eyes were swollen, his cheeks grazed and blood was pouring from his puffy and swollen lips and nose, on to his dark funeral clothes. His head throbbed, in fact his whole body ached, and yet in a way he felt better. He knew why Con and Sean had beaten him up, he'd expected it, and he didn't really blame them.

He'd wished many times he could have gone back to the previous Saturday and done things differently. But saying sorry didn't come easy to Barry and while he shouldn't have hit Kathy, there was no denying the affair she'd been conducting while he'd been overseas, but he wouldn't tell anyone about that, and let them all know how he'd been so duped.

Molly was listening to the wireless, drinking her bedtime cocoa, when Barry almost fell in the door. She gave a cry of alarm when she saw the state of her eldest son, but when she realised who had administered the beating, Barry got scant sympathy. She'd seen Kathy's face herself, and blamed the O'Malley brothers not a bit for taking to task the man responsible. But Barry would not answer any of her questions and said it was his business. In the end, defeated, Molly took herself off to bed, and Barry lay down on the sofa and tried to sleep.

During the first week of Kathy's lying-in period, she was very low in spirits, and this was made worse by the fact that she was totally unable to feed the little mite she'd given birth to. However much the doctor said it was to be expected after such a traumatic birth that her milk supply would dry up, she felt a failure. She also knew the doctor was wrong that national dried milk was just as good; breast milk was better for babies, particularly premature babies, because it protected them from infection.

Laura was a week old when the holidays began, and then it became more difficult for Maggie to come every day. A couple of times Maggie and Rose came together, and Padraic was delighted to see his cousins, but there was only really the bombed buildings to play in. After Josie sprained her ankle quite badly and Pete cut himself on a jagged piece of glass partially hidden by rubble, both Maggie and Rose decided that the bombed buildings were a dangerous playground.

Instead, after the second week of Kathy's lying-in period was over, they suggested taking Dan and Padraic to stay for a wee while with them.

Kathy knew she'd miss Maggie's visits greatly, but she couldn't refuse to let her sons spend time with the cousins they got on so well with. She was just glad her mother and Molly were there to lend a hand with the shopping and the washing, because she still had days when she felt very weak and was glad in a way she didn't have the boys to worry about too.

They'd not been gone very long when there was a knock on Kathy's door and she was surprised to see Bridie outside. 'Hello, Bridie,' she said guardedly.

'Oh, you're up then?' Bridie said. 'Are you sure you're up to be doing everything?'

'I'm well enough,' Kathy said shortly. 'Mammy still helps.'

'Aye, she'd need to,' Bridie said. 'From what I hear, that man of yours is no use to you.'

Kathy flushed. 'What d'you mean?' she snapped.

'Common knowledge,' Bridie said. 'I'm only telling you what everyone's saying, so don't snap the head off me.'

'And what exactly is everyone saying?' Kathy said, and then could have bitten her tongue off. Did she want to know? Would it help?

But it was too late. 'Only that he's never away from the pub and seldom sober,' Bridie said. 'Course, I always had that trouble with Pat.'

'You did not!' Kathy burst out, thinking how odd it was that she found it easier to defend her brother than the stranger her husband had turned out to be.

'You know nothing,' Bridie said dismissively. 'I had a life of it with Pat, you don't know what I had to put up with.' She leant forward conspiratorially and went on, 'The point is, I know better than most what you're going through and can sympathise.'

'I don't need sympathy,' Kathy said sharply. 'Barry and I are fine.'

'That's not what I heard,' Bridie said. 'And Sadie was telling me he takes not a whit of interest in the baby.'

'How the hell would she know?'

Bridie gave a little laugh. 'Och, Kathy, sure, your life's not your own in this place, surely to God you know that. If you turn over in bed, half the street knows it and the other half are told.'

Kathy knew that all she said was true. Living tightly packed back to back, in houses opening on to either the streets or dingy courtyards, one person's business was soon everybody's.

'Strange, isn't it, when he was so taken with the other weans,' Bridie said. 'Everybody's saying it's odd, that. They say he thinks the sun shines out of Padraic's arse, but he hasn't said a word about his baby daughter. When you think how he was with Lizzie, and from her being very wee too. Cock-a-hoop, my Pat said he was.'

Kathy caught her breath sharply. Didn't she already know what Bridie was saying, and it tore the heart out of her? But how could she answer her, and could she stop her voice from breaking if she did? She tried. 'Barry's . . . Barry's . . . not been himself since he came home,' she said. 'He's . . . Terrible things happened.'

'Och, sure, I know that,' Bridie said. 'Terrible things happened to them all, for God's sake. It wasn't a Sunday school outing they were on. At least he did come back, even if it did turn his hair white.'

'Bridie, I'm very tired.'

'Aye, so would I be,' Bridie said almost sympathetically. 'Tired of my bloody husband and tired of making excuses for him.'

'I'm not, and anyway it's my business.'

'Course it is. I'm not one to pry,' Bridie said with a smirk. 'Still, after what Sadie said she'd heard, I said I'd come and see you, tell you what's been said.'

'I don't want to hear it.'

'Course you do,' Bridie said. 'The thing is, with Barry home in December and you giving birth in July, well, you know how people talk. And then with Barry taking no notice of the child at all, getting drunk every night . . . you can't blame them for getting a bit suspicious.'

Kathy was having trouble drawing breath. She stared at the woman in front of her, hardly able to comprehend what she'd just said. She'd had no idea people had jumped to conclusions like that, but she shouldn't be surprised; rumour and speculation often started with far less. She said stiffly, 'She's premature. The baby was premature.'

'Of course she was,' Bridie said soothingly, but with a sardonic sneer in her voice. 'I told them that, people who mention it to me, Kathy. But then there was your face all bashed in, and no use denying it. I wasn't the only one to comment. Everybody that went in to see the baby was on about it. It was the talk of the place. And then people were saying that if a man like Barry lashes out, he must have a bloody good reason, and they know he lashed out, for wasn't his fist all swollen and bleeding?'

'Oh, God!'

'Don't take on,' Bride said. 'Be a nine-days wonder I should think, but I thought you should know about it. Now, shall I pop down the cellar and make a nice cup of tea for us both?'

440

She came every week after that. Kathy never knew when to expect her. She never brought the children; Matt couldn't travel on a bus easily, she said, and Sheelagh wouldn't come. 'She said she was glad enough to get out of the place and has no desire to return,' Bridie told Kathy.

Kathy was glad Sheelagh didn't come, for she'd be another to taunt and torment. Every day she came, Bridie made allusions to the paternity of the tiny baby in the cradle and further observations about Barry. 'I hear he's very friendly with that Connie McIntyre again,' she said once. 'You want to put your foot down there, should have put it down in the first place, you know what she is. Pat might have liked a skinful now and then, but he never took up with the likes of her and he wasn't getting it off me either. I told him to tie a knot in it after Matt was born. I wasn't a bloody brood mare, and I told him so.'

Another day it was, 'Your Barry had a load on him a couple of nights this week, Sadie told me. Young Dennis had to lead him home, seemingly. Shouting his mouth off about all women being bleeding whores and wives the worst of the lot. Are you all right, Kathy? You've gone quite white.'

Kathy never passed on to her mother the disturbing things Bridie told her. She was too ashamed. She knew also that her mother must be aware what people were saying and thinking, for there were those who'd delight in telling her, and Molly O'Malley too. Carmel had probably heard things as well, but none of them had mentioned a word to her, and she hoped to God Lizzie was ignorant of the rumours. Everyone in the family knew about the gigantic rift in their marriage, but Kathy refused to explain anything.

She battled on regardless, her nerves shot to pieces with trying to create a near-normal atmosphere for three youngsters, a wee baby and an embittered husband who seldom spoke to her and then only to find fault.

It was mid-August, and Laura was a month old, when Lizzie received a letter from Hereford. The post hadn't been when she'd left for work in the morning and the envelope had been pushed behind the clock on the mantelpiece. Kathy handed it to her as she got in that night.

The letter was from the Barracloughs. Lizzie felt a bit guilty because she hadn't written for a while and they had been good to her. She opened the envelope and drew out a card which invited Lizzie – and Dan, if he wished to go – to the wedding of David Alexander Barraclough to Rosamund Caroline Harrington on Saturday 14 September 1946.

Lizzie wasn't surprised. She'd known that Rosamund was out to get David and that he wouldn't be able to stand against her, and she could feel it in her heart to feel sorry for him.

Sophie, however, had been completely unprepared. They were all awaiting the results of the Higher School Certificate David had taken, when he stood one evening before his mother and, trembling slightly, said he was going to marry Rosamund. He had to marry her, he went on, because she was carrying his child, and they must do it without delay.

Sophie was astounded and bitterly disappointed, while Chris told his young brother that he was a bloody fool. Sophie couldn't bear to write to Lizzie and tell her that David had got Rosamund in the family way. She knew how Lizzie had always looked up to David, and she'd have hated her to think less of him.

Knowing recriminations were of little use, she planned to make the best of it. A simple service in the village church would have done her, but she had reckoned without the Harringtons. Rosamund was their only child and she was going to have the wedding they'd always dreamt of. Marjorie was quite glad to get her daughter safely and respectably married at last. Knowing her to be a sensual young woman with strong sexual needs, she decided it would not do at all for David to become a pilot. Dear God, no, that would leave Rosamund to her own devices too much, and that, she knew, would be disastrous. She'd speak to Gerald. Surely with his contacts he could get David something more suitable? Not that she'd tell him the reason; he'd not believe her anyway, for in his eyes Rosamund could do no wrong.

Sophie knew nothing of Marjorie's planning, but she did know that the wedding was to be taken out of her hands completely and she wasn't totally happy about it. The gilt-edged invitation cards were far too fancy to her mind, but she made no protest. When Marjorie expressed surprise that she should invite her little evacuees, however, Sophie was angry. 'They lived with me for five years, Marjorie,' she said. 'It isn't as if they were here for the odd weekend.'

'They're of a different social class.'

'So's Millie. In fact, I suppose half of the village are,' Sophie said, and then caught sight of Marjorie's face. 'Don't tell me you were thinking of not inviting Millie?'

Marjorie coloured slightly and then said, 'Well, I suppose we must have her, seeing as she lives in the same house, but she'll be out of her depth totally. As for Elizabeth O'Malley and her brother . . .'

'They are being invited as my guests,' Sophie said firmly, and she put in a little note with the invitation urging Lizzie to come at least, even if Danny couldn't be persuaded.

'Do you want to go?' Kathy asked.

Lizzie thought. Did she want to go and see David tie himself to Rosamund for life? Could she even face him naturally after the brush-off letter he'd sent her? Well, she wouldn't risk it, why should she? 'No,' she told her mother. 'Not really. The service is midday on Saturday, so I'd have to get the Saturday off work, and anyway, I'd rather see Kenny.'

Kenny had been a life-saver for her in those hectic weeks after Laura's birth, coming to Edgbaston to take her to the pictures, or for a long walk. She'd always been glad to get out of the house, because the atmosphere had become so strained. Kenny was easy to be with, and good fun too. With David, she'd been like a willing slave, hanging on his every word, and doing things to please him that she later felt uncomfortable about, and knew were wrong. She wasn't sure she loved Kenny, but then she'd had little experience of it. She certainly looked forward to seeing him, and a certain look he had always turned her legs to jelly, and when he took hold of her hand, her whole body tingled.

But best of all, she could talk to him about anything, and he was fast turning into her very best friend. She wondered why she'd thought David so wonderful, and knew Kenny was worth ten of him. One thing she didn't mention to him though, was the problem she could see developing between her parents. She didn't think she should discuss this with anyone. It didn't seem right for her to voice her concerns outside of the family, but she did mention the fact that her father seemed to take no notice of the baby. Kenny didn't think it odd at all. 'He's probably nervous of picking her up,' he said. 'I mean, she's so small, isn't she? I'd be nervous if she were my babby.'

'But he doesn't talk to her, or even look at her.'

'Men don't feel the same way about babbies that women do,' Kenny told her. 'After all, they're not very interesting. He'll probably like her fine when she's older. He might have been the same with Padraic if he'd been here to see him when he was a nipper. But look at him now. Your dad thinks the sun shines out of his backside.'

'Oh, Padraic,' Lizzie said impatiently. 'He needs his bottom skelped, and often. He's a horrible spoilt brat.'

'Well, your dad didn't see him for five years.'

'That doesn't give him the right to ruin the child now.'

'Maybe not,' Kenny said with a sigh. 'It just might explain why he feels he has to make it up to him.'

Lizzie heard Kenny's sigh of exasperation and impatience, and though she didn't agree with him for a minute and knew there was more to her father's indifference to the baby than he thought, she knew he was fed up discussing it and she'd have to drop the subject. Kenny thought Lizzie was making a mountain out of a molehill, and much as he liked her family, especially Kathy, he didn't want to waste the precious few hours he spent with Lizzie talking about them.

He was glad Lizzie had decided not to go down to Hereford, but he didn't pry into her reasons for not attending the wedding. He didn't know how Lizzie really felt about David now, because he'd never asked her and she'd not volunteered the information, and neither of them had ever referred to David's letter again.

'Won't she sort of expect you to go, his mother?' Kenny asked.

Lizzie shrugged. 'Maybe,' she said. 'I'll explain I'm needed at home, with Mammy having had a new baby and her daddy dying and all. Danny definitely doesn't want to go, and Mammy doesn't want the expense of dressing him up in a suit he'll probably never wear again. In fact I'll write tonight and tell her.'

Sophie's response to Lizzie's letter was swift. She expressed sympathy for the death of Lizzie's grandfather and congratulations to her parents on the birth of their daughter Laura. The parcel in which the letter was enclosed contained two matinée jackets and a pram suit complete with bonnet, mittens and booties. It reduced Kathy to tears of gratitude, though she said ruefully that she didn't know when the tiny scrap she'd given birth to would grow big enough to fit into the things.

Lizzie hugged her mother tight. She knew that she, Mary and Molly were busy knitting tiny garments to fit little Laura, as ordinary baby clothes swamped her still. 'By the winter she'll need the things Sophie's sent,' she said. 'You just see if she doesn't. She's getting bigger by the day.' She didn't know if this were true or not, but she knew Kathy needed reassurance. Seamus, the baby who'd died, had been much more robust than frail little Laura and yet he'd died, and that fact had haunted Kathy since the day her new daughter had been born.

There was just one week until David's wedding – for though Lizzie told no one, she had been keeping count – when a frantic letter came from Alice. She was coming to Birmingham with Lena Carstairs for an exhibition the weekend after the wedding and would have a few hours to spare on the Saturday afternoon and would like to meet up with Lizzie.

Lizzie knew she would like to see her friend, but she didn't want to bring her home. Kathy had decided on a different plan for Saturdays once the schools opened again. With Maggie's agreement, Dan and Padraic would go to her house on Friday and then to the match with their uncles and cousins the next day, and make their own way home after. Barry kicked up about it at first, but Kathy said he was too fond of his pop to have the care of the lads, and she wasn't having them hanging around a saloon bar all of Saturday afternoon and evening.

Barry didn't complain again. Anyway, it meant he was free to go for a few pints with his brother before the match, and back to the pub after it until closing. Lizzie had been at work when these arrangements were being, discussed, but she was usually home when her dad returned from the pub, and was always disgusted by his drunken state. She was also nervous of him, and knew her mother was too, for where once Barry had been an amiable drunk, now he was unpredictable.

446

Kathy knew what was in Lizzie's mind and suggested she write to Alice and arrange to meet her in town. 'It's you she wants to see,' she said. 'Anyway, this house is no place to bring anyone these days.'

It was the first time Kathy had admitted to there being anything wrong at home, and the look in her eyes tore at Lizzie's heart. 'Oh, Mammy,' she said.

'Don't, Lizzie,' Kathy said, hearing the break in her daughter's voice. 'What can't be cured must be endured, and there you have it. There's no point crying over it.'

But though she spoke the words bravely, she'd cried many a night for her and Barry, the love between them shattered by a letter from a GI now dead and gone. She'd also cried for the baby so precious and delicate, ignored and rejected by her father. She guessed it had nothing to do with Laura, but was just another way for Barry to punish her. It cut her to the quick, especially as she remembered how he'd been with Lizzie and Danny as babies. Padraic he adored, and though she'd complained in the past that he was spoiling the boy, still she had to admit he loved the child, and deeply.

But now she spoke to Barry only when she had to. She couldn't get over the fact that Laura might be lying screaming in her crib while she was up to her eyes in something in the cellar, and he'd not only not lift her up, but seemed not even to hear her. Fortunately she cried little and was a placid, happy baby, but despite that, Kathy cuddled her more than she'd done the others, as if to make up for her father's neglect. She blessed her own mother and Molly for their presence and constant support, and knew that without them she'd have found life almost intolerable.

TWENTY-SIX

Kathy was dog tired. The baby had caught a cold, though where the hell she'd caught it from when she didn't go anywhere puzzled Kathy. She was glad the lads were away, it being Saturday, and hoped she'd be able to grab a few hours' sleep in the afternoon, for she'd been up all night, in fact for the past few nights, with Laura.

Despite her own weariness, she was worried about her child, for she wasn't feeding properly and her snuffly nose made breathing difficult, and Kathy wasn't sure she didn't have a slight wheeze in her chest. It would have to be the doctor for her on Monday, she thought to herself, for the warmed camphorated oil she'd rubbed on Laura's tiny chest had done no good at all.

She laid the sleepy baby down in her crib and began to collect up the dinner plates. She and Barry had sat opposite each other during the meal, and later he had read the paper while she fed Laura, and all that time not a word had passed between them. Kathy was used to Barry's silences, when one or other of the children were not around to break them, and so she took no notice now and still without a word went down to the cellar to begin the washing-up. In a minute she would take Barry a cup of tea, which she would place beside his chair, and though he wouldn't thank her, he'd drink it. Then he'd pull on his coat and go out of the door to collect his brother for a drink before the match – she knew his routine.

She hated Barry at that moment. She didn't hate him for hitting her – she felt she deserved that, and if he'd have punished her further she'd have taken it, too. She doubted her brothers would have agreed with her. She hadn't at first been aware of their involvement in Barry's injuries. He'd hidden out at his mother's the weekend following her father's funeral, but the marks on his face had not faded completely when he came in from work on Monday evening. Kathy assumed he'd been involved in a drunken brawl at the pub over the weekend. She wondered whether to ask him how he'd got such a bruised and battered face and whether he'd bother to answer her if she did. Danny and Lizzie had both looked at him askance and then at Kathy, but were wary of inflaming his anger by saying the wrong thing.

Padraic had no such qualms and asked his dad straight out what had happened and Barry said he'd walked into a wall. Padraic might have been fooled, but no one else was, and when Mary came around later and told Kathy what had really happened, she wasn't even surprised.

She'd tried so often, since she'd been up and about, to talk to the man she'd once loved so much, even staying up and risking his drunken rages, but he always pushed her away. She was tired of trying to make things better between them.

But worst of all was the way he ignored the baby. It was as if she didn't exist and that hurt. It was totally beyond Kathy's understanding and she had no defence against it.

Back upstairs, Barry was only pretending to read his paper. Surreptitiously he'd watched Laura for weeks, but had made sure no one saw him. She was very tiny still, and delicate, very like Lizzie but much smaller, and with her down of black hair, heart-shaped face and rosebud mouth she was the image of Kathy. Being premature, she hadn't been smiling very long, only about a fortnight or so, but when she did, it was enough to melt anyone's heart. And she *was* premature, he'd checked it with the doctor. He hadn't doubted it himself, but the comments of his drinking partners had forced him to find out, because everyone knew you couldn't go on size. But the doctor had assured him that Laura had been at least six weeks early.

He told himself it didn't matter anyway. The child she should never have conceived in the first place. If he'd read the letter first, he'd never have touched Kathy. But the child had been conceived and born before he'd known his wife had been unfaithful. He'd told himself he wouldn't feel the same about the baby: he certainly had lost respect for its mother.

But he'd reckoned without the charm of Laura as she grew. When she cried he'd ached to pick her up and nurse her the way he had Lizzie and Dan when Kathy had been busy, but he held his arms stiffly by his sides and tried to ignore the wails. He'd watched her as she slept, marvelling at the tiny fingers with minute nails, and the little feet encased in white booties. He'd often wanted to touch her face with its fair skin tinged to pink on each cheek, and the little snub nose all weans seemed to have. He felt a swell of pride in her. She was his yet he wouldn't acknowledge her, and when she smiled at everyone but him, he felt as if a dagger had twisted in his heart.

He'd listened to her snuffly breathing for days now with concern. He'd heard Kathy soothe the baby over and over, night after night in the bedroom below his and guessed she must be worn out with it, but the child seemed to have got worse if anything. She was so small every breath seemed to shake her little body, so that it hurt him to watch her.

They should call the doctor, he thought, and whatever was between him and Kathy he'd tell her so before he left. She'd be surprised he'd even noticed, let alone cared, but he was worried for the child. She wasn't big enough or strong enough to fight things off the way others could.

Suddenly he was aware of silence. Downstairs he could hear Kathy still clattering the plates, but in the room he sat was silence. He put down the paper and listened. Had the snuffling stopped? Surely it shouldn't stop just like that?

He got up from the chair and crossed the room. Laura had been lying on her side, but now she'd rolled on to her back. A dribble of milk had escaped from her mouth and lay in a thin line across her cheek and settled in a crusted pool on the sheet beneath her head. But it was her chest that drew Barry's attention, for it wasn't rising and falling, not even a little, and he couldn't hear anything. He knew small babies breathed only shallowly, and he'd had a couple of frights with Lizzie as a wean, but Laura was utterly still, and as Barry watched, horrified, her red lips turned pale, with a bluish tinge to them.

For a second or two he stood rooted to the spot, as realisation hit him that his child had died while he'd been sitting in the same room scanning the paper. 'No, bloody hell, she can't just die!' his mind screamed. 'That sort of thing doesn't happen.'

He pulled the blankets away and lifted the child up, shaking her frantically as he yelled for Kathy. Kathy, even while she was amazed that Barry had shouted for her, was alarmed at his tone. She galloped up the stairs and at the doorway stood stock still for a moment, looking with horrified eyes at her husband shaking the baby as if she were a rat.

'What the hell are you doing?' she cried as she ran across the room and grabbed the child from Barry's arms. His shaking had roused her and she began to cry, a thin, plaintive wail. Barry, still in shock at what had almost happened, said, 'She stopped breathing.'

Kathy looked down at the crying baby. The colour had returned and her cheeks were bright pink with the exertion of crying, but there was still a bluish tinge around her lips. She put Laura over her shoulder to try and soothe her and patted her back rhythmically. She glared at Barry. She didn't doubt Laura had stopped breathing, but why? Babies didn't just stop breathing. She knew she had a cold, but still it didn't make sense.

'What did you do to her?' she said coldly.

'I didn't do anything,' Barry said. 'I found her lying in her cot like that. I shook her because it was all I could think of.'

'You found her lying in her cot?' Kathy repeated in an incredulous voice. 'I don't think so. You've not looked on the side the child was on since the day she was born.'

'God, Kathy,' Barry cried. 'I swear to you, I never touched the baby, not in that way, not to harm her. She stopped snuffling and I went to see if she was all right. That's all, I swear.'

Kathy was still cautious. 'Are you sure you didn't try and hurt her in some way?'

'No, I didn't. Christ, she's my daughter.'

'Not many would know that.'

The baby lay over Kathy's shoulder; she had stopped crying, but her tortured breathing was clearly audible. Kathy's eyes met Barry's, and both of them were scared.

'I'll go for Mammy,' Kathy said.

'You'll not,' Barry said, suddenly and firmly. 'We'll not wait in for any bloody doctor either. Wrap the child up well and we'll take her straight to the General Hospital.'

When Kathy hesitated, Barry yelled, 'We haven't time to waste. She's stopped breathing once and she could do it again. She's ill, listen to her.'

Without another word, Kathy wrapped the baby in the cot blankets and handed her to Barry while she put on her own coat. 'I'm ready,' she said, and with Barry still holding Laura, they walked briskly down the road to the bus stop.

As her mother and father hurried into the city centre, Lizzie was making her way to St Phillips churchyard in Colmore Row to meet Alice. David Barraclough had been married one week, and she hoped Alice could fill her in on what sort of wedding it had been, for both she and Kathy had guessed it would be a classy affair.

In one way she couldn't miss Alice, for she stood out amongst the milling shoppers, but in another way the figure scanning the crowd looked nothing like the young girl she'd not seen for over a year.

She had on a green coat, not olive green, nor lime, but a colour somewhere between. It was fitted at the bust, and a belt at the waist indicated what a lovely figure Alice had. It finished halfway down her calves, and there was fur at the collar and trimming the matching hat she had on. Her legs were nylon-clad and her black leather court shoes matched the handbag she clutched, and suddenly Lizzie felt shy of her friend. She looked too smart and stylish, and about twenty years old.

Lizzie felt glad she had on the blue woollen coat that had once belonged to Rosamund and not some dowdy old thing cut down from one of her mother's. She looked around her and realised that most people looked dull. They'd all been making do and mending for more years than anyone cared to remember, and now their clothes were downright shabby.

In contrast, Alice stood out as fresh and bright as a lone flower on a dung heap. Lizzie stepped forward hesitantly, almost nervous of speaking to someone so stylish.

453

But she soon found out she was the same Alice. Spotting her friend, she came running forward with a cry of delight and enveloped Lizzie in a hug. 'Oh, I've longed to see you. It's such an age and letters are never the same.'

Lizzie laughed and hugged her friend back. It was great to see her again. She disentangled herself and stood back from Alice, surveying her, although she still held her hands as she said, 'Alice, you look just marvellous. These clothes! I've never seen you look so smart.'

Alice smiled. 'I know, it's great, isn't it?' she said. 'Lena made the coat and hat from bales of melton cloth she'd had in from before the war. The point is, we're making marvellous dresses and gowns for people and she says we have to look the part. I mean, if they see us going about in dingy-looking, unfashionable clothes, they wouldn't want to give us a free hand with creating marvellous things for them.'

'I suppose not,' Lizzie agreed. 'It's grand anyway to see you looking so good.'

'Come on,' Alice said, drawing Lizzie to a bench. 'I haven't come all this way to talk about my clothes. I've got lots to tell you and we haven't got that long really.'

'When do you go back?'

'Tomorrow morning, early, but Lena's booked us into the Grand Hotel and I have to meet her there for dinner at eight.'

'Oh, gosh, it's two now,' Lizzie cried. 'What shall we do? Do you want to go somewhere to eat?'

'No, not yet,' Alice said. 'Anyway, the point is, you're invited to dinner too. Lena wants to meet you.' She looked her friend up and down and said in a mock disparaging voice, 'Can't see why, myself, but there you are. No accounting for taste.'

'Well, you haven't changed,' said Lizzie with a laugh. 'For all you look so smart, you're still a cheeky bugger.'

'Thank God for that,' Alice said, and both girls burst out laughing.

'You can come, though, can't you?' Alice said. 'Your mam's not expecting you home at any special time or anything?'

'No,' Lizzie said. 'And how could she anyway, with your vague letter? It just told us when you were coming, nothing about how long you were staying. Mammy said she'd expect me when she saw me, and I arranged not to see Kenny tonight.'

'Ooh, Kenny, the boyfriend,' Alice said, almost rubbing her hands with glee. 'Come on, tell all to your Auntie Alice.'

Lizzie laughed. 'Maybe later,' she said. 'Tell me about David's wedding first. I'm sure it was a very interesting experience.'

'Well, that's one way of describing it,' Alice said dryly. 'It was very classy and very expensive, I'd say. A few local women came to us for their outfits, so of course we knew all about it beforehand, and one woman, Mrs Symmonds, came back a couple of days ago to tell us how it went. She's a friend of Lena's and knew we'd both want to know.'

'Is she pregnant, Rosamund?' Lizzie asked. 'It seemed such a rush job.'

'Well, no one is supposed to know that,' Alice said. 'Rumour has it she was, or said she was and named David, and the marriage was arranged hurriedly. Then she lost the baby, though it was all hushed up, but people got to know. Mrs Symmonds said she doubted there ever was a baby at all, and to be honest so do I. Anyway, David was all for postponing the wedding. I think he'd have liked to have cancelled the whole thing, but apparently Rosamund was hysterical and her father went down to the Barracloughs' house threatening to sue David for breach of promise.'

'How d'you know all this?'

'Come on, Lizzie, you know how it is. I suppose their servants talked,' Alice said. 'Anyway, it set the village alight. You know how they've always been interested in the doings of the big house. It even reached my mother's ears. She said it was all everyone was talking about on market days.'

'So the marriage went ahead as planned?'

'You bet, and in style,' Alice said.

Lizzie smiled and said ruefully, 'David is really no match for Rosamund and her family. They'll devour him.'

'You said that before,' Alice reminded her. 'But he only has himself to blame. He's not a baby.'

'No, I suppose not,' Lizzie said. 'Who was his best man?'

'His brother Chris, and what a looker he is. Even better than David.'

'Did you go to the wedding then?'

'Course, I wouldn't have missed it for the world. The whole village crammed into the church,' Alice said. 'The two Barracloughs stood together at the front like film stars. I can't understand why no one's snapped up Christopher yet.'

'Maybe he's wilier than his little brother,' Lizzie suggested with a grin.

'Or choosier,' Alice said. 'David's two friends were there too, you know, those that came down for the holidays sometimes, Philip and John.'

'Oh yes, I bet they've changed a bit.'

'I'll say. They're quite nice-looking, only not as good as David. Mind, according to Mrs Symmonds, that didn't stop Rosamund flirting with both of them.'

'She always did,' Lizzie said, remembering. 'It used to drive David wild.'

'Nothing much has changed then,' Alice said.

'What d'you mean?'

'Well,' Alice said, 'it seems Rosamund disappeared at the reception in the evening, and so did Philip. Of course no one linked the two at first, but a search was made for Rosamund and they were found in a very compromising position together with their clothes in total disorder. Of course everyone tried to cover it up, but . . . well, it's hard to keep people quiet over that sort of thing. Everyone loves a bit of gossip. Mrs Symmonds said the place was buzzing, and when the happy couple left to go on their honeymoon, they weren't speaking.'

'They'll make each other totally miserable,' Lizzie said. 'Still, I don't suppose David will see that much of her once he's flying.'

'He's not going to be flying.'

'Oh, I thought it was arranged,' Lizzie said. 'Mrs Barraclough said if he got the grades in his Highers it was what he intended doing.'

'It was, and as far as I know he got good passes. He had even applied to British Airways and was all lined up for his medical.'

'Then what happened?'

'Rosamund, in a word,' Alice said. 'Complained she didn't want a husband flying around the world all the time. She said she might as well not marry at all. Then her father used his connections to get David a job in Broadcasting House in London. Apparently it's the place to be. He said television is going to be the next thing and everyone will have one in their homes.'

'Television!'

'You know. Like a wireless, except the television will have pictures as well as sound.'

'I can't see everyone having one of those, can you?' Lizzie said. 'We haven't even got electricity. Our wireless works on an accumulator and a battery. I doubt we could have one of those new televisions even if we could afford it.'

'Yes, and they're going to cost something, I'd say,' Alice said. 'It would be like having your own cinema in your living room.'

'Anyway, David has got a job there?'

'Apparently,' Alice said. 'But that's enough about them. This is my first visit to Birmingham and I want to see everything.'

'Right,' Lizzie said, and giggling together, the two friends crossed the churchyard and started down Needless Alley into New Street.

'I don't understand,' Kathy said to the white-coated doctor with the stethoscope hanging around his neck. 'How can a baby just forget to breathe?'

The young doctor ran his hands through his hair and admitted, 'We don't really know, but what we do know is that premature babies are more affected than others. However, in your baby's case, there is also a trace of infection in the lungs.'

'Oh God!' Kathy said.

'It should clear up with no adverse effects whatsoever,' the doctor said. 'These new antibiotics work wonders these days.'

'So you will treat her?' Barry said. 'And she'll be all right? Is that what you're saying?'

'I'm saying, Mr O'Malley, that your daughter is very sick,' the doctor said firmly. 'We'll run some further tests and then get an ambulance to take her to the Children's Hospital in Broad Street.'

'I must go with her,' Kathy said.

'I'm afraid that wouldn't be allowed, Mrs O'Malley.'

'But she can't go on her own,' Kathy argued. 'She's just a wee baby.'

'I assure you, she'll be well looked after,' the doctor said. 'Parents hanging around only upset the patients unduly and get in the way of the medical staff.'

Barry looked at his wife's stricken face and his anger at her evaporated. She looked so lost and so very, very frightened. He couldn't walk away from this, though God, he was frightened too. 'Come on, Kathy,' he said. 'The doctors know best.'

Kathy hardly seemed to have heard Barry, but she did feel the hand he'd put on her arm. She looked at it, slightly puzzled, as if she wondered what it was doing there, but she didn't shake it off. Instead she said to the young doctor, 'When will she be taken to the Children's Hospital?'

'After the tests are completed, but certainly today.'

'Can I see her?'

'She's asleep at the moment.'

'Please,' Kathy pleaded. 'I won't wake her.' She looked across at Barry still holding her arm and said, 'We'd like to see her.'

But when they saw her lying in her plastic hospital cot, she looked so ill that Barry thought they were probably bidding her goodbye. Tears stood out in his eyes, but Kathy was crying unrestrainedly as she bent to kiss her baby, and a wave of tenderness swept through Barry. Whatever Kathy had done, she didn't deserve this, he thought, and he put his arm around her shoulders and was ashamed when she flinched at his touch.

'As it's Sunday tomorrow, you'll be able to visit from two till four p.m.,' the doctor told them.

Barry nodded, but Kathy said nothing. Her baby, her Laura, was being cared for and looked after by strangers, well qualified, but still strangers, and she'd only be allowed two hours with her. She couldn't stand it! She wouldn't! It was inhuman!

'How long will she be in hospital?' Barry asked.

'Ah, now that's impossible for me to say,' the doctor said. 'Have a word with the doctors tomorrow, they'll be able to tell you more accurately than I can.'

Barry sighed. 'Give us some idea, man,' he said irritably. 'You've examined her already. You must have an idea what's wrong.'

The doctor looked at the parents and was glad the husband was there for his wife, for she looked ready to collapse, but to keep the truth from them was not a kindness. 'I think your baby has developed pneumonia,' he said.

Kathy gasped, and even Barry looked appalled. How in God's name could a tiny baby fight the disease that had been such a killer in his youth?

The doctor saw the distress he'd caused and tried to remedy it. 'We'll know more when we get back the results of the tests we've done,' he said. 'And then of course the Children's Hospital has the expertise for dealing with serious illnesses in the very young. Try not to worry too much.'

What a trite phrase that was. Barry led Kathy from the room, and as he glanced back at the baby from the doorway he wondered bleakly if it was the last time he'd see her alive. Kathy seemed to be in shock, and Barry didn't even know if she was aware of him. He took her to the reception area and sat beside her, rubbing her hands as if she were cold. 'Do you want a drink?' he asked.

Kathy shook her head.

'It might help, Kath, calm you down a little,' Barry said. 'Hot, sweet tea is supposed to be good for shock.'

'I don't want a cup of tea,' Kathy said coldly. 'I'm not in the least shocked and I don't need calming down.' She looked at Barry and said, 'What I need is to know why you're being nice to me all of a sudden. Why you're treating me like a human being instead of some slug you'd rather grind beneath your heel.' Before Barry could reply she went on, 'Our baby is dying, is that it? The baby you never wanted and have ignored since she came into the world is soon to be no more, and perhaps then you'll consider I've been punished enough for my one indiscretion.'

'No, Kathy, no . . . God, I don't want the baby to die.'

'How can you say that when you took no notice of her when she was well and healthy?' Kathy cried. 'You've only begun to care now she's sick.'

Barry knew that that was how it must seem. He wanted to run from the hospital and pretend these awful things weren't happening to him. He wanted to find a pub and drink himself senseless, but he knew he could do neither.

Kathy was right in a way, for in her distress he felt a tenderness for her he'd not felt since he'd returned from the war. She'd appeared so strong, so capable then, as if she had no need for him. But now she was vulnerable, and though she was accusing him of not caring for the child, even that was better than the bitter silences he'd felt powerless to break.

Both of them, he realised, had been deeply unhappy, and for months he'd covered his misery with drink and the company of women his Kathy wouldn't even shake the hand of. He knew that if their marriage was ever to have a chance, he had to talk to Kathy; even with their child desperately sick, that was important. In fact maybe it was more important *because* Laura was so ill. If she didn't survive, Kathy could easily go under, Barry thought, looking at her strained white face, and he would be suffused with guilt, guilt that he hadn't loved her, or protected her enough, and that could destroy him too. He didn't kid himself his character was particularly strong. If he lost that baby, and he and Kathy hadn't attempted some form of reconciliation, he could go to the dogs altogether.

'Kathy,' he said. 'Could we talk?'

Kathy's dead eyes looked into his. 'Talk!' she said, with tears streaming down her cheeks. 'What about, for Christ's sake? How many times have I wanted to talk to you? I've begged pleaded, ranted and raved, and each time you've pushed me away.'

'I know, I'm sorry,' Barry said. 'I acted badly, and then shame and pride kept me from admitting it.' Kathy had never seen Barry in this light, or at least not for years. Apologising and admitting he was wrong had never come easy to him, even in the pre-war years, but she wondered whether what he'd done could be wiped out with just a few soft words. She searched his face to see if there was sincerity there behind the sad, troubled eyes.

Eventually she nodded. 'We'll talk,' she said. 'I'd like to explain things to you. I will be totally honest, and after I have finished you can decide whether you want me for your wife or not. But,' she warned, 'if you are not prepared to live with me as my husband and be a proper father to our children, you must move out. How we're living at the moment and how you're behaving is upsetting them all badly.' She turned in her seat and faced Barry. 'Those are my terms and will stay my terms whether . . . whether Laura . . . lives or . . . or dies.'

Barry watched Kathy dash the tears from her eyes almost impatiently and square her shoulders, and he felt immense respect for her. 'I know how things have been,' he said. 'You're right. It's been worse than if I'd moved out altogether.'

He looked round the corridor in which they were sitting. It was anything but private, with patients awaiting treatment and people newly arriving all the time. Cheerful porters pushed the incapacitated or seriously ill past on stretchers or in wheelchairs, while nurses in starched uniforms looked disapproving at any sudden or unexpected noise or movement, and harassed young doctors seemed to be in a constant hurry. 'Let's go home,' Barry said.

'No,' said Kathy. 'Everyone in the place will know by now. You don't run down the street with a baby on a Saturday afternoon just to go into town to shop. If we go home, they'll all be in on top of us.'

Barry knew she was right. 'Well, we can't stay here.'

Kathy looked round. 'No,' she said.

'Come on,' Barry said. Kathy didn't ask where, and when he stretched his hand out, she looked at it for a minute but didn't take it. Instead she swung away from him and walked out of the hospital, and he followed behind.

TWENTY-SEVEN

Kathy didn't really want to talk to Barry; she wanted to sit beside her baby and will her to live, but she knew she wouldn't be allowed to, and she also knew that this might be her only chance to talk things over with her husband. She didn't know whether she wanted him to understand or whether she really cared about his good opinion anymore, but she knew that marriage, certainly a Catholic marriage, was for life, and she owed it to the children to try and bring some normality to their home.

Without being aware of it, she turned towards the city centre, not really caring where she went, conscious of Barry striding beside her, close but not touching her and as silent as the grave. She wondered if he was just waiting for her to speak, or if he'd sunk once more into one of the sullen periods he'd indulged in since Laura's birth when he'd speak not a word, not even when he was asked a question.

She glanced at him, but his set profile gave little away, and she knew she would have to say something before she lost her nerve altogether. She cleared her throat and Barry glanced at her, his face slightly anxious, not at all sure he was ready to hear Kathy's explanations.

But the uncertainty on Barry's face gave Kathy courage, and she said, 'To understand what happened between Doug Howister and myself, you really need to understand how it was for us all back home here. I don't mean just the raids, though God knows they were bad enough, day after day and hour after hour, cowering in the cellar while the pounding went on above, wondering if any of us would be alive after it and if the house would be still in one piece or bombed to a pile of rubble above us. But it was more than that. The drabness and sameness of it all got to us, the horror of trying to feed a family on the rations allowed was a constant nightmare, and in the end the monotony was depressing, because the only thing anyone had a surplus of, they didn't want.'

She gave a grim laugh and went on, 'They used to run articles in women's magazines and between the films at the cinema. Gripping stuff, like fifty million ways to serve potatoes, swede or carrots, or how to make a cake with no sugar, not much fat and no eggs either. There was a woman called Mrs Sew and Sew encouraging us to make do and mend, but after a few years of shortages, with people losing all they owned in the Blitz, there wasn't a great deal to make do and mend with.'

She looked directly at Barry and said, 'I took a job to do my bit, save some money and get out of the house, if I'm honest. Your mother and I were falling over each other to keep the place clean and look after Padraic, and I felt it was better for one of us to be out of the way. But the factory hours were often long, and while overtime wasn't exactly compulsory, you felt obliged to stay if others did, and so to make our dreary lives a wee bit better, I started to go to the pictures once a week with Maggie, like I wrote and told you.'

Kathy fell silent, and Barry beside her had for the first time an inkling of how it had been for the women left at home. In her letters Kathy had told him little of any of the restrictions she'd just described, and despite the raids he'd heard about, he'd never given much of a thought to how they were all managing without him.

Kathy had begun speaking again. 'That's how people were living when the GIs started to arrive in Britain in the summer of nineteen forty-two. They came to a world of shortages and monotony and war-weary women missing their men and any semblance of a normal life. They hadn't already suffered three years of war and seemed full of life and vitality. They seemed to have more money than the occasional British lad home on leave and no problem about spending it. The young girls' heads were turned, and they can't be blamed altogether, for many had not seen a man for some time and a normal courtship was a thing of the past. The Americans wooed them with chocolates, nylons, decent cigarettes and chewing gum, and though some were loud and brash, others were decent, sometimes a bit homesick and, after all, on the same side.'

Barry made no comment. He'd been staggered by the thought that Kathy had known the man for two or three years. 'Is that when you met this Doug fellow, nineteen forty-two?' he asked.

'No,' Kathy said. 'I didn't meet Doug till February forty-four.' She paused and went on, 'We met at the cinema.'

Barry gave a sigh of relief, but Kathy didn't notice. Her face was set, remembering it all again, and she said, 'We were making our way out of the seats when a GI knocked me over. It wasn't done on purpose, it was a total accident, and he couldn't apologise enough. He had a mate with him, Phil Martin, and they took Maggie and me for a drink at The Trees to say sorry. Then we said goodbye and went home and as far we were concerned that was that.'

Kathy paused and went on, 'The next time I saw him was some weeks later when I bumped into him in Calthorpe Park.

You'll mind I wrote and told you Maggie and I were taking the afternoon off to see if we could get the wee fellows a place in Rea Street Nursery?'

Barry gave a brief nod.

'Well, it was that day,' Kathy said.

'Was it by design?'

'Of course it bloody well wasn't,' Kathy burst out angrily. 'I told you, we hadn't seen them for a few weeks. I just happened to be there that one day with Padraic and Maggie's Tim and met Doug, and when I got home I told them all about it. Padraic was very taken with him, and I met him the following week because he'd promised to bring a ball for him and Tim to share. You probably don't know this, but at that time it was easier to obtain the crown jewels than a rubber ball.'

Barry stared at Kathy. What she'd just said about the Yank and a ball had stirred a memory in his brain. He remembered the day he'd returned home, and how shocked his family had been. Kathy had been odd with him and Padraic had been prattling on about a man giving him and Tim a ball, and then someone called Doug saying his daddy would play with him. 'Was it the same Doug Padraic mentioned that time?' he asked. 'The day I came home, was that him?'

'Oh, aye,' Kathy said. 'That day you came back. That's what upset me so much. It was seeing you standing there, so much changed; it was obvious you'd been through it. When I hugged you, it was like holding a bag of bones, and then when Padraic mentioned Doug, I remembered it all again and felt full of guilt. It made things awkward between us.' She turned to Barry and said, 'I'm sorry.'

'Was that why you didn't want sex that night either?'

Kathy gave a brief nod, though it wasn't the whole truth, but Barry seemed satisfied. She was not to know that he understood, because Madelaine had flashed into his mind as he'd taken Kathy in his arms. And if he was honest, when he lay panting and spent on top of an unyielding Kathy in bed at night, he'd often wished it were sensual, erotic Madelaine beneath him.

'There was nothing illicit to it, Barry,' Kathy said. 'Doug and Phil went along to tea at Mammy's a few times, just like our Carmel's Ricky. Apart from that, the only outing we had with Doug was when he took Maggie, myself and the two boys to the Lickey Hills for the day. We went twice altogether.' Then she shrugged and said, 'That one fateful evening you read about was the sum total of my torrid romance with Doug Howister.'

'But you were attracted to him?'

Kathy took a deep breath and said, 'Yes, I was attracted to Doug, and I know also he felt something for me. But now I think that part of the way I felt was because I was missing you so much, and I don't just mean the sex either. I wasn't the only one; lots of women felt the same, sometimes we'd talk about it at work. Barry, I had a job where I was surrounded by people, I had my own house chock-a-block and my family beside me, yet sometimes I was so bloody lonely.'

She looked directly at him and said, 'You were everything to me, Barry, the light of my life. In all my life I'd never looked at another man. There were none before Doug and there's been none since. I'm not the whore you accused me of being, but I'm not the person you left behind either, and neither are you the man who went away. A war like we've both lived through is bound to change a person, and yet I want you to know that once I loved you very much.'

Barry heard Kathy's use of the past tense and felt his heart plummet. He had tears in his eyes as she continued. 'But still, I was aware of this pull Doug had, and I knew it was wrong, so I avoided any situation where we might be alone together.' She glanced at Barry and went on, 'If

Maggie hadn't been taken ill that day and had come to the cinema with me as arranged, then what happened might not have done.'

They'd reached Lyon's tea shop on New Street, and without a word they went inside and ordered tea and scones. Kathy was glad to sit down, for she felt suddenly weary. She knew she was coming to the embarrassing part of the story, and that what she said in the next few minutes would determine whether she still had a marriage or not.

She sat silent, twisting the strap of her handbag nervously between her fingers, until the tea and scones had been placed before her, and even then Barry had to say, 'Go on,' before she started her tale again.

'We'd arranged to see *Mrs Miniver*,' she said. 'They'd all been from work and kept on about it, and so we said we'd go. We hadn't seen Doug and Phil for a couple of weeks then and thought they'd been shipped out, as Carmel's Ricky had, but still, when Maggie was taken ill, I was all for calling it off. I hadn't a notion of going on my own, but they all pressed me to go and tell them about it later. Mammy said I was sure to see someone in the queue I could sit beside.' She gave a rueful laugh and said, 'And she was right. I did see someone, and that was Doug Howister. Hardly what Mammy had in mind.'

'So you went in together?'

'Well, of course we did,' Kathy cried. 'It would have been stupid not to. But before we'd gone in, he'd told me they were moving out the next day, and when we were outside, saying goodbye, I suddenly thought I would never see him again. Then all the faces of people already dead flashed before me. Pat, your two brothers and all the other husbands and brothers and sons from round here, and I reached up and kissed Doug. It was meant as a kiss to wish him well, but . . .' She spread her hands helplessly and went on, 'It . . . it turned into something else.'

469

She sipped at her cup of tea, but made no effort to eat the scone which she crumbled between her fingers. Barry didn't speak; he had the feeling Kathy was miles away. She suddenly took a gulp of tea, looked directly at Barry and said, 'I slept with Doug Howister once, and that was it, and yet it totally disgusted you and caused you to lay into me and then ignore me for weeks.'

'It wasn't that alone,' Barry protested. 'It was the bloody letter.'

'He wrote that because he was lonely and beside himself, because his best friend had been killed,' Kathy said. 'Who else could he write to?'

'Och, don't treat me like a wean,' Barry snapped. 'I read the bloody letter, don't forget.'

Kathy raised her head high, two spots of colour stood out on her cheeks and her dark eyes flashed. She knew this was make or break for their marriage and she might never have the opportunity again. 'Barry,' she said, 'I made love to an American soldier on the dusty floor of a house near bombed to bits, and it was a wonderful experience.'

Barry laid his cup down in the saucer with a clatter, his hands balled into fists at the implied criticism and he leant across the table, his face flushed, and demanded, 'What d'you mean by that? That's a fine bloody insult to make to a man.'

'Aye, if you take it that way,' Kathy agreed. 'But it had to be said if we're ever to have a chance to put things right.'

'What fancy talk is this?'

Kathy had never felt easy talking of sexual matters, and she didn't now. She blushed and said, 'You are my husband and you have certain rights over me, and I would never refuse you unless for a very good reason, but . . . but I don't enjoy it, Barry. You take me as if you must, almost as a duty, and that's the way I feel too.'

'But you didn't feel the same with the American?' Barry said sarcastically. 'Of course,' he added, 'he had no rights, seeing as it was someone else's wife he was having it off with.'

'Ssh,' Kathy said, looking around fearfully in case Barry's outburst had been overheard. 'And no, I didn't feel that with Doug Howister. I'm sorry if that hurts you, but it's true.' She reached across the table and grasped Barry's clenched fist. 'Don't fight me, Barry,' she pleaded. 'Please don't. Look, I was a virgin when we were first married, and I often enjoyed sex then, but since you came back, it's . . . well, just different.'

And if Barry were truthful, he could never have described the sex he'd had with Kathy in anything like the same tones as the Yank had done. He realised suddenly that while he'd missed his family and longed to see them again, he'd wanted to come back as head of the house, with no thought for anyone else. He'd expected Kathy, who'd supported the family emotionally and financially for five years, to step aside meekly as he walked over the threshold of his home.

And when he'd found out she'd been unfaithful, he'd given her no chance to explain, but instead had lashed out at her and behaved little better than a thug. He hadn't made much protest the first night Madelaine had slipped into his bed and seduced him, and he hadn't given Kathy a thought then, nor in the rapturous sex-filled nights afterwards. He'd thought he couldn't treat his Kathy the way he'd done Madelaine. He'd thought he had to treat his wife with more respect – well, just look where respect had got him.

Kathy watched the frown on Barry's face with a sinking heart. She thought she'd shocked him too much. She wondered what he'd say if she went on to tell him now that she had been pregnant by Doug Howister, but she'd miscarried the baby. Maybe he should know; maybe there should be no secrets between husbands and wives. She knew it would be the death knell for their marriage, but it seemed to be that way already. She opened her mouth, but instead of what she'd intended, her voice came out bitterly: 'Didn't you learn anything useful from Connie McIntyre?'

Connie McIntyre? Barry remembered the evening he'd stumbled from the pub with her arms wrapped around him, the night before Laura's birth. 'God, Kathy, I never touched her.'

'I bet. Runs a benevolent home for poor misunderstood husbands, does she?'

'Honest to God, Kath, I swear I didn't lay a hand on her,' Barry said. 'I think I'd have been too drunk anyway, but I passed out in the gutter outside her house and she couldn't move me. Old Sam Patterson came along with his son and they took me to their house. I spent the night on their settee.'

Kathy knew Barry had to be speaking the truth about that time – she could easily check it out – but Bridie had hinted at other occasions. 'What about the other nights? Our Bridie said you've been more than friendly a time or two.'

'Bridie's a liar,' Barry burst out. 'She came on to me, Connie, aye, I'll admit she did, and in the end I took myself off to Dennis's local, the Cross Keys. But I swear to you, I've never touched Connie McIntyre.'

Kathy let her breath out in a large sigh and decided that this wasn't the time to admit she'd become pregnant by Doug. Barry watched her face and knew he'd gained a measure of her trust, and thought that now wasn't the time to tell her of his wartime romance.

The two were silent for a while, looking at one another, and then Kathy said sadly, 'It's a shame that our baby lies desperately sick before you and I could talk together.'

'And that's been mainly my fault,' Barry said, getting to his feet. 'But it will be better from now on, Kathy, I promise you. I'm not much good with fancy words, but I want you to know I love you and have always loved you.'

And when Kathy lifted her head, she didn't see the prematurely aged man with white hair and lines of suffering on the face that had never recovered its pre-1939 glow. She saw the young man she'd grown up with and loved all her life, and a lump rose in her throat. But she couldn't say she loved her husband, not yet. She bent her head in confusion, but when Barry held out his hand, she hesitated only a moment before taking it.

'Oh, my darling girl, let's go home,' Barry said.

The two girls at a nearby table watched the couple leave, and Lizzie's eyes opened wide in shocked disbelief. She'd had a wonderful day with Alice, who'd been in her element searching amongst the fashions of Lewis's, Greys' and C & A Modes. Lizzie had wanted to show her friend the Bull Ring that she'd told her so much about, but they decided to have a cup of tea and a sandwich at Lyon's first.

She was describing it all to Alice again while they waited for their order, when Alice suddenly said, 'Hey, Lizzie, isn't that your mam over there?'

Lizzie looked across and was totally amazed when she saw both her parents at a nearby table. 'And my daddy,' she said, and wondered what they were doing there.

They looked very serious, she noticed, and she hoped they weren't having a row. Surely they wouldn't do that in so public a place? She wondered if it was a good sign that they were talking, because they didn't do much of that any more. Maybe they'd come out together to sort things out. About time if they had. It certainly seemed important, whatever they were talking about, important enough to leave Laura behind with someone. She felt embarrassed watching them. It was like eavesdropping, and she wished she'd seen them before she'd given her order. There were plenty of other places to eat.

The tea and sandwiches were placed in front of them as Alice said, 'I think they're going. Aren't you going to say hello?'

'No,' Lizzie said. They'd probably be embarrassed. She saw her father hold out his hand to Kathy, and noticed the slight hesitation before she took hold of it. Lizzie let her breath out slowly, not aware that she'd been holding it as she watched the interchange between her parents.

'Isn't that just too romantic?' said Alice dreamily.

'What?'

'Your parents holding hands like that,' Alice said. 'I mean, you wouldn't think they would be bothered after all this time. I'd have thought they were too old for that sort of thing.'

Lizzie was glad then that she'd not told Alice of the difficulties since Laura's birth. She agreed happily that she too would have thought they were too old for holding hands at their age, but really her heart was lighter than it had been for ages.

'Come on, then,' Alice said, taking a large bite of her sandwich. 'Eat up quickly, I want to see this precious Bull Ring. And,' she added, 'I need to look around the Market Hall you told me about, because Lena wants me to buy some lace and ribbons, fancy buttons and anything else I think we might use to decorate gowns. She said it's likely to be cheaper here and they'll probably have more choice.' She leant forward and whispered, 'I've got twenty pounds to spend.'

'Twenty pounds!' cried Lizzie. 'To buy buttons and stuff? God, Alice, you could probably buy shares in a button factory for that.'

Alice laughed and said, 'I don't have to spend it all, you fool, it's just if I see something special.'

'There will be something special all right,' Lizzie said. 'They have oceans of fancy stuff like that. But there will be plenty of other entertainment too.'

'I can hardly wait,' Alice said. She hadn't been nervous of the city as Lizzie had been on her first day back; she'd been excited by it, and wanted to see and experience everything. She loved the shops and the hordes of people everywhere, and the rattling trams that went swaying down the road on those little rails, and it seemed a waste of time to sit drinking tea in a café with the world waiting outside. 'Come on, Lizzie,' she said. 'Drink your tea and let's go.'

Lizzie did as her friend bid her, and they went out together arm in arm towards Jamaica Row.

Back in Bell Barn Road, the news had spread rapidly that Kathy and Barry O'Malley had sped down the road just after dinnertime without looking right or left or replying to any greetings, with the baby in Barry's arms. While Mary and Carmel were digesting this news, brought to them by neighbours, and wondering what to make of it, Molly arrived. Dennis was raging, she said. He'd waited for Barry until he was almost late for the match, but he hadn't turned up and he wasn't at the Cross Keys either. She wondered if he was ill, or whether there was some other reason for his non-appearance. She was further intrigued when she found the O'Malley door locked and no sign of Kathy either, but Mary – whose house she went to next – could throw no further light on where either of them were.

Mary was annoyed that Kathy had gone somewhere without discussing it with her – she'd never done it before – and all the neighbours said Barry had been carrying the baby, and yet she'd not known him lift the child since the day she'd been born. And why take the child anyway, if they had to go somewhere together, though she couldn't think where Kathy would go without telling her. Why hadn't she asked her or Carmel or even Molly to mind the baby? Any one of them would have done. 'She shouldn't have taken the child out with that cold she has on her,' she said at last and testily. 'It might be fine and warm now, but as soon as the sun goes down, there's a definite nip in the air.'

'Maybe they won't be away long, Mammy,' Carmel said soothingly.

'They've been long enough now,' Mary said. 'Well over an hour, from what the neighbours say.'

In fact the neighbours were saying far more than that. They were saying that there was more upset with that O'Malley family, and really you had to admit there was never a dull moment living near them. It was more entertaining than the pictures.

Then Con arrived with Dan and Padraic. Although the lads normally made their own way home after the match if they didn't meet up with their father, that day Con had decided to take them. Rose and Maggie had been concerned by the children's behaviour the last couple of weekends. Both had seemed too quiet, almost withdrawn, and Padraic had let slip some of the things Barry had said to his mother and how he'd sit without a word in the house – not that he spent that long in there at all, because Padraic had told his aunt that his dad went to the pub a lot and got drunk.

'It's not right,' Maggie told her husband. 'Someone has to go and have it out with him and tell him to shape up.'

So Con took the boys, thinking he'd see Barry at the match. But he didn't, and though he spotted Dennis, he was too far away to talk to and ask where Barry was. He'd thought Barry would make for the pubs, but he checked all his usual haunts on the route home and couldn't find him. He was tired and hungry and wished he hadn't volunteered to talk to his brother-in-law at all. But he did feel sorry for Kathy, and once he'd arrived in Bell Barn Road, he decided to go and see her anyway and ask her how things really were between her and Barry.

He was surprised to find Kathy's house empty and locked up – few locked their doors in the street – and intrigued, he went along to Mary's, sure he'd find Kathy there, or that they'd at least know where she was. But all he found were his mother-in-law, Carmel and Molly, and none of them knew where Kathy and Barry had gone with their baby daughter.

Kathy and Barry, preoccupied with their sick baby and their re-emerging feelings for one another, had no idea of the time or the anxiety they were causing their family. Kathy hated to leave the town, for Laura was there and she felt she wanted to stay close, so Barry suggested they visit the hospital again before going home.

The young doctor they'd spoken to earlier recognised them as they came through the door and went forward. 'Your baby has been transferred to the Children's Hospital,' he said.

'Already? So soon?'

'Early treatment of pneumonia in a baby so small is essential,' the doctor said. 'But although the child is tiny, you got her to us early, so she could make a complete recovery.'

Kathy and Barry both heard the doubt in his voice, and Kathy felt her heart sink. She was no fool; she knew how serious pneumonia was.

'You won't be allowed to see her this evening,' the doctor said. 'They've probably already started her treatment and the staff won't like her upset at this juncture.' He saw the distress on the face of the parents, the mother in particular, and went on gently, 'Go tomorrow. You can have a couple of hours with her and possibly have a word with the doctors.'

'Yes,' Kathy said, but still she stood with Barry's arm around her shoulder.

'Have you other children?'

'Aye, two boys and a girl.'

'I suggest you go home,' the doctor said. 'They'll be wondering where you are.'

'Aye, they will,' Barry said, glancing at his watch. 'The lads will be back from the match, Kathy. We must go home before they send a search party out.'

They hadn't actually done that, but the whole street knew about the strange goings-on of the O'Malleys, and most had their own theories on what had happened by the time Barry and Kathy turned into Bell Barn Road. The road was almost deserted, for it was teatime for most families, but they were spotted, and the whisper went round that they were home, but without the baby, and that the pair who had been snarling at each other like mad dogs for weeks were now holding hands like a couple of weans.

Kathy was glad of Barry's comforting grasp. She felt very close to screaming in frustration and confusion. How in God's name could a baby become so sick so quickly? True, Laura had been snuffly; all babies had snuffles now and then, she was sure the others had. But how had that ordinary common complaint become so serious?

She was so tired she didn't know whether she could cope with the barrage of questions the family were bound to fire at her. She felt their sympathy would make her break down completely. She looked across at Barry, suddenly panic-stricken, and he, knowing how Kathy felt, gave her hand a squeeze and said, 'Come on, love, we're in this together.' Immediately she felt a little calmer. They passed their home without pausing, knowing where everyone would be, and when Kathy opened her mother's front door, she saw them all turn and stare at her.

That night, after Con had come home with the distressing news, Maggie went down to see if she could be of help, while Sean went off to tell Bridie and the Sutcliffes what had happened. They didn't hold out much hope for Laura. Pneumonia killed the very old and the very young, the weak and the frail, and many knew of whole families wiped out by it. Even with modern drugs, Laura O'Malley, premature and delicate anyway, would have little chance of survival.

None of this was said to Kathy, nor communicated in any other way as Maggie took over the care of the boys, cooking an evening meal and organising baths for them both. Kathy, exhausted, had gone to bed when Lizzie arrived home ecstatic from her day out with her friend, which had culminated in a meal at the Grand Hotel. She had met Alice's friend, employer and saviour, and found her a thoroughly nice woman. She went home more eagerly than she had done for months, the apprehension she often felt lessened by what she'd seen in Lyon's tea shop, and she hoped that whatever had ailed her parents was now beginning to be mended at long last.

Her Aunt Maggie met her with the news about Laura, and instantly the day's happiness was wiped out. She felt almost angry that her parents had dumped the baby in hospital and, instead of staying with her, had walked around the town as if they hadn't a care in the world. It was Maggie who calmed her and told her about the hospital rules that forbade parents to stay with their sick children however much they might want to. 'Your mother is exhausted,' she said, 'and your father is worried sick. They need your support, not your criticism.'

Lizzie was ashamed, and when she went up later to see her mother she put her arms around her and they cried together. 'Will she die, Mammy?' Lizzie asked at last, and her voice wobbled with the effort of not crying again.

Kathy wasn't going to lie to her daughter. 'She might,' she said. 'No one knows. Pray for her, pet, she's in God's hands.'

Lizzie moved her head impatiently. Wasn't Uncle Pat in God's hands, and Charlie Sutcliffe, and her grandad, and the thousands and millions of others who'd died?

Kathy saw the thoughts swimming around her daughter's head and grasped her hand tightly. 'I know,' she said. 'I don't understand it either, but it can do no harm.'

'No, I suppose not.'

So that night Lizzie knelt beside the bed and said a decade of the rosary and began a novena to the Blessed Virgin. She'd almost finished when she heard her father open the door at the bottom of the stairs. She said a hasty Amen, made the sign of the cross and slipped between the sheets. She always liked to be in bed by the time her daddy came into the attic. But as she lay there, she realised that her father's footsteps had stopped on the floor below, the bedroom he'd once shared with her mother. She listened intently and heard the mumble of voices and the creak of the bed springs, and she knew her father had got into bed beside her mother, and she smiled, turned on her side and went fast asleep.

Kathy had not long returned from nine o'clock mass the following morning, when Enid and Sid Sutcliffe called in. Enid knew how Kathy and Barry must be feeling, for she and Sid had had a child too who'd hovered for days between life and death, and she hoped sincerely that Laura might pull through.

But she was a practical woman, and she knew that though worrying and anxiety had a stupefying effect on a person, other members of the family had to live too. So she'd brought two home-made pies with her, and a large apple tart, while Sid had brought carnations from his garden to cheer Kathy up, though she was cheered more by their corning straight over to see her than anything they brought. She knew they'd suffered the loss of a child, and was grateful for their thoughtfulness.

'When are you visiting?' Enid said.

'Today between two and four,' Kathy said, and gave a little shiver.

'It's a wonderful hospital,' Sid put in. 'They'll do their best for her, I can guarantee that.'

'We intend to try and talk to the doctors today,' Barry said.

Enid looked up as he spoke. Kenny had told her that Lizzie was worried about her father ignoring the babby, but he was concerned for her now well enough, Enid thought. He was probably nervous of her, with her being so small and delicate; a lot of fathers were nervous of babbies, in her opinion. And judging by the look that she saw pass between Kathy and Barry, any of the awkwardness she'd witnessed at his return to the house after so long had passed too.

Lizzie had seen the look too and didn't fully understand it. But Kathy knew her husband was as worried and scared for Laura as she was herself. The previous evening when he'd come into her room again, for the first time since the day he'd found the letter, she'd been frightened. Surely to God he can't want sex tonight? she thought. And her body shrank from him as he crossed the room and stood beside the bed. 'Don't be frightened, Kathy,' he said, guessing her apprehension. 'I just want to hold you, that's all.'

And oh, Kathy wanted that too, for she needed comfort more than she'd ever needed it. She flung the blankets back and Barry climbed in beside her. He held her in his arms while he gently stroked and caressed her body, and despite her initial feelings, she felt desire mounting in her and kissed Barry with passion. He didn't make any further move towards her, though, which surprised her. 'Not yet,' he said at last, and when she pressed him, 'We need to rediscover each other first. Relax, Kathy, you need sleep more than sex at the moment. We have all the time in the world.'

All the time in the world, an echo of Doug. Kathy knew that once and for all she had to banish Doug from her memory.

'Barry, please,' she said. 'I need you, Barry, now, tonight. It's been so long.'

Barry raised himself on his elbow and looked at Kathy in the half-light. 'D'you mean it?'

'I mean it,' Kathy said.

Barry took his time, gently massaging her breasts till the nipples stood up, and then, taking them in his mouth, he kissed them tenderly while Kathy gave little moans of pleasure. He kissed between her breasts and down her belly, while Kathy, trembling with excitement, wound her legs around her husband. She felt him throbbing against her and tried unsuccessfully to stop the cry of excitement escaping from her. The joy Barry was bringing to Kathy increased his own desire for her, and suddenly he could wait no longer.

Kathy thought she would die with happiness. Never, ever had she experienced such pleasure with her husband, and looking at his eyes shining with tears he would not allow to fall, she knew it was the same for him. 'Goodbye, Doug,' she said silently, and she kissed Barry on the lips and at last was able to say, 'I love you.'

'I love you too, my darling girl,' Barry said, and silently added, 'Thank you, Madelaine,' and entwined together, Kathy and Barry slept the night through.

TWENTY-EIGHT

Barry and Kathy returned home on Sunday evening after visiting their baby, shocked by the pitiful state of her. She'd been clad just in a nappy that seemed to drown her and a light vest, fed by a drip, with a monitor plugged to her tiny, heaving chest. She'd seemed unaware her parents were there, and they were unable to do much more than stroke her hands gently and tell her how much they loved her. Her body was clammy to the touch, but her hands were hot, like her little face, which was reddening and sweating with the exertion of taking enough air into that tiny body to keep her alive.

The doctor spoke to them before they left and stressed the seriousness of Laura's condition. He said that though she was holding her own, she wasn't responding to treatment as they'd like. 'She should reach the crisis sometime in the early hours of Monday morning,' he said.

'And then?'

'After that we talk further,' the doctor said. Barry and Kathy both knew what he meant by that, and Kathy was glad of Barry's arm supporting her.

Maggie and Mary had gone to the hospital with them, though they hadn't been allowed to see the baby, and they parted at the O'Malleys' door. Kathy was glad Molly had the boys. She was so tired she was barely able to put one foot in front of the other and she could have cried to see Bridie and her children sitting in her house.

'Hello, Bridie, I suppose you've heard the news?' she said, sitting on the settee facing her sister-in-law.

'Aye, Sean came over and told me. I must say, I was surprised. You knew the child was delicate and sick. Why didn't you look after her properly?'

'I did,' Kathy protested, taken aback by the attack.

'Did you? Pneumonia, your Sean said?'

'Aye, but it was just a cold at first.'

'And where did she get a cold from?' Bridie said, enjoying needling the pair before her. 'You couldn't have wrapped her up well enough.'

'Shut up, Bridie,' Barry snapped. 'A cold is nothing to do with being wrapped up well.'

Bridie ignored Barry and, turning to Kathy, went on, 'If you ask me, you've forgotten how to be a proper mother. After all, your two older weans were sent away for years and Molly reared Padraic, and as for Laura, you didn't even breast-feed her.'

Kathy started. Barry knew she'd always felt guilty about not being able to breast-feed Laura, and he also knew he must take some of the responsibility for her failure. 'Come on, Bridie,' he began in a conciliatory tone, but Kathy cut in.

'I couldn't feed Laura. I tried. My milk dried up.'

'Aye, so you said,' Bridie went on in a tone that said she didn't believe a word of it. 'I would have thought you might have persevered a bit, with the poor little bugger being prem and all.' There was a pause, and she continued, 'That is of course if she was really prem at all.'

Barry had had enough. 'Christ, Bridie, will you shut your mouth,' he said. 'We can both do without your vindictive and untrue charges being thrown at us. Have you no shame to behave like this when our baby lies desperately sick in a hospital cot?'

'Don't you talk to me about shame, Barry O'Malley,' Bride said. 'God, you've got a nerve. And now all this so-called concern for Laura that everyone knows is just a sham, when you've not cared a whit for that wee mite since the day she was born.'

Barry's face blanched. He knew that Bridie was just echoing what everyone else must be thinking, but that hardly mattered at that moment. 'Look, Bridie,' he said. 'You're not helping by bringing this up now.'

'Well, aren't you the grand fellow altogether?' Bridie said with a sneer.

'Oh, shut up,' Barry said wearily. 'In a few hours' time we'll be back at the hospital. Can't you lend a hand at a time like this and still that malicious tongue of yours? I'm not really interested in anything you have to say.'

'Oh, I'm sure you're not,' Bridie snapped.

'What d'you mean by that?' Barry said threateningly.

Kathy put out a hand. She wanted to warn Barry, to tell him not to retaliate. He might have forgotten the power of his sister-in-law's tongue, but she hadn't, and she was afraid that in a minute or two Bridie would rip their world and their fragile peace apart. But no sound came from her moving lips.

'I'm sure you don't want to know what people are saying about you,' Bridie said, her voice low and menacing. 'Or your precious Kathy either, who gave birth to a baby a scant seven months after you arrived home.'

Kathy gasped. Barry sat beside his wife and looked at her chalk-white face, wondering if he should just put Bridie out of the house physically. But there was Sheelagh to contend with too, and what if the pair of them should stand outside, shouting their accusations to the street? No, whatever Bridie said had best be kept within their four walls, and so he glared at Bridie and almost shouted, 'She *was* premature, you mean-minded bitch. Laura was premature, do you hear?'

'Oh aye, I hear,' Bridie said with scorn. 'Is that why you were out celebrating the night Kathy gave birth to her? Tipping beer down your throat as if there was no tomorrow, you were, and nursing bleeding knuckles like you'd been in a fight, they said. And who had you been in a fight with? Ah now, that's the question, isn't it? Well, I'll have a guess it was Kathy, because her face was all black and blue when I came out to see her on Monday.'

No one noticed Lizzie enter the room. Pressed into making tea for her unwelcome visitors, she'd added another two cups to the tray when she heard her parents come home, and had come up the cellar steps quickly, intending to hear how her baby sister was. Instead she heard Bridie accusing her parents of something beyond her understanding. What puzzled her most was that neither of them denied the things she was suggesting.

Eventually Barry said, 'All right, Bridie, you've had your say, but for God's sake, now is not the time to go into it. Have a bit of compassion.'

'Oh aye, like you did, you mean?' Bridie said. She'd seen Lizzie putting the laden tray down on the table and had a sudden urge to destroy Barry in his daughter's eyes once and for all. 'Did you have compassion when you staggered out of the pub with Connie McIntyre that night?' she asked.

Lizzie's eyes opened wide with shock, and Kathy wanted to scream and scream. Bridie was blowing everything wide apart. She felt as if she'd been stripped naked and left in the street. 'Please, Bridie,' she begged. 'Please stop this.'

'But it's you I'm thinking of, Kath,' Bridie said insincerely. 'God knows, my heart's been sore for you the last months. Married to a drunken sot of a husband who lays into you with his fists for whatever reason, and lies with common whores and lets the whole world know of it.'

'You understand nothing,' Kathy said coldly.

'Oh, don't I?' Bridie said, annoyed by Kathy's tone. 'Well, I understand a good hiding when I see one. God knows I've had plenty in my time from my old man.' She stopped and went on sneeringly, 'Unless, of course, your Barry had a good reason for thumping you.'

'For pity's sake,' Barry began wearily, but Bridie cut in.

'Did Kathy tell you about her war? Did she tell you of the Yanks she and Maggie ran round with? I tell you, so friendly did she get with one of them, I wouldn't have been a bit surprised if she hadn't presented you with a little American bastard for you to rear on your return.'

Lizzie wanted to leap in and accuse Bridie of lying. She knew they couldn't be true, the things she said, and she wondered why her mother wasn't shouting and screaming at Bridie's ravings, but Kathy said nothing, and that alone stayed Lizzie's voice. Kathy was too weary and sorrow-laden to fight Bridie. She just wanted her out of her house and her life, and she only said, 'Do your worst, Bridie, Barry knows it all.'

Bridie's eyes narrowed. She couldn't understand this feeling she sensed between Kathy and Barry. Sadie had told her things were bad. They seldom spoke, and when they did, they snapped and snarled like a couple of mongrel dogs. At least Barry did, Kathy was much quieter altogether, ashamed likely. Not of course that Barry was in the house much. He virtually lived at the pub when he wasn't at work and had done since the wee one's birth. But here they were, Kathy saying she'd told Barry everything, and Barry himself fine and sober when she might have expected him to be sleeping it off in the room above.

But she wondered if Barry knew how far things had gone with the Yank. Not that she did herself, of course, not totally, but she could guess, and so she said, 'Everything, Kathy?

Are you sure? Did you tell him about the night you met your Yank outside the Broadway and kissed him in front of everyone? God above, all those leaving the cinema had an eyeful. Eating you, Sadie said he was, and his hands all over your body and you lapping it up.'

Kathy watched the blood drain from Barry's face, and she realised he hadn't known that the kiss she'd told him about might have been witnessed by anyone. He thought the black-out would have hidden it from straying eyes. But obviously it had been seen, and he had to deal with that knowledge, and Kathy felt faint with apprehension.

Lizzie's own senses were reeling from what she'd heard. She couldn't understand why they were allowing Bridie to hurl accusations around, and today of all days too. Her eyes were drawn to Sheelagh, who had a smile of satisfaction plastered to her face, and Matt on a stool in the corner, as red as a beetroot and embarrassed as hell, and wishing he were anywhere but in the O'Malleys' house.

Lizzie regarded the cups of tea turning cold on the tray. She hoped only to deflect her aunt's anger as she said, 'Doesn't anyone want this tea I've poured?'

Kathy started at her voice, further dismayed and upset when she realised that Lizzie had heard much of the exchange between themselves and Bridie. Barry felt almost as bad. Bridie, who knew she'd scored a hit, had no need of tea, and Sheelagh just stared at Lizzie with a smirk.

Lizzie remembered the years she'd suffered under her cousin's hand. She reminded herself that the day war had been declared, she'd decided that the next time she hit Sheelagh it would be for real. With this thought in mind, she almost bounced in front of her and demanded, 'What are you laughing at, you skinny bastard?'

Sheelagh looked down her nose scornfully at Lizzie and said, 'At you and yours, and I have every reason to laugh, I think.'

The strength of the slap took even Lizzie by surprise, and the power of it jerked Sheelagh's head back as if she were on strings. 'Laugh now, then,' Lizzie snapped.

Sheelagh's shrieks mingled with shouts from Bridie, but Lizzie seemed unaffected by it. 'Get out!' she yelled at Bridie. 'You're no earthly use and never have been.'

Kathy and Barry sat as if mesmerised by Lizzie's outburst. Bridie, her arm around her hysterical daughter, stabbed Lizzie in the chest with a bony finger, accentuating every word as she said, 'You think your parents are saints, don't you? Well, I know different. You come from rotten stock and you'll come to a bad end.'

With a shriek of rage, Lizzie fell on her aunt, scratching her cheeks and slapping and kicking at her. Barry, shocked at last into action, leapt to his feet and held Lizzie tightly around the waist. 'Enough, enough,' he said soothingly, stroking Lizzie's hair to calm her as he hadn't done since she was a baby. Her rage dissolved to heart-rending sobs, and Barry said bitterly to Bridie, 'You've achieved your objective and near destroyed us all. Go now, there's nothing else you can do here.'

Bridie, her face red and with scratch marks under one eye, said, 'Oh, I'm going, don't worry. And I'd get that young one seen to,' and she indicated the weeping girl in Barry's arms. 'Tempers like that should have been knocked out of her years ago.'

'Get out!' Barry yelled. 'Before I lose control altogether. Get out of my sight.'

Bridie surveyed them all and opened the door before she said, 'I'm going, but I'll tell you now, so that you can sniff and disapprove of it to your heart's content.' She paused for effect then said, 'I'm getting married in a month's time to a lovely man called Arthur Weatherington. He brought me here today in his car and he'll be along to fetch me

489

very soon, and glad I'll be to be away from the whole lot of you. So chew on that.'

As she slammed from the room, Sheelagh in tow, everyone felt the tension ease, although Barry knew that his hopes of keeping the disagreement and Bridie's tirade from the ears of the neighbours were forlorn. Those around them would have heard everything, and those who hadn't actually heard it themselves would have every word told by those who had. Oh well, it was no use worrying about it.

Lizzie, her sobs easing at last, began to tremble as reaction set in. She sat down in one of the armchairs. She was deeply shocked by her actions, but not at all sorry, and she said to Barry, 'You shouldn't have pulled me off her, Daddy, you should have let me scratch the bitch's eyes out.'

The minute the words were out of her mouth, she caught sight of Matt, who was feeling so ashamed of his mother he wished the ground would open up and swallow him whole. 'Oh God, Matt, I'm sorry,' Lizzie said.

'Don't be,' Matt said, struggling up from the stool. 'Mammy doesn't like you and never has, but then she don't like me much either. I don't think she likes many people except Sheelagh and now Uncle Arthur. But,' he went on miserably, 'she shouldn't go on like she does. I'm really sorry she upset you all.'

Kathy looked at the young boy beside her. At almost thirteen, he looked so like Pat she was stunned by it. He had Pat's eyes, mouth and nose, the same shaped face, the same lock of hair that refused to lie down and would keep trailing across his forehead. Only his voice, as yet unbroken, was his own, and he was more solemn than Pat. His father, Kathy remembered, had had an almost permanent upward quirk to his mouth, and his dark eyes had seemed to twinkle constantly with devilment. Mind, it wasn't to be wondered that Matt should be solemn, living with that virago of a mother. Kathy put her arm around his thin shoulders and said, 'It's all right, it's not your fault.'

Barry also felt strangely protective of the son of his best mate who'd been blown to bits in the English Channel. He wondered about the man Bridie was to marry. Was he another such as herself, or a poor blind bugger like Pat? For the boy's sake he had to ask. 'What's he like, this chap your mother's marrying?'

Matt was surprised by the question, but answered readily enough. 'He's all right, Uncle Arthur,' he said. 'His wife's dead and he's got a daughter at the convent with Sheelagh, and that's how he met Mammy. Mammy's better since they got together. At least –' he bit his lip in embarrassment and gave a wry smile – 'at least she is when he's around. He says he's always wanted a son and he doesn't even mind that I'm a cripple. He's took me to a couple of football matches and taught me to fish.' He gave a shrug. 'He's OK, you know.'

Limping across the room, he said, 'I'd better go or Mammy will be raging.' He stopped just before opening the door, turned and said, 'By the way, we're moving to Sutton Coldfield after the wedding. Uncle Arthur has a house there. I'll send you the address when we're settled.'

'Do that,' Kathy said. 'We wouldn't want to lose touch with you altogether.'

As the door closed behind the boy, Barry said, 'Poor little bugger.'

'Aye, at the moment,' Kathy said. 'I have it in my head that he'll probably make a great turn-out at the end of it all, though. But just now I'm sick, sore and tired of Bridie and her problems. We have plenty of our own at this time.'

Kathy looked across at Lizzie and said, 'Are you all right now?'

'No, I'm not,' Lizzie snapped back. 'Isn't anyone going to tell me what's going on? Auntie Bridie said terrible things about you both and you just let her. Why didn't you tell her to shut her mouth and take her filthy lies somewhere else?'

Lizzie saw her parents' eyes meet across the room and felt horror creep through her as she realised that they couldn't deny Bridie's claims because they were true. Tears of shame stood out in her eyes as she got to her feet and faced them. The things Bridie had accused them of were hammering in her head as she asked, 'Was there any truth in the things she said?'

'This isn't the time, Lizzie,' Barry said shortly.

'Not the time,' Lizzie snapped. 'No, of course not. Course it isn't the time. Auntie Bridie can come here and slander the two of you and none of it can be explained to me. Well, when will be a convenient time for you both?'

'Your mother can't deal with it now,' Barry said. 'She's all in.'

Lizzie ignored her father, and although she saw that Kathy was dead on her feet, she faced her and asked again, 'Was there any truth in what Auntie Bridie said about you?'

Kathy said, 'Yes, Lizzie, but it wasn't . . .'

Lizzie then demanded of her father, 'And you? The things she said about you, was she right?'

'Not the way she said it, no.'

'Is there some other way to say you punched Mammy unconscious and went with a common prostitute like Connie McIntyre?'

'Lizzie,' Kathy pleaded. 'Please let us explain.'

Lizzie said incredulously, 'I attacked Auntie Bridie because of what she said about you. I thought it couldn't be true and yet now I find . . . I find . . .'

She couldn't go on. She wrenched the front door open and ran into the street.

'Come back!' Barry shouted. 'Lizzie, come back!'

Lizzie, tears streaming down her cheeks, ran unheeding down the street, and women gossiping on the steps, discussing no doubt the latest unholy row going on in the O'Malley house, shook their heads over the distressed girl as she ran. But Lizzie was past caring what anyone thought, for her world had been blown wide open.

Kenny found her in Calthorpe Park about an hour later, hiding behind the shrubbery bushes, away from the shrieking children in the playground and the families on the grass. When she saw him approaching, she turned crossly away. She'd stopped sobbing, but her eyes were red-rimmed and puffy and it was obvious she'd been crying for some time. Kenny made no mention of it, but just sat beside Lizzie without a word. She glared at him and snapped, 'What d'you want?'

Kenny laughed. 'Well, that's nice. I came over to spend some time with me girl on a Sunday afternoon and that's the welcome I get.'

'Shut up, Kenny. I'm not in the mood.'

'Maybe not, but you're in a mood of some sort, I'd say.'

'Well, perhaps I have reason.'

'Yes, maybe you have,' Kenny said. 'I've been to the house and spoken to your dad. When he said you were upset I knew you'd be either here or at Cannon Hill. You always head for grass when you're bothering over something.'

Lizzie was surprised at what Kenny said, but knew he had a point. She always seemed to be able to think better with grass under her feet and the blue sky above her head, but she wasn't going to discuss it, she had more important things in her head. 'Did he tell you what happened?'

'He told me Bridie came.'

'And what she said?'

Kenny gave a laugh. 'God, what does she ever say but things to annoy and upset others?'

'I know that.' Lizzie bit her lip, not knowing if she should go on, if it was disloyal to her parents, but she had to talk

493

to someone and Kenny wasn't the sort to tell or carry tales. At least he cared about her, and at that moment she wasn't at all sure her parents did. 'Bridie said Mammy had been running around with Americans in the war. And . . . and Daddy beat her up because of it and went out whoring with Connie McIntyre.'

Kenny sighed. He'd got the whole story from Barry, who'd been worried to death about the effect Bridie's wild accusations would have on Lizzie, and Kenny knew he was right to be worried. 'Lizzie, listen to me,' he said. 'Remember, I was here, living in the same house as your mother, all through the war, and she never, ever ran round with any Americans. Her and your Aunt Maggie met two at the Broadway one night and there was no secret about it. One nearly knocked your mother on her face, she said, and she had us all laughing about it.

'After that they were asked to tea at your grandmother's and one of them took a shine to Padraic and Tim and brought them a ball from the camp and took them to the park a time or two.' Kenny looked at Lizzie and said, 'As far as I know, your Mammy never went out alone with anyone, English or American.'

'She was kissing a GI, Bridie said so, outside the Broadway,' Lizzie cried.

'Maybe she was,' Kenny said carelessly. He knew where the kiss had led to – Barry had been straight with him – but he didn't think Lizzie needed to know. 'What's a kiss in wartime, Lizzie? It was maybe a goodbye kiss, for I know most of the Americans were leaving about that time. Carmel was real miserable because Ricky was gone, and I know that the one GI your mam knew, a man called Doug, and his friends were involved in D-Day because he wrote after his friend was killed.'

A goodbye kiss. The way Bridie had described it it hadn't seemed like a goodbye kiss, but that was Bridie for you. 'He wrote to Mammy?' she said.

'Yes, and your dad found the letter, and as he admitted himself, he went mad for a minute or two and lashed out at your mother.'

Lizzie's eyes opened wide. So Bridie had been right about that. 'He punched her, she said. And so hard his knuckles split.'

'No, he split his knuckles punching the bedroom wall after he'd read the letter and thought your mother was cheating on him,' Kenny told her.

That was news to Lizzie. 'Did he tell you that?' she asked.

'Yes, he did. But he did hit your mother, and afterwards he could barely live with what he'd done. Probably his actions caused Laura to be born prematurely and he was so ashamed he could hardly look at her.' He glanced at Lizzie and went on, 'So you were right when you said your father ignored the baby. He also said he's been drinking heavily since Laura's birth. You never said anything about that.'

'I was ashamed,' Lizzie said. 'He's been horrible to Mammy too. I couldn't understand any of it, but for God's sake, to hit her . . . I couldn't ever imagine him doing anything like that.' She shook her head, confused, and then, remembering her aunt's words, went on, 'Auntie Bridie said the baby had come so early it might not even be Dad's. D'you think he thought that himself and that's why he couldn't take to Laura?'

'For crying out loud, Lizzie, Laura was premature. It was obvious to everyone that she was,' Kenny cried. 'Your dad knows Laura is his. He was filled with guilt, that's all. And you've got to remember too what he'd been through. Anyway, he and your mother have sorted things out now and she's forgiven him.'

'Oh, that's all right then,' Lizzie snapped.

'Come on, Liz,' Kenny went on. 'It's part of being grown up, realising your parents aren't perfect. Everyone has done something they're ashamed of later.'

Lizzie was silent, remembering how she would once have let David Barraclough do anything to her, when all the time he was seeing Rosamund. She remembered with a feeling of embarrassment how stupid she'd been, and she felt the tell-tale flush of crimson on her cheeks.

Kenny saw it but didn't comment, though he guessed the direction his question had led Lizzie in. Instead he took her hand. 'Come on,' he urged. 'Your parents are worried sick about the baby and they don't want to have to fret over you too.'

Lizzie saw the sense of what Kenny was saying, and how wise and considerate he was, and she allowed herself to be drawn to her feet and into his arms. The kiss was different to any they'd experienced before, and Lizzie felt the faint stirrings of the excitement she'd had with David Barraclough. She realised with slight amazement that she was falling in love with Kenny Sutcliffe. When Kenny released her, both were slightly breathless, and she knew he'd been affected in the same way. 'Cor blimey, Lizzie O'Malley, you're a smasher,' he said in his broadest Brummie accent, to hide his embarrassment, and Lizzie smiled at him and they kissed again.

She still didn't understand much of what had happened between Bridie and her parents. One day she might ask her mother to tell her all about it. After all, she was no wean any longer, to be palmed off with half-truths or blatant lies, as might suit Padraic. But today she had to show her maturity by supporting her parents and, as Kenny had said, not giving them further cause for concern.

'Come on,' she said, pulling herself from his arms and taking his hand. 'Let's go home,' and hand in hand they left the park.

For hours they sat on either side of their baby daughter in the small room allotted to her because of the seriousness of her condition. At first they'd held or stroked her hand, the only part they could reach, and talked to her constantly and gently, but in the end it was hard to keep going, and they were both so tired anyway. The family had said the rosary on Saturday and Sunday evening, and the first mass on Sunday morning had been offered for Laura's recovery, but there in the bare hospital room they felt horribly isolated.

Kathy didn't dare ask Barry if he thought Laura would make it, because she guessed he didn't and she wasn't ready to face that yet. Instead she tried to think of other things besides the unconscious baby with the wheezy chest, taking gulps of air in tiny little gasps. She remembered coming down earlier from the bedroom where she'd lain for over an hour, desperately tired but unable to sleep, and seeing Lizzie and Kenny walk through the door hand in hand. She'd recognised the glow in their faces and knew something had happened to both of them.

At first her heart sank, for Kenny, much as she thought of him, was a Protestant, and she couldn't see him turning just to please the priests. But then she realised that Lizzie could marry a Catholic man who wouldn't be half as good to her as Kenny Sutcliffe. Lizzie must have her chance of happiness and choice of who she'd marry, for it was for life and not always an easy path to tread, and Kathy wouldn't let anyone, even Father Flaherty, ruin it for her.

Barry broke into her train of thought, worried by her pensive air. He too began to speak about the children, confessing to Kathy that he'd been jealous of the control she'd had over them, over the whole household, on his return home. He'd felt superfluous and almost a visitor in his own home, and not always a welcome one either. He admitted he'd spoilt Padraic, doing him a severe disservice, and virtually ignored the other two, and promised that things would be better in the future.

For the first time, Kathy realised how he must have felt. It was as if the war had robbed him of everything: his place in the family, his children, even his health. When he'd read the letter, it must have seemed as if he'd lost his wife too. 'Oh, Barry,' she said. 'If only we'd talked earlier, much of this could have been avoided.'

Kathy felt guilty as she realised she hadn't even tried to understand how Barry would feel and had pushed him out, refusing even the comfort of her body until he'd had to take her by force. 'I'm sorry, Barry,' she said.

'No need to be. I was a brute.'

'No, you were hurting. I could have tried harder to understand.'

One thing still bothered Barry, though. With the imminent arrival of Ricky Westwood to finally marry Carmel and take her back to the States with him, he wondered if Kathy's GI would turn up one day and try to claim his wife. He didn't really want to bring it up, but he'd probably never have the courage to do so again. He began tentatively. 'You know the American fellow that wrote to you?'

'Doug Howister?'

'Aye. Did he ever write to you again?'

Kathy knew immediately what was eating Barry, and she smiled sadly as she said, 'It was his one and only letter, Barry. He was killed shortly after he wrote it.'

Barry felt the breath leave his body in a sigh of sheer relief. He wasn't sorry the man was dead, for now Kathy was safe from him. He didn't ask how she knew; he didn't care. He took her hand and gave it a squeeze. Her eyes, he noticed, were glazed with tiredness and there were black rings around them. He said, 'Why don't you close your eyes for a few minutes to try to rest?'

'No, no, I'm fine.'

'You're far from fine,' Barry said. 'Come on, I'll watch her. Don't worry, I'll wake you if . . . if anything happens.'

Kathy couldn't remember feeling so tired since the Blitz, when her sleep had been disturbed night after night, and her smarting eyes felt as if they were full of grit. The hard, uncomfortable hospital chair was not conducive to sleep, but just to be able to shut her eyes was a relief.

She woke slowly, as if from a drug-induced sleep, stiff and uncomfortable and for a while not certain where she was, wondering why Barry was shaking her. Then she remembered and was alert, and her eyes shot round to the baby. Barry's eyes were shining, though tears ran down his cheeks as he exclaimed, 'She's going to be all right, Kathy! She's going to live!'

And Kathy realised that the baby's fever had gone and the wheeze in her tiny chest was much less. 'She's sleeping normally,' Barry said. 'I've rung for the nurse.'

'Oh, thank God,' Kathy said fervently, and she crossed the room to gaze down at the little child as a doctor burst in.

After he'd examined Laura, the doctor turned to Kathy with a smile. 'The fever's broken,' he said. 'She'll be in hospital for a little while yet, but she's turned the corner.'

Kathy felt as if she and Barry had been given a second chance to get things right and in time she guessed she would be the only one of the family left. But if it was too late for her she wanted a better life for her children, even if it meant them living miles from her. For now though, Kathy thought, the baby would be a consolation for Mary who'd miss Carmel, her baby, more than she yet realised. And Molly would have another O'Malley to spoil, but this time both Barry and herself would be around to see it didn't get out of hand.

She hadn't heard Barry come up behind her until his arm crept around her shoulders. 'She's a beauty,' he said as he stroked the baby's tiny hand. 'Just like her mother, and she can fight like her too.'

'I'm tired of fighting, Barry,' Kathy said. 'The children have all been disturbed or upset in some way by how we've gone on lately. Let's try and pull together now to give them as decent a life as we can.'

Barry was so moved by the emotion in Kathy's voice that he took her in his arms. 'I love you, Kathy O'Malley,' he said, and though Kathy didn't say the words, Barry felt her whole body responding to his embrace.

The nurse coming to take Laura O'Malley's temperature stopped outside the door. Through the glass panel she could see the couple clinging together and kissing passionately, and she knew that neither would welcome her intrusion at that moment and returned to the main ward.

If you liked this book, why
of Anne Bennett's

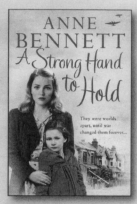

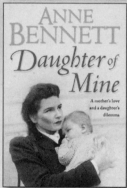

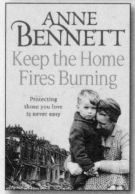

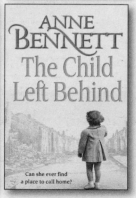

not dip into another one fantastic stories?

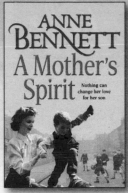

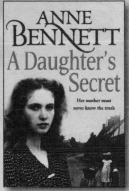

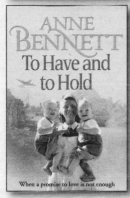

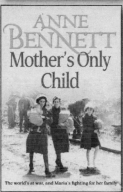

'The beauty of Anne's books is that they are about normal people and are sewn through with human emotions which affect us all'

Birmingham Post

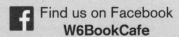